DONN'S LEGACY

CARYN LARRINAGA

DONN'S LEGACY
Published by TWISTED TREE PRESS

Twisted Tree Press, LLC
PO Box 540836
North Salt Lake, UT 84054
www.twistedtreepress.com

Donn's Legacy
Copyright © 2020 Caryn Larrinaga
ISBN-13: 978-0-9990200-5-0

1st Edition | December 2020

For Amuma. I'll never stop missing you.

CHAPTER ONE

A moving truck sat in front of Primrose House, its front tire bent inward by the concrete curb. I glared down at it through my apartment window as several men and women wearing matching navy blue jumpsuits ferried furniture from the truck to the house. They weren't supposed to be here yet; the morning sun had just barely risen over the hill, and when I went to sleep the night before, I'd been sure Graham and I would be on the road before the truck arrived.

"Best laid plans," I muttered as I went back to stuffing clothes into my suitcase.

This was the second such truck to mar the view outside my window that month. The first had come just two weeks before to carry my best friend, Kit Dyedov, off to Los Angeles to chase her dreams. In a classic case of adding insult to injury, she'd had the nerve to force me to carry her furniture from her second-floor apartment to the U-Haul, then complained when I wasn't "Tetris-y enough" about arranging it.

I still couldn't believe she took everything with her. When she decided to help her girlfriend launch a new paranormal documentary series called *Hidden Truths with Amari Botha*, I

expected her to pack a few weeks' worth of clothes into a backpack, test the waters, and send for the rest of her things when
she was sure this was the right decision. But then, she had
seemed pretty sure when she and Amari pulled away from
Primrose House and left Donn's Hill together. And from the
excited texts she sent me on a daily basis, she didn't have any
regrets.

She didn't seem to miss me half as much as I missed her.

Now this second truck was delivering the furniture for Primrose House's newest resident, a man I hadn't yet met. He would
fill the empty second-floor apartment with his own things, his
own personality. Would he be friendly and outspoken like Kit?
Stingy about coffee creamer and personal space but generous with
everything else? Hilarious, brusque, driven, and the absolute
funnest scary-movie-marathon partner in the world?

I doubted it.

A light tap sounded at my door, and Graham Thomas strode
into the room. My landlord-turned-boyfriend's heavy eyebrows
knit together over his glasses when he spotted my half-packed
luggage.

"You're still not ready?" he asked.

"I'm almost there." I ducked into the bathroom for my
toiletries as Graham peeked out the curtains.

"Maybe I should stay and help them," he called to me. "Just
for an hour."

"I thought you said the guy hired a moving company." I
dropped an armload of shower bottles into the suitcase and
glanced pointedly at my wristwatch. "Besides, we're late
already."

"Uh-huh. And whose fault is that?"

"Striker's."

He smirked. "Right."

"It is! I packed yesterday—you saw me do it. And I could

swear I zipped up my bag before I went to bed, but this morning it was open on the floor and... well, look what she did."

The clothes I originally intended to take with me to New Mexico were strewn across the braided rug that covered most of my studio apartment's floor. Several of my T-shirts had bite marks in them, and every item was covered in a thick layer of cat fur. The destruction was too thorough to be accidental. While I slept, she had pulled everything out of my luggage, dragged it purposefully around the room, and rolled back and forth on top of it until she left a suitable mark.

Honestly, if I'd been able to watch it, I wouldn't even be angry.

Graham covered his smile with one hand and shook his head. "Sorry. I shouldn't laugh."

"She's a menace, and it's your fault," I accused. "You spoil her constantly, like with that cat door."

"Hey, you were just as bothered by her moping around as I was."

He was right. Striker was an outdoor kitty, used to coming and going as she pleased through my window. The sloping roof and sturdy tree outside the turret were her own private staircase, and throughout the warmer months she scampered up and down the three stories all day long. But a feline arthritis diagnosis and the recent cold weather convinced me it was better to keep the window closed and force her to go in and out through the ground-level doors like a civilized cat.

She hadn't been pleased.

Her constant howling at the back door broke our hearts and irritated the other tenants of Primrose House, so Graham installed a cat flap in the kitchen. In a typical show of feline gratitude, she thanked him by vomiting into both sides of his suitcase when he got it out to pack for our trip.

A troubled look crossed Graham's face as he stooped to pick

up one of my cat-fur-crusted shirts. "Maybe she's trying to tell us something. First my luggage, now yours. Do you think she wants to stay home?"

I recoiled from the suggestion. "What, with a sitter or something?"

"I don't know. It's a long drive. Maybe it would be better if she didn't come."

As I knelt on the slightly overfilled suitcase to zip it closed, I considered his suggestion. My boss, Yuri Dyedov, would probably be willing to check in on her twice a day. We might even be able to leave her in the care of my masseuse, Elizabeth Monk. We were only planning to be away for a week. Striker would survive being apart from us for a quick burst.

But I had a vision in my head of how this trip should be. I couldn't call it a vacation; to me, vacations were schedule free, lazy spans of time spent relaxing or casually taking in the sights. Our journey to New Mexico had several overlapping agendas, and I wasn't sure how much time we'd really have for napping or meandering strolls.

On paper, we were going to check out a few art galleries in Albuquerque that Graham had connected with earlier that year. Being able to write off the travel expenses was the only way we could justify splurging on our lodging—there was a fine line between "affordable" and "wake up murdered" that I was never willing to cross again. Plus, the places that let you bring cats along charged an extra fee.

The real reason we were taking this trip was simple: my gut had been screaming at me to go for weeks, and my instincts told me I needed Striker with me.

This idea had first popped into my head after Graham and I found a van smashed into a boulder outside the city limits. Two men had been ejected from the vehicle, and by the time we found them, they were already dead. I had been trying to make contact with their spirits since, because what we found in their van raised way too many questions to ignore.

First, I wanted to ask them about their cargo. Their van was packed full of moldy old cabinetry and wood paneling from a notoriously haunted cabin, and while I couldn't prove it, I was sure the wood contained the spirit of a man named Richard Franklin—a murderous poltergeist I'd been trying to banish. They also had a small wooden jewelry box containing an equally malevolent force—a box they had stolen from Graham's garage the night before the crash.

Both spirits had escaped into the night sky as the van and its contents went up in flames. I felt their negative energies evaporate as they moved on to the next plane of existence. There had been no reports of paranormal activity at the haunted cabin since. But those facts brought me little peace; there was still too much I needed to know.

How had they extracted Richard Franklin from his hunting ground? Was his spirit already tied to the things they stripped out of his cabin, or had they somehow bound him to the wood? Either way, where were they taking him, and for what purpose? Whose ghost was trapped in the jewelry box? What was the purpose of the Seal of Solomon on the bottom?

Only three people knew the answers to those questions. Two of them had died on the side of the road that night, and if their spirits lingered between worlds, I hadn't been able to reach them. It didn't help that we didn't know their names. The sheriff's department ran into so many dead ends identifying the men that they passed the case on to the state police, who were still investigating. The third person... well, I had his name. And if I wanted to take off the black tourmaline necklace I wore to protect myself against negative energies, I was sure he would appear.

My hand unconsciously leapt up to the stone, and as my fingertips stroked the cool, smooth surface, I let out the breath I'd been holding. The necklace was still there. It still protected me. As long as I wore it, he couldn't find me.

But I wanted to find him.

The man who called himself Horace had psychically stalked me, pretending to be a ghost trapped in the attic of a local inn. He tricked me into going into a haunted forest to find a jewelry box I was sure he had left there for me in the first place and, equally suspiciously, had ordered the men to steal back. He'd been toying with me from afar, astral projecting from an unknown location.

I didn't know enough about astral projection to even guess where he might really be. But the van his lackeys crashed bore license plates from a familiar state: New Mexico.

It was my only lead. My friend in the sheriff's department told me the van had been stolen from long-term parking at the Albuquerque International Sunport, so the plates were real. Odds were Horace was down there. And if I was going to find him, I needed all the help I could get.

"I want Striker with us," I told Graham as I picked up my suitcase. "I'll just feel safer if she is."

"Okay. It's your call." He looked around my apartment. "Where is she?"

"At your place."

He looked startled. "My place? No, I thought you had her up here."

Our eyes widened in unison, and we took off running out my door. Our footsteps pounded down the wide, angular staircase to the second floor, where I narrowly avoided colliding with a man carrying a typewriter.

"Easy!" the stranger snapped, yanking the machine back as though I'd tried to snatch it from him. "This is a '49 Adler!"

"Sorry, Reggie." Graham pulled me backward. "We're just looking for our cat."

Reggie—who I assumed had to be Primrose House's newest

resident—looked vaguely familiar to me. He was taller than Graham, with salt-and-pepper hair rapidly receding from a wide forehead. His dark eyes showed no sign of recognition when they met mine, but I knew I had seen him before—on TV maybe, or in a magazine.

"Do I know you?" I asked.

He tightened his grip on the typewriter. "Doubtful."

"You look so familiar," I pressed. "Are you an actor or something?"

"I'm a writer."

"Oh!" I took a few steps toward him. "I love to read. What have you written?"

"Uh…" He looked me up and down. "Nothing you would know."

That stopped me where I stood. His tone of voice made it clear he wasn't being modest about the popularity of his writing. Whatever his books were about, he didn't think I was… well, *something* enough to have read them.

It wasn't a compliment.

Without another word, he ducked through the open door into Kit's old apartment, leaving me to gape after him. I'd known, obviously, that whoever moved in after she left couldn't possibly match her friendliness. But I hadn't expected my new neighbor to insult me within five seconds of meeting me.

Before I could ask Graham what Reggie's deal was, my boyfriend sprinted for his own closed door. I left him to search his apartment and hurried downstairs to comb the first floor, checking the unoccupied apartment in the converted butler's pantry and the large living room off the vestibule. Graham found me as I was on my hands and knees in the kitchen, hoping to find Striker loafing on the heat register beneath the table.

"She up there?" I asked.

"Nope." He eyed the cat flap in the back door. "She's outside somewhere."

I groaned. She could be anywhere in town, and we were already running late. By the time we found her and got on the road, we'd be guaranteeing ourselves a midnight arrival in New Mexico. I just wanted to be there already.

As I silently debated whether it would be better to delay our departure until the next day or leave her here and arrange for someone in the house to put out fresh food and water, my phone buzzed in my pocket.

"You left town yet?" Elizabeth Monk said when I answered. The voice of my massage therapist made my shoulders reflexively relax downward a full inch.

"No, we're still at home. Why?"

"Good. Thought you left your little puff behind."

I nearly dropped the phone in relief. "Striker's with you?"

She chuckled in my ear. "Showed up half an hour ago, howlin' and scratchin' at the front door. Don't think she knew you canceled this week. Or that she was six hours early for her usual appointment."

"Let me guess: you gave her a massage."

"Can't say no to that face."

"Trust me, we know the feeling." I rolled my eyes at Graham. "Thanks, Elizabeth. We'll be right down."

We packed our luggage beneath the camper shell on a borrowed pickup truck. Graham's faded yellow Geo Metro couldn't be trusted to make it more than a few hundred miles at a time, and his father insisted we take the truck for any longer journeys. In the cab, Graham carefully fastened an oversized pet carrier with soft, tentlike sides on the back seat and tucked a fresh bag of kitty treats into the glove box.

A few minutes later, we arrived at The Enclave, a neighborhood within a neighborhood that catered exclusively to psychics, occultists, and other intuitives. I had been spending a lot of time in The Enclave lately, filming special episodes of *Soul Searchers* with Yuri. We were shorthanded, since our former cameraman, Mark, had gone to LA with Kit. But we had bills to pay, so while we waited for responses to our help wanted ads, Yuri scrounged up work where he could. His girlfriend happened to be the deputy mayor of Donn's Hill, and together they cooked up a scheme to keep us busy on the town's dime by shooting short featurettes about the local psychic community that the tourism commission could post online.

It was far from my favorite thing to do. We were essentially making commercials, and none of them gave me any opportunity to use my psychic gifts. I missed the thrill of reaching out to a spirit and feeling their answer. I craved the high it gave me to help people deal with a haunting. Anything less just felt like a chore.

Halloween decor was still strung up between The Enclave's brightly painted row houses, and scattered orange candy wrappers from last night's trick-or-treaters littered the ground. At the far end of the cobblestone footpath, a hulking two-story building housed the Ace of Cups, a gastropub with a deliciously carb-heavy menu and a popular Sunday brunch. My stomach growled, but we didn't have time to stop for food. It would have to be a protein bar on the road at this point.

From the porch of a pink building between us and the pub, a gangly man in his early forties swept fallen leaves from his shop's steps. Stephen Hastain was a rune caster, Irishman, and Graham's best friend. He cupped his hands around his mouth, and his voice echoed off the surrounding storefronts. "Hey, Mac! When's my interview, eh? Elizabeth's getting all the attention!"

I flapped a hand at him as I sprinted down the path, futilely trying to get him to lower his volume. "Good grief, are you always this loud this early? Your neighbors must hate you."

The smile lines around his eyes crinkled as he jerked his chin toward Elizabeth's shop. "Only one. Not that I blame her."

That was generous of him. The Enclave was a small neighborhood with a lot of open secrets, like Stephen's now-ended affair with a married woman. Elizabeth hadn't approved. And honestly, when I first learned about it, I had thought less of him. But the woman he was sleeping with was a master manipulator, and I couldn't fault him for falling for her tricks.

I had fallen for them too.

His former paramour had been a tarot card reader named Daphne Martin. Unlike Stephen and me, her psychic abilities had been a sham, and her need to perpetuate that hoax drove her to murder. Her shop now sat empty beneath Elizabeth's more respectable day spa.

"Yuri said he'll call you to get your interview scheduled," I told Stephen. "You'll get your fifteen minutes of fame after I get back from vacation, I promise."

He grinned. "I'd better. I saw the fan mail Elizabeth's been getting, and it is stee-ee-eamy."

"Liar." Graham laughed beside me. "There's no way she would show you something like that."

"Fair enough," Stephen admitted. "But can't you just see it? The old girl's face would be so red!"

His cackles followed us across the street to Elizabeth's building. A simple wooden sign above the door read Massage - Reiki - Furrapy, and the glass door at the top of the stairs was etched with silhouettes of humans and animals in a variety of active poses. Inside, Elizabeth stood behind the check-in desk. Her lean face was covered in a dense network of fine lines, and a loose white braid flowed over the shoulder of her long-sleeved dress. Her serious mien was somewhat undercut by the friendly crinkle at the corners of her eyes as she glanced down at my cat.

Striker lay next to Elizabeth's keyboard, her yellow eyes watching tendrils of frankincense-scented steam rise from the oil diffuser toward the ceiling. She rolled over to show me her multi-colored belly when I walked in the door, trilling, "Brrrllll."

Her sleepy expression was normal after a furrapy appointment with Elizabeth. The brief sessions were a fraction of what I paid for my monthly visits and specifically designed to relieve Striker's arthritis symptoms. Along with talking to ghosts and working on the crew of a paranormal TV show, paying someone else to massage my cat was one of many things I never thought I would do before coming to Donn's Hill.

"Hey, sneaky girl," I told Striker as I pulled out my wallet. "Took matters into your own paws, huh?"

"Should'a heard the racket she was makin'," Elizabeth said with fondness in her voice. "Miracle she didn't wake the whole street."

Graham gathered the cat into his arms. "I hope she didn't wake you."

"Never get much sleep, and less now than I ever have. Don't know if it's age or a restless mind." Elizabeth eyed me. "Suspect you'll be the same when you're as old as me."

"If I get to be half as tough as you are, it'll be worth a few sleepless nights. Any news about what might move in downstairs?"

Elizabeth shook her head. "Won't be long yet. Some new pretender'll be down there soon."

"What this place needs," I decided, "is an occult-themed bakery. Ouija board cakes, sugar cookies with runes on the frosting, tasty little muffins…" My mouth stopped moving, but my mind ran wild with the delicious possibilities. An after-massage pastry sounded like the perfect self-care day.

"We heard you've been getting a little fan mail," Graham said.

Elizabeth huffed out through her nose. "Never should'a let Yuri talk me into doin' that. Phone's ringin' all day and night, people wantin' me to come teach classes on the craft."

I wasn't surprised so many people had connected with her through our promotional video. Her unique treatment strategy and her skills as an Empath made her a top priority for the tourism commission, but it had taken both Yuri and I wheedling and cajoling her before she agreed to go on camera. We filmed right in her day spa, where she demonstrated her furrapy practice on a certain volunteer tortoiseshell cat and discussed the differences between being an Empath and having empathy.

Now she held out her hand, and the dozens of tiny stones around her wrist tinkled. "Let's get you out that door before your energy knocks me off my feet. Never seen you so wound up."

Her bracelets, one on each wrist, were made of the same black tourmaline she had given me to wear around my neck. She wore them to protect herself from absorbing any negative energy during reiki or massage, but no crystal could muffle her natural ability to read someone's emotions, and apparently it didn't do much to block out the waves of anxious excitement rolling off me now.

"Sorry." I winced. "I'm just antsy to get going."

"Go on and get movin'. I'll phone my cousin, let him know you're on the way."

"Thanks again for recommending his place to us. I'm excited to see it."

Striker was still limp as a noodle when we packed her into the truck, and I crossed my fingers that her state of quiet relaxation would last a few hundred miles. After our ridiculous morning, I fully expected at least two or three more distractions to delay our departure, but none came. We were two hours late but finally on the road.

Traffic was easy at this early hour on a Sunday, but cars still streamed onto Main Street from the highway. The tireless tourism efforts the deputy mayor had been driving for the last several months had not only increased weekend traffic but grown the permanent population of Donn's Hill as well. Everyone from private residences to the Ace of Cups was renting out spare rooms, and the large modern apartment complex behind the gas station on Main had a full parking lot, including two moving vans like the one Reggie had brought to Primrose House.

A sudden wave of nausea slammed into me as we passed the apartments. I jolted forward and gripped the dashboard for support.

"You okay?" Graham asked in alarm. "Are you carsick?"

I shook my head. The iron grip on my insides didn't feel like motion sickness. The nausea pressed down on me, trying to flatten me from all sides. Buzzing filled my ears, and I had a sudden flashback to coming down this road from the other direction, cringing in pain as we unknowingly carried a haunted jewelry box in the trunk. Bile crept up my throat at the memory. I scrambled to open the glove box, praying there was an old grocery bag or something inside that would spare me the embarrassment of explaining to Graham's father that I'd vomited all over the inside of his truck before we even left the city's limits.

The feeling passed. It disappeared as suddenly as it had come, and I slumped against the cold window glass beside me, panting slightly.

I felt the truck's wheels slowing, and I shook my head. "I'm fine," I told Graham.

"Are you sure? We can head back to the station, get you some ice or something."

"Really, I'm okay." And I was. The nausea had lifted, leaving no trace behind. "I'm just tired. And hungry. Do you have any of those granola bars?"

I tried to put the weird bout of sickness out of my mind as I chewed. If it had lasted much longer than that brief flash, I would have asked Graham to turn around and take us home.

And maybe that would have been for the best.

CHAPTER TWO

Thirteen hours and sixty-eight million cat howls later, my navigation app instructed us to turn off the interstate. The sun had set long before we crossed into New Mexico, but I could see the glint of water in our headlights as the Rio Grande snaked back and forth beside the two-lane highway.

It was a vaguely familiar journey, one I had taken with my mother the first eight springs of my life. Driving from Albuquerque to Donn's Hill for the Afterlife Festival was our one big vacation every year, and it was weird to be making the trip the wrong way around. Several of the gas stations felt like places we had stopped at on our way home, but I couldn't say for sure. Was that the same rest stop where I puked after ignoring my mom's warnings about doing puzzle books in the back seat? Or did they all just have that same green paint and white powdered soap?

My clearest memory of our time on the road was listening to her favorite Oingo Boingo cassette over and over, singing along to "Dead Man's Party" as loudly as we could. Graham had the same album on his iPod, and we mixed it in along with the R.E.M. and Oasis playlists he needed to stay focused on the road. During my turns as copilot, I texted pictures of the scenery to Kit, who replied with helpful tips from her own recent journey west: *Don't forget to pick up those gummy twin snakes next time you stop. They're road-trip fuel!*

Striker did better than I expected, mostly napping in her carrier. Graham pulled over frequently to let her stretch her legs on the truck's seats, drink some water from her travel dish, and nibble a small pile of crunchy treats from his hand. But that level of first-class travel still left plenty of room for complaints. Any time we sped up to pass another vehicle or went around the gentlest of curves, she let out a guttural yowl that zinged straight into my heart.

"What's this place called?" Graham asked.

"Yurt in Luck." I checked my phone. "Two more miles."

He chuckled. "Oh man, we have to tell Penny about that one. She hates punny stuff like that. I think it physically pained her when Tom named their motel E-Z Sleep."

When I pictured our accommodations, I imagined something similar to that now-demolished motel outside Donn's Hill: one long row of connected rooms strung together in a single building. The name of the place, plus the fact that Elizabeth had recommended it to us, should have warned me that Yurt in Luck would be a little different.

Rows of twinkling lights marked the entrance to a parking lot flanked by eleven small round structures. They were arranged in a wide *V*, with the end units closest to the road. The large center building beside the river had the word Office etched into the front window. An enormous sandstone slab welcomed us to Yurt in Luck Riverside Resort, and a pair of rustic wooden signs pointed toward Curios on one side and Critters on the other.

I left Graham in the truck with Striker and paused outside the office for a few moments, inhaling the sweet scent of the desert. I'd forgotten how good piñon pine smelled, and I let the freshness of the night air clear out my lungs and chase away the last of the day's stress. After a few more greedy breaths, I left the soft gurgle of the river behind and stepped into the office.

Inside, a reedy man with a wild, gray beard munched on hummus and pretzel sticks at a messy desk. His weather-beaten face suggested he was in his seventies or eighties, but he leapt to his feet with the spry energy of a younger man and rushed forward to hold the door open for me.

"Come in, come in!" He patted my shoulders as I passed, then let the door fall closed and hurried back around to the business side of his desk. "How can I help you?"

"We have a reservation under Mackenzie Clair." I handed over my driver's license and my credit card.

He took them and sat down, frowning at the name printed on the cards. It wasn't the facial expression I usually expected to see when checking in somewhere, and my unease mounted as he typed something into his computer and gave a slow shake of his head. "Hmm. I'm sorry, miss, but I don't have anything under that name. Are you sure this is where you booked your stay? We are a little... uh... niche."

"Shoot. Maybe it's under Mac? I'm not sure which name my friend used when she booked it."

"Nothing under Mac.... What's your friend's name? We might have put it under that."

"Elizabeth Monk?"

The man's cheeks split like baked sand as he grinned. "Cousin Lizzie! How do know you her?"

"She's my massage therapist."

"Lucky you! She's famous now, did you know that?"

"So I've heard." I was glad people outside Donn's Hill had seen the video; that meant Yuri and Penelope's strategy was working, and our work hadn't been wasted.

"Well, let's get you checked in. I'll just update your name, Miss..."

"Clair," I repeated, holding out my hand. "Call me Mac."

"Fred Hawkes. Pleasure to meet you." He pecked at his keyboard with two long, slow fingers. "Traveling alone?"

"No, my boyfriend is outside with our cat."

"Cat?"

"Yeah. That's okay, right?"

"Hmm." A deep divot formed between his eyebrows. "We had you in one of our pet-free units. We can't allow a cat in there. Allergies, you know."

My earlier tension returned to my chest, squeezing tightly, as I imagined how expensive it would be to find a room somewhere else for tonight. "Is there another room available?"

"Not on the Critter side." He frowned and glanced at the keys on the wall. Five hung beneath gold labels that matched the signs outside: four beneath Curios and one beneath Critters. "Well, maybe. I'll have to check something."

He picked up the phone and turned his back to me, murmuring into the mouthpiece at a volume too low for me to effectively eavesdrop. Meanwhile, I tried to remember if we had passed any other lodging within the last hour. Would they have a vacancy? Would they allow cats?

Just as I was pulling out my phone to see if it would be too cold to sleep in the truck tonight, Fred swiveled back around in his chair to squint at something on his computer screen.

"Well, can't we just swap them in the system? ...And what about her bags?" He glanced up at me and turned away again, but his volume wasn't quite low enough to keep me from hearing him ask, "What did the police say?"

My eyebrows and my curiosity both shot into the stratosphere. What did the police have to do with our reservation?

When he hung up the phone, his mouth was pulled into a grim expression. "Okay, we're all set."

"Really?"

He leaned back in his chair, snatched the lone Critter key off the row of hooks, and hopped to his feet once more. "Let's get you settled."

Fred led me down the row of yurts on the right. Pools of yellow light from the bulb above each porch illuminated placards with words like White Elephant, Ladybug, and Scarab instead of numbers. Our unit was on the southernmost end, closest to the wooden round-rail fence that marked the edge of the property. It was a strange little structure; it looked as though someone had taken an enormous maroon sock and stretched it over a soup can large enough to live in, then punched in windows and a door as an afterthought. Whatever the material was made of, it was taut enough that it didn't so much as flutter in the night breeze.

"Here you are: Tortoiseshell." Fred slid the key into the door, jiggling the handle up and down as he turned it. "You have to give it a bit of a shake sometimes." When the door still refused to budge, he gritted his teeth and glared at the handle for a second before giving the door a little kick. It popped open. "Ah, there we go! After you."

The yurt felt larger inside than it looked from the outside, and the interior was pleasantly bright and clean. The walls—or *wall*, really, since it was a single rounded surface that stretched all the way around with no corners—were made from floor-to-ceiling cedar boards that had been polished to a high sheen. The linoleum bore a few deep scratches and scuffs, hinting at the structure's age, but the familiar scent of Pine-Sol assured me the floor was cleaner than the average motel carpet.

The night sky was visible through a circular window at the peak of the ceiling from which the canvas roof cascaded gently down to the yurt's sides. Most of the space was taken up by a queen-sized bed, above which hung a portrait of a tortoiseshell cat. The cat looked like she had two faces combined into one, creamy tan on one side and dusty black on the other.

"This is so weird," I told Fred. "We have a tortie."

"Lucky you!" he said for the second time. "Literally. All our units are named after good-luck charms, and I can't think of a cuddlier one than a tortoiseshell cat."

A wooden dresser, a small kitchenette, and a pine table with two chairs stood around the curved wall. I was relieved to see that none of the furniture was fabric or wicker. Everything was catproof.

"The bathroom and laundry are through here." Fred disappeared through a door that had been cut into the yurt beside the kitchenette. When he reappeared a moment later, he was pulling a large piece of rolling luggage behind him.

"What's that?" I asked.

"Oh, just something the last guest left behind. Nothing to worry about." He leaned the luggage against the main doorframe and turned back to me. "Now let's see. Pots and pans are in the dresser's bottom drawer, and spare toilet paper is in the cupboard above the washing machine. Any questions?"

I had several, but they were all about the silver suitcase, so I shook my head and smiled politely. "Nope. Thanks for doing whatever you had to do to make room for us. I think we'll be really comfortable here."

"Good." He dropped the key onto the little dining table and pulled the left-behind luggage out the door, calling over his shoulder, "Don't hesitate to call if you need anything, anything at all."

Graham pulled the truck around to our side of the little triangular parking lot. As we ferried our luggage and Striker's accessories into the yurt, I snuck a glance at our nimble host. Rather than taking the suitcase into the office, he put it in the farthest unit on the Curio side of the complex.

There was no time to wonder what he was doing. Striker's sharp, high-pitched yowls set my priorities, and I found a place for her litter box between the sink and the tub. Not willing to take any chances, I locked her in the bathroom so she could acclimate to her surroundings and take care of business.

Graham was grinning at the photo above the bed when I closed the bathroom door. "This has to be a good sign, right?"

"I think so." I gave him a quick kiss. "This is already a great trip."

We took our time settling into our temporary home, tucking a week's worth of cat food into the dresser drawers and unpacking our clothes. After such a long car ride, it felt good to stretch out on the large bed for a few minutes before releasing Striker from the bathroom.

She inspected every inch of the building's interior with quivering whiskers and a wet nose. The furniture must have met her approval because she settled down on top of the pine table in a compact bundle and stared at the desert that stretched out beyond the fence.

"Let's leave her here while we grab dinner," Graham suggested. "We passed a taco place a few miles back that looked open."

We left Striker to guard the yurt and drove back up the road to the restaurant Graham had seen. The all-night eatery took up the right half of a gas station, with counter service inside the convenience store. Graham ordered our food, and I wandered the shop, selecting sour candies, mini donuts, and potato chips to keep handy in the yurt. My purchases made, I joined Graham in a faded yellow booth to wait for our dinner.

He leaned against the hard plastic mold of the bench and leafed through the Arts section of the Albuquerque Journal. His posture was lazy, with one leg crossed over the other and the newspaper suspended between his elevated hands. I couldn't see his face, but I knew his expression would be one of easy contentment, as though we were sitting in the kitchen of Primrose House instead of a Chevron.

I had always assumed Graham's relaxed attitude had been because of his surroundings. Prior to this trip, I'd only seen him on his home turf. But he had carried that calm demeanor through every rest stop on the long drive here, and I realized that, in addition to his talent for sculpture, Graham had a knack for being comfortable anywhere he went. He could settle into any chair, pick up an abandoned copy of the local paper, and lose himself in the moment.

I envied that. No matter where I was or what I was doing, my mind wanted to focus on being somewhere else and doing something different. There always seemed to be some errand that needed running or question that needed answering. Like right now. How could I relax when tomorrow we would be visiting my childhood home?

"You okay?" Graham asked.

"Yeah, why?"

"You're shaking the whole booth."

I pressed down on my bouncing leg, forcing my foot to stop tapping. "Sorry. Now that we're here, I'm excited to start seeing everything again."

"Here." He handed me a section of the paper. "This might help distract you while we wait."

Attempting to mimic his Mr. Cleaver-like posture, I flicked open the paper and skimmed the current events. None of it interested me—I doubted I would care about local government business even if we were back in Donn's Hill. As a tourist, I felt especially disconnected from New Mexico's news.

Then a headline caught my eye with a word I had never seen before today but with which I was now intimately acquainted: YURT RESORT DEATH RULED ACCIDENTAL.

A woman found dead in the Socorro County desert died from hypothermia, officials said Friday. Camila Aster, 24, of Gainesville, Ga., was found in her pajamas just a few hundred yards from her motel outside Escondida after an unusually cold overnight low of 26 degrees Fahrenheit.

Aster was reported missing on Oct. 28 after failing to check out of her room on time. Resort staff found the door to her unit ajar and no signs of a struggle. She was in the Socorro area on vacation to visit the Very Large Array and was traveling alone, according to police.

"This was a shock to all of us," said Lucille Hawkes, owner and operator of the Yurt in Luck Resort. "Our guests are like family."

A chill ran up my spine, and I checked the date at the top of the page. The paper was only a day old. Within the last week, this woman had been staying at our exact same motel. What were the odds hers was the Tortoiseshell room?

One in ten, my brain chirped helpfully. But I knew in my gut that the luggage Fred Hawkes carried out of our unit hadn't been left behind by anyone who'd gone home alive. Our room had last been occupied by the now-deceased Camila Aster.

I kept reading, rabidly curious to know more about the woman whose suitcase had so recently been wheeled out of our bathroom.

Authorities warn that hypothermia can set in at tempera-tures as high as 50 degrees, especially if alcohol or other substances are involved. Aster is the 22nd person to die of exposure this year...

My vision fuzzed, and my mind stopped processing the words in front of me. Suddenly, I was no longer sitting in a cheap taco shop. I was crying on the swing set in my mother's backyard, clutching the chains at my sides and struggling to process her death. I hadn't seen her die. I hadn't even been allowed to see her body. All I had was a single word, a nonsensical bunch of syllables I hadn't understood and hadn't wanted to.

Exposure.

The word unleashed a tidal wave of emotions that would have knocked me over if I wasn't already sitting down. As the cashier dropped a paper bag full of burritos onto our table, I burst into tears.

CHAPTER THREE

My plans for our first day in New Mexico were simple: sleep in to recover from the drive, take Graham to visit my mother's grave, and stop by the house where I had spent the first eight years of my life. There was just one problem: sleeping in required falling asleep in the first place.

After my unexpectedly emotional response to such a simple word, Graham and I returned to the yurt to gulp down our dinner. He heroically tried to stay awake and talk to me, but there wasn't much to talk about. We both knew the real reason I was crying was that I was completely exhausted from the trip, and hunger tended to bring out my emotional side.

Graham was snoring as soon as I turned out the light. I tried to follow suit, but my mind kept going back to the day my mother died. It returned again and again to the word I had never wanted to hear again.

Exposure.

Back then, it was only when my father arrived that I heard anyone ask the important question: what had my mother been doing out in the desert in the middle of the night? She was supposed to be covering the graveyard shift for a friend at the call center while our neighbor Darlene watched me.

Nobody had an answer for my father. And when I got older and asked the same question, he didn't have an answer for me. He thought she might have been exhausted and delirious from picking up too many extra shifts. He felt guilty about that. If she hadn't been a single mother, if he'd known about me sooner and been able to help, would she have been working so much?

As I lay awake in the yurt, I wondered if my father had been right. Did she really wander into the wilderness in a fit of delirium? What if she meant to go out there? What if she was looking for something?

What had she seen?

And had Camila Aster seen the same thing?

I didn't know why a stranger's death was eating at me so much. Camila and my mother were just two women who happened to freeze to death in the same state. As far as I could tell from one newspaper article, their similarities ended there. But the word nagged at me, tugging at the corners of my mind until my brain folded in on itself like origami.

Exposure.

I forced myself to stay awake and stared at the stars thought the yurt's skylight, terrified that if I fell asleep, I would wake up alone in the cold, dark desert. It wasn't until the glow of dawn peeked through the window that I finally allowed myself to drift off.

TOO FEW HOURS LATER, the pinging of my phone dragged me back into consciousness. It was a message from Kit: *How's the trip?*

OK so far, I typed back, too tired and groggy to even attempt to tell her what had happened the night before. *Going to visit Mom's grave today.*

Wish I was there with you, Kit sent. *Lay a flower for me.*

I snuggled back against my pillow. Imagining Kit standing beside me at my mother's grave washed away a layer or two of the sorrow that had drenched my soul after reading the article about Camila Aster's death. I wished Kit were here now. We could catch up over breakfast and laugh a few of our troubles away.

Will do, I sent back. *What are you up to today?*

Well…

A moment later, an image popped up on my phone. Kit grinned at the camera, green hair wild and thick eyeliner smudged around her eyes. She looked like she had just woken up. The skin at one of her temples looked slightly red and swollen, and silver gleamed above and below her eyebrow.

Did you get a new piercing? I asked.

While I waited for her reply, my brain processed the other details in the picture. Kit was somewhere crowded. Behind her, I could see the curly red hair of our former cameraman, Mark, who also left our show in favor of working with Amari. And behind him—

I sucked in a breath through my teeth.

Behind Mark, I could just make out the boarding area of an airport gate.

Holy crap! I typed. *Where are you right now?*

Yes to new piercing LOL. And NYC, baby! We had to wake up super early but it's gonna be worth it when I'm in FREAKING PARIS in eight hours!

She sent another photo. This one was a double selfie with her girlfriend, Amari. They both grinned from ear to ear as they held up their plane tickets. Kit had used an app to add a curly French mustache to her face and put a digital beret on

Amari's usually shaved head. A ghost emoji completed the picture.

My fingernails scraped down the back of my phone's case as I gripped the screen. We didn't even have the budget or the manpower to film in Moyard, and they were going to France? She was going to Europe without me?

For once, I was glad we were communicating via text and she couldn't see the envy on my face. It made it easier to fake the right emotions. *Exciting! How long will you be there?*

Just a week. Hoping to sneak in a visit to the Louvre while we're there. Don't know if my phone will have service but I'll send pics when I can!

Another message from her interrupted me as I was typing a reply. *Have to board now—talk soon!*

I tossed my phone back onto my nightstand.

"Everything okay?" Graham asked.

The aroma of a rich, dark roast reached my nose. He had packed his percolator from home, not trusting the motel to have a decent one. The bag of mini donuts was already open on the table.

"I'll be better with some breakfast in my stomach," I said as I climbed out of bed. "Did you bring any cream?"

An hour later, Graham filled a pair of thermoses with more coffee for the road, and we headed out the door. Striker wasn't invited on this portion of the trip; the yurt resort was nearly an hour from the cemetery, and we decided it wasn't worth putting her through that long of a journey just so she could wait in the truck. After so many hours wincing every time we passed another car, it was a relief to travel without any yowls from the back seat.

My mother had been buried in a large memorial garden that, from the outside, looked like it could be a soccer field if not for the flat grayish rectangles set into the grass. A tall chain-link fence protected the cemetery from vandals, and an unnaturally wide variety of conifers, oaks, and shrubs dotted the park.

We picked our way through the rows of in-ground headstones, using a printout from the cemetery's website as a guide. The closer we got to my mother's marker, the worse I felt. I hadn't been back here in over ten years, not since before I started college.

I should have visited her more frequently.

I should have known my way here by heart.

By the time we reached her tombstone, my guilt had latched onto my shoulders and compressed my chest. I forced myself to exhale slowly as I crouched beside her grave. With a shaking hand, I ran my fingers over the inscribed letters:

Evelyn Clair

She passed through nature to eternity

"What does that mean?" Graham asked.

"It's from Hamlet." I smiled, recalling my father's explanation for choosing the inscription. "My dad and Darlene came up with it together. They thought my mother never seemed afraid of death the way people sometimes are. She knew it was just another phase of the journey."

As the words left my mouth, I heard them in my father's voice, and I felt the truth of them. My mother had traveled the country looking for what she called "spiritual nexuses," places where the veil separating the living and the dead was the thinnest. She had spent spring after spring in Donn's Hill, trying to connect with the other side through her friend and psychic medium, Gabrielle Suntador.

She wouldn't have been afraid to cross over.

She wouldn't have lingered here.

Just the same, I stood and leaned against Graham, closing my eyes and mentally feeling for her presence. While the black tour- maline protected me from unwanted energy, it was more of a one-way mirror than a brick wall. Slowly, as my breathing grew more regular, I allowed my consciousness to spread out.

The longer I waited, the sharper my other senses grew. I could smell woodsmoke in the air and hear footsteps in the grass, but I felt nothing else.

As I suspected, there was no trace of her here.

The guilt I had been feeling detached from my chest and evaporated into the chilly air. I might not have made the pilgrimage to my mother's grave as often as other people visited their departed loved ones, but I thought of her every single day. I carried her memory with me. Wherever she was, I was confident she didn't resent me for not placing flowers on her grave every week. And if she wouldn't blame me, why should I blame myself?

A smile settled onto my lips. I opened my eyes and instinctively looked for the source of the footsteps I had heard. An elderly man shuffled by a few rows away from us. He stooped to collect a bundle of dried roses from the base of a wide tombstone, replacing them with a fresh bouquet. He stood there for a few silent moments, clutching his feed cap to his chest.

Something about his posture sent my mind back to the first time I had been in this cemetery.

"There was an old man there," I remembered aloud.

"Where?" Graham glanced around until his eyes landed on the man with the roses. "That guy?"

I shook my head. "No, not him. My mother didn't have a funeral. Not like they do in Donn's Hill anyway, with the big church service and the procession to the cemetery. We just had a few prayers at her grave."

"That sounds nice. Intimate."

"I guess. I didn't really have anything to compare it to. I could barely process any of it. But my dad was there, and Darlene, and this little old man I'd never seen before."

Graham's brows furrowed together. "You didn't know him?"

"No. Is that weird?"

He watched the elderly mourner in front of us, then shrugged. "I don't know. Maybe he worked with your mom, or maybe he just happened to be here and stopped to pay respects or something."

"Yeah." I chewed my lip, then sighed. "Holy crap, I'm so tired. My brain keeps fixating on the weirdest things. I've got words and images flashing on repeat in my head, and I can't make any sense of them."

"Let's head back to the yurt," Graham suggested. "We're on vacation. Vacations mean naps."

"That sounds phenomenal."

I knelt and rested my hand against my mother's tombstone one more time. It felt like the right thing to do, but even as my skin touched the cool stone, I knew it was an empty gesture. My mother's spirit wasn't hanging around her coffin. I didn't need to trek all the way to New Mexico to see her.

All I had to do was dream.

CHAPTER FOUR

I stood in my mother's backyard. My gaze passed over the weedy flower beds and empty bird feeders to rest on the swing set, where a pair of vacant seats creaked and twisted in the wind. The swings pulled at me, begging me to sit down, pump my legs, and soar into the air. But the rusty chains—and the memory of the last time I'd sat in that spot—kept my feet rooted where they were, glued to the cracked concrete of the patio.

I closed my eyes and inhaled deeply, expecting the clean scent of lavender I remembered from my childhood. Instead, the foul stench of rot and decay invaded my nostrils. My eyelids flew open, and I glared at the overflowing garbage bins by the back door.

Reality so rarely measured up to dreams.

If this was a dream, I could stand still, awash in nostalgia until my mother's shimmering form took shape at the edge of my vision. Then I would hear her voice, clear as the tinkling of wind chimes from the neighbor's yard, calling my name.

But this was real life. I wasn't likely to see her here.

Despite being fully rested from my nap, I felt like the world around me was cloaked in a layer of surreality, almost real but not quite, like an optical illusion my eyes were on the verge of seeing through. Darkness slowly gathered as the sun set behind the low hills far to the west, but I half expected to blink and find myself in total blackness. Then, just as they had too often in my nightmares, a pair of glowing red eyes would open in front of me.

I turned and squinted at the kitchen window, sure *he* would be standing there, watching me the way my mother always had. The window was empty, but I still reflexively checked for the piece of black tourmaline on the cord around my neck.

"Doing okay?" Graham asked. He sat on the patio, rubbing Striker's ears as he watched me.

Her yellow eyes followed me around the yard as well, wide and upside down from her position in Graham's lap. She lay on her back with each of her four legs sticking out in a different direction, in protest of her harness.

"I'm fine," I said.

"Has it changed a lot?"

I closed my eyes again and pictured the yard as I'd known it as a child—and as I'd known it in my dreams. "It's too quiet. In my memories, it's always summer."

"I like picturing tiny Mackenzie playing tag on the lawn with a bunch of other little kids."

"Well… it was usually just me."

"Really?" He raised an eyebrow. "No friends?"

I shrugged. "Not that I remember. Not here anyway."

"Hmm." He narrowed his eyes, but his lips curled upward in a sly smile. "Okay, I'm revising the image in my head. Now I see little Mackenzie hitting her goth phase a few years early, telling the kids at school about the ghosts in her bedroom and freaking everybody out."

"I was *not* goth." I didn't bother disputing the rest. His imagined scenario was too close to reality for comfort, and it was only my extreme laziness toward makeup that kept me from wearing heavy eyeliner and purple lipstick. "And most people don't have the luxury of growing up somewhere like Donn's Hill, okay? In places like this"—I waved a hand at the back fence, indicating the suburban area around us—"people like to throw words like *freak* around."

His smile vanished. "Oh, don't worry. There were plenty of tiny tyrants at Donn's Hill Elementary. Kids always find a way to make somebody feel bad for being different."

I sat beside him and wrapped an arm around his waist, pulling him into a lopsided hug. "I wish we'd met earlier. I would've loved having a friend like you around."

He squeezed me back. As we sat there, the breeze picked up and shook the surrounding trees. I shivered. My loose-knit pullover left far too many gaps and spaces to effectively block out the wind, and the cold seeped through my jeans from the concrete.

"It's getting chilly." Graham let go of my waist and rubbed my back with one hand. "I wish we could go inside."

"Me too," I said automatically, but it was a lie.

When we had first pulled up to the house, I just stared at it for a while, taking in the sameness of it. It was identical to the one in my memory, as though I'd only been gone twenty minutes instead of twenty years. Whoever bought the house after my mother's passing hadn't made any changes, not to the light pink stucco or the bark chips and succulents that crowded the tiny front yard.

It took me longer than I would have expected to find the strength to climb out of the truck. My legs felt limp beneath me as I crossed the short distance from the sidewalk to the front porch, and when I rang the doorbell, I found myself hoping nobody would answer.

Nobody did.

Reluctant as I was to step foot inside the house, I hadn't been able to resist sneaking down the driveway and slipping into the backyard through the unlocked gate. Now, just in case this was my last chance to be here, I heaved myself to my feet and wandered over to the swing set. My fingers dragged lightly down the metal links, as cold as the last time I sat there. In my mind's eye, I saw our neighbor Darlene round the corner from her driveway. A grim expression clouded her features as she explained to me how completely my life was about to change.

A sharp voice yanked me back to the present. "Excuse me, can I help you?"

Graham was on his feet, tucking Striker into the front of his zippered hoodie and backing toward me protectively as an angry-looking woman let herself through the back gate. I focused on her face and let out a tiny shriek of surprise.

There she stood, as though summoned by my very thoughts.

Darlene.

I hadn't even bothered checking to see if she still lived in the house next door. I assumed that, like me, she had moved away a long time ago. Looking at her, I realized how little sense that made. Just because my life upended completely didn't mean everyone else's didn't carry on as per usual. Obviously, Darlene had stayed right where she was, looking exactly the way I remembered her.

No, I realized as she squinted at Graham. *She's aged.*

For some reason, that surprised me too. It was jarring to see the crinkles around her eyes and mouth and the encroaching gray at the roots of her hair.

She moved a few steps closer and asked Graham, "Do Jack and Diane know you're here?"

A smile spread across my face. This was classic Darlene: bold, brave, and in everyone's business—but in a good kind of way. She wasn't the sort of neighbor who would ignore questionable activity in the next yard. She would put on her best housecoat, march back there, and make sure everything was on the up-and-up.

"Darlene, it's me." I waved at her, pulling her attention away from the tall man with the cat in his sweater. "Mackenzie Clair."

The instant she saw me, recognition sparked in her eyes. She placed a hand over her heart. "Macky-bug?"

I cringed. I had forgotten that awful nickname. Graham coughed in a way that sounded suspiciously like laughter, and I realized with horror that he would *never* forget it.

"It's just Mac these days." I rubbed the back of my neck with one hand and ducked my head, feeling like a little kid.

Her body slammed into mine before I had a chance to look up, and her arms wrapped around me in a suffocatingly tight hug. Just when I thought I would have to shove her away so I could breathe again, she released me, pulling back to examine my face.

"Look at you! You're all grown up. And—" Her voice broke, and she finished her thought in a whisper. "God, you're just your mother's clone, aren't you?"

Her face was close enough to mine that I could trace her eyes as they landed on each of the features I inherited from my mother: the dark blue in my irises, the sharp edges of my cheekbones, the loose waves in my dark hair.

I cleared my throat and stepped backward, then introduced my companions. Darlene gave Graham an awkward half hug to avoid smashing Striker.

"How long are you in town?" she asked. "Do you have time for a cup of coffee?"

Graham perked up. "You don't mind if we bring our cat?"

Darlene waved a dismissive hand. "No, no, that's fine. Come on over whenever you're ready."

She slipped out through the back gate, and I looked at Graham.

"We can stay out here as long as you want," he said.

I shivered, once more feeling the chill through my sweater. "It's okay. I'm ready. Besides, it's freezing."

"Brrrllll," Striker agreed, snuggling deeper into Graham's hoodie.

We slipped out the way we'd come, closing the back gate behind us and returning to the sidewalk. Next door, Darlene's house looked just the way I remembered. It was one of the few two-story homes in the neighborhood, and she'd painted the siding a vibrant green that exactly matched the Astroturf covering her front yard. Unlike my mother, Darlene hated gardening.

She threw open the door and ushered us inside, clearly excited to have guests. I stared around the living room, trying to recall if I'd ever actually been inside her house before.

I decided I hadn't.

If it had looked like this when I was a kid, I would have remembered.

Furniture, plastic totes, and cardboard boxes crowded the room from edge to edge. A narrow, winding pathway had been kept reasonably clear, but we had to step over a toppled pile of newspapers to follow her into the kitchen.

"Sorry it's so tight in here." Darlene squeezed between a tall dresser and a television stand that held no television. "Nobody ever comes to the front door, so I mostly use this room for storage."

The kitchen was blessedly uncluttered. Cupboards ringed three of the walls, leaving an open space in the center for a small table. Pale light from the setting sun peeked into the room from the window above the sink, which provided a clear view across Darlene's driveway and into my mother's old backyard. A door by the fridge led outside.

I wondered again if I had been in her house before, at least in this room. Everything from the pale yellow refrigerator to the sunflower-printed hand towels felt undeniably familiar.

"Sit down, sit down," she said. "Cream in your coffee?"

"Yes, please." I lowered myself onto a spindly stool I suspected had been rescued from a dumpster somewhere.

Graham took the metal folding chair next to me and released Striker from the indignity of her harness. She shook herself vigorously before setting to work investigating the crumb-littered recesses beneath the cupboards.

After pouring the coffee, Darlene leaned her elbows on the table and stared at me, joy still lighting up her face. "I can't believe it's really you. Tell me everything. What do you do for a living? Are you a librarian like you wanted?"

"Librarian?" I frowned. I had enjoyed Saturday morning story time at our local branch, but when I cast my mind back on my earliest career aspirations, all I could remember wanting to do was hang out with the Muppets or live in a castle in some unspecified—but probably royal—capacity.

"Do you remember that little card catalog you made out of a shoebox?" Darlene rested her chin in her palm, eyes dancing. "You wouldn't let me borrow so much as a magazine from your mom unless I wrote my name on an index card."

I laughed. "I don't remember that at all."

"She's still pretty stingy about letting people borrow her books," Graham said.

"That's not true!" I protested.

"Really?" He raised one thick eyebrow. "I wanted to borrow your copy of *For Whom the Bell Tolls* last month and you said I was welcome to read it, but only in your apartment."

"That's because you read in the tub, and I don't want my books to get wet. If you'd read like a normal person—"

"What, hunched over a bowl of cereal at the table?"

Darlene reached out and patted my hand. "You two are adorable."

"I'm not a librarian." I shifted in my seat, debating how to explain my profession. For one thing, I'd never had to tell someone I was a paranormal investigator before; someone else always seemed to, or people already knew before meeting me. "I work on a TV show called *Soul Searchers*. We... well, we sort of look into potential hauntings—you know, try to figure out what's really going on."

"You're kidding," Darlene said.

I blushed again. "Nope. That's really what I do. I know it sounds kind of silly, but—"

"This is perfect." Her eyes were very round. "I'm so glad you're here. I've got a ghost upstairs."

CHAPTER FIVE

I laughed at Darlene's words, but I was the only one who found them funny. As she and Graham stared at me with serious— and in her case, confused—expressions, I realized she wasn't joking. Even Striker paused her efforts to fish something out from under the fridge to gaze at me with reproachful eyes. My laughter faded away until the ticking of Darlene's wall clock was the only sound in the kitchen.

"You're serious?" I asked.

"Of course." She cast an anxious glance at the ceiling above us and shuddered.

"Oh."

Investigating a haunting was not what I expected to spend my evening doing. And since prior experience had taught me that burning sage did nothing to dispel Horace when he appeared, I hadn't bothered to pack anything more than the single emergency bundle I always kept in my purse. On top of missing most of my supplies, my track record with solo attempts to summon or banish spirits wasn't great.

But the thought of reaching out into the next world and feeling something reach back stirred something in me. If my psychic gifts had a stomach, it would be growling louder than an angry cat. Not getting to do any real *Soul Searchers* investigations lately had starved me, and Darlene was offering me the fix I'd been craving for weeks.

"Okay," I said, straightening up in my chair and putting on my most confident smile. "We'll get to the bottom of this together. Why do you think your house is haunted?"

"I hear footsteps," she said. "Every night, right above my head. There's a master bedroom upstairs at the front of the house, but I haven't slept up there in years. My knees don't like the stairs, so I moved my bedroom into the den down here."

She pointed to the adjoining room. Through the open door, dozens of pieces of furniture loomed. A sudden sense of claustrophobia pressed in on me, even from my seat in the kitchen. How did she manage to sleep surrounded by so many shapes in the dark?

"I went up there once to investigate," she said. "I told myself nobody could be in the house. I figured it had to be my imagination."

"Did you see anything?" Graham asked.

"No." She glanced up toward the ceiling again and lowered her voice. "But I could hear someone whispering."

I found myself unconsciously matching her low volume. "What did they say?"

"I couldn't understand the words. It might have been a different language. Spanish, maybe?"

I traded a look with Graham, who simply shrugged.

"There's something up there." Darlene stared back and forth between us with wide eyes. "Can you make it go away?"

Her earnest expression tugged at my heart. Even if I hadn't already been on board with helping her, those eyes would have sold me. Kit and Yuri had always fielded the requests for the *Soul Searchers* team to investigate a haunting. Did everyone who came to us look this frightened and desperate? How did Yuri ever manage to say no?

"I'll try," I told her. "I can't promise anything. Usually when I do this, my team has a lot of equipment—EMF meters, thermometers, cameras…"

"We have cameras." Graham held up his cell phone. "And flashlights."

Darlene brightened. "So you can do it?"

"I don't know if there's anything up there," I hedged, not wanting to get her hopes up higher than I could deliver. "But I'll do whatever I can."

After we finished our round of coffee, Darlene led the way back into the living room. I had thought the room only had two doors—the front entrance and the little archway into the kitchen. But she pushed aside a tall pile of cardboard boxes marked BEDDING, revealing a narrow carpeted staircase leading to the second floor.

"When's the last time you went upstairs?" Graham asked.

"Oh my, let's see… It's been a few months at least." She cringed. "You must think I'm a foolish old woman, not even using half my house."

"It's hard to downsize." Graham's voice was smooth and soothing. "We completely understand."

His words erased the worried crease between Darlene's eyebrows. I stared at him in wonder; he was perfectly channeling Yuri's famous bedside manner, the quiet confidence that made people comfortable letting us into their homes for our investigations.

"Do you need anything?" Darlene asked.

I pulled the sage bundle from my purse and squeezed it. The faint crackle of the dry herb was always a comfort. "Matches and a candle, if you have them."

She ducked back into her kitchen and returned a moment later with a sheepish expression, handing me a small green lighter in the shape of an alien's head.

"It was an impulse buy," she explained. "I got it years ago in Roswell. I don't know why. I don't even smoke."

"It's cute." I clicked the button where one of the alien's ears would be, if it had them. It took me a few tries, but the lighter finally sparked and a thin blue flame hissed out of the nozzle. I lifted my finger off the button, expecting the flame to extinguish, but it was a persistent little thing.

"Sorry, it's always been like that. Sticky." Darlene reached out a hand and popped the button back up with her fingernail. The flame went out. "Just be careful with it."

"I will be. Thanks."

"Do I have to come with you?" she asked.

Her expression begged for a negative. When I shook my head, she visibly relaxed.

"I'll just wait down here then," she said, retreating into the kitchen.

I took a deep breath, then began creeping up the narrow staircase. It was clear Darlene hadn't been up here in some time; the light from the living room hit the photos of her extended family at a sharp angle, illuminating a thick layer of dust on the glass. The air grew warm and stale as I neared the top of the stairs, and I sneezed.

Striker padded along beside me on silent feet, for once not trying to trip me. She also wasn't trying to race me to the top, a fact I forced myself to ignore before my imagination could run amok with reasons my furry companion might be reluctant to beat me upstairs.

Graham brought up the rear, following behind us with pursed lips and tense shoulders.

At the top of the stairs, I groped around the corners for a light switch. I found one and flicked it up.

Nothing happened.

"Is there a light up here?" I called down to Darlene.

She reappeared in the living room doorway. "The bulb burned out. I kept meaning to fix it, but"—she shrugged—"didn't."

I pulled out my phone and switched the camera function to record video. The screen was gray and grainy until I turned on the flash. There was a burst of light, and then the hallway was illuminated. Beside me, Graham did the same.

Our twin lights swept the walls. Despite the clear signs of hoarding on the main floor, I still wasn't prepared for the amount of furniture and boxes above. The clutter began in the hall, which was lined with packed shelves and rows of cardboard boxes. Faded black permanent marker announced their contents, with lines drawn through the original labels and all-caps descriptions like AUNT DEBBIE and TAXES—1998 scrawled below.

Through the three open bedroom doors—one on each side and a third at the end of the hall—more furniture was visible. Every flat surface was stacked high with boxes, baskets, loose piles of clothing, and bric-a-brac. The sensation of claustrophobia I'd felt downstairs crept back up my spine. I shuddered.

"Feel anything?" Graham asked.

"Uncomfortable," I whispered. "I can taste the dust in the air. I really don't want to go into any of these rooms. God knows how much mold might be up here."

"So don't," he suggested. "Let's just set up right here."

He propped his phone against a pile of sewing patterns and angled it so the camera pointed down the hallway. Then he took my phone out of my hands and aimed the camera toward me.

Striker, always the brave one, immediately ducked into a bedroom. I would have preferred her to sit in my lap; she was my good-luck charm, and I felt stronger with her nearby. But the logical part of my brain reasoned that the footsteps Darlene thought she heard were nothing more than an ancient pile of magazines toppling over. If there was no ghost up here, it didn't matter how weak or strong my psychic abilities actually were, so I let the cat explore the maze of stale smells that permeated the collection of preserved garbage.

For an instant, I considered going downstairs and telling Darlene my theory. I could encourage her to start clearing out some of her accumulated junk. But though Yuri pushed a "supernatural second" approach with the *Soul Searchers*, trying to rule out mundane answers before turning to paranormal ones, he still set up our ghost-hunting gear. He always made sure.

With my back against the frame of an open bedroom door, I settled myself into a relaxed, cross-legged seat on the floor. I placed the sage and the campy lighter on the floor in front of me, within easy reach in case they were needed. Then, eyes closed, I took a deep breath in through my nose. The dusty air burned my nasal passages, but I did my best to ignore the sensation, holding my breath for a moment before slowly releasing it out of my mouth. I repeated the process, focusing on a different part of my body with each breath until I could slump, relaxed, against the doorframe.

The breathing technique was relatively new to me. Elizabeth had shown me how to do it during a recent massage session as a way to help me clear my mind. Once I was no longer thinking about my surroundings or worrying about the future, it was easier to cast my consciousness outward.

I did so more thoroughly than I had in the cemetery. There, I had only been feeling for my mother—and half-heartedly at that. In my experience, cemeteries were some of the least haunted places around. I'd had far more hair-raising experiences in libraries, motels, and private residences than within the serene surroundings of a graveyard.

Here, I felt outward for anyone and anything at all. I sent my mind down the hallway and into each bedroom, allowing my sixth sense to creep along like invisible tendrils, touching and feeling the air as I went. I pictured the whole of Darlene's house, what I knew of the inside and the outside, and even into her yard and along the fence line.

I sensed nothing.

For a moment, I considered taking off my black tourmaline necklace. Was it preventing me from feeling whatever presence lurked here? Its protective energy shielded me from malevolent forces; I would be able to feel a friendly ghost but was essentially numb to anything that would want to harm Darlene.

The thought sent a chill through my bones.

The worst-case scenario—the most dangerous possibility— was that something truly dark lurked up here in this forgotten part of her house. What if I had been right, and the sounds she heard *were* caused by things falling over, but those things didn't fall on their own? What if these things Darlene hoarded up here came with more history than she realized? Kit's girlfriend, Amari, had opened my eyes to the world of haunted objects. Could Darlene have picked up something like that and squirreled it away up here with everything else she couldn't let go of?

If that kind of spirit lingered here, Darlene could be in real danger. My fingers crept toward the back of my neck, where a single silver clasp was all that separated my senses from everything that hid from me now.

And from Horace.

My hands froze in midair. If I took my necklace off, I would be vulnerable. Horace would find me. I didn't know how, but he was able to feel me the same way I was trying to detect any spiritual presence now. I had to assume it was because he was hundreds of times more powerful than I was, and I had to assume he was looking for me all the time, waiting until his sight could penetrate my defenses.

No, I couldn't take it off. And as I made that decision for the second time that day, I realized I didn't need to. None of the original *Soul Searchers* team had any psychic abilities, but Yuri, Kit, and Mark had managed to identify and banish plenty of spirits before I came along.

I forced my hands back down to their original position, palms resting on my knees, and thought about what Yuri would do if he were here right now. He would probably start by going from room to room, assessing the situation while he considered everything he had learned in his pre-filming research... of which I had done exactly zero.

Just as I was about to suggest we hit the library tomorrow and come back another day, I heard them.

Whispers.

My eyes flew open. The sound was muted but unmistakable. Multiple voices, blending together, murmuring in the darkness. They spoke too quickly and too quietly for me to make out the words.

I kept my voice low. "Do you hear that?"

Graham nodded. His attention was fixed on the doorway at the end of the hall.

My hands were around the sage and the lighter in an instant. The butane torch lit the dried herbs more easily than a match, for which I was grateful. I blew out the flame, and the end of the bundle glowed comfortingly as the cleansing scent chased away the stale odors around us.

Graham pulled me to my feet by my free hand. Together, we crept down the hallway toward the nearly closed bedroom door.

The whispers grew louder.

I gripped the sage in both hands and held it in front of me like a shield. Graham reached out and pushed the door open, and the light from the cell phone in his hands illuminated a space as cluttered as the living room had been.

I pawed the wall for a light switch. Thankfully, this one

worked. As the overhead light flared to life, I felt my jaw go slack.

"What is it?" Graham whispered. "Do you see something?"

My mouth worked in silence for a few moments, opening and closely uselessly while I tried to process what I was seeing. For an instant, I forgot where I was. I forgot *when* I was. A wave of memories slammed into me, knocking me backward into Graham's arms.

He steadied me and gripped my shoulders. "Mac, what's wrong?"

"This is my mother's bedroom," I said.

"What?"

"All of this"—I gestured to the bed, dresser, vanity table, and bookshelf crowded into the small space—"was in my mother's bedroom."

It was arranged differently than it had been next door. The bed was on the wrong wall, and the vanity was smashed into the corner by the closet instead of sitting under the window. There were no fresh flowers anywhere, and my mother would never have tolerated this much chaos on every flat surface. But there was no mistaking it: this was my mother's furniture.

Before I could fully process what I was seeing, the whispers sounded again. This time, we were closer to the sound, and with a seventy-watt light bulb shining overhead, it was easier to focus on the noise and make out the details.

It wasn't a whisper.

It wasn't even a voice at all.

Scratch, scratch, scratch, scratch.

"Do you hear that?"

"Yeah." Graham frowned. "What is it?"

I listened again, cocking my head toward the sound. "It's coming from the corner, by the closet."

The scratching began again, and an unwanted image popped

into my mind. The noise was far too much like the sound I imagined fingernails scratching at the inside of a coffin would make. If I heard a bell ringing, I was sure I would need a new pair of jeans.

As I inched my way across the crowded bedroom, I tried and failed to stop myself from wondering how someone could have been buried alive inside—or beneath—Darlene's house. What would it feel like to be stuck in the wall between rooms, unable to move, no space even to breathe? What if someone had fallen into the pit when they dug out the foundation and been crushed by falling dirt and rocks?

My chest constricted. My feet stopped moving. I gasped for air, clawing at my throat.

"Mac?" Alarm sent Graham's voice up a full octave. "Do you have asthma? What's happening?"

I couldn't suck in enough air to answer. All I could do was shake my head before the panic filled me, taking up all the room in my mind and my lungs. Shadows fuzzed at the edges of my vision.

If Darlene's house isn't haunted now, it will be soon, I realized, clutching Graham's hoodie for support.

"Brrrllll."

Striker's muffled trilling replaced the scratching sound from the corner of the room. Then she made a noise I'd never heard before, howling in a strange way that sharply increased in volume before abruptly cutting off. She did it again, and the second "MmOOOWWWWww" snapped me out of my panic.

"Striker!" I gasped in air and broke away from Graham, stumbling toward the source of my cat's little voice.

She had to be under my mother's vanity. It was a small, shallow piece of furniture with a narrow stack of drawers on the left and a dainty space for a pair of legs on the right. There was no mirror attached; I remembered my mother using a freestanding one she could tuck away in the top drawer when she wasn't putting her makeup on. Now, instead of her small collection of cosmetics, the top of the vanity was stacked high with a miniature red cooler, a metal toolbox, and several cardboard boxes marked CAMPING.

When I got to the vanity and knelt down to check beneath it, Striker wasn't there.

"Striker?" I called. "Where are you?"

"Brrrlllll."

Her answering trill was close. I stared at the stack of drawers holding up the left side of the vanity; Striker was a wily cat, but I'd never seen her open a drawer before. There was no way she was inside one.

I was immediately proven wrong. When I opened the bottom drawer, Striker stared at me from the rectangular space with wide eyes.

"How did you get in there?"

Graham peeked behind the vanity. "There's no back on this thing, and the drawers aren't as tall as they look on the front. She must have slipped in the spaces between them. And— Ew! There are mouse droppings back here."

"Gross. I guess that's why Darlene heard scratching." I picked up the cat and lifted her to my chest. "Is that what you're doing? Hunting little mice?"

"Careful," Graham warned. "She's probably filthy. Don't touch your face until you've had a chance to wash your hands, and we should probably give her a bath."

Striker heard the B-word and twisted around in my arms, squirming and struggling to get down. She slipped out of my grasp, landed on the floor, and immediately settled back down into the drawer. Paper crinkled beneath her furry bottom, and she pawed beneath herself with the intense focus of a grad student excavating an archaeological site.

Scratch, scratch, scratch, scratch.

"What did you find?" I murmured, lifting her back out again.

A messy pile of envelopes half filled the drawer. I assumed they were Darlene's old electrical bills or something else that should have been thrown away two decades ago, but I shined my flashlight inside to be sure.

My mother's name—Evelyn Clair—was written on the front of the top envelope in a flowing, formal script I recognized. And even if I hadn't known my former mentor's handwriting, I certainly knew her name.

The return address confirmed it: *Gabrielle Suntador, Donn's Hill.*

CHAPTER SIX

"I hope you don't mind I kept your mother's furniture." Darlene chewed off a bit of her lipstick and glanced at her kitchen towels, which I now recognized weren't just similar to the ones my mother had owned. They were the actual ones from our house. "It was just sitting out on the curb, waiting for the garbageman, and I thought I could use a bedroom if I had visitors or you came to stay, and—"

I cut her off before she rambled herself into exhaustion. "It's okay. Really. If you let it all go to the landfill, I wouldn't have found these."

The clean envelopes—the ones that had been buried deeply enough to avoid being soiled by Darlene's industrious little housemates—were stacked into tight bundles on Darlene's kitchen table. Many of them had already been bound together by rubber bands; I pulled back their edges and scanned through their return addresses like a flip-book but saw only utility companies and mortgage lenders.

The more interesting finds had been at the top, and after Graham carefully removed the letters from their filthy envelopes, I organized them into piles according to the sender. Striker sat atop the letters from Gabrielle possessively, her yellow eyes narrowed in smug satisfaction. I let her keep her prize for the moment and gleefully surveyed the collection as a whole.

It felt like I'd found a gigantic missing piece to the puzzle of who my mom had been. I knew her as my mother, but it wasn't until the prior spring that I'd discovered who she was outside of that role. She was a psychic, a traveler, a seeker of unseen truths. I had unlocked more about her personality and her life from a box of letters her favorite pen pal, Gabrielle, had kept in her attic. But now I had the other side of that conversation, plus letters from several other people my mother decided were important enough to keep.

Like from my father.

There was only one, but the sight of his precise, small-caps writing made me snatch it up the second Graham set it onto the table. It had been addressed to Springville, Utah, and was shorter than I would have liked.

Evie,

Thanks again for a great night. Sorry about your shirt. Next time, let's go somewhere without any marinara.

The invitation to stay with me in Colorado is always open.

Until then,
Henry

To my surprise, reading my father's decades-old words didn't fill me with sorrow. I didn't dissolve into the kind of body-spasming sobs that had accompanied any thought of him after he first passed away. Part of me felt guilty about that, like I should never stop mourning him as intensely as I did the day I lost him. But as

I smiled down at his handwriting, I realized that somehow—without me noticing—I had been healing.

Now I had the freedom to remember my father as often as I wanted, without slamming any protective walls around my crushing grief to prevent it from spilling over in mixed company. Like my mother, I could give him free reign in my mind and allow him to come and go as his memory pleased.

"I didn't even know those were in there," Darlene said, her nose wrinkled in distaste at the brown splotches on the envelopes. "Nobody ever came to stay, so I didn't take the time to clean out the drawers."

That was clear from my rummaging through the rest of the furniture she had hoarded away in that tiny guest bedroom. The dresser was still full of my mother's clothes, now stiff and musty. Even the tightly wrapped bundles of lavender at the back of each drawer hadn't been enough to stave off two decades of disuse. The nightstand held expired Tums, over-the-counter painkillers, a small metal ankh, and several bundles of wild blue sage, lavender, and rosemary tied together with purple string.

The herbs and ankh had immediately gone into my purse. I thought about telling Darlene I had taken them, but they felt like they were mine to take. Besides, she would never even know they were gone.

"Well, the mice sure found them," Graham called from the sink. He had been washing his hands for several minutes now and shuddered occasionally as he rinsed his skin clean of the pooped-on, chewed-up, and shredded envelopes left behind by Darlene's tiny "ghosts."

"You're sure that's all it was?" Darlene asked. "Mice?"

"Yep," I said. "I think you just heard their claws scratching around up there. It sounds creepy as hell, but it's more gross than scary."

"It's still pretty scary." Graham dried off his hands and took a seat at the table. "You've got to get rid of those mice, Darlene. They can be dangerous to your health."

"I will. Thank you both for going up there. I feel like it's safe enough for me to start using those rooms again."

She and Graham kept talking about mice and exterminators, but I stopped listening. There was nothing they could possibly say that would be more interesting than the letters in front of me. I combed through the other half of my mother's correspondence with Gabrielle, filled with everything from advice about the best herbs to use in smoke cleansing to reassurances that a six-year-old Mackenzie wasn't in any danger from the ghosts who visited her in the middle of the night.

I couldn't imagine how terrifying that must have been for my mother. She put on a brave face when she fibbed and told me the people who sat on the edge of my bed at night or visited me in my dreams were just an unusually large number of "imaginary friends." She called them the Travelers because they often told me they missed their homes and families; she never let on that I was having nightly conversations with wandering spirits.

It's likely a phase, Gabrielle wrote. *All children see more deeply into the untouchable world around us than adults. Rest assured, the Travelers will do her no harm.*

I wanted to laugh. She had partially been right; nothing I ever saw as a child hurt me. But as an adult... Well, not every ghost was as peaceful as the Travelers.

Graham leaned over and peeked at the letter. "Find something good?"

"Just a letter from Gabrielle, filled with optimism."

"Who's Gabrielle?" Darlene asked. "Your mother never mentioned her."

"Really? That's weird. They were very close. I don't remember her from when I was a kid, but she's who my mom was always visiting in Donn's Hill when we went there every spring."

"Hmm." Darlene was thoughtful for a minute before shrugging. "I don't remember the name. But then, Evelyn was always a very private person. She was a great listener, always happy to hear about my life and my family and my problems. But she didn't talk much about herself unless it was work stuff."

"Did she tell you about me?" I asked. "About the Travelers I saw?"

Darlene laughed. "Oh, sweetie, *you* told me about those. Every time I babysat, you had a pile of stories about the imaginary friends who came to visit. You had such a vivid imagination. You came up with whole family trees, careers, all kinds of stuff."

I stared at her. "That's what you thought they were? Imaginary friends?"

"Well… yes." She narrowed her eyes and looked at me strangely. "Who else would they be? It's not like your mom ever had anybody else watching you, and I didn't see many friends come to call."

The words *they were ghosts* perched on the edge of my lips, ready to leap out into the air and blow Darlene's mind. But I hesitated, unsure if telling her was the right thing to do. On the one hand, she hadn't even blinked when I told her I made my living looking for ghosts. But on the other hand, we had only just convinced her that her house wasn't haunted. She'd been so terrified by the sounds of a few scratching mice that she blocked off half her house. If I told her literally hundreds of ghosts had passed through the house next door, would she ever be able to sleep again?

On top of that, as far as I knew, my mother had only told one other person what was really going on with me. She had chosen to limit that information to Gabrielle, a psychic with decades of experience with the paranormal. She hadn't confided in Darlene about it, and I had to assume she had good reasons for playing her cards close to her chest.

I swallowed the words down and forced a smile onto my face. "It was pretty quiet over there, huh? I don't remember any visitors besides you."

"I guess your mother preferred pen pals. I don't know any of these names either." Darlene walked her fingers through a pile of unsoiled envelopes, then paused and plucked one out. "Oh, except Anson Monroe. I remember him."

"Anson Monroe?" The name tickled a memory. I'd heard it before but couldn't place it. "How do I know that name?"

"Brrrllll," Striker chimed in, shifting on her brisket. She sniffed the letters beneath her, no doubt searching for any lingering traces of nag champa from Gabrielle's house.

I slapped my forehead, realizing at once where I'd heard—or rather read—the name Anson Monroe before. It had been in a letter my mother had written to Gabrielle before I was born, one I'd found in the box in Gabrielle's former attic just weeks before. I checked the return address on the letter in Darlene's hand: Seattle, Washington.

"I met him at your mother's funeral," Darlene said, handing the envelope to me. "Such a nice man."

"Wait, he was at the graveside service?" Graham asked.

She nodded. "He was one of the few. It was just me, Mac, her dad, and Anson there."

"That's what Mac told me this morning," he said.

"He was just as distraught as I was, the poor guy." She smiled at me sadly and squeezed my hand. "Your mother may not have left many friends behind, but the ones she did loved her dearly."

I yanked my hand out of hers, suddenly desperate to read the contents of Anson's letter. My fingers fumbled with the envelope, struggling to untuck the flap and finally ripping the back of it to get the letter free. I quickly scanned the cramped handwriting on the unlined sheet.

I need to get out of Seattle. I'll tell you more when I see you, but for now, does your offer still stand? New Mexico has always intrigued me, and I believe the desert would provide a welcome change. I'd like to pick up our work where we left off—I think we can crack it. You always were my most promising student.

The letter was undated, but the postmark on the now-torn envelope was from six months before my mother died.

My mind raced. My mother had written to Gabrielle to tell her Anson Monroe was a powerful psychic. Before I was born, she traveled all over the country, searching for a place with enough spiritual power for her to tap into that she could go where few living people dared to tread: the astral plane.

Had Anson moved to New Mexico? Had my mother started studying with him again? If so, where and when had she possibly managed to do that? He had never come to our house, and she didn't go anywhere except for work.

"Holy crap," I murmured.

All those late nights. All those extra shifts. Had she really been at the call center?

There was only one person who would know if she had actually been spending those nights working with Anson Monroe. Was he still alive? He had seemed like an old man then, but to an eight-year-old, even twenty-eight was ancient. And unless he moved again after my mother died, he was still in New Mexico.

He could be here.

I could find him.

And maybe, just maybe, I could learn what really happened the night my mother died.

CHAPTER SEVEN

Graham and I stayed up deep into the night scouring the internet for any record of Anson Monroe. He wasn't on any social media sites and didn't come up in any of the online white pages. A few websites promised they could find information on anyone in exchange for my credit card number, but Graham was skeptical they could dig up anything if we couldn't find so much as a whiff of him anywhere else.

"It's way too late," Graham announced after several hours of fruitless searching. "You need to get some sleep. Let's keep looking tomorrow, okay?"

I hated to give up before finding any trace of Anson Monroe. All I needed was some indication—anything—that he still lived in New Mexico. Then I would know if it was worth delving deeper or if we were at a dead end. But the words on the screen were beginning to blur, and I found myself rechecking the same sites multiple times by mistake. Reluctantly, I agreed to put a pin in the search for the night and climbed into bed, and for once, I was able to fall asleep before Graham started snoring beside me.

I opened my eyes in the backyard at Primrose House.

The yellow siding gleamed in the sun, and a warm summer

breeze tinkled the wind chimes hanging over the back porch. From my position in the middle of the blacktop parking lot, I marveled at the explosion of color in the planter boxes. They overflowed with strange species of flowers, ones I'd never seen before, certainly not in our yard. Nobody at Primrose House was particularly good at horticulture, and Graham was usually content to manage the wild growth with a Weedwacker.

As I moved toward the garden to get a better look, the edges of my vision fuzzed. The surrounding houses shimmered, and a single step propelled me all the way to the picnic table beside Graham's garage. Without moving to do so, I sat on the metal bench, which had been baking in the summer sun but was somehow cool to the touch.

The venue was different, but I didn't need to be standing on my mother's old patio to know where I really was. This was a dream. And when my dreams took on this strange, surreal glow, it usually meant I wasn't alone. Part of me worried *he* would appear —that if I peeked beneath the picnic table, I would see his glowing red eyes staring at me from the shadows. But the other part of me waited. It was worth the risk of getting ambushed by Horace if it meant I could see her again.

"Mac!" a woman's voice called from the doorway.

My mother stood there, just inside the kitchen. She looked clearer than she had ever looked in one of my dreams before, as real as anyone I'd seen in my waking life. Her brown hair curled gently back from her face, and her blue eyes glimmered in the light from the unnaturally bright sky. But her lips were pulled into a deep frown, and deep creases lined her forehead.

"Hurry!" she shouted. "She needs your help!"

"Who does?" I stood and tried to move toward her, but the ground beneath me turned like an invisible treadmill. I couldn't get any closer to her.

Frustration grew on her face. She tried to take a step off the porch, as though she wanted to come to me, but she was bounced backward by an unseen wall.

I tried again, putting all my energy into my legs. They propelled me forward, but just before I reached the steps, I tripped over my own feet and tumbled into the blooming flower beds. My face landed in a large orange rose. I inhaled deeply, recoiling immediately.

It stank like rotten fish.

The rose had no eyes, but I could feel it watching me angrily, as though it was offended I had trampled on its friends. It leaned forward and sniffed me, snuffling my face like an inquisitive animal.

"Brrrllll!" the rose said.

My eyelids fluttered open against the bright sunlight shining down through the round window at the yurt's peak. Striker stood on my chest, eyes bright and intent. She needed something, and she communicated this in the subtle way only a cat can manage: by putting her entire weight onto my sternum and blowing cat breath up my nose.

"There's food in your bowl," I reminded her, shoving her away with one hand.

She returned immediately with another low "Brrrllll!" One of her paws touched my lips, claws extended.

"Ouch!" I sat up and shot a glare at her. She bounced away down the bed, quickly escaping my reach while avoiding stepping on Graham. Whatever she wanted, it clearly wasn't important enough to require waking up her favorite person. The smaller of her two servants would do.

I rubbed my eyes and checked her bowl. "Told you, you've got plenty of food."

But she wasn't interested in breakfast. She plunked her bottom down in front of the yurt's door and glared up at me.

"I can't let you outside," I told her.

She scratched at the door.

I knew this would happen. She had gotten used to having free reign of Primrose House, its yard, and anywhere else in Donn's Hill her little legs could take her. We should have waited to install the cat door until after we got back; clearly, she had gotten used to it and was pissed the yurt didn't have a similar way to let her come and go as she pleased.

There was no way to explain to her that we couldn't risk that here. We were in a strange place with an abundance of new smells to lure her into the desert hunting grounds of too many predators.

However, Graham and I had packed a compromise. I pulled on jeans and a windbreaker, then retrieved her purple harness and its accompanying leash. Like the day before, she seemed disgusted by the entire notion of wearing it, biting my fingers as I fed her legs through the openings. As soon as the clasps latched into place, she collapsed onto her side and glowered up at me, eyes aglow with all the righteous indignation she could muster.

"It's this or nothing," I told her.

"MeeOOWWW!" she protested.

Her shriek woke Graham, who sat up blearily. "What's going on?"

"Taking Striker for a walk."

"Good luck with that." He chuckled and lay back down, pulling the covers over his eyes as he went.

"Enough shouting," I whispered to the cat. "Stop being difficult."

In response, she squirmed on the ground, flopping like a fish in a vain attempt to shake the harness off. I tightened my grip on her leash and opened the door.

The early morning sunshine streaming through the skylight had been deceptive. A surprisingly cold breeze tickled my cheeks as I plopped Striker onto the sidewalk. She stood awkwardly for a moment, then raised her nose to sniff the surrounding air. Apparently, the lure of a million new scents was enough to overcome her hatred of the harness, and she took a few tentative steps forward.

"Good girl," I urged. "You can roll around if you want, or we can— Hey!"

The leash slipped out of my hands as she equipped a pair of invisible feline rocket boosters and took off into the parking lot.

"Striker!" My heart leapt into my throat, muting my surprised shriek, and I raced after her. My eyes flicked to the highway; we were so close—dangerously close—to the speeding cars. If she darted out there...

I couldn't think it.

My heart wouldn't be able to handle it.

"Striker!" I shouted again.

Either she couldn't hear the panic in my voice or she just didn't care. She dragged her leash behind her, paws barely touching the ground as she tore across the asphalt with an elated energy. I couldn't see her face, but I was sure she wore the same determined expression she always did when we raced each other up the stairs at Primrose House. I cursed myself for playing that game with her; I had accidentally trained her to think racing me was a game.

She always beat me to the top of the stairs, but I couldn't afford to let her win this time. Not when the stakes were this high. Losing this race could mean losing her in the desert or watching her disappear beneath the wheels of a semi.

A cramp zapped up my side, but I pushed through it.

The gap between us closed.

I was gaining on her.

Then, suddenly, the race was over. Striker reached the sidewalk on the other side of the parking lot and came to an abrupt halt in front of the last yurt. My feet put on the brakes, but the top half of my body sailed forward, arms windmilling at my sides. I stumbled over my shoes, lost my footing, and somersaulted over the sidewalk.

For an instant, I was airborne. No part of my body touched the ground... until I landed in an awkward heap in the dirt.

"Owww," I groaned.

Striker tilted her head to look at me, her lamplike eyes filled with concern. Sympathy, but no guilt. I could practically hear her thoughts in my mind: *Silly Mac, why didn't you stop more gracefully?*

While she enjoyed her victory, I snatched up her leash and wound it around my elbow. I would happily let her win this round as long as there was no second one. She didn't seem to mind being tethered to me, and she turned her focus to inspecting the small patch of grass beside the yurt's door.

I pulled myself to my feet and checked for any sore spots. The only damage seemed to be a few minor scrapes on my arms and a tear in my jeans at the knee. A small trickle of blood dripped onto the ripped denim. I glared at my cat. Now that I knew she wasn't about to be snatched by a hawk or run down in the street, I had enough emotional energy to be furious with her.

"Was that fun, you little hellion?"

She squinted happily at me as she munched on the grass. After a few bites, she raised her head and rubbed her jaw on the yurt's doorframe. The small placard beside the door read SHAMROCK.

"Oh, I suppose you think this is your property now, huh?"

"Brrrllll," she replied, rubbing the other side of her face along the wood.

"This one isn't ours. We're over there." I pointed across the parking lot toward our unit, where Graham was still asleep and blissfully unaware of Striker's misbehavior.

My hand froze in midair as I realized where I was standing. We were exactly opposite our yurt. That meant this was the same unit Fred Hawkes had visited immediately after checking us into ours.

This was where he had stashed the dead woman's luggage.

As I stared at the door handle, little tendrils of thoughts—my mother, exposure, the desert, death—weaved together to form an idea. If we weren't able to find Anson Monroe, we might never know where my mother had really gone the night she died. But he wasn't my only lead. If I could ask Camila Aster what she had been doing alone in the desert, I might be able to find out if my mother had been doing something similar.

It was a long shot, but one I immediately decided was worth taking. After all, I knew it was possible to channel the dead and ask them questions. I had seen it.

All it took was a connection to that person. Some psychic mediums used living connections, like the people the dead left behind. But I also knew that through the course of our lives, we leave our mark on so much more than just the people around us. We imprint onto the places we spend our time and the things we carry with us.

Things like luggage.

Or the clothing packed inside the luggage.

Before I could stop myself, I reached for the door's handle and tried to turn it. It was locked, and I thought about walking away. But instead of turning and carrying me back to my yurt, one of my feet jerked out and gave the door the same swift, low kick I'd seen Fred use on our unit.

It popped open.

I hesitated on the threshold. If someone walked by right now, I could plausibly claim the door had opened on its own. Clearly, the latches weren't super reliable. But how could I explain walking into another room? What would I say if someone found me inside?

As I debated with myself, Striker sauntered around me and

into the yurt, leaping with casual grace onto the bed and settling down to clean her paws. She paused midlick to look questioningly at me, as if to ask, *Aren't you coming?*

With a last glance at the parking lot to be sure nobody was watching, I stepped inside and closed the door.

CHAPTER EIGHT

The blinds were drawn, protecting me from being noticed by any other guests. Nevertheless, the knowledge that I was somewhere I wasn't allowed to be compelled me to hunch down and creep across the floor on my tiptoes. Even in the dim light, I could tell this yurt was identical to ours. The only difference was the portrait above the bed. Where ours had a tortoiseshell cat, this one depicted a vivid green field of shamrocks.

Striker spread the toes on her white hind foot, eyes crossed as she chewed her toenails.

"Try not to get too much fur on the bed, okay?" I told her. "This is supposed to be a pet-free room, you know."

She glanced up at me, then whipped her head toward the bathroom.

Through the open door, something moved.

I froze. Was Fred in here cleaning? Had he heard me?

My heart pounded as I debated whether to stand here until I was discovered or shuffle backward toward the door as silently as possible. I couldn't envision grabbing Striker *and* getting out without being seen or heard, so I stayed where I was. With my eyes locked on the bathroom doorway and my breath locked inside immobile lungs, I waited.

A light sound—like fabric brushing across fabric—made me jump. My eyes were drying out, but I didn't dare blink them. Then, just as my lungs clamored for fresh air, I saw it.

The shower curtain fluttered. A moment later, it quivered again.

My breath rushed out in the form of a muttered curse. I stalked angrily into the bathroom, ready to slam shut the window Fred must have left open and block the breeze from scaring me again. But the window above the toilet was closed. The air in the bathroom was still and smelled faintly of peppermint soap.

The curtain rustled again.

Tiny pinpricks marched up the backs of my shoulders and up my neck. I had always known, deep down, that something terrible would happen to me in a motel bathroom. On some level, I had even been sure it would be a serial killer who leapt out from behind a shower curtain to end my life.

Well, I wouldn't go without a fight.

My hand shot out, and I yanked the curtain back.

Nobody waited for me in the bathtub. But there, resting on the molded plastic, was the silver-sided rolling luggage Fred had wheeled out of our yurt two days before.

I paused before hauling it out of the tub, feeling the same way I had outside the yurt's open door. This was a turning point. I might be able to fib my way around trespassing inside an empty room, but there was absolutely no way to explain rummaging around in another woman's luggage.

As I contemplated what I would tell Fred if he chose that moment to collect Camila Aster's suitcase, I felt momentarily disoriented. Why had I decided to come in here? What had possessed me to think this was a good idea?

I glanced over my shoulder. Through the bathroom's open door, I saw Striker lounging on the bed, quietly depositing her fur all over a comforter the exact same color and pattern as the one in my yurt. That's where I should be right now—in my own room, in bed beside Graham, asleep for another half hour before our alarms went off.

My fingers uncurled from around the suitcase's handle. I couldn't open it.

But as I took a step back from the tub, my scalp tingled. A heartbeat later, something landed on my shoulders.

A mouse, my brain decided. *A mouse just fell out of the ceiling and into my hair.*

I couldn't bring myself to raise my hand to check. Instead, I turned my head one millimeter at a time until I could see the mirror over the sink in my peripheral vision.

Nothing sat on my head. No rats, bats, or spiders.

But as I watched, a section of my hair rose into the air. It hung there for a moment, just long enough to erase any possibility of a sudden gust of wind being responsible for its movement, then fell back onto my shoulders.

"Striker," I whispered. "Pssp, pssp, pssp. Come here."

A pair of soft thumps behind me told me she had heard my quiet call. As she weaved between my ankles, her gentle purrs floated up to me. Most of the time, she purred when she was happy.

Sometimes, she purred when we were no longer alone.

I lifted my chin and my voice. "Camila? Camila Aster?"

The shower curtain was still. Not a single hair on my head moved.

"Once for yes, twice for no," I said.

The curtain fluttered once. Then all was silent.

I swallowed. If I died while I was on vacation and some strange woman started poking around my luggage, I would be pretty angry. Maybe even angry enough to graduate from spirit to poltergeist.

Poltergeists could interact with the living world.

Poltergeists had a tendency to break things.

Striker hopped up onto the side of the tub and reached a paw toward the suitcase. As her claws grazed the handle, a strange thought popped into my head. Camila hadn't lifted my hair until after I decided not to rifle through her belongings. Had she been trying to stop me from leaving before I did what I had broken into this empty room to do?

There was only one way to know for sure. I lifted her luggage out of the tub. In the space of a breath, it was open on the floor and my hands were sifting through her belongings.

I didn't even know what I was looking for. I had originally come here to find something personal, something with a strong enough connection to her that I could use it to reach into the void between this world and the next and try to pull her back. But she was already here. And I took the lack of any crashing furniture or breaking glass to mean that I had been right and she had been telling me to open the suitcase.

This wasn't about what I wanted to find anymore.

It was about what she *needed* me to see.

One at a time, I picked up and set aside her personal items— her hairbrush, a half-empty bottle of Maker's Mark, a T-shirt printed with a saucer-shaped UFO. Nothing my hands touched gave me any strong feelings. Then, as I gingerly lifted her undergarments out of the case and set them onto the linoleum floor, my fingers scraped against something hard.

A wooden box, just bigger than the palm of my hand, rested on the suitcase's fabric lining. Its hinged lid was open. Nothing sat within its red velvet interior. It was empty, but I knew what it had been designed to hold.

This was a jewelry box, sized to fit a single bracelet, pair of earrings, or other beloved bauble.

But it wasn't the size of the thing that sent a lightning bolt of fear into my stomach. It was the fact that I had seen it before—or one very like it.

This box looked exactly like the one that had turned my life upside down weeks before. The one the psychic stalking me had sent me to find. The one that had been haunted by a malevolent spirit capable of clawing at the back of my brain from a half mile away. The one I had seen reduced to cinders in the back of a vehicle fire.

This was an exact duplicate of the box Horace had used against me.

CHAPTER NINE

I pressed my back against the bed rail. Through the bathroom's
open door, I could see the edge of Camila Aster's luggage
where it had landed when I kicked it away before crabwalking to
safety as fast as my body would let me.

The box, I assumed, still sat in the suitcase. I wanted to leave
it where it was, get the hell out of that yurt, and never look back.
But my mental commands to my limbs to hoist me off the floor
were half-hearted at best, and my body didn't listen. I just sat
there, staring at a dead woman's luggage from an uncomfortable,
hunched position on the floor.

At least I knew what had possessed me to commit a felony
and break into an empty motel room. That had become crystal
clear the instant I saw the box. I had conjured up a decent enough
reason for trespassing here, but the seed of the idea hadn't come
from my own mind.

It had been planted there by the box.

The box had called to me, just as Horace's jewelry box had
done in the clearing in the woods weeks before, just as it had
while it was locked in Graham's garage on the night Horace's
men stole it from us. I now suspected it had even drawn me to

look in the back of the van with New Mexico plates, the same van that had given me the idea to come back to my first home.

My fingers curled around the piece of black tourmaline around my neck. I clung to the cool stone, unsure if the protective powers it offered had stopped working. Would Horace be able to find me? If I closed my eyes, would he be standing above me when I opened them again?

Striker trilled from the bathroom as she rubbed her jaw on the zipper running along the suitcase's open edge. Then, as daintily as a model stepping into a swimming pool, she climbed inside the luggage.

I frowned. She had reacted much differently to the first box, bolting down the stairs at Primrose House to attack something only she could see, something that floated just above the box's polished surface. Her calm demeanor now was enough to tilt the scales in my indecisive brain. I stood to get a better view of her.

She loafed inside the suitcase, paws tucked under her chest and eyes closed contentedly.

"Striker?" I asked uncertainly.

"Brrrllll."

I moved closer, feeling as though an invisible hook had wrapped itself around my waist. Unseen hands tugged me into the bathroom, pulling me toward the box like a magnet. As the word entered my brain, a nervous laugh bubbled out of my lips. A deputy I was friends with liked to call me the Donn's Hill Body Magnet, and whenever she said it, I imagined corpses and spirits being drawn to *me*, a stationary object with some kind of ghostly gravitational pull. All this time, I'd had it backward. *They* were the magnets, and I kept getting sucked toward them like a stray piece of metal with no will of its own.

It was a disturbing thought.

But as Striker's purrs rumbled up from the open suitcase, I remembered the other times I had been drawn to a spirit. Striker never hesitated to make her feelings known when unseen entities were present. She attacked a violent poltergeist in my apartment, went ballistic about the first jewelry box, and growled like a dog when Horace appeared.

She didn't growl at this box. Instead, she purred as throatily and contentedly as she might while sitting in the lap of someone she trusted.

Carefully, I crept forward and lowered myself onto the ground beside the suitcase. I wanted to be close to the floor in case I experienced a repeat of the time I had picked up Horace's box in the woods. I wasn't super excited to black out again.

I had only briefly seen the inside of that first box. It had a red velvet interior, just like this one. And I knew in my gut that when I lifted this box out of the suitcase, it would have a matching Seal of Solomon on the bottom.

Gingerly, I picked up the box and flipped it over.

The bottom was empty. No interlocking star waited for me there.

I ran my thumb over the smooth, varnished wood.

"It's got to be here somewhere," I muttered, turning it over and inspecting every side. All were bare. But as my fingers explored the box's surface, part of the velvet lining puckered along its lip. I slid my finger into the opening and along the inside edges, popping the thin fabric away from the weak adhesive that held it in place.

The velvet fell away. Beneath it, on the bottom of the box's interior, a series of symbols were burned into the wood. They looked similar to the ones Graham's friend Stephen had carved into one of his rune sets: sharp, angular letters you might get if you were trying to spell out a message with nothing but popsicle sticks.

Striker swatted the back of my hand. She sniffed the corners of the box and scraped her teeth along the bottom edge.

"What?" I asked. "Done napping already?"

She pulled the box down with her paw the way she often did when I was holding a crumpled ball of paper. I let her tug the box downward a few inches, then raised it back up, teasing her.

That was a mistake. She lunged at the box, knocking it out of my hands and sending it flying across the bathroom. In a flash, she pounced on it and rooted around inside with an urgent industry usually reserved for her litter box.

"Hey!" I shouted, standing to retrieve it from her. I needed to take her back to our room as fast as possible, or at least outside where she could do her business in the dirt.

As I stood, it felt like I was stepping out of a fog. My head—which I hadn't even noticed was fuzzy—cleared. I was as alert and refreshed as I felt after a solid night's sleep followed by a cup of Graham's atomic coffee.

"Give me that," I scolded Striker, snatching the box and inspecting it for damage.

One of the hinges was slightly squashed, so the lid no longer closed correctly. The inside of the box had borne the brunt of her razor claws. Several long, deep scratches ran through the runes that had been carved into the bottom.

A few possibilities ran through my mind. None of them made much sense, and a few were barely more than half-formed ideas. While my brain struggled to handle the overload, my hands tucked the mango-sized box into my jacket pocket.

"Great," I muttered. "Now I'm officially a burglar."

Having stolen property bulging out of my windbreaker felt like a good cue to exit. I stooped and hastily refolded Camila's clothing, tossing it back into the suitcase in roughly the same order I had taken it out. I zipped the luggage and stood it back in the tub, hoping nobody would have any reason to open it and notice how messy its contents had become.

The thought gave me a moment's pause. Who had packed the suitcase after they found Camila's body?

It was a question for later.

"Goodbye for now, Camila," I told the bathroom. "I'll reach out as soon as I can, and I hope you'll answer."

Then I grabbed Striker around the middle, tiptoed to the front window, and peeked through the blinds.

The coast was clear.

Like a criminal fleeing the scene of a crime, I slipped out the front door and yanked it closed behind me. Then, as casually as I could manage, I ducked around the back of the yurt and let Striker down onto the ground. I let her lead the way for fifteen minutes or so, following as she sniffed and scratched and explored the open area between the yurts and the river.

"Okay, baby," I muttered as I picked her back up. "I think that's a good enough cover. Let's go wake up Graham."

But Graham wasn't in the yurt when we got back. A note in his messy hand sat on the bed: *At the office.*

I swallowed. Why was he at the office? Had someone seen me? Had they come to tell him to pack our stuff and get out? Was he in there now, pleading with them to let us stay? I couldn't let him fight this battle on his own. I had to go apologize.

After giving Striker a post-walk treat and depositing Camila's jewelry box into my purse, I strolled to the office with what I hoped was the casual air of a woman who hadn't just broken into one of the vacant rooms on the property. I rested my fingertips on the central yurt's front door for a moment and took a deep breath. I would tell them the truth, I decided. Or as much of it as I could without terrifying them.

A burst of laughter met me when I opened the door. Graham leaned back in one of the office chairs with a mug in his hands, shaking his head from side to side as he chuckled about something. Fred Hawkes was pounding on his desk, clearly overcome with mirth.

"What's the joke?" I asked by way of greeting.

Graham turned and grinned at me. "Oh, hey, Mac. We're just swapping stories."

"I couldn't handle being a landlord," the older man said, wiping tears from beneath his eyes. "Folks do enough damage staying here a few nights. I've never had to paint over someone's mural, though."

I looked questioningly at my boyfriend.

"It was a few years before you moved in," he said. "This guy who lived in Kit's old apartment told me he was an artist. He used to come into my studio and critique my sculptures, especially the… uh… female ones. He thought their proportions were off."

Fred shook his head ruefully. "You should have seen it coming, son."

"When he moved out, he left behind a mural he'd done right on the walls. Paintings of—" Graham flushed. "Well, you can guess."

Fred exploded with laughter again. After a few moments, he settled down enough to offer me a cup of coffee and gestured for me to sit beside Graham. I hovered by the door for a few moments, not yet confident that my adventure in the empty yurt had truly gone unnoticed. Or at least that nobody had said anything to Fred about it yet.

Across from his desk, a console table sat beneath a portrait of Fred with his arms around a smiling woman with frizzy white hair. A box of donuts waited there, its lid open invitingly. I helped myself to a large powdered-sugar-dusted creation that looked like it had pastry cream peeping out the top. As Graham and Fred dove back into comparing tenants versus motel guests, I sank my teeth into the still-warm dough.

Sweet, tangy lemon custard danced across my tongue. A hint

of lavender added a note of floral richness. My eyes closed, and I briefly stopped listening to the men, choosing instead to lose myself in the simple pleasure of a damn good donut.

"I'm hoping to get my work into a few galleries here," Graham was telling Fred when I tuned back in to the world outside my taste buds. "With a little luck, we'll be back next year to deliver some sculptures."

"You're welcome here anytime," Fred said. "We'll make sure we've got a room on the Critter side for you two and your little cat."

An errant thought pulled me out of my lemon-curd reverie. The question flew through my mind and out of my mouth before I had a chance to stop it. "Why was Camila Aster staying in our room? Did she have a pet?"

Fred's eyes went wide, and he ran a hand over his wispy hair. "How do you know that name?"

"We found a newspaper article the other night about her passing," Graham explained. "We're so sorry you had to go through that. Losing a guest must be difficult."

"You don't know the half of it." Fred slumped in his chair. His face lost all the youthful animation his laughter had given it, and he suddenly looked like a very tired old man. "She asked for an end unit so she could hike out to do some stargazing, and Shamrock was taken, so we put her in Tortoiseshell. We think that's what she was doing out there in the middle of the night. Lucy, my wife, found her just a hundred yards out, not breathing, unresponsive. Lucy tried CPR until the paramedics got here, but they told us the poor girl was gone long before Lucy arrived. Doesn't stop us from thinking about what more we could have done."

"It sounds like your wife did everything she could," Graham said.

"Well, we didn't even go looking for Camila until after noon. It's our slow season, and we don't like to chase folks out of their rooms unless there's somebody else checking in that day. So Lucy came up with the idea to do these early-morning meet and greets." Fred gestured toward the donuts with his coffee cup. "It's been working out pretty well, and it's a great excuse to make some new friends."

Graham raised his mug. "Hear, hear."

I took a second donut and settled into the chair next to Graham. "I think it's a great idea. I'll come back just for another taste of these babies."

"Be sure to mention that in your review." Fred laughed, and some of the life came back into his eyes for just a moment before a troubled look settled onto his face. "Actually, if you two wouldn't mind leaving us a review online, that'd go a long way. Last thing we want is to become another Arcane Oasis."

"What's that?" I asked around a mouthful of custard.

"One of our competitors. This couple from back east reno-vated an old thirty-room motor lodge a few years back for the summer festival crowds. You see that a lot here—motels with UFO or paranormal themes. Tourists love a themed room, and Arcane Oasis styled their whole place on this psychic power mumbo jumbo."

Graham and I exchanged glances. Fred could have been describing the Donn's Hill bed-and-breakfast strategy, especially during the Afterlife Festival.

"You don't believe in psychics?" I asked.

"Well, I hope I'm not about to offend you here, but no. A lot of our summer guests try to read my palm or tell my future, and it's a load of bunk." He paused. "Don't tell Lizzie."

"I won't," I promised.

"Aliens, now—they're all over this desert."

I buried my nose in my coffee cup to hide my smile. I didn't want Fred to think I was laughing at him, and I needed a moment to quash my knee-jerk desire to call Elizabeth and out her cousin as a skeptic. It was tempting to hear her launch into one of her trademark rants about true psychic abilities. But I liked Fred and didn't want to spoil his close relationship with her. After all, when we came back, I was counting on more donuts.

"Anyway," Fred said, "we thought Arcane Oasis would be the juggernaut around here and we'd have to pick up the crumbs when their rooms filled up. Then the disappearances started."

I raised an eyebrow. "Disappearances?"

"Every year, one or two of their guests just up and vanished in the middle of the night. Skedaddled without a trace."

"Seriously?" I stared at him. "They never found them?"

"Never. The owners couldn't take it. Before long, they sold the land to a condo developer and went back to New York." His eyes lifted to the portrait on the wall. "Lucy and I don't have anywhere to go back to. This is it for us. We'll do whatever it takes to hang on to this place."

We sipped our coffee in silence for a few minutes. I didn't know what was going through the men's minds, but I was trying to decide what would be worse: knowing someone I cared about had died or only knowing they had disappeared and never finding out what really happened to them.

I tried to force the thoughts out of my mind. It was an unwinnable game of Would You Rather that I had no interest in playing.

After a while, Graham set down his mug and slapped his knees. "Well, we should head into the city. Ready, Mac?"

We made our goodbyes, and Graham stepped out onto the sidewalk, but I paused on the threshold. Something had been eating at me since before I snuck out of the Shamrock yurt, a question I couldn't leave without asking.

I turned back to Fred. "This is going to sound like a weird question, but chalk it up to some psychic-power mumbo jumbo."

He smiled indulgently. "Shoot."

"Somebody had to pack up Camila's things, right? After she passed?"

He nodded. "I took care of that. We're still waiting on her next of kin to tell us where to send it."

"Did you..." I paused. Was there a way to word this that wouldn't tip him off to what I'd done? "There's an image I can't get out of my mind. I keep seeing it when I close my eyes, and I can't shake the feeling it's related to Camila. Did she happen to have a small hinged jewelry box? One with red velvet inside?"

Fred's eyes went wide, and the hand holding his coffee mug slowly sank down to the desk. When he spoke, his voice shook ever so slightly. "Well, I'll be. I figured with you being from Donn's Hill, you might fancy yourself a psychic. But I didn't think you could actually *be* one."

"So she did have one?" I pressed.

"When Lucy found her, Camila's body was hunched on the ground, curled around that box. We had to..." He swallowed. "We had to pry it out of her hands."

CHAPTER TEN

I followed Graham to our yurt without processing the world around me. When he paused to open the door to our unit, I walked right into his back and stepped on his heel. He turned in surprise.

"Crap, sorry," I said, steadying myself against the doorframe with one hand.

The minor note of irritation vanished from his face when his eyes met mine. He ushered me inside, eased me down into a chair, and poured a glass of water from the sink. "Here, drink this."

He watched me take a few long, deep sips. The cold water helped bring the world back into focus and chased away the mental image of Camila Aster—whom I had never seen, which left my brain no choice but to substitute my own body for hers—dying in the desert while clutching a jewelry box in my hands.

"What's going on?" Graham asked. "You're really pale."

"I need to tell you something, but you can't get mad."

"Okay." He lowered himself into the other chair. "Is this about you going into that other yurt this morning?"

I whipped my head toward him. "How did you know?"

"You're not as quiet as you think. After you and Striker went outside, I couldn't fall back to sleep, so I sat here and started going through the rest of your mom's mail." He tapped the shoebox on the table. "A few minutes in, I glanced out the window and saw a very suspicious figure slink out of that yurt like a cartoon cat burglar. Then Fred knocked on the door, and I thought for sure he saw you and was coming to kick us out." Graham would have been justified delivering those words in anger, but his voice was level.

"You're not mad?"

"I mean, I am a little. I thought you were done barreling into everything alone. I thought you trusted me."

"I do trust you." I sighed. "But I don't trust myself. That's what I want to talk to you about. I don't think I should be alone down here. I'm worried I might... I don't know"—I gestured at the endless desert outside the window—"disappear."

"Why?"

I told him everything that had happened inside the yurt. Graham's eyes grew wider and wider behind his glasses. When I pulled the little jewelry box out of my purse and put it on the table, he recoiled.

"You took it?"

"I know what you're thinking, but this isn't like that first box. Look at Striker."

She hopped onto the table and was rubbing her face along the box's edges, purring enthusiastically as she marked it with her scent.

Graham stroked a hand down her back. "She likes it."

"Exactly, and she hated the other one. But she did attack this one for a minute." I opened the box and pointed to the scratched-up runes. "And as soon as she did, my head cleared. I felt like I was in control again." My fingers found my necklace, and I squeezed the crystal tightly.

Graham's eyes darkened. "Is that thing still working? Have you seen Horace?"

"I can't feel him. But I can't shake the feeling that he's connected to this somehow. The box can't be coincidence, right? Or am I just paranoid?"

He considered the question for a long time. "I don't know," he finally said. "The box you brought back to Donn's Hill didn't look handmade or anything. I remember it looked weirdly new. For all we know, those boxes could be mass-produced in a factory somewhere and sold in every gift shop in America. There wouldn't be anything special about them. But on the other hand, you wouldn't be drawn to something for no reason, right?"

The best I could do was a half shrug. I honestly didn't know.

He ran a finger over the runes. "These could have been added later. If Horace did have something to do with this box, he could have bought it and burned these in with a pyrography pen or even a soldering iron."

I tried and failed to picture Horace, red eyed and black cloaked, hunched over a workbench. He didn't strike me as an artist or crafting enthusiast, but my encounters with him left me with the distinct impression that he was a control freak. Whatever the purpose behind these boxes, whatever the meaning behind the runes, I could see him making—or at least modifying—them himself.

"In any case, I think we better assume the two jewelry boxes are related," Graham said. "And after that story Fred told us about people just up and vanishing, I don't really want to be alone either. So let's just do everything together today, okay?"

A little bit of the tension left my shoulders, and I managed a weak smile. "Deal. I wanted to see those galleries anyway."

It was a lie, and he knew it. Art was Graham's world, not mine. He could lose himself in a museum or exhibition the way I lost myself in a good book, seeing stories and emotions in abstract works that completely eluded me. I had originally planned to drive over to the Albuquerque Main Public Library while he chatted with the gallerists he'd been emailing, but that plan held zero appeal now.

"And once I finish my meetings, what if we go here?" He slid a folded sheet of paper across the table.

It was a piece of stationery about the size of a paperback novel. The pale lavender paper and cactus watermark immediately evoked a memory of my mother writing grocery lists at our kitchen counter. But the handwriting on this sheet wasn't in her sloping cursive; it was in the same painfully small print I had seen in Anson Monroe's letter from Seattle.

And it was an address.

"Holy crap," I breathed. "Where did you find this?"

"Pinched in a stack of old electric bills. We were sorting the clean envelopes so quickly at Darlene's, we missed it."

I stared at the address. "Do you think this is where he lived?"

"I don't know. But I looked, and it's only two hours away, so it's worth checking out, right?" He glanced down at his watch. "Um, after my meetings anyway. The first one is in an hour, so we better hit the road."

Before we left, I tucked Camila's jewelry box back into my purse. We weren't able to take our furry little good-luck charm with us, but something told me the box from the Shamrock yurt might bring us some good fortune.

GRAHAM DRUMMED his fingertips on the steering wheel and whooped with excitement as we got back onto I-25 that afternoon. His meetings had been in Albuquerque's Old Town, a historic neighborhood populated by flat-roofed buildings with creamy adobe walls. And despite his anxious, philistine girlfriend hovering awkwardly nearby, he had managed to secure an invitation to submit his work for consideration from the first gallery. The second gallerist had previously met Graham at an arts exhibition in Chicago and fallen in love with his work, and she made an outright offer to mount a show of Graham's sculptures after the new year.

Now, as he mused aloud about which pieces to recreate versus which sketches were worth finally bringing to life with clay, I thought about what a perfect day this was turning out to be. I hadn't thought anything could balance the specter of Horace's presence, but Graham's artistic career was literally going farther than it had ever gone before, and we were on our way to meet my mother's old mentor.

Every time the thought entered my mind, I tried to temper my own expectations. Our assumption that the address on the stationery belonged to Anson Monroe could be incorrect. He could have moved sometime during the last two decades. Even if he still lived there, his memories of my mother could be locked away behind the walls of Alzheimer's or dementia.

My anticipation grew as the road took us through the dusty black vistas of the Valley of Fires. On any other day, I would have insisted we pull over to explore the ancient lava flow, but today I had to bite my tongue to keep from asking Graham to fudge the speed limit a little—or a lot—more.

We found the address among the low foothills surrounding a tall peak. Six letters stenciled onto a signpost at the foot of the driveway sent my hopes into outer space: MONROE.

Unable to tear my eyes away from the name, I groped for Graham's hand, squeezing his fingers. "He's still here!"

"Let's just hope he's open to visitors."

Graham's voice was strained, and I quickly saw what was making him nervous. A tall chain-link fence ringed the property, hung every few feet with rusted white signs reading KEEP OUT and NO TRESPASSING. But the open gate did nothing to prevent us from pulling up the drive, a sign of hospitality that made me brave enough to step out of the truck as soon as Graham parked it.

Anson Monroe's house was a wide, prefabricated building. A large propane tank sat off to one side, and sloping sheet metal covered the empty carport. The smell of burning piñon pine from a wood fireplace filled the air, but no smoke rose from the chimney.

Tall weeds sprouted and withered in the network of cracks in the driveway. As I picked my way through them, I looked for any sign of recent activity. I listened for the sounds of a television or a radio but heard only the wind rustling through the overgrown and untamed trees that grew too close to the house.

My heart sank. Nobody lived here. It had been empty for a long time.

"Maybe he's just not great at keeping up on the yard," Graham suggested as we climbed the steps onto the front porch.

I stepped around a rusted deck chair. "Maybe."

"Well, only one way to find out." He raised his fist to knock on the door, but before he could, a gust of wind knocked into us from behind.

The door creaked open.

I shivered. It felt like the house was inviting us inside. Part of me wanted to accept that invitation, but of course we couldn't. This old abandoned place was probably condemned. The county could have put up the fencing and the signs to keep teenagers from turning a dangerous building into a party house.

But the name on the driveway post suggested Anson Monroe had been the last person to live here. I wondered when he had left and why. Had he left anything behind? Maybe a photo or something that could help us find his next address?

"Mac, hey." Graham grabbed me by the arm.

"What?"

"You can't go in there."

"I wasn't going to."

But as I spoke, I realized I had taken two steps toward the threshold. I forced myself to reverse course and backed all the way off the porch and onto the driveway.

"This is what I'm talking about," I said once I was a safe distance away. "I can't trust myself."

He followed me off the porch and wrapped his arms around me. "Do you feel the way you did when you were outside that other yurt?"

I tried to assess my own thoughts. It was a slippery sensation. Nothing *felt* wrong. And really, what would be the harm in looking around a little before we left? It's not like we would ever come back here again.

This was our only chance.

"Let's just check it out real quick," I said.

"Are you serious?" Graham looked back and forth between me and the front door. "We can't walk into somebody's house uninvited."

"This doesn't feel like anyone's house. Nobody lives here—that's obvious. Let's just take a quick look inside. Please."

He shook his head. "No way. I'm not going to get arrested for criminal trespass in another state."

A frustrated groan escaped my chest. Why was he being so difficult? "Listen, remember how pissed you were when I didn't wake you up the night those two guys broke into the garage? You were furious that I went downstairs alone, even though I had no idea they were out there."

An irritated frown settled onto his face. "Of course I remember. That's why I was kind of ticked off you went into that other yurt alone this morning."

"Well, my gut takes me places. Or maybe it's not my gut. Maybe it's... I don't know." I flicked the side of my head. "It could be the same busted thing in my brain that lets me see ghosts. But whatever it is, you have to admit it leads me to some pretty interesting stuff. And even though the things I find scare the hell out of me sometimes, I would rather *know* what's out there than wonder."

He opened his mouth to reply, then closed it again. The muscle in his jaw twitched a few times. Finally, he said, "I think I know where you're going with this, and I don't like it."

"Because you know I'm right. If you want me to tell you everything I'm thinking, all the irrational psychic urges or anxious worries, I need to know you'll support me."

He glared at me, rivaling Striker's ability to pack twelve megatons of emotion into a single expression. Then he stared at the house for a while. When he looked at me again, I could see in his eyes that I had won.

"Okay, we can go inside," he said.

I suppressed the urge to hold up my hand for a high five, sure he would leave me hanging.

"But when we get back to Donn's Hill, you need to talk to Elizabeth about all of this. Whatever's"—he spat out the next word like a bad piece of cheese—"*calling* to you obviously isn't fazed by your necklace. There's got to be something else we can do to protect you."

"Deal," I said, and I meant it. I hated not knowing if something was really my idea or not.

I hated it almost as much as I hated not knowing what was inside this house.

With Graham close behind me, I stepped inside.

CHAPTER ELEVEN

My only prior experience with abandoned buildings was a dilapidated old cabin in the woods outside Donn's Hill—a building with three decades of mold, mildew, rot, and vandalism added to its rustic charm. I expected to find some serious dirt inside the house, but it didn't feel as abandoned on the inside as it looked from the outside. It felt more like an apartment that was between renters: a little dusty, a funky smell in the kitchen, and a living room carpet that could use a good cleaning.

Despite his reluctance to come with me into the house, Graham proved to be an able burglar. We moved quickly through the kitchen, opening cabinets and drawers to check for anything Anson Monroe might have left behind.

"Just plastic utensils and some fast food napkins," Graham announced.

I gingerly peeked in the refrigerator, sure it was the source of the rotten stench that permeated the kitchen. The foul odor of spoiled milk exploded out into the air around me as soon as the door's seal broke, and I spotted a chunky white substance oozing out of the top of a gallon jug. I slammed the door closed, hunched over the counter, and willed the bile back down my throat.

Graham pulled his sweatshirt over his nose. "Did that look as gross as it smells?"

"Stop." I clamped my hand over my mouth. "Please don't make me remember it."

It took several minutes of fighting off dry heaves before I felt safe to stand up straight again. I fished a piece of gum out of my purse—I had learned to carry gum with me everywhere after the first time I threw up on set with the *Soul Searchers*—and popped it into my mouth. Even though I hadn't actually vomited, the sharp spearmint made me feel better, banishing the ghost of the rotten milk from inside my nose.

The master bedroom was off the living room, and it, too, was empty. So were the two smaller bedrooms beyond the kitchen. Apart from the appliances, not a single piece of furniture remained in the house, but rectangular impressions in the carpet convinced me Anson Monroe had lived here. But when? How long ago did he—or someone—empty these rooms and pull the pictures off the walls, leaving nothing but miscolored sections of paint as evidence that this had once been his home?

The more we searched, the more my body felt like a wind-up toy that was running out of juice. As we checked the last closet, finding nothing but a few forgotten wire hangers, the last of my enthusiasm escaped in a deep sigh. I could barely muster the energy to follow Graham through the kitchen and into the back-yard, where nothing lurked but an empty chicken coop.

I had been so sure I would find answers in New Mexico, answers to questions I couldn't even put into words. But all I found were dead ends. I mean, what had I learned, really? The name of an old man?

Most frustrating of all was my gut's stubborn insistence that we had missed something. Even as I stared at the overgrown yard, the feeling in my belly persisted. It screamed that there was something here, something important. It warned me that if we left before we found it, I would never, ever be able to let it go.

Stop being absurd, the rational half of my brain lectured. *There's nothing here, and if you had any sense, you'd be relieved.*

That much was true. But even as I acknowledged the fact, I still felt cheated. Tricked. Had the box in Camila Aster's luggage really called to me, or had I imagined it? Was I just desperate to believe there was some mystical force informing my instincts?

Was everything I did, every discovery I made, really just luck?

I mentally grasped for someone or something to blame for this disappointment, but if I wanted to point fingers, I would have to point them in the mirror. This vacation had been my idea, but it was all as useless and empty as this house. I turned away from the building in disgust.

"That's odd," Graham said from behind me.

I craned my head over my shoulder to peek at the house. Graham stood inside the back door, where a small mudroom granted access to the kitchen. His back was to me as he peered into a closet.

"What is it?" I asked.

"I didn't think houses in New Mexico had basements."

"They don't. Not that I've ever seen anyway." My curiosity aroused, I allowed myself to be lured back into the building. "I remember thinking my dad was super rich when I moved into his house in Colorado because he had a basement."

"Well, look at this." Graham stepped aside so I could look in the closet.

It wasn't a closet at all. I had assumed it must be; we'd explored the entire house, and there wasn't enough space for another room. But beyond the door lay a wooden staircase leading down into pitch blackness.

Behind us, the back door creaked in the wind.

Before us, something moved in the darkness.

My heart stopped. "Did you see that?"

"See what?" Graham asked.

Without waiting for me to answer, he leaned around me and found a light switch on the wall. A fluorescent bar above us flickered to life, illuminating the light gray floor below. And at the edge of the visible space, just before the ceiling blocked everything else from view, I recognized the unmistakable quilted blue pattern of a mattress.

My feet refused to move. I stood at the top of the stairs for a good five minutes, listening, waiting to see if anything moved again.

"I swear I saw something down there," I whispered.

The back door creaked again. Graham pulled it closed.

"What was it?" he whispered back.

"I don't know."

"Should we leave?"

I wanted to. I really, really wanted to. But I worried if I didn't get to the bottom of this now, I would find myself back here later.

Possibly alone.

Probably in the dark.

I shook my head. "We have to check it out."

We crept down the stairs together, wincing with each creak of the wooden treads and pausing every few steps to listen for any sign that we weren't truly alone. Slowly, more of the basement came into view.

It was a small space, only about a third the size of the floor above and not nearly as nicely finished. The gray concrete beneath our feet was as unfinished as the drywall on the walls and ceiling. Beyond the stripped mattress stood another bare bed. A pair of tall dressers faced the beds, and a small table and two chairs took up the center of the space. At the far end of the basement, a trio of empty shelves looked sad without any books to hold.

Like the rest of the house, it was clear someone had lived here before. Possibly recently. There were scuff marks on the footboard of one of the beds, and the sagging mattresses were dotted with stains. But unlike the rooms upstairs, the walls down here weren't blank.

These were covered, from floor to ceiling, in strange symbols.

Some were familiar, like the Egyptian hieroglyphs above the empty bookshelves. Others almost looked random, like they'd been doodled in a moment of boredom. All looked like they had been painted with the same wide brush, in thick black paint that seemed to glisten in the glow of the fluorescent bulbs.

Graham reached out a cautious finger and touched an abstract sun that had been painted above one of the beds. "Weird. It looks wet, but it's completely dry."

"I don't get it." I stared around the room, trying to make sense of the overwhelming variety of shapes that covered nearly every square inch of wall. The sheer sensory overload threatened to short-circuit my brain, but the feeling that I was supposed to be here remained in my belly. I felt sure there was a good reason I had come into the basement, but nothing around me made sense. "Is this some kind of cult thing?"

"Whatever it is, they're mixing and matching from a lot of sources. Hieroglyphs, Judeo-Christian religious symbols, the zodiac." He gestured toward different parts of the room, then raised a hand to point above me. "And those look Norse, but I can't be sure. It's been a while since anyone commissioned me to use Futhark runes on a sculpture."

As I looked up to see what he was pointing at, my stomach plummeted into my shoes. Directly over my head, scrawled on the ceiling in slick black paint, were the same four symbols I had seen inside Camila Aster's jewelry box. Needing to be sure, I pulled the box out of my purse and raised it with shaking hands.

Looking at them side by side left no doubt. They were the same.

"Hey," I squeaked, letting out just a little of the breath I was holding in. "Can you... break that?"

"Break what?" Graham narrowed his eyes at the paint above me. "The ceiling?"

"No, the shapes."

Despite my nonsensical instructions, Graham did as I asked. He picked up one of the wooden chairs by the table and heaved it above his head. I couldn't get my legs to carry me out of the way, so I covered my head with my arms as he gouged a hole into the ceiling's drywall with one of the chair's legs. He repeated the process, tearing a chunk out of each of the four symbols.

"Are you okay?" Graham asked, sweat glistening on his chalky forehead from the exertion of wielding a chair like a sledgehammer.

I took my time answering. My heart raced in my chest, my lungs screamed for air, and my stomach felt stuck between wanting to vomit and wanting to collapse in on itself. But my head felt clear, just as it had after Striker attacked the jewelry box in the Shamrock yurt. I released my held breath in a rush and sucked in a new one.

"I'm fine." Even though the symbols no longer tugged at my mind, I didn't want to stand beneath them. I took a few steps toward the stairs. "Can we go?"

He set the chair down. "I thought you'd never ask. Let me just get a few photos. Stephen might know some of these symbols better than me."

"Make sure you get that Eye of Ra above the bookshelves," I said. "I used to think that would make a cool tattoo."

"That's the Eye of Horus," he corrected me as he snapped a picture of it.

"Are you sure?"

"Yeah, the Eye of Ra faces right. The Eye of Horus faces left. And see? There's the symbol for Horus right next to it." He pointed to a hieroglyph of a falcon, which, like the eye, faced left.

I stared at the hieroglyphs as Graham's words echoed in my mind.

The Eye of Horus.

Horus.

My name is Horace, the so-called ghost at the Oracle Inn had told me.

Or rather, I thought he said Horace. I had spelled it in my mind as he spoke it aloud. H-O-R-A-C-E, like the poet.

But couldn't it have been H-O-R-U-S?

In my mind, I saw his shadowed face, his pale skin, his red eyes. I saw his smile as he claimed, "My name is Horus."

No matter how he spelled it, the name was a lie. I knew now who he really was.

Horace—no, *Horus*—was Anson Monroe.

And I was standing in his basement.

My brain overloaded. My body took charge. With Graham's footsteps thundering behind me, I fled up the stairs and out of the house.

CHAPTER TWELVE

"We should call the cops," Graham said.

"And tell them what?" I countered. "'Hi, we just broke into someone's house and found a bunch of weird graffiti in the basement'?"

He said nothing, but the muscles in his jaw worked overtime as he guided the truck back down the winding road. Soon, we were on the long, straight path back toward the yurt resort, and I felt safer with every mile we put between us and that house.

I didn't know where Graham's mind was during the two-hour drive, but mine was trapped in that basement. The seemingly random array of symbols kaleidoscoped inside my brain as I futilely tried to make sense of the few things I knew. It felt like trying to put together a jigsaw puzzle with pieces from different boxes. There was no way to fit them together, and even if the edges miraculously lined up, the picture made no sense.

Anson Monroe, the man who had been a stranger to me at my mother's funeral, was Horace. I refused to change the way his name appeared in my brain. I wasn't going to think of him as an Egyptian deity. He may have been the most powerful psychic I had ever encountered, but he was still just a man.

Right?

Yes, I decided. If I let him grow into anything else in my mind, I would never be able to think rationally about him.

Not that rational thought was doing me much good. With growing horror, I realized exactly how much I had underestimated Horace's abilities. Not only could he astral project—something I had never thought possible—but he could change his appearance. Anson Monroe had to be more than ninety years old, but he wore Horace like a mask that made him look half his age.

Still, I had seen his true face. It might have been twenty years ago, but I knew who he really was. And that was an advantage I hadn't had before.

Knowing his identity only increased my confusion. How could the man my mother so excitedly wrote about be the same person who psychically stalked me? How could someone she trusted test me, toy with me, and terrify me with obvious glee?

It made no sense, but it had to be true. There was no other explanation.

I had been reasonably certain the two men who broke into Graham's garage and took the haunted jewelry box were connected to Horace. Who else could have known it even existed? But now, I was absolutely sure. They had been driving a van with New Mexico plates, and his house—his strange, empty house— was here too. Those beds in the basement had to belong to his lackeys.

Is that why the furniture in the basement had been left behind when the rest of the house was emptied? Did Horace know they were dead, or did he just think they bailed on him? When did he leave—before or after their van crashed and burned?

And more importantly: where did he go?

As we neared the resort, my eyes swept the desert. It was cold out there, especially now that the sun had set. I thought of Camila Aster freezing to death beneath the stars.

Was Horace connected to her somehow? Or was it just some kind of freaky coincidence that she had a similar jewelry box?

No—it wasn't just similar.

Those runes were his calling card. They were the one thing that connected him to everywhere I had been down here.

I was still trying to work it all out by the time we stumbled into our yurt. Striker stood next to her empty bowl, tail thrashing and yellow eyes defiant. Graham gave her a scoop full of dry food, picked up his suitcase, and started throwing things into it.

"Whoa." I stood in front of the dresser to stop him from grabbing any more clothes. "What are you doing?"

"Packing." He moved into the bathroom and scooped up an armful of toiletries. "We're getting the hell out of here."

"Now? Graham, it's late. We'll be driving all night."

"I don't care."

"And you have another meeting tomorrow, right?"

"I don't care." He dumped the toiletries onto the bed and faced me with his hands on his hips. "Why are you playing devil's advocate on this? Don't tell me you want to stay here."

"I… I don't know."

Part of me did want to stay. I had more questions now than when we first started planning this trip, and I hated walking away before I had the answers I needed. What was the point of coming if we left now?

But could I answer those questions from here?

Could I answer them at all?

Striker, having finished her snack, hopped up onto the box of letters on the table and began the lengthy post-meal task of cleaning her face. She loudly licked her paws until the fur there was as damp as an old washrag, then swept it up over her ear, down across her eyebrow, and over her cheek. She repeated the process several times on each side before moving on to a deep cleaning of her fangs.

I couldn't resist walking over to scratch beneath her chin. In the face of my mounting stress, I envied her easy happiness. I wanted to be part of it. She looked up at me with half-closed eyes and purred throatily.

As soon as I was away from the dresser, Graham started dumping the drawers out onto the bed and arranging the clothes into our luggage. I settled down into the chair beside Striker, too exhausted to fight with Graham about packing.

The wailing guitar intro to Bush's "Everything Zen" made me jump. Graham silenced his ringtone and answered his phone with a brusque, "Hey, Stephen."

I couldn't hear what Stephen was saying, but as Graham listened, the irritated scowl on his face faded away. His features crumpled, pulling downward into a sorrowful expression.

"Which Elizabeth?" he asked.

Striker's head snapped up. Her pupils narrowed into thin slits as her purring ceased.

Graham lowered himself onto the bed, one hand cupped over his face. "How did it happen?"

How did what happen? I wanted to scream. Instead, I leapt up from my seat and climbed across the bed to Graham's side. I pressed my ear against the back of his cell phone in case I could hear what Stephen was saying.

Only Graham's voice was audible. "When's the funeral?"

That was more than I could handle. I snatched the phone out of his hands and mashed the button to put the call on speaker.

"... Penelope is helping Cynthia with all the arrangements," Stephen was saying. "It's awful, just awful. Nobody knows what she was doing out in the woods, and she must have been there awhile—"

"Stephen, it's Mac," I broke in. "What's going on?"

"Oh, hi, Mac. Sorry to be the bearer of bad news, but I figured you'd want to know." Stephen delivered his words in his usual calm Irish brogue. "Elizabeth Monk passed last night."

My heart flew up into my throat. "*What? How?*"

"It's the damnedest thing. She was out in the woods off the main highway in her bathrobe and froze to death. They're still trying to figure out what she was doing out there."

The phone slipped out of my hands and clattered to the floor.

Elizabeth had frozen to death.

Just like my mother.

Just like Camila Aster.

I suddenly knew exactly why she had been out in the woods and who had lured her there. And even though Stephen hadn't used the word, I knew what would appear on the final autopsy report.

Exposure.

CHAPTER THIRTEEN

E xposure.
   Exposure.
Exposure.

The word rang in my mind like the striking of a gong, tolling over and over as we drove back to Donn's Hill. Each time I tried to break my thoughts out of the pattern, they inevitably returned to the fact that when we got home, our lives would be changed.

Yet another person had been taken away from me—like my father, like Gabrielle, like Kit. How many more would I lose? How much more change could I survive?

Then a wave of guilt squeezed my chest as I remembered that as much as my life was constantly changing, at least I was still alive. Elizabeth Monk hadn't gone to prison or left town to pursue her filmmaking career.

She was dead.

From exposure.

Exposure. Exposure. Exp—

"I'm so sorry we couldn't swing through Colorado to visit your dad's grave, Mac." Graham's voice snapped me out of the loop.

"It's okay," I said automatically.

He took a hand off the wheel to squeeze mine. "We'll go another time."

"Sure."

Striker was quiet for most of the drive, only complaining when we had to speed up to pass a truck. Graham and I made little conversation, relying on the radio to keep ourselves awake and alert, occasionally commenting on a news report or forgotten song. We kept our stops to a minimum, switching drivers every couple of hours.

By the time we reached the outskirts of Donn's Hill in the small hours of the morning, my eyeballs were raw, and I wasn't sure what I needed to do more: sleep or cry. Fluffy snowflakes drifted lazily downward over the yard at Primrose House as we ferried everything inside, but the yellow structure seemed determined to be sunny and cheerful in the face of the oncoming storm.

This will be my first winter here, I realized. More than half a year before, on my very first day in Donn's Hill, a friendly barista had warned me about the snow and cold. I had reassured him that after living among the Rockies and the Wasatch, I was ready for anything.

That barista was dead now.

So was Elizabeth Monk.

From exposure.

"No!" I shouted, slapping myself lightly on the cheek before the loop could suck me back in.

Graham rested a hand on my arm. "Why don't you go up and lie down? I'll finish getting everything into the house."

My exhaustion was so complete that I didn't actually remember climbing the stairs to my apartment or crawling into bed. It wasn't until I woke up a few hours later that I was even sure we had really gotten home. In my fitful dreams, we were still driving, trapped forever on an endless road. Once awake, I buried my face into the sheets and inhaled the fresh scent of my own detergent. Even though I hadn't wanted to cut our trip short, it was good to be home.

Striker snoozed in her usual spot across the top of my pillow, but Graham wasn't beside me. Either he had slept in his own apartment or he hadn't come to bed yet. I showered off a little more of my travel fatigue, changed into jeans and a clean Led Zeppelin sweatshirt, and set off to fill my empty stomach.

Primrose House was even quieter than usual for a—I had to check my watch to be sure—Wednesday morning. I looked at my watch again and drew to a halt at the bottom of the staircase as the date and time fully penetrated the fog around my brain.

It was Wednesday.

How could it possibly only be Wednesday? We had left Donn's Hill on Sunday. Somehow, a month's worth of change, heartache, and stress had been crammed into the last three days, and I felt like I'd only had one night's worth of sleep to process it all.

I wanted to turn around and retreat back to bed. Surely, I had earned a week or two of uninterrupted sleep. But my stomach gurgled and squeaked. Its demands were clear: *Food first, sleep later.*

Graham wasn't in the kitchen, and the glass carafe beneath the coffee maker was clean and dry enough to make me suspect he was still zonked out in his own apartment. Our luggage sat in a small pile by the table, but I was too tired to ferry it up the stairs just yet. Instead, I poured myself a large bowl of cereal, nudged a suitcase out of the way with my foot, and collapsed into a kitchen chair to mull while I chewed.

I couldn't wrap my head around the reality of Elizabeth's death. It didn't feel real. I suspected it wouldn't sink in until her funeral, but the thought brought me no comfort. I didn't *want* this to feel real. I didn't want it to be real. A light like hers wasn't supposed to go out like this.

It occurred to me that Elizabeth's shop would join the unit below it on the list of available spaces in The Enclave. I tried to imagine something—anything—inhabiting her space, but just kept picturing her smiling as she carried Striker out of the pet therapy room.

Then, unbidden, I suddenly saw her lifeless body on the forest floor.

Exposure.

"Urngh," I groaned through a mouth full of cereal as I squeezed my eyes closed. My hands found their way into my hair, and I clawed at my scalp to chase the image away.

"Excuse me," a sharp voice asked. "You used my milk."

I raised my head to find Reggie glaring at me from beside the refrigerator. His broad, shining forehead was wrinkled in frustration, and he held a milk carton in his hand.

"See?" He pointed to the carton's label, which had the letters *RA* scrawled across it in fat black marker. "I put my initials on it."

"Whoops, sorry. I didn't notice."

He huffed out through his nose and stuffed the milk back into the fridge, grumbling something I couldn't quite hear. As I went back to my cereal, he tossed something heavy onto the counter and started filling a French press with water.

"Graham will probably make some coffee soon," I said. "But I've got to warn you, it's potent stuff."

"Oh, I know." Reggie made a face. "It's too strong for me. Besides, judging from the snores rumbling through the second floor, he's not going to be down here anytime soon."

I buried my face in my bowl to hide my sudden grin. Graham's snores were usually as soft as a cat's, but when he was particularly exhausted, he rattled the shingles. He must have decided to sleep at his own place to spare me from hearing them, but I wondered if the sound might be enough to make Reggie regret moving in here.

Only if we're lucky, I thought and nearly choked on my Froot Loops while trying to smother a laugh.

When I got up to rinse out my bowl, I caught sight of what Reggie had tossed onto the counter. It was an unopened ream of paper.

"Is that for your typewriter?" I asked.

"Yes." He didn't elaborate.

I had enough social sense to realize he wasn't in a chatty mood, but I couldn't help myself. Everything about the guy rubbed me the wrong way, but I couldn't contain my curiosity. "What are you working on?"

"Nothing you would be interested in."

There it was again, the implication that I wasn't smart enough to read whatever it was he wrote. My cheeks warmed, but before I could figure out a way to call him out for the insult, he took his paper and his French press and left me alone in the kitchen.

"I do not care for that man," I muttered to myself. The least he could have done was share his coffee with me.

I wanted to call Kit, just to hear a friendly voice and have a sympathetic ear to talk to, but her cell phone didn't seem to be working in Paris. I hadn't gotten a response to any of my messages since she texted me from the airport. Her radio silence irked me. Couldn't she borrow a phone? Call me to check in? Even if she did, I grudgingly admitted to myself, she would probably get the time zones wrong and call while I was sleeping.

What I needed was someone to talk to *here*. I had so much to talk about—the trip, the letters, the jewelry boxes, Anson Monroe's house, Elizabeth's death...

The cruelest irony of losing a friend is that you can't talk to them about what losing them feels like.

That earlier sense of surreality returned. It just didn't make sense to me that she was gone, and it made even less sense that she had died in the same way my mother and Camila Aster did. Could it be coincidence?

And if Anson Monroe/Horace was involved with both my mom and Camila, could he be involved with Elizabeth's death too?

I couldn't be sure. I didn't know enough. All I knew was that I didn't want him to be. Tragic though losing Elizabeth would have been under any circumstances, if I could rule out any connection to Horace or a wooden jewelry box, I felt like I would be free to mourn her without also feeling afraid for myself. Because if Horace was involved, that could only mean one thing: Horace had come to Donn's Hill.

A shiver ran through my body. I couldn't afford to put my faith in assumptions. I had to know for sure.

There was one person in town who would not only have access to helpful things like the coroner's report, but who also knew about and believed in the psychic world. If anyone could help me confirm my suspicions, it was Deputy Cynthia Wallace of the Driscoll County Sheriff's Department. She didn't answer her cell phone, so I grabbed my coat and Graham's keys and headed out the door.

Graham's car was a cantankerous old Geo Metro he had named Baxter fifteen years before. Baxter didn't seem to like me much; even in ideal conditions, the car was reluctant to start or shift gears. In the midmorning cold, with snowflakes sticking to the windshield, the old engine complained even more than usual before finally agreeing to turn over.

The banana-yellow beater rattled and sputtered across town to the sheriff's station, but it got me there safely. As I climbed the short flight of concrete steps at the front of the building, a heavyset man with a large mustache sauntered out the main doors with his thumbs tucked into his pockets.

"Miss Clair." Sheriff Harris touched the wide brim of his felt campaign hat and gave a slight nod. "What brings you down to the station?"

I returned his nod with a polite one of my own, but it took some effort. The sheriff and I hadn't gotten off to a great start. Our first meeting had been in an interrogation room where he left no doubts about his opinion of me. My opinion of him had flat-lined pretty hard by the end of that conversation; getting called a fraud and being accused of murder has a tendency to do that, I guess.

Judging by the set of his mouth, he didn't look any more excited to be running into me than I was to be seeing him.

"Hey, Sheriff. I'm just here to see Deputy Wallace."

"She's off today." He shifted his belt. "Anything I can help you with?"

For a moment, I considered asking him what he knew about Elizabeth's death. But I had a feeling he would laugh me right off the steps.

"No, just wanted to chat. Will she be back tomorrow?"

He shook his head. "She took some personal time. Death in the family. You might have heard her grandmother passed away."

"Oh no! That's awful. When did that happen?"

"Night before last. Very unexpected. Elizabeth was fitter than I am—we all thought she'd live to be a hundred at least." He assessed the expression on my face and chuckled. "You look surprised. I thought you were supposed to be psychic?"

I didn't need to explain myself to him, but the words reflexively popped out of my mouth anyway. "I'm not that kind of psychic."

Even if I had the kind of omniscient powers people like Sheriff Harris loved to accuse me of pretending to have, I shouldn't have needed them to realize Deputy Wallace and Elizabeth Monk were related. In retrospect, it was obvious. They both shared the same broad-shouldered build, and they even wore their hair the same way.

I wondered when Wallace's braid would turn white.

"I'm just surprised Elizabeth was old enough to have a grand-daughter around my age, that's all." I pulled my hood up against the chill wind and shivered. Then, since he had raised the subject, I asked, "How did she die?"

"Hypothermia. She wasn't dressed warmly enough for the cold snap." He delivered the facts about her death in a detached manner that I found disturbing. How many tragedies did someone have to deal with before being able to talk about them so casually?

"Did she…" I hesitated, not sure how to phrase the question in a way that would sound like any regular person with a passing interest in local news. I couldn't come out and ask, *Did she happen to die with a small wooden box in her hands?* "Was there anything strange about her when you found her?"

Sheriff Harris's eyes hardened. "Strange? Miss Clair, there's nothing about finding an elderly woman alone in the woods in her pajamas that isn't unsettling. It's a tragic situation. But that's not what you meant at all, is it? I know all about your involvement in the apprehension of Thomas Bishop's killer last spring. One of these days, I'll get to the bottom of how you knew so much about his death, and I won't be at all surprised to learn you were more involved with Gabrielle Suntador than you claim."

His accusation made my heart thump inside my chest and my fingers curl into fists at my sides. Gabrielle had been my friend and my mentor, and it had broken my heart to learn that she helped two local men commit a series of burglaries before accidentally killing her co-conspirators. She had begged me not to tell the police what I discovered, and I could have let her get away with it.

But I hadn't.

"You're way off base," I snapped at him. "Deputy Wallace can back me up."

He rolled his eyes. "Oh yes, she told me all about you and your psychic detective skills. So what? You heard about Elizabeth's death and now you can't wait to get out your magnifying glass and your deerstalker hat and go hunting for clues?"

I opened my mouth to object, but he had no interest in hearing anything I had to say. He raised his voice and steamrollered right over me.

"How about I save you some time? Elizabeth was an insomniac who often took walks when she couldn't sleep. Her neighbors confirmed it. And do you know what happens when your body temperature drops below eighty-nine degrees? You get confused. You start walking in the wrong direction." As if to illustrate his point, he ambled toward me, forcing me backward into the cold metal railing at the top of the steps. "We found her in her pajamas, but she likely left the house with an overcoat on and stripped it off as she got colder. They call it paradoxical undressing."

He leaned toward me so close that I could smell the subpar coffee on his breath. I sidestepped him and moved down a few stairs.

Once more, I tried to defend my interest in the case. "I'm not—"

"The bottom line, Miss Clair, is that as awful as the way Elizabeth died is, there is absolutely nothing suspicious about it." He was leaning toward me again, nearly shouting now.

Nothing about this situation was remotely funny, but I felt laughter welling up inside me as my brain crept closer to full panic mode. Clearly, despite the fact that I had been completely cleared of suspicion in Raziel Santos's death last month, Sheriff Harris still didn't like me. And he was going to punish me for my innocence by yelling at me until I died right here on the station's front steps.

I mentally amended my earlier thoughts about how the years on the job must have made him so detached from emotion; anyone who could rant this long at a near-stranger had to start off detached from a lot of things.

"We found no signs of drugs or alcohol in her system, and no evidence that she was forced or coerced into leaving her home." He finally straightened back up and adjusted his hat. "There's just nothing here to concern you at all, got it?"

His pause left a window for me to speak, but I didn't dare try. As soon as I opened my mouth, I was sure he would launch back into his tirade. I nodded, which was apparently good enough for him, because he strode past me and down to his black truck.

I stayed still until he pulled out of the parking lot. Only then did it feel safe to climb back into Baxter. Like the sheriff, the car hated me, but at least I didn't have to listen to it talk.

CHAPTER FOURTEEN

When I pulled back into the parking lot at Primrose House, Stephen Hastain was walking up the path to the back door. The large white box in his hands looked suspiciously like the kind of thing you might get at a bakery, and I hustled to catch up with him in the kitchen where Graham was pouring fresh beans into the coffee maker's hopper.

"All right, Mac?" Stephen asked.

"Depends on what you brought and if I can have some."

"Thought you two might need a pick-me-up." He set the box onto the table and flipped the lid open, then wafted his hand over it to send the sweet-scented air my way.

The aroma of maple syrup tickled my nose and lured me closer. I slid into a chair and immediately had to put a hand to my mouth to keep from drooling on the twelve intricately decorated donuts Stephen had brought with him.

I swallowed back the rush of saliva. "Where did you get these?"

"New bakery in Moyard. Just opened. I thought you two could use a good treat after rushing home like that." Stephen raised an eyebrow and peered into the box. "I have to admit, I can't quite decide where to start."

He wasn't the only one. Between the maple-frosted creation that looked like it was topped with crystallized bits of syrup, the glazed donut covered with jagged multicolored pieces of sour Skittles, and the cloudy pink-and-purple fluff that had to be some kind of cotton-candy frosting... it was impossible to know where to begin.

"Let's slice a bunch up and sample all of them," I suggested.

Stephen grinned and tilted his head backward to address Graham, who was still getting the coffee sorted out. "Smart woman you have here. You got a knife?"

After several minutes of tasting the designer donuts, ranking them, then retasting and reranking based on the way pairing them with coffee changed their flavor profiles, the general consensus was that the chocolate cake donut smothered with crushed Oreos was the best overall.

Graham dusted his hands off on his coveralls. "Thanks a lot, Stephen. Now I'm going to have to drive out to Moyard twice a week for these monstrosities."

"Maybe Penelope can get them to have a booth at the Afterlife Festival," I suggested. A fantasy played out in my mind of the owners falling in love with Donn's Hill and deciding to relocate here. "And then they could open a shop here year-round."

"Mmm," Stephen agreed. "We could use a good bakery."

"We could use a lot of things." Graham rested his hands behind his head and leaned back in his chair to gaze at the ceiling. "An art supply shop, a bookstore, more varied restaurants..."

"Nah, you don't want that stuff," Stephen said. "Donn's Hill is a perfect little pocket of oddities. If you bring in all that, we'll be just like everywhere else."

"I guess we'll have to wait until Gabrielle comes back for that bookstore," I said.

Graham pursed his lips but didn't look at me.

"Do you think she will come back?" Stephen asked. "I'd like to meet her."

"Of course she will." I reached for another chunk of the Oreo donut. "This is her home."

A loud *thunk* sounded as the front legs of Graham's chair landed back on the tile floor. He hopped up and rummaged through the pile of luggage we'd left in the kitchen after our late-night arrival. "Mac, where'd you put the jewelry box you found?"

"Oh, with my toiletries."

A moment later, he found what he was looking for and set it on the table in front of Stephen. The Irishman picked it up and studied it with furrowed brows.

"Is this… for me?" he asked.

"No, there are some runes inside," Graham explained. "We thought you might be able to tell us what they mean."

"Oh, thank God." Stephen opened the box. "I thought this was some kind of weird souvenir you thought I'd like."

Graham and I exchanged glances, and I shifted uncomfortably in my chair. In all the chaos of our sudden departure from New Mexico, we had forgotten to bring back anything for our friends.

Stephen seemed to notice our silence. "Eh, not that I was expecting anything. Not really."

I cleared my throat and flicked the red velvet. "There's something under that loose piece."

As he pulled back the cheap lining, I found myself holding my breath. I no longer felt the strange pull that had led me into the empty yurt, but I was still fascinated by the little jewelry box. It was like when you walk into a gift shop filled with inexpensive trinkets, but there, among the personalized keychains and mass-produced bumper stickers, you manage to find something truly unique. Something that captures the energy of the locale and the spirit of the moment.

We may not have brought back any souvenirs for other people, but for me, this box embodied everything about our trip—the strangeness, the sadness, even the abrupt way it had ended. When I looked at the box Camila Aster had been clutching when she died, I felt it all.

I mentioned none of that to Stephen, and I was glad Graham left out any context as well. I was curious to see what the rune caster sensed from the box, if anything.

Stephen frowned at the symbols burned into the wood.

"Do they mean anything?" Graham prodded.

"Hard to say. It looks a bit like *lathu*, but they're really scratched up."

I winced apologetically. "Yeah, Striker did that. What's a *lathu*?"

"If I remember right, it's an invitation rune. Well, a word, really. See how it's made up of these four runes together? But it doesn't really come up much in divination, so I'm not completely sure."

"Invitation, huh?" My attempt at casual curiosity was spoiled somewhat as the hand holding my coffee mug began to shake. "Where would you typically see it? Like a slab of stone with a wedding invitation carved onto one side?"

Stephen chuckled. "I suppose it could have. But I've only ever seen it in a more supernatural context."

A sudden chill ran up my arms. "Like how we invite ghosts to speak to us during a séance."

"Yeah, that kind of thing." He set the box back on the table. "Where'd you get it?"

From a dead woman, I wanted to say. Instead, I shrugged. "Another guest at the motel in New Mexico left it behind when they, uh… checked out."

"Odd." He looked at his watch and stood. "Well, I had better get back down to The Enclave. Penelope asked a few of us to help

Elizabeth's family gather up some photos and things for the memorial service."

"When will it be?" Graham asked.

"Saturday. I guess Elizabeth had friends all over the country, and her kids want to give everybody enough time to get here."

Delaying the funeral until the weekend made sense. I supposed we could have stayed in New Mexico longer instead of rushing home in the middle of the night, but then again, Graham hadn't really wanted to hang around.

"Can we do anything to help with the service?" I asked.

"Only if you have pictures of Elizabeth you want to give them."

I didn't. It never occurred to me to take one of her. The old woman had seemed so vital. I wished now that I had thought to take a photo of her with Striker.

After Stephen left, I found it difficult to focus on anything for too long. Part of it might have been the persistent sugar rush from snacking on leftover donuts, but I felt like I was in a sort of time-less limbo. All I wanted to do was sleep, but I knew if I let myself go to bed too early, I would screw up my sleep schedule for days, so I kept myself in the waking world by keeping busy.

There were plenty of small tasks around Primrose House to keep my hands moving and my blood pumping: unpacking and putting away our luggage, sweeping the wraparound porch, changing the furnace filter, replacing a few burned-out bulbs along the staircase. Household maintenance usually fell to Graham, but he dove into rebuilding his inventory the moment Stephen pulled out of the parking lot.

"I need to push myself," he told me as he lifted an enormous block of clay onto his workbench. "The gallery wants twenty original pieces, and I've got to plan for next year's Afterlife Festival too."

"Brrrllll." Striker sat in her usual spot atop Graham's filing cabinet. It was the perfect height for supervising his work and conveniently close to his stash of kitty treats.

"Can I help?" I asked.

"Just take care of yourself." He kissed my forehead, then pulled on an apron and got to work under Striker's watchful eye.

The light in the garage stayed on well into the evening, and when I finally decided I had been awake long enough to avoid the kind of faux jet lag that often followed all-nighters in college, I went to bed alone. Thanks to its position at the top of the house, my apartment collected all the excess heat from the units below and managed to stay warm with little additional effort on my part. All the same, I snuggled beneath the heavy quilt on my bed before closing my eyes.

For the second time that week, I opened them in the backyard of Primrose House.

I blinked a few times, unsure if I was awake or not. The world lacked the Technicolor sheen of my usual dreams, and unlike the perpetual summer of my imagination, the yard around me looked the same as it had when I had last gone outside to check on Graham: nearly bare tree limbs; flat, dormant grass; masses of unraked leaves scattered across the ground.

Had I been sleepwalking? I had never done it before, but it had been a long time since I'd been this sleep-deprived. I rubbed my eyes, which still fuzzed and blurred with the remnants of my slumber. I was debating whether to go into the garage and talk to Graham or go straight back up to bed when I realized not *everything* in the yard was the way I had left it that evening.

The leaves weren't their usual array of autumn reds, golds, and browns. Like everything else coming into focus around me, they were in varying shades of gray.

I couldn't see any color at all.

My feet made my decision for me, and I sprinted for the garage. I needed Graham to check my eyes, maybe even drive me to the emergency room in Moyard. Had I hit my head before going to sleep? Did I have a concussion?

Leaves scattered as I plowed across the lawn, and I drew to a sudden halt. My footsteps should have been crunching on the frozen grass. I should have heard the leaves crackling beneath my feet.

But there was no sound. I clapped my hands, snapped my fingers, and tried to speak.

Nothing.

Please, please, please let this be a dream. At least I could hear my inner monologue, even if my actual voice had been silenced.

Something touched my leg, and I jumped backward. This had all the qualities of a nightmare, which meant a dog-sized tarantula or a swarm of snakes could appear at any moment.

A black-and-gray cat with gray eyes blinked up at me from where I'd just been standing. Its color pattern was familiar; the grays swirled and blended into each other at random, and one of its hind feet was nearly white.

"Striker?" I tried to speak her name, but no sound left my mouth.

She lifted her chin. I couldn't hear it, but I was fairly certain she had just trilled at me.

I scooped her up into my arms. Her heavy purr was inaudible but still rumbled against my chest comfortingly. I squeezed her, grateful beyond words that she was here to help me face whatever terrifying things my brain was about to conjure.

Striker's head snapped toward the house. Her strangely colorless eyes held the same curious gleam she often had when she was looking up into the corners of the ceiling. I didn't want to know what she was looking at, but I couldn't help peeking over my shoulder anyway.

A woman stood in the kitchen doorway.

Mom?

No. It wasn't my mother. This woman was tall and rail thin, and her black hair was much curlier than my mother's. She looked like she might be a college student, but it was hard to guess her age in grayscale.

She walked across the lawn and stopped a few feet away from me. Her face was illuminated from the light spilling out of Graham's garage's window, and she looked both happy and relieved to see me. I got the feeling she knew me, but I had never seen her before in my life.

"Who are you?" I mouthed.

Her lips moved, but I couldn't hear what she was saying. My rudimentary lip-reading skills were only good for a few syllables at a time, and only if there was plenty of context to inform my guesses. She tried again. When my expression made it clear I didn't understand her, frustration clouded her beautiful features. Then she reached out, lifted a section of my hair, and dropped it.

"Hey." I stepped back, not sure what she was trying to do.

She held up both hands, palms out, like she was trying to soothe a feral cat. With two baby steps toward me, she did it again, this time grabbing a larger piece of my hair. The strands tickled as she dropped them back into place.

I shivered. The sensation was familiar. It had happened in the empty yurt in New Mexico. Only back then, I hadn't been able to see the person doing it.

"Camila?" I said soundlessly. "Camila Aster?"

She nearly collapsed with relief. She clapped her hands silently and nodded.

"What are you doing here?"

Camila stood very still, and her face grew serious. She mouthed something to me, slowly and deliberately. I focused as hard as I could, trying to read her lips.

It was impossible. I couldn't make out a single word, and the lack of any sound was unnerving. Half of my brain kept groping in the silence for any noise, and when it couldn't find any, it distracted the other half of my brain by freaking out about it.

Camila's expression grew more and more agitated. Striker's silent purring intensified, rattling my sternum.

"I want to help you," I mouthed. "What can I do?"

In answer, Camila shook her head. Her hair thrashed violently back and forth, and she balled her hands into tight fists at her sides. She opened her mouth and screamed.

I heard it.

The grayscale world around me blinked out into darkness. When I opened my eyes again, I lay flat on my back in my bed. Camila's scream still rang in my ears—

No. *I* was screaming.

I snapped my mouth closed, and the faint sound of my teeth clicking together was literal music to my ears. I had never noticed how many ambient sounds were always in the background—the slight *whoosh* of the heated air from the vents, the little whirring of my mini fridge's fan, and Striker's purr from my pillow, where she was wrapped around my head.

As I moved to reach up a hand to stroke her fur, something shifted on my chest. The box I had taken from Camila's luggage rested over my heart. My left hand gripped it so tightly that it took a moment of effort to uncurl my fingers.

I sat up slowly, examining the box. I didn't remember bringing it to bed.

"Brrrlll," Striker trilled from my pillow.

I held the box up for her inspection. "Do you know anything about this?"

She stood and rubbed her face along the corner of the box. One lip curled upward, exposing a fang, but she didn't look menacing.

She looked affectionate.

After a moment, she switched to head-butting my free hand until I scratched her chin.

"I dreamed about you, sweet girl. I was feeling pretty freaked out, and then you showed up and made me feel better."

She drew back, and her yellow eyes glinted. I shivered. I had a strange feeling she didn't need me to tell her anything that had happened in that dream.

She already knew.

CHAPTER FIFTEEN

My body ached when I climbed out of bed later that morning. My feet felt like I'd been hiking in crappy shoes, and even walking across the room to the kitchenette made my leg muscles scream in protest. As I tucked Camila's box into the cupboard above my sink, I wondered if I should call Elizabeth and make an appointment for a massage.

My phone was in my hand before I remembered she was gone.

I slowly sank down onto a stool at my counter. I hadn't expected to feel this way until the funeral, but here it was. For the first time since receiving the news, her death felt real. I had to acknowledge it. The final period at the end of her story had been hammered onto the book of her life—or at least the part of the story I had been privileged to read. Her next chapter would be written on the vellum that separates the living world from the next plane of existence, and not even a psychic like me would be able to see it all.

A sob bubbled up my throat as the finality of her loss sank in. I would never be able to talk to her again. I would never get to listen to her opinions about the way an intuitive should use their gifts for the benefit of the world. I wouldn't even get to tell her about New Mexico and see her gray eyes flash with indignation when I let her know her cousin Fred didn't really believe in her psychic abilities.

"Crap," I muttered.

Fred. He didn't know why we left early. Graham had left our room key in the late checkout box outside his office when we hightailed it back to Donn's Hill. I meant to call Fred after we got back, but my run-in with Sheriff Harris had driven it right out of my exhausted mind.

He and Elizabeth had been close. They were family. He needed to know she had passed away. How did that normally work? My father had no extended family for me to contact when he died. His friends at the university helped me spread the word about his services. Was someone here making the difficult phone calls to the people who had known and loved Elizabeth?

Just in case, I called the Yurt in Luck office and got no answer, so I left a message asking Fred to call me as soon as possible. Death didn't seem like an appropriate topic for a voicemail.

When my phone rang later that morning, I expected it to be Fred calling me back. Instead, Yuri's accented voice greeted me warmly.

"Good news," he said. "We have two new crew members."

"Really? That was quick."

"We got lucky. Our new cameraman just moved here from Los Angeles and can't wait to get started."

"Oh, cool," I said half-heartedly. I found it hard to get excited about working with anyone who wasn't Mark or Kit. "How about a producer?"

"I wanted to talk to you about that. You are doing a great job with the sound equipment on our little minisodes. Would you like a promotion? To take over the rest of Kit's duties?"

I winced, glad he couldn't see the look of distaste on my face. I had watched Kit edit several episodes, and the software she used was terrifyingly complicated. Plus, the process of clipping, cutting, rearranging, and generally wrestling the footage into a TV-ready format looked more tedious than I could handle. "I don't think anyone would want to see an episode I edited."

"I should have said, her duties except for that. We can outsource the editing to the same team we used for our commercials and the recent minisodes. You would handle the scheduling, making arrangements, keeping us on track. That sort of thing." When I didn't answer right away, he added, "It would come with a significant increase in your pay."

Striker reached up and hooked one of her claws into my phone's protective case. She yanked it downward toward her mouth like she was going to bite it, and I swatted her paw away.

"Mac? Are you still there?" Yuri asked.

"Sorry. Striker's trying to take over. She wants to know if she'll get a raise too."

I expected him to chuckle, but his voice was serious as he said, "I can offer her an extra bag of fishy treats per month."

Just like that, I lost the game of phone chicken and burst into laughter. Yuri joined in, which made me laugh harder and longer than the joke deserved. But it felt good. I wanted to keep laughing forever. I had been too long inside my head, and for the first time since Kit left, I found myself feeling genuinely excited to get to work.

"Deal," I told Yuri. "So do you need to hire my replacement now?"

"Already done. Stephen Hastain recommended a friend of his. Do you know Kevin Lund?"

"I don't think so."

"He impressed me quite a bit during our interview. He has a passion for what we're doing."

"Sounds good to me. When can we get started? Or is finding our next gig my job now?"

I could hear the smile in his voice as he said, "You can take over starting with the next one. The Ace of Cups has asked us to investigate some unusual activity. We'll start shooting Sunday evening."

"I thought their whole bit about psychic bartenders was just a shtick to get around The Enclave's rules?"

"It is, though we won't mention that on the show. But some of their staff live on the second floor of that building in the tenant apartments. They claim to have seen a ghost up there. I think it will be a fitting bridge between our tourism series and the next season of *Soul Searchers*."

After we hung up, I mentally amended my resumé. My career had doglegged sharply to the left when I decided to start over in this town. A string of administrative support jobs had suddenly ended, replaced by production assistant—a job I hadn't previously known existed. Now I was going to be a producer on a television show.

I had to look up what I had agreed to become.

According to the internet, it sounded like producers were sort of like the managers I had worked for at previous jobs. They hired crew members, managed schedules, and oversaw the budget. I frowned. I had never really thought about the *Soul Searchers* budget before. Did Yuri actually expect me to manage the money? I raked our conversation over in my mind. He'd only mentioned the schedule, so I decided to focus on that piece until we could talk about it more.

I knew most of our prior investigations were booked in one of two ways: either someone reached out to us through our ScreamTV website and asked us to come look into suspected paranormal activity, or Kit and Yuri contacted people who owned notoriously haunted locations—like the Grimshaw Library or the

Franklin cabin—and made arrangements to film an episode there. If I was going to be scheduling upcoming investigations, I decided I had better start making a list of possibilities to pitch to Yuri.

Down into the rabbit hole of online research I went. My entire day disappeared, sucked into an endless sea of personal blogs, message boards, and social media threads about paranormal activity in and around Driscoll County. If everything I read was true, almost every public building had at least one ghost associated with it. I started a list of the most promising places and kept digging.

It was satisfying to actually find something in my research for once. Funny how casting a wide net let me catch more leads than trying to hunt for an Anson Monroe–shaped needle in the haystack of the entire American population.

My hands froze on the keyboard. When Graham and I had been looking for Anson's contact information, we'd only been searching for him by name. We had chosen the most specific possible thread to follow. Of course it hadn't yielded many results.

Tentatively, I typed in a few other search phrases, things I knew Anson specialized in. Between my mother's letters and the conversations I'd had with Horace, I had way more to go on than just a name.

Astral projection. Spiritual nexuses. Crossing over.

Even in the endless sea of the internet, the resources I found were comparatively thin. It wasn't as easy to find instructions for astral projection as it was to find a recipe for super chewy chocolate chip cookies. But hunched over my laptop with a bowl of potato chips at my side, I spent hours sifting through what little I could find.

Compared to scouting potential filming locations for the *Soul Searchers*, this was a slog. A strangely combative argument on a now-dead forum about whether astral projection or transcendental meditation were to blame for the hauntings in Amityville nearly made me give up and snap my laptop shut. But near the bottom, just before the conversation petered out, I read a comment that made me lean forward toward the screen.

If you really want to astral project, you have to disconnect from your body, the poster wrote. *You'll need one of these flying ointments.*

I had no idea what a "flying ointment" was, but the idea that the answer to the question my mother had spent so long asking could be found on the internet both saddened and intrigued me. When she died, we didn't even have a computer in our house. She wouldn't have been able to resist clicking the link at the bottom of the comment, and neither could I.

It took me to a blog post that was over ten years old. With as much authority as a free website can muster, the author claimed to have unearthed the only genuine flying ointment recipe in the world. It listed a dozen herbs—some I recognized, like ginger and chamomile, and others I didn't, like hemlock and thorn apple. According to the site, witches as far back as the middle ages would rub the salve on their skin to "facilitate the separation of their spirits from their bodies, which allowed them to fly above the earth and pass freely through walls."

I frowned. Anson definitely ignored walls when he appeared to me as Horace in places like Elizabeth Monk's day spa. But the idea of someone's spirit detaching from their body to literally float around like a cartoon ghost? Even living in Donn's Hill, where the impossible happened every day, something about that just didn't sit right with me.

It didn't sound like astral travel.

It sounded like death.

The first comment at the bottom of the page backed up my suspicions. They emphasized their warning in all-caps: *DO NOT*

USE THIS! These ingredients are dangerous! If you're lucky, you'll hallucinate your brains out. If you're not, you will seriously die.

Another reply agreed. *Belladonna? Wolfsbane? You're kidding, right? That's literally poison.*

The first commenter added, *Yup. And you don't even need an ointment to astral project. You just need to be in a place of power.*

"A place of power" sounded like the spiritual nexuses my mother had spent years exploring—places like Donn's Hill, where the wall separating the living and the dead was thinner than normal. But she hadn't stayed in Donn's Hill. She had gone looking for somewhere even more powerful. Had she known about these ointments? Had she tried them?

My stomach turned.

A third poster chimed in, claiming, *You can't just find somewhere powerful enough to cross over. You have to make one.*

To that, the original author of the blog replied, *You're all missing the point of the salve. If astral projection was easy, everyone would be doing it. Your mind has to separate from your body completely to pull it off. If you have to be on the edge of death to get there, so be it.*

I sat back from my computer, momentarily stunned by the ideas I had just consumed. Where were these people getting their information? Experience? Had the person who wrote the blog actually used the recipe to successfully astral project?

It didn't feel likely. It seemed too close to something Kit's girlfriend, Amari, had told me about how to tell if a psychic is real or fake.

"The real ones," she had said, "don't advertise."

If someone had knowledge this powerful, I couldn't picture them just posting it online. I couldn't imagine them sharing it at all. How would you even know who you could trust with it? What if you taught someone and they used it for evil?

The question brought a deep frown to my lips. Had Anson Monroe discovered the secret to astral projection on his own, or had he learned it from someone else? I knew my mother had considered him a mentor. She had been convinced he was going to help her do it, so he must have told her he could. Had he ever intended to teach her? Or had it all just been a trick, part of some sadistic plan that ended with her dying alone in the desert?

I didn't want to imagine it, but the images filled my mind nevertheless. I saw her curled around a jewelry box just like Camila Aster, cold beyond shivering and no longer aware of her surroundings. I wondered if, as the link between her spirit and her body weakened, she was able to astral project at all. Did she realize her dream before she died? How long did it take for her soul to detach completely, leaving her body on the ground for the New Mexico State Police to find?

"No!" I shouted, shoving my laptop away from me. It flew off the countertop and clattered to the floor.

Tears streamed down my face as I fled my apartment. I needed to find Graham, needed to feel his arms around me and hear his voice in my ear. But no matter how fast I ran down the stairs, the vision in my mind followed.

No matter how far I went, I could never escape the past.

CHAPTER SIXTEEN

I spent the next two nights in Graham's apartment in the hopes that being in a safe place, somewhere I had never been literally or figuratively haunted by the ghosts of the past, would give me a peaceful night's sleep. But even there, my nightmares found me. Visions of Anson Monroe's basement and the endless space of a freezing desert sent me shooting upright every half hour, gasping for breath and clutching the sweat-drenched sheets.

Graham had taken to sleeping on his couch—within earshot if I needed his help but far enough away that I wouldn't wake him up or kick him with my thrashing legs. I felt guilty for chasing him out of his own bed, but as he drove us up Main Street to Elizabeth Monk's memorial service, I glanced at his unbagged, not-at-all puffy eyes with envy. He looked handsome and well-rested in a navy blue suit. I knew I looked frumpy in my unironed skirt, but I hadn't had the energy that morning to do much more than dab concealer under my eyes and wrestle my hair into a black velvet scrunchie.

Elizabeth's service was held in the same place all respected citizens of Donn's Hill were eulogized: Hillside Chapel. The gray stone building at the top of the hill for which the town was named marked the end of Main Street and typically seemed a fitting place to mark the end of someone's life. But unlike the last service I had attended here, which had been formal and structured, Elizabeth's didn't take place in the chapel itself.

Instead, mourners were directed down the stairs into a large, surprisingly high-ceilinged basement with a stage at one end and a kitchen at the other. As we entered, we passed through a cloud of incense that someone close to Elizabeth must have chosen. Frankincense oil had been part of the blend she diffused throughout her massage parlor. She told me once that frankincense helped establish rituals, and she believed few things were as important as the ritual of self-care. I inhaled deeply, allowing the earthy scent to relax my stiff shoulders as I prepared myself for another important —but far less pleasant—ritual: saying goodbye to a dear friend.

Her ashes sat atop a black-draped pedestal on the stage in a polished gray urn. It felt more fitting than an ornate casket would have been; she was such a practical woman. But her sensible, down-to-earth nature had clearly attracted many people into her orbit. The hall was packed with mourners, and their voices echoed off the walls, nearly drowning out the strains of "Amazing Grace" from a string quartet in the corner.

The energy down here was nothing like the mournful atmosphere I had expected. There was a joy in the air that I didn't have to be an Empath to sense. It felt like a wake, a celebration of the life Elizabeth had led, and I added it to a mental list I had never thought to make before: how I would like to be mourned when I died.

Someone had enlarged photos and hung them all around the space: a young Elizabeth in a long bridal gown with an uncomfortable-looking amount of lace; Penelope and Elizabeth posing at the entrance to The Enclave, pre-renovation, with hard hats on their heads and shovels in their hands; a family portrait with a lot of tall people who shared Deputy Wallace's broad build and dark hair; Elizabeth scowling at the counter of her spa as though she thought getting her photo taken was the silliest idea she'd ever heard.

I took a picture of that one with my phone as a fresh wave of grief squeezed my chest. I wished I could tell her how right the photographer had been to capture her in that moment.

Penelope Bishop, deputy mayor of Donn's Hill, greeted us at the guest book with a pair of quick, tight hugs. Her honey-blond hair was carefully coiffed into a high bun from which a few delicate strands had "fallen" in strategically flattering places, and she looked a full decade younger than her fifty-five years in her designer pantsuit.

"How are you holding up, Mac?" she asked.

"I'm doing okay," I fibbed. "How are you?"

"Devastated." She sighed and shook her head. "Elizabeth and I grew quite close this past year. If she hadn't volunteered to lead The Enclave's tenant association, I don't think we would have been able to fill the spaces so quickly. I don't know what I would have done without her."

"I didn't know she helped with that."

"She had connections all over the country." Penelope gazed around the assembled mourners. "I wish she could have seen how many of her friends made the trip to say goodbye."

It was an impressive amount of people, and I didn't know very many of them. Of course, I wasn't the friendly extrovert Graham was and could only name the few dozen people I regularly talked to in the course of my daily life. But I had grown accustomed to the faces in Donn's Hill, and I recognized few of them here.

The realization that I was surrounded by strangers stiffened my spine. How many of them were truly unknown? Could Anson

Monroe disguise himself as effectively in the real world as he could on the astral plane?

No. I couldn't accept that. As much as psychic abilities sometimes felt like magic, and even as often as psychics had been tried and murdered for being "witches," I couldn't believe Anson Monroe could walk around a funeral wearing Horace's face. I felt safe assuming that if and when we met again, he would look like an older version of the man I had seen two decades before.

Of course, that still wasn't much to go on. I didn't have any photos. All I had was a faded memory from a day when he had been the least of my worries. To my eight-year-old mind, he had been an older, gray-haired man. There were many people here who matched that description, and people changed a lot in twenty years.

A number of informal receiving lines had formed throughout the room, each leading to someone with Monk family features. I studied my fellow mourners with a focus so intense that I didn't notice Stephen Hastain until he jiggled my elbow.

"All right, Mac?" the rune caster asked.

"Fine." I forced a small smile. "How are you doing?"

"As well as you might expect." He nodded toward the urn. "We got off to a rocky start, but I'm going to miss her."

Graham patted his shoulder. "She was a tough lady. It's hard to believe she's gone."

"You looking for someone, Mac?" Stephen asked. "You're squinting pretty hard there."

"Oh." I made an effort to relax my face. "Just looking for anyone familiar."

"Like him?" Graham spotted someone behind me and waved his arms, raising his voice above the hubbub to call, "Fred!"

I turned around to see Fred Hawkes making his way toward us through the crowd. At his side was the same white-haired woman from the portrait in the Yurt in Luck office. She dabbed at her eyes with a handkerchief; he looked stricken. Exhaustion radiated off them both.

"Graham." Fred smiled weakly. "Great to see you."

"I didn't think you'd make it."

"We left as soon as we found your note in the drop box. Took us a few days, but we did it." Fred patted his wife's hand. "Lucy doesn't like to drive too many hours a day."

"Oh, posh." She frowned at him. "You just hate missing your evening shows."

"They're the best part of autumn," he protested.

"Don't I know it," Stephen put in. "Have you seen that new improv show? Hilarious."

As the men compared notes about their favorite fall programs, Lucy looked at Elizabeth's urn on the stage and sighed deeply. "I never thought she'd be the first to go. She had so much spirit. She always made us feel younger when she was around."

I smiled. "You two are pretty youthful and vibrant already."

"Thank you, dear," Lucy said. "It's the desert air that does it. Although, looking at these photos... Well, maybe there's something in the air here too."

"You can say that again. I didn't know Elizabeth was a grandmother. I knew her age, but she still didn't seem old enough." I glanced at the line snaking around Deputy Wallace. "Speaking of which, I should go talk to her granddaughter."

"We'd like to talk to Lizzie's daughter," Fred said. "Better get in line now or we won't get out of here before dark."

"Where are you staying?" Graham asked.

"Not sure yet. We like to look for vacancy signs, check out a few places." Fred grinned. "Scope out the competition."

"We have a lot of cute bed and breakfasts here—" I started to say.

Graham interrupted me. "One of my units will be vacant for

the next couple of weeks. It's fully furnished. Would you like to stay with us?"

"That depends." Fred's eyes twinkled roguishly. "Any murals on the walls?"

"I'm afraid not. But there's a TV, and we have cable."

Fred grabbed Graham's hand and shook it. "Sold!"

"Find us when you're ready to leave," Graham said. "You can follow us there."

Our impromptu houseguests moved toward one of the receiving lines, and Stephen led Graham away to talk shop with some of the other local artists who usually exhibited at the After-life Festival. Left to my own devices, I meandered over to the buffet tables by the kitchen and filled a small plate with finger foods before taking my place in the line leading to Wallace.

It was strange to see her here, out of uniform and in a boxy black dress. I thought about teasing her about it, then decided it would be inappropriate. Besides, looking at her now, I suddenly realized how many traits she had inherited from Elizabeth. It went beyond the long braid and the tall build. Wallace had always exuded a calming energy, and her features—though stern—were beautiful.

Someone stepped into line behind me. I glanced over my shoulder and stiffened. A pair of men who looked far older than Elizabeth stood shoulder to shoulder in matching black suits. One wore a blue cap with a red letter C embroidered on the front, and the other had yellowish wisps of hair curling out from behind his ears. I didn't recognize either of them, and I didn't have Graham beside me to fill in the gaps in my local knowledge. Were they from out of town?

Could one of them be Anson Monroe?

"What's the matter, missy?" the man in the cap asked in a reedy voice. "You a Redbird?"

I blinked, startled by the strange question. "What?"

"You're lookin' at us like we're the devil," he said. "Must be a Redbird."

I had no idea what he was talking about. Birds?

"Leave her be, Nicholas." The second man sighed and turned to me. "Ignore my husband. I told him it wasn't right to wear a baseball hat to a funeral."

"Elizabeth would have wanted it this way, William," Nicholas said loudly. "She loved the Cubs!"

I couldn't help but smile as I tried to imagine Elizabeth watching a baseball game. I couldn't see it. And unless Anson Monroe had changed his name, he wasn't either of the two gentlemen standing in front of me.

I would know if he was, I decided. As soon as I saw his face, I would know it. Whether it was his real face or the false one he wore when he came to me as Horace, I would recognize him.

The line moved forward a few paces, and I asked, "How did you two know Elizabeth?"

"She was my second cousin," William explained. "And you?"

"She was my friend." The last word caught in my throat, and tears blurred my vision.

William smiled sadly. "She had a lot of those."

It was my turn to give my condolences to Deputy Wallace then. As the people in front of me stepped aside, she pulled me into a bear hug. We stayed like that for several moments before the pressure at my back softened, and I pulled away.

"I'm so sorry for your loss," I said, blinking back tears. "Elizabeth was an incredible friend. She must have been the best grandma."

Wallace sniffed and nodded. "She really was. And she liked you a lot. She was so excited to have another real psychic around." Her voice hitched. "I guess you're the only one now."

I didn't know what to say to that. There were others people in Donn's Hill who had a genuine gift—Stephen Hastain, for one—

but I supposed I now had the uncomfortable distinction of being the most powerful.

"Thank you so much for coming," Wallace said.

"Of course. If there's anything I can do for you, let me know."

"Actually, there is." She hesitated. "I need to box up everything from Grandma's place at The Enclave and take it to my house. Would you mind helping me?"

It was my turn to pause. The memories of boxing up and dealing with my father's things earlier that year were still raw. I had done it alone, thanks to my then-boyfriend's refusal to help with or even attend the funeral. Most of my father's possessions had gone to friends of his from the university where he worked. A lot had gone to Goodwill. But some things—his favorite chair, a good chunk of his books, nearly everything from the walls of his office—had been too difficult to say goodbye to at the time. It all sat in a storage unit in Denver.

But as I thought about it, I felt another wave of the peace and strength I'd felt at Darlene's while I was reading Dad's letters to my mom. The pain of losing him was still there, but it was a dull ache now. It didn't sting the way it had at first.

Maybe it was time to bring his things here. He'd never been to Donn's Hill, but I thought he would have liked it.

And maybe if I'd had some help going through his things, it would have been less painful. Maybe I would have made different choices, had the strength to take more of him with me.

"I'd love to help," I told Wallace. "Just call when you need me."

I gave her another quick hug and got out of the way of the rest of the mourners. Graham was still talking to the other artists, so I made a second trip to the buffet table. I was trying to decide between the bite-sized pecan pies and the miniature pumpkin chocolate chip cookies when an elderly woman elbowed me.

"Take them both," she whispered.

I laughed and acted on her recommendation, not needing much encouragement to give in to my gluttonous side. "Thanks. I needed the nudge."

"I know." She winked at me and took a seat at an empty table.

Something about her reminded me of Elizabeth. They didn't look very similar; this woman was at least ten years younger, with a silver bob and purple cat-eye glasses. But I couldn't shake the feeling they had something in common.

"Care to join me?" she called. As she lifted a hand to wave me over, a collection of black stones tinkled at her wrist. "Don't be shy."

She's an Empath, I realized. She wasn't reading my mind, though sometimes it had felt like Elizabeth could. Like her, this woman had read my emotions.

I sat next to her.

She nodded at the piece of black tourmaline hanging from my neck. "Elizabeth give that to you?"

"Yeah." I pointed to her wrists. "Did she give you those?"

Her eyes crinkled as she smiled. "No, honey. I gave her *hers.* You an Empath?"

"No, I'm just a medium."

"*Just.*" She snorted. "You got the gift of gifts and you say *just.* You do séances? At the Afterlife Festival?"

"Oh, no. I'm not strong enough."

"'Not strong enough.'" She shook her head. "Honey, I could feel your power from across the room. You listen and you listen good. If there's something you can't do, it's probably not worth doing. Let me ask you: do you see the dead in our world or just in dreams?"

I stared at her for a few seconds, then finally found the presence of mind to ask, "I'm sorry… Who are you?"

"Don't apologize. That's on me. I get feelings from people. Strong ones. So strong I feel like I know them before we've been introduced, and then I forget to tell them who I am." She held out a hand. "Call me Grey."

"Mackenzie Clair."

"Pleased to meet you, Mac."

I didn't bother asking how she knew my nickname. This woman was on an entirely different level, sensing things I wasn't sure even Elizabeth would have picked up on.

"Do you come to the Afterlife Festival often?" I asked.

"Used to. Don't think I'll be back next year, though." She shivered and pulled her wrap tighter around her shoulders. "The energy here is off."

"Here?" I looked around the room.

"No, in town. Can't say for sure what's wrong, but I don't like it. To be honest, I'm canceling my reservation at the inn and heading back home right after this."

"Where's home?"

She glanced around and lowered her voice. "I'd rather not say, if that's all right."

I raised an eyebrow. Her open, friendly expression had gone tight. She looked afraid, and I had no idea why.

Suddenly, she brightened. "Tell me about the ghosts you see."

"I've seen a few. Mostly at work."

"What do you do for a living? Graveyard shift somewhere?"

"No, I'm a paranormal investigator for a television show." I grinned. "So it's on purpose."

"You've very lucky. Not many people can make a living with their gift."

"It does feel rare, even around here." I paused and replayed her earlier question in my mind. "What did you mean about seeing the dead in my dreams?"

"Dream visitations. Real common, more than people realize. I see my late husband at least once a week in my sleep. He pops in to check on me and asks how our cats are. Sometimes our old dog is with him." She considered me for a few moments. "Yes, you've had them. I'm not surprised. Most people do. They just dismiss them as dreams, nothing more."

Her words reminded me of the Travelers who had sat on my bed at night and told me their life stories while I slept. It had been years since they visited me, decades since I'd had one of these dream visitations Grey was describing. And yet—

I blinked.

No, it hadn't been that long. It had only been years since a *stranger* stopped by to say hello.

"I see my mother," I blurted out. It felt strange to spill that ultra-personal detail. "Kind of. She's usually fuzzy... like a bad TV signal. I get a few words here and there, but that's it. And then there's this other woman, Camila, who died recently. I didn't even know her, and she's been showing up in my dreams, trying to talk to me."

"What does she say?" Grey asked.

"I don't know. I can't hear her. I can't hear anything." I studied Grey's face, which had gone back to the tight, drawn state it had been in a moment before. "Is that normal? I mean, you can hear your husband, right?"

"I can," she said softly. "In dreams, anyone can touch the other side. Our world is solid ground. The next is a great rushing river. The water flows too fast for our minds to keep up. If we don't know how to swim, we get swept away."

I suppressed a shudder. I had never been a huge fan of swimming, and finding a dead body in a lake earlier that year had solidified my desire to keep my feet firmly on dry ground. I didn't like Grey's metaphor, and I especially didn't like how accurate it felt.

Her eyes drifted to the photos of Elizabeth on the walls, and her voice softened. "She's there now, in the water where I can't follow. But soon, I'll sleep and find myself in that river. Because

I'm sleeping, I won't think to fight the current. It won't try to take me. I'll flow with it. And Elizabeth will reach back, grab my hand, and sit with me for a spell."

Grey smiled at me, but I couldn't return the expression. I stared at her, stunned into silence by the matter-of-fact way she described speaking to the dead. Was it so easy for her? She just fell asleep and *bam*, she had her own personal séance going on?

Why wasn't it ever that easy for me?

"That's not how my dreams go," I said.

She tilted her head and studied me for a few moments. "You've got so much power, it's getting in the way. When I dream, I don't know it. I simply wake up and remember the visits I had."

That didn't make any sense to me. If I was so powerful, if I had this amazing gift, why couldn't I have what Grey had?

"So what am I supposed to do?" My words were rough and irritated, which surprised me. My cheeks flooded with warmth. "I'm sorry, I didn't mean to snap at you."

Grey didn't seem upset, but her eyes remained concerned. "You have two choices: fight the current or try to swim."

"Swim?"

"Accept the moment. Accept the dream. Walk in it. Be part of it. But be careful." She glanced at the photos of Elizabeth again. "Dive too deeply, you'll get swept away. Then you'll be the one waiting in the water for your friends to fall asleep."

CHAPTER SEVENTEEN

I arrived at the Ace of Cups on Sunday powered by caffeine, sugar, and anticipation—but not sleep. My conversation with Grey at Elizabeth's memorial left me unbalanced, and I felt hyperaware of my psychic energy whenever I tried to fall asleep. As my mind neared the edge of consciousness, I imagined I could feel the next world lapping gently at my feet like the waves of a very deep lake. It pulled at me, inviting me to walk into the water. I considered giving in; I wanted to have a real conversation with my mother or even hear Camila's voice.

But before I could give in, a sudden fear gripped me. My eyes flew open. I couldn't let go of consciousness. I couldn't let the current take me. I was sure that if it did, I would never wake up again.

Then drowsiness would sneak back up on me, and the cycle repeated again and again until I gave up and went down to the kitchen to make coffee.

Now I sighed heavily as I stared up at the wide, two-story building that anchored the far end of The Enclave. I was so tired that climbing the short flight of stone steps to the bar's front entrance seemed like an impossible task.

"Carry me up there?" I asked Graham.

He frowned. "Are you sure you should even be here? Don't take this the wrong way, but you don't look like you slept at all."

I wanted to give him crap about how you never tell a woman she looks tired but lacked the energy. "I'll take a little nap after work."

"Okay…" he said uncertainly, glancing up at the late afternoon sky. "It'll be night then, so maybe take more than a nap."

"I will, I will." I waved a hand impatiently. "I just need your help getting up the stairs. Come on, it'll be romantic. You can carry me up over the threshold like in the movies."

"In the movies, those people have just gotten married and the threshold is to their honeymoon suite, not the local bar. Plus"—he hoisted Striker's carrier—"you know she doesn't like to share."

"Fine," I grumbled.

With genuine effort and focus, I made the climb. If I wasn't so excited to be doing a proper investigation again, I think I would have toppled backward halfway up and tumbled down the stairs like a Slinky. But I knew that at the top waited the promise of doing what I loved doing best. Even if Graham refused to carry me up the stairs, my driving need to use my gift propelled me forward.

Inside the pub, a heater vent belched hot air at us, prompting me to shrug out of my coat and hang it on the row of hooks along the waiting area's wall. As I did, the aroma of freshly baked soda bread tickled my nose.

I perked up a bit. Since opening in the summer, the Ace of Cups had quickly become one of my favorite places in Donn's Hill. The building had originally been a boarding house for miners, but the main floor had been completely gutted and redesigned to fit a gastropub. The public space now looked like a castle basement: stone walls, rounded doorways, and a steeply curved ceiling that was cozily close to the ground at the edges.

Graham hated sitting in any of the booths along the perimeter. I didn't blame him; I was short enough to sit comfortably, but he had twice bumped his head when getting up to use the bathroom.

We were frequent customers despite Graham's enmity with the ceiling for one reason: the food.

Hearty stews, fish and chips, colcannon, and soda bread were best sellers, and it was here that I had been introduced to a battered potato masterpiece called boxty. The owner rounded out the menu with American bar favorites like fried pickles and nachos, and her Sunday brunch—complete with mimosas—brought in crowds from the surrounding counties every weekend.

All residents of The Enclave were required to have some kind of connection to the psychic industry that made Donn's Hill famous. Despite being exempted from the rule due to the nature of her business, the owner leaned into the spirit of the town by claiming her bartenders all had the gift of second sight. No matter what drink you ordered, they could sense the drink you really needed.

Or in my case, the dessert.

"Mac!" Alexi Ash, owner and chief mixologist of the Ace of Cups, waved at me from behind a row of beer taps. "Come here. I saved something for you."

The brunch rush was long over. I weaved through empty tables and leaned against the ornately carved bar. Caramel and honey liquids glittered under spotlights, and a rainbow of liquor labels advertised the fact that the bartenders here could make you any drink you could name and a few you couldn't.

"Busy day?" I asked.

"Off the walls," Alexi confirmed. "I expected a slump when the cold weather hit, but it's been nuts all weekend. I don't know what witchcraft Penelope is working to keep the crowds coming, but I'm going to need to hire some more staff."

"Lots of customers, lots of orders," I mused. "Any leftovers?"

Her corkscrew coils bounced as she skipped down to the dessert case and back. With a grin that rivaled the Cheshire Cat's, she slid a small plate holding a quadruple-layered slice of chocolate cake across the bar. Silky ganache dripped down the white cream cheese frosting, and to an untrained observer, it looked like a regular slice of Death by Chocolate. But I had long since learned that desserts at the Ace of Cups were rarely as simple as they seemed.

"What is it?" I asked.

"Whiskey and stout cake. It's our special this week."

Despite the heavenly aroma of cocoa swirling above the plate, I wrinkled my nose. "I'm not much for heavy alcohols. Whiskey is a little…" I couldn't think of a word to describe it that wouldn't insult my host's taste, so I didn't finish the sentence.

She rolled her brown eyes and reached for the plate. "Fine, if you don't want it—"

I snatched it out of her reach. "Hey, I didn't say I won't eat it."

"Attagirl." Alexi leaned to the side and waved at Graham. "Is that Striker in the carrier?"

"Yeah. Yuri let you know she's part of the crew, right?"

"I figured she would be. Mind taking her into my office until everyone gets here? We can't have animals in the restaurant area." She pointed to a door at the far end of the room. "I'm just closing up for the day. I'll find you guys wherever you are after we lock up."

I carried my cake into her office, which was richly furnished in blocky faux leather chairs and a heavy mahogany desk. Once the door was closed behind us, Graham gingerly released Striker from her carrier.

"Not a single scratch on the furniture, okay?" he warned.

She stared up at him with defiant eyes. The message was

clear: if she did or didn't do anything, it was because *she* wanted to.

"Are you going to hang out for the investigation?" I asked Graham as I took a bite of the cake. It was surprisingly sweet, with no hint of the bitterness I usually associated with hard liquors. The cream cheese frosting was tangy and bright, and the cake itself was fluffy and moist. I thought about offering some to Graham, but that would leave less for me.

I didn't share.

"Do you want me to stay?" he asked.

I shrugged. "I love your company, but if you have other plans, I understand."

"What about"—he glanced around the empty office and lowered his voice to a whisper—"Horace?"

At the name, I automatically reached up and touched my necklace to be sure it was still there. "I was thinking about him a lot at the memorial yesterday. For a while, I was convinced he was there."

Graham pursed his lips. "Was he?"

"I don't think so. No, I know he wasn't. Especially after talking to that friend of Elizabeth's." I stroked Striker's fur as I remembered my interaction with Grey. "She knew I was psychic without even asking. She could feel it. And I think I can feel it too. Like with Stephen."

"I keep telling him he's got a real gift. He says it's all in the stones."

I rolled my eyes. "He tried to sell me that line too. But I swear I can sense his talent. And I think I would be able to feel power as strong as Horace's."

Graham looked doubtful. "Did you feel Elizabeth's power? Or that woman you were talking to at the funeral?"

"I think so. I mean, I didn't think that's what I was feeling, but

I was so instantly drawn to both of them. If I meet someone who could be Anson, I'll watch for that feeling."

He seemed unsure until we heard Yuri's voice outside the office door. Graham stood to kiss the top of my forehead. "I'll just be over at Stephen's. If anything weird happens—and I mean anything—call me."

"I will."

As Graham left, Yuri pulled a flat cart into Alexi's office. Stacks of equipment cases were tethered together to keep them from falling off as he eased the cart over the raised threshold. Striker's tail poofed, and she scurried under the desk to escape the contraption, but I whistled in approval.

"Pretty cool, right?" Yuri asked as he unclipped the bungee cords.

"I love it," I said. "I thought I'd have to help schlep those up the sidewalk two at a time."

"Our new production assistant had the idea. It's his cart." Yuri glanced back into the bar. "Where did he go? He was just—ah, Kevin, this is Mac, our medium."

The newbie stepped into the room shyly, and I wondered how he had gotten past the door. He didn't look nearly old enough to be in a bar. He had the skinny frame of a high school student, and his pasty chin and cheeks were devoid of even a hint of hair.

There was something familiar about him, though. As I squinted at him, he coughed and tucked a long strand of straight black hair behind his ear.

My eyes went wide. I did know him. It was just a little strange to see him wearing jeans and a hoodie. The last time I saw him, he'd been wearing a floor-length robe while getting strangled by a fake psychic. "Fang?"

Heat filled his otherwise chalky cheeks. "You can call me Kevin, if you want."

I stared at him for a second before turning my frown on Yuri.

"You know he's a fraud, right? He scams tourists by pretending he can read palms."

"Yes, Kevin was open about his—shall we say—checkered past." Yuri clapped the younger man on the back. "It is behind him."

"I closed up the shop," Fang said hurriedly. "Gave up my lease. I'm sleeping on Stephen's couch. I don't want to lie anymore. I want to help people."

I didn't like it. Something about the situation irked me, and I couldn't let it go. Forgetting for a moment that Yuri had already interviewed and hired Fang, I launched into a line of questions.

"How old are you?"

"Twenty-one," he said.

"That's pretty young," I argued. "Do you even have any experience?"

Yuri dipped his chin and eyed me over his glasses. "Mac, come with me to check on something while Kevin unpacks the equipment. Kevin, make sure everything on the checklist is accounted for."

We stepped out of the office, and Yuri closed the door behind us. I looked around expectantly, not sure what he needed my help with.

He didn't move except to fold his arms across his chest. When he spoke, his voice was low and stern. "Mac, what's going on?

"With what?"

"Why are you interrogating Kevin?"

I glanced at the closed door and lowered my voice. Fang was close to Stephen, and I didn't want my criticisms to get back to Graham's closest friend. "It just feels like a bad fit. I mean, the kid's a con artist."

"Was," Yuri corrected.

"So he claims. What if our viewers find out what he used to do? It's already an uphill battle with the skeptics out there. Every week, somebody calls me fake in our video comments. They call me a liar. How are we supposed to defend ourselves against those kinds of attacks if somebody on our crew really *is* a fraud?"

"I won't pretend to be thrilled about the choices he made in the past. But listen to your words, Mac. Don't you believe in second chances?" When I didn't answer, he pressed on. "Gabrielle will be free someday. She will need to find a home, a job. How do you hope people respond to her when they learn about the terrible choices she made?"

I opened my mouth to object. Their situations weren't at all similar.

Yeah, my inner voice chided. *The stuff she did was way, way worse. And you still take her calls. You still let her put you on the prison's visitor list.*

Damn it. I sighed deeply and scratched at my hairline with both hands, sending my hair flying. "Fine. I'll give him a chance. But I still think he's too young."

The corner of Yuri's mouth twitched upward. "He's older than Kit was when she and I started this."

Having soundly defeated all my arguments, Yuri pushed the office door open and gestured for me to go back inside. I found Fang crouched on the floor, dragging a bungee cord back and forth in front of the narrow space between the desk and the carpet. One of Striker's black paws shot out, and she hooked her claws into the braided material.

Fang giggled. "I see why you named her Striker."

"Actually, I didn't. She already had that moniker when I adopted her." I studied him as he tugged lightly on the cord. "What happened to your accent?"

"Accent?" He glanced up at me, then flushed again. "Oh. You mean my"—his voice deepened and took on a pompous quality I associated with old presidential speeches—"soothing psychic voice?"

In spite of myself, I smiled. "Yep. That's the one."

He shrugged. "I don't need it anymore."

"What about 'Fang?' Where did that come from?"

"It started as a gamer tag. When I opened my shop, I thought it sounded more mysterious than Kevin."

"Which name do you prefer?"

He was silent for a few moments as he bounced the end of the cord up and down in front of the desk. He kept his eyes fixed on the floor as he said, "I don't know. I want to leave all that behind, all the lying and scamming. So I sort of feel like I should be Kevin again. But the weird thing is, even though it wasn't my real name, calling myself Fang never felt like lying. It just felt... like me." He looked up at me. "Is that dumb?"

I smiled, relieved by his answer. "I don't think so. I'll be honest, I wasn't sure about it at first. But now I'm having trouble calling you anything else."

As I spoke, Striker yanked the cord back under the desk and sank her teeth into it. One of her wild yellow eyes shone from the shadows, and her purr was audible even across the room. Our production assistant crouched down to wiggle his finger in front of her face, and she proved that she had some fangs of her own.

"Striker!" I rushed forward and nudged her face away from his hand. "Did she bite you?"

Joy lit up his face. He held up his finger for my inspection. "She's just playing. See? She didn't break the skin. She just wanted me to know she could have, like flag football."

"Brrrllll," Striker agreed.

Fang rocked back on his heels and hopped to his feet. "Sorry. I got distracted. I'll finish unpacking."

"It's okay. Hopefully Yuri told you in the interview, but entertaining Striker is actually the production assistant's most important job."

"Oh, he told me," Fang said seriously. He reached into his pocket and pulled out a bag of cat treats.

Striker immediately materialized in front of the desk. She pawed at Fang's pant leg and yowled vociferously. When he reached down with a treat in his hand, she snapped it right from between his fingers.

"Hey, I need those," he teased, then gave her a second treat.

Yuri elbowed me. He didn't say it, but I felt his silent "I told you so" in my ribs. And honestly, I didn't mind. It had been the fake things about Fang—the bogus accent, the flowery manner, the phony palmistry—that irked me. I hadn't been able to stand the fifty-year-old Vincent Price wannabe in the twenty-one-year old's body, but his real personality and bubbling enthusiasm were quickly growing on me.

I helped him unpack the gear and explained what a few of the less-obvious items on the packing list were. Kit's shorthand had taken me a while to get used to; she preferred nicknames like *shinies* for the light reflectors and *sneks* for the extension cords. It was the kind of thing she had only gotten away with doing because she worked with her father, and a fit of laughter nearly overwhelmed me as I imagined her trying to use a similarly ridiculous naming system with Amari's crew.

I had just finished explaining how the EMF meters worked when there was a tap on the door. A stranger poked his head in, and his face split into a smile when he saw us.

"Oh, good. I'm in the right place." He stepped into the room and shook Yuri's hand. Dark circles sagged beneath his eyes. "Sorry I'm late. I totally underestimated how long it would take to walk across town."

"No problem," Yuri said. "We were just about to start setting up. Mac, Kevin, this is Noah Westhouse."

Noah stared at me for a long, awkward moment. I returned the favor with a raised eyebrow, studying his features. Like Fang, something about him was vaguely familiar, but I couldn't place his face. He looked older than me, maybe forty or so. He had large frame with broad shoulders, and his short sandy brown hair swooped up and away from his forehead in a messy pompadour.

Maybe it was just how completely exhausted he looked. Those same dark circles had been greeting me in the mirror every morning for a week straight.

He blinked and grabbed my hand to shake it. "Sorry, I just can't believe it's really you. Mackenzie Clair, psychic extraordinaire, in the flesh."

Heat rushed into my cheeks. I still wasn't used to people knowing who I was before I introduced myself.

Before I could respond, he moved on to Fang, who gazed at him with a sort of starstruck awe, forgetting to pull his hand away when Noah stopped shaking it.

"Is it true you used to work on *First Date Worst Date*?" Fang asked.

Noah laughed and raised his right hand. "Guilty."

"What is that?" I asked.

Fang turned to me, excitement lighting up his eyes. "It was this awesome show where they paired up couples at random and told them they were sending them on this amazing first date. But then everything would go wrong, like the limo would get a flat tire and the driver would pretend not to know how to fix it or all the food at the restaurant would come out with bugs in it."

I cringed. "That sounds awful."

"No, it was great!" Fang said. "Some of the people were like, 'Screw this, I'm out.' But every episode there would be at least one couple who, like, made the best of it, and you just knew they were gonna make it."

"Okay, guys." Yuri clapped his hands together. He was addressing all of us, but I felt sure his next question was just for me. "Are you ready to begin?"

Excited as I was about finally getting to do a proper para-normal investigation again, I hesitated before answering. Our once-perfect crew was now rounded out by a former charlatan and someone with more experience dealing with angry couples than angry spirits.

Hopefully the audience would never know the difference, but the truth was the old *Soul Searchers* was dead. We were a zombie crew now, a ghost of our former selves.

Even if I was ready, were we as a whole?

It didn't matter. Ready or not, our first job with the new *Soul Searchers* was about to begin.

CHAPTER EIGHTEEN

Noah jabbered away constantly as he positioned the tripods, or maybe it just seemed that way compared to the quiet way I was used to things happening. Our old cameraman, Mark, would bustle around wordlessly, only occasionally asking Yuri to confirm that the framing or the angle was what Yuri envisioned. Noah, on the other hand, had opinions about everything: the lighting, the way the chairs were staged, whether or not Striker should be on someone's lap. Yuri considered each suggestion thoughtfully, seeming to enjoy the endless discussions.

I hated it.

Noah struck me as the kind of person who automatically assumed he was the smartest in the room. He probably wondered how on Earth we had managed to film a single episode without his expertise.

I imagined an alternate timeline where Kit and Mark had never left. Right now, Kit would be figuring out how to get a little more life out of a secondhand piece of equipment, and Mark would be quietly scowling at his camera. After filming, we could grab a beer together or take a dozen donuts back to Primrose House to sustain us through a movie marathon.

Is that what they were doing right now in Paris? Bonding with their new crew over a box of croissants and Kit's new favorite horror flick?

"Hey, Mac, how do you work these mics again?" Fang asked, snapping me back into the moment.

I coached him through attaching the lavalier mic to Yuri's lapel and again to Alexi's when she finished locking up the bar and joined us in the office.

"What, no makeup?" she joked, patting a copper cheek as she settled into her high-backed desk chair.

Soon, the cameras were rolling, and Yuri was asking Alexi about the history of the bar and the building it occupied. I found it strangely difficult to focus on their conversation. My mind was with Kit and Mark. What were they investigating in France? Did they have better equipment? How big was their crew? Did they miss the chaos of a smaller operation, always having to do more with less?

Did they miss me?

"… She was the first bartender to bring it up, and she ended up quitting just a few weeks after we opened," Alexi was saying. "Honestly, I'm having trouble getting staff to stick around because of this."

"What about the other employees?" Yuri asked. "The ones who aren't also residents?"

"They like to spread the stories. They'll tell the new hires about a 'lady in white' in the basement by the napkin refills, but I don't think they really believe in anything they're saying." Alexi glanced at the ceiling. "If there's anything supernatural going on here, it's upstairs, not in the basement."

Yuri looked directly into the camera. "Let's go find out."

We stopped rolling and prepared to go mobile. Noah transferred the camera to a shoulder rig, and I put on one of the lavalier microphones. From here on out, I would be on camera. Even after six months with the *Soul Searchers*, I still wasn't super comfortable with it. My voice seemed to shift upward in pitch as soon as the little red light came on, and I had to fight to sound postpubescent.

"Hey," I whispered to Yuri as we climbed the back stairs to the apartments. "I sort of spaced out back there. What have people seen up here?"

He threw me a surprised glance. "Are you feeling all right? It's not like you to be inattentive."

"Yeah, I'm fine. Just tired, I guess."

His mouth opened, and I thought he was about to fill me in on the disturbances Alexi's staff had reported, but he abruptly pursed his lips. A mischievous smile crept onto his face.

"This is perfect," he said. "I can do a voice-over later to explain that you don't know the background of the reported haunting. Then if you sense something, our viewers will know that it wasn't an idea Alexi planted in your head."

Before I decided whether I agreed with his idea or not, we reached the second floor. A strange feeling settled over me as my feet crossed the creaking floorboards on the landing.

If someone told me we just went back in time, I would have believed them.

From the looks of it, Penelope's team had taken the exact opposite approach up here from what they did downstairs. Instead of gutting the space and starting over, they had opted to repair and restore as much of the original construction as possible. A narrow hallway stretched out before us. Twelve identical doors lined the walls, six on each side. If I stood in the middle of the hall, I could easily grab the knobs of two opposing doors. I imagined doing that while the occupants of the old miners' apartments pounded to be let out.

Striker immediately began running her nose along the tall

baseboards, pausing at the first apartment to thrust her paw into the crack beneath the door.

"Is anybody home?" I asked.

Alexi shook her head. "I chased all the tenants out for the night. It's just us."

"Noah, go ahead and shoot some B-roll while we get the GoPros up," Yuri instructed. "MOS, okay?"

"MOS?" Fang asked Noah.

"Uh—"

"We'll be filming without sound," I interrupted, pleased to not be the new kid for once. "Yuri probably wants to do some voice-over stuff on top of the footage."

We divvied up the tiny, mountable GoPro cameras, and I showed Fang the places he should put them in the hallway. Yuri pointed me to a door and gestured to the case containing our measuring instruments.

"I want a camera in every corner of that room," Yuri said. "That's where most of the activity has been centered."

"Got it."

The apartment on the other side of the door looked as old and carefully restored as the hallway, with eggshell paint and twelve-inch baseboards. It reminded me of my college dorm room, if my dorm had been built in the early 1900s. The space was long and narrow, but a tall window at the far end helped it feel cozy rather than claustrophobic. Through a narrow doorway, I spied a cramped bathroom. And it had two things my apartment didn't: a stove and a full-size refrigerator.

Striker hopped up into the sink and sniffed the faucet handles with quivering whiskers. I turned one on, just a trickle, so she could drink from the stream. Noah brought his camera closer, and a deep growl rumbled out of her chest.

"She thinks you're going to turn off the water," I explained.

"I just want to get some footage of her. Beautiful cat." He

backed away and slowly panned around the room. "This place isn't too shabby."

The red light glowed on his camera. I stiffened, then had to remind myself to relax. *This is your job, Mac. Be cool.*

He tracked me as I set up the thermometer, EMF meter, and audio recorder on the kitchen counter.

"Nervous?" he asked.

"No," I lied.

He chuckled. "I don't want to freak you out, but viewers can totally tell you're not comfortable in front of the camera. It's okay, though. Adds to your charm."

I clenched my jaw as I climbed up the stepladder to mount the first GoPro. Why did he have to tell me that? Now it would be even harder to act natural.

"So what are you going to go with?" he asked.

"For what?"

"For the ghost. You should do another poltergeist. Everybody loved the ghost at that cabin."

I paused in my work. "What do you mean, 'do another poltergeist'?"

He couldn't be asking what I thought he was asking. But from the uncomfortable expression on his face, I realized there was no other alternative.

I glanced at the open door and lowered my voice. "Do you think we fake the hauntings?"

"Well, yeah." He frowned. "I mean, come on."

My silence hung in the air. I had no idea what to say to his accusation. What was he doing here? Why would someone take a job with a crew they thought was faking evidence?

"Look." The red light blinked off, and Noah lowered the camera. "It's just you and me in here. No cameras. No mics. You don't have to pretend ghosts are real around me, okay?"

"I don't pretend *anything*." My palms suddenly hurt, and I

realized I was digging my nails into them. It took a conscious effort to unclench my fists. "Did you mention this to Yuri? That you're a skeptic?"

"It didn't come up." He laughed. "Neither did leprechauns or unicorns."

"I can't believe this. I haven't even gotten used to dealing with this kind of crap from viewers yet, and now I'm supposed to work with somebody who thinks this is all some big joke?" I shook my head. "No way. I need to talk to Yuri."

"Wait." He grabbed my arm as I walked toward the door.

From the sink, Striker issued another low growl.

Noah dropped my arm and took a step back. "Whoa, I'm not going to hurt her. Chill out, cat."

She shifted on her haunches but didn't take her yellow eyes off him. I made a mental note to tell Graham that Striker was playing the part of the jealous type on his behalf.

"Come on," Noah said to me. "You're not seriously going to ask Yuri to can me just because I don't believe in ghosts. I don't believe in love either, but that didn't stop me from working on dating shows for a decade. I'm good at my job. What I believe doesn't matter."

I considered it for a few seconds. In fairness, I hadn't really believed in ghosts until I had seen one on my first day with the *Soul Searchers*. I hadn't considered myself a skeptic before then; I just hadn't really had an opportunity to see something real.

Maybe that was all Noah needed. If he had ever seen real love on one of those dating shows, he would probably be a little more romantic. So once he saw us investigate an actual, verifiable paranormal event, he would realize we weren't faking things.

If he still refused to believe after that, then I would talk to Yuri. I could let Noah's skepticism ride until then.

"Okay," I told him. "But I have to warn you, I'm going to make a believer out of you."

He winked and switched his camera back on. "I look forward to it."

I thought it would take a few investigations before we ran into something real. As per usual, the universe was eager to prove me wrong while simultaneously proving me right.

CHAPTER NINETEEN

We made the empty apartment our main base of operations for the investigation. Once the cameras and instruments were all set up, we filmed one of the most classic elements of a *Soul Searchers* episode: Yuri's lecture.

In documentary terms, the shot was called a talking head. Yuri sat with his back against a neutral background—in this case, a section of blank wall where a future resident might put a dresser —and addressed someone just off camera. The viewer only saw his torso and head, hence the terminology. But to me, it always felt like Yuri was delivering a lecture in one of his history classes —an engaging one, full of death and tragedy, but a lecture none- theless. It would later be cut into sections and sprinkled throughout the episode, but we filmed everything he knew about the allegedly haunted location in one large chunk.

Before Kit left, giving Yuri someone to look at had been her job. Now it was mine.

"Before its renovation into a restaurant and apartments, the building anchoring The Enclave was one of many boarding houses for underpaid and overworked iron miners," Yuri told me as the camera rolled. "The property was owned by the Bishop

Mining Company, who also employed the miners. This was a common tactic at the time. Mining companies would deduct the cost of their employees' lodging, food, tools, and more from their paychecks. Frederick Bishop was largely considered fair compared to some of the more notorious mining barons, but even with a paternalistic employer, the life of an iron miner was difficult and dangerous."

Because he was talking to me, I kept wanting to break in with questions. I had to purse my lips to stop myself from interrupting his flow to ask where the other boarding houses were and how closely intertwined the mining and psychic communities were.

"As the economic landscape of Donn's Hill shifted, the need for the boarding houses dried up. The mining company sold the land to residential developers, and most of the original buildings were demolished. But due to its proximity to the industrial and manufacturing district, this particular neighborhood was the last to continue catering to Bishop Mining Company employees. After the company formally shut down their boarding program, the buildings here sat vacant for decades.

"An empty property such as this can be a magnet for trouble from both the living and the dead. It would hardly be surprising for the sightings reported by the residents here to be genuine. But we need to find out if there's really something going on or if the staff of the Ace of Cups is concocting more than cocktails."

He waited a beat, then nodded and stood. Noah gave him a high five, which was something I had never seen Yuri give or receive.

"That was great," Noah said. "What's next?"

Yuri nodded to me. "Now you'll see why I begged Mac to join our team."

My cheeks warmed as Noah, Fang, and Alexi all turned their eyes on me at once. I wasn't used to having this many strangers with me at this stage of an investigation. Previously, it had always been just Yuri, Kit, Mark, and Striker. On the one occasion we had pulled together a larger group, I had known nearly everyone there from numerous prior encounters. The only exception had been a paranormal debunker named Raziel Santos who had crashed the séance just to try to prove we were frauds.

A sense of déjà vu washed over me. This moment felt strangely similar to that day. Only this time, the skeptic was our cameraman. Still, if there was anything here, anything at all, I had to do my best to make contact with it.

I took a deep breath and squared my shoulders. "Okay. There's a nice open area in the center of the room. Alexi, you've seen stuff up here before, right?"

She nodded. "Yeah. I'm in the first apartment by the stairs, and I've seen—"

Yuri held up a hand to stop her from saying any more. "We are doing an experiment this time. Mac will be calling out with as little direct knowledge of the incidents as possible."

Alexi frowned. "But she was in the room when I explained it all downstairs."

"She wasn't listening." Yuri's tone was one-part apology to Alexi, one-part guilt trip for me.

Noah rolled his eyes. I knew exactly what he was thinking, and I couldn't wait to wipe the smug, all-knowing smirk off his face.

"Alexi, since you have a strong connection to this place, I'd like you in the circle." I pointed to a spot on the floor. "You can sit there, and Yuri will sit there. I want to lean my back against the cupboards, so I'll be over here."

"What about me?" Fang asked hopefully. "Do you want me in the circle?"

I shook my head. "I want you over in the corner by the bath-room. You can monitor sound from there. And Noah, you can move around wherever you think you'll get the best shots. Just don't walk between the three of us, okay?"

"Prop open that door," Yuri told Fang. "I want to be able to hear any movement in the hallway."

Everyone took their positions. I fished two souvenirs from my trip out of my bag: an herb bundle from my mother's nightstand and Darlene's alien head lighter, which I used on a black three-wicked candle that I rested on the floor beside the herbs. As soon as I was settled, Striker took possession of my lap.

"Ah, I see." Yuri nodded at the cat. "Striker makes four."

"Next best thing to nine," I said, grinning.

The warm glow of the candle's flame reflected off his glasses. "If you believe it will strengthen your power, I believe it will too."

Fang switched off the lights. The candle illuminated Alexi's and Yuri's faces, but I couldn't make out much detail outside of our little circle. That was a relief; I didn't think I would be able to concentrate if I could see Noah's doubtful expression.

I closed my eyed and focused on Elizabeth's breathing exercises. It took longer than it had in Darlene's house, but within a few minutes, I managed to block out all other distractions. Like I had done there, I sent my consciousness outward. I pictured my psychic sense like a fog that spread from room to room, touching everything, feeling for anything that didn't belong to the living world. I retraced our steps back to Alexi's office and the bar, calling with my mind all the way.

Hello? Is anyone here? Come talk to me. I'm upstairs.

When nothing answered, I slowly pulled my senses back toward my body. Back up the stairs. Back down the hallway. Back into our circle.

Striker began to purr.

A sudden thrill ran through me. There it was—the feeling I had been missing. The sensation of something reaching back.

A door slammed shut. My eyes popped open.

The young man standing just inside the closed door gave off a soft, flickering glow, as though lit by another candle I couldn't see. He didn't look at me—or at anyone else in the room for that matter. As I watched, he walked to the corner, sat on thin air, and started taking off his boots.

The rest of the crew still watched the door.

"There's someone here," I whispered to Yuri.

I expected the man to look up when I spoke, but he ignored me. He just sighed heavily and stared down at his feet.

"Where?" Yuri asked.

"In the corner." I pointed to the back of the room. "He's sitting on something. Can you see him?"

"No. What does he look like?"

"Young. Maybe Fang's age." A lump formed in my throat as I studied him. "He's thin. Really, really skinny. I think… I think he's sick."

The spirit's hands shook as he pulled his second boot free. His cheeks were hollow, and watching the way his shoulders contracted with each shallow breath made me want to cough.

"What is he doing?" Yuri prodded.

The man stood and stretched, then walked a few feet and bent slightly. He brought his hands to his face a few times then patted his cheeks. Like watching a mime, my mind filled in what I couldn't see.

"He just washed his face. Now he's drying it with a towel. Not at the sink, though. Over there, by the wall."

"These apartments used to be set up like dorms," Alexi whispered. "Just bunk beds and washbasins with a shared toilet down the hall."

The man went back to the place he had been sitting before—only this time, he stretched out. It looked like he was lying down, but his form hovered a couple feet off the ground.

"I think he's going to bed." I looked at Yuri. "Do ghosts sleep?"

His brow furrowed. "I'm not sure. It seems unlikely."

For a few minutes, Striker and I watched the dead man as my team watched me. Just as I started to wonder if his form would fade away once he zonked out for the night, he swung his legs out and hauled himself to his feet.

"He's walking back to the door," I whispered.

His hand closed around the knob. The door opened, and he left it that way as he slipped out of the room.

"He left. Did you get that?" I asked Noah. "The door opening?"

"Got it," he murmured. His voice trembled.

My legs tensed. I wanted to stand, to follow the ghost out into the hall, but I didn't dare break the circle for fear I wouldn't be able to see the spirit if and when he came back. I could guess where he went; there was one thing I always had to do before falling asleep, and if I forgot, my bladder chased me out of bed again within seconds of lying down.

But what kind of sense did that make? He was dead. Why go through the motions of washing a face no dirt could stick to and emptying a bladder he could never fill?

Unless...

"He doesn't know he's dead. He's just going through the motions." I turned to Alexi. "I'm guessing the door opening and closing is what's freaking out the staff, right? They hear it at night?"

She nodded.

"Is it at the same time every day?"

Her eyes widened. "Same time, down to the minute."

"I think he's stuck in a loop. Maybe it's a random day, or maybe it's the last day he was alive. But he's just redoing the same thing over and over."

"A psychic impression." Yuri rubbed his chin. "Interesting."

"What does that mean?" Fang asked.

"Wait." As I felt another of Yuri's lectures coming on, I heard Kit's voice inside my head, screaming at me not to miss the moment. "Fang, will you turn the overhead lights back on? And grab that ring light. Noah, make sure you get this."

Noah moved in closer. "Do we need to change backgrounds?"

"No, he's fine where he is."

Yuri's lips rolled into a paternal smile. Once we were back in position for a talking head, he dove into answering Fang's question. "There are a few names for these phenomena. Psychic impressions. Residual hauntings. Spiritual afterimages. Whatever you call them, they are one of the most widely reported types of paranormal activity in the world. Have you ever seen the images from Hiroshima? The shadows burned into stone? Many paranormal researchers believe psychic impressions are formed in a similar way, by an event as shocking to the soul as an atomic bomb."

"An event like what?" I asked.

"Dying," he said simply.

I gave a small involuntary shudder.

"Obviously, there are many other circumstances that can cause a powerful impression," Yuri went on. "I once met a man who moved into his deceased mother's house. His mother had been very abusive to him while he was growing up, and he hated being back in his childhood home. In the night, he was repeatedly awakened by the sound of a child crying inside his old bedroom closet. He remembered hiding there when his mother came home drunk."

"He was haunting himself?" I asked.

"Essentially. Often, these imprints are auditory only. Guests on the *Queen Mary* report hearing sounds of splashing in an empty pool. Workers remodeling an old children's hospital swear they hear laughter from rooms that have been vacant for years.

But what Mac is describing is either a less common version of this type of haunting—where a visual impression has been left—or it is simply something only those with a higher level of psychic sensitivity can discern."

"So you're saying it's just like a movie?" I asked. "His spirit isn't actually trapped here?"

Yuri bobbed his head from side to side. "It is impossible to say."

"If he comes back, I'm going to try to channel him," I decided. "Maybe if we tell him he's dead, he can move on."

Alexi frowned. "If this is a ghost and not just some kind of spooky recording, won't that piss him off? If somebody showed up in my bedroom and said, 'You're dead, get out,' I'd be mad."

I looked at Yuri. "What do you think?"

"It could work. But"—he nodded his head toward the door-knob—"he is already able to interact with our world. If he does get angry, you might push him into becoming a poltergeist."

I swallowed. I'd had enough of those to last a lifetime. "I'll tread lightly."

My words implied a confidence I didn't truly feel. Channeling a spirit—inviting them to speak or write or otherwise interact with the living world through your body—was something I had never actually done. But I had seen it. Gabrielle did it at her séances, and I had personally witnessed an elderly man say goodbye to his deceased son, who spoke with Gabrielle's voice.

It was the kind of experience that left a mark.

I remembered with a start that I had meant to channel Camila Aster. In the moment, it was only an excuse I had given myself for breaking into the empty yurt, but it was something I still wanted to do. Finding Anson Monroe's house, learning about Elizabeth's death, hightailing it back to Donn's Hill, and getting absolutely no sleep since coming back had driven that plan from my mind, but I still wanted to do it.

This could be my practice run.

Looking at it that way gave me the strength I needed to square my shoulders, straighten my spine, and nod at the others that we were ready to begin. I held Yuri's and Alexi's hands. Fang turned the lights down, and we went back to waiting.

Before long, Striker's purring increased in volume.

The spirit stepped into the room and closed the door.

I thought about the way Gabrielle had seemed to communicate wordlessly with the spirit before he spoke through her. She must have been calling to him with her mind, just the same as I did when trying to make contact with a ghost. How did she deepen the connection? How did she get them to speak?

Well, I had to start somewhere.

He was halfway across the space when I called to him, but with my mouth and my mind in tandem. "Can you hear me?"

Either he couldn't or he didn't feel like responding to the strange woman in his bedroom. He continued past me and lay down.

I tried again, pushing harder, imagining the words wrapping around the two of us and connecting our wrists as I spoke them. "Can you hear me? Please talk to me."

Still nothing.

"Any response?" Yuri whispered.

"No. He's back in bed."

It felt strange and rude to talk about the spirit while he was right in front of us, but I had to assume he couldn't hear us. Frustration grew in my chest, and I squeezed Yuri's and Alexi's hands. There was some kind of invisible barrier blocking my words from reaching the ghost, and I didn't know how to break through it. Was he too far gone? Could only the recently dead be channeled? Did I need a more personal connection, something more meaningful than, *Hey, look, I see a ghost, so let's talk to it*?

No. Or rather, maybe. It could be one or all of those things, but the main problem—the key issue—had to be me.

I wasn't strong enough.

I was no Gabrielle.

With a sigh, I released my grip on the others in the circle. "I'm not getting a response."

"Maybe if you knew his name," Yuri mused. "I might be able to find it. I can look into the historical records and see if there's anything about deaths of the miners who lived here."

"Sure," I said half-heartedly.

Yuri stood, and as he broke the circle, the sleeping spirit faded away. Striker hopped off my lap and went to sniff the floorboards where the ghost had been, but I took my time getting to my feet. Disappointment and frustration warred with elation and exhaustion inside my body, and I worried I might keel over if I stood too quickly.

Fang switched on the overhead light, face jubilant. "Holy crap! You guys, that was awesome. I mean"—he grabbed his long hair with his hands and pulled it straight against his cheeks—"the door just *whooshed*, and then Mac was all, 'It's a ghost!' And I felt it. I *felt* it!"

"Yeah, kid," Noah muttered. "We were all there."

Our new cameraman looked even more stunned than I had dared to hope. I fought the smile off my face and asked casually, "Believe me now?"

"I want to see what the cameras picked up before I say for sure. But…" He ran a shaking hand down his face. "Damn."

"Are you okay leaving the spirit here a bit longer?" I asked Alexi, who still sat on the floor across from me. "I guess I could try to help him move on with a smoke cleansing now if your tenants are really uncomfortable."

Banishing a spirit didn't require any level of personal connection. It was something I had done on my own, and I knew it was well within the limits of my abilities.

Limits being the key word, I thought sourly.

I expected her to take me up on my offer, but her eyes danced. "Are you kidding? Do you know how many people will want to spend a night in this room now? The ghost can stay forever."

CHAPTER TWENTY

It seemed I had left all my luck in the New Mexico desert. Sleep—that easy, natural thing that had come so easily to me before our trip—eluded me yet again. The morning after our investigation at the Ace of Cups, I slumped across the table in Primrose House's shared kitchen and watched Graham pull apart packaged cinnamon rolls. He arranged them with more care than they deserved on a cookie sheet and put them in the oven before finally tackling the task I had been dying for him to do all morning: brew some blasted coffee.

"Need a pillow?" he asked.

"No," I grumbled. The table wasn't exactly soft, but my face had already stuck to the polished wood. I was too tired to lift my head back up, so there was no point in him bringing me anything soft to rest it on.

The door to the butler's pantry opened. Fred and Lucy Hawkes sauntered into the kitchen. They had the relaxed, happy expressions of a couple on vacation, and I envied their disposition.

"Good morning." Lucy beamed.

"Morning," Graham returned. "What are your plans for the day?"

"We're going to drive out to Moyard, check out the town," Fred said.

Graham grabbed a sheet off the grocery list pad. "I know you love donuts, Fred. Let me write down the name of this bakery. You don't want to miss it."

"'Preciate it," Fred said.

"We've just been eating our way around town." Lucy pinched a nonexistent spot of fat on her stomach. "Elizabeth's family was kind enough to include us in a big breakfast yesterday, and I still feel full from it all. I've always heard food is the primary love language for country folk, but this is the first time I've gotten to experience it."

With much effort, I finally forced myself to lift my head off the table. "Aren't you guys 'country folk' all the way out there by the ranches?"

"Fred maybe, but not me." Lucy smiled. "I'm a Seattle girl."

I sat up very straight. "Seattle?"

"And let me tell you," she said. "We know how to be hospitable in the Pacific Northwest. But Donn's Hill is like nowhere else."

I knew I should have said something then, but my brain wasn't sending the right things to my mouth. Eventually, I managed to choke out, "And where are you from, Fred?"

"Oh, here. There. Everywhere. Travel keeps you young." He grinned at his wife. "Didn't want to settle down till I met Lucy, and by then, she had fallen in love with the desert life."

She glanced at her wristwatch and elbowed him. "If we want to catch the breakfast menu at the diner, we better skedaddle."

"Whoops. Can't start my day without pancakes." Fred shuffled after her toward the door. "We'll be back tonight. Save one of those cinnamon rolls for me."

I stared after them, feeling more awake than I had any right to be. Through the kitchen window, I watched Fred's face from every angle as he settled Lucy into the passenger side of their car and rounded the sedan to get into the driver's seat.

Their Seattle connection bothered me. Where had he and Lucy met? *When* had they met? Had Fred ever gone by another name?

I felt foolish for not asking these questions before. I hadn't recognized Fred at all when we met, but my memory of Anson Monroe's face was fuzzy at best. The more important question was: had Fred recognized me when I checked into the Yurt in Luck Resort? If so, he was a heck of an actor. He played the part of a gracious host perfectly. But then, Horace was quite an actor too. He had twisted me into his world of lies, and I'd bought everything he told me.

A frustrated, guttural growl choked its way out of my throat. Horace had twisted me up, all right. He made me so anxious and paranoid that I was second-guessing myself at every turn. Of course Fred wasn't Anson Monroe. Like I'd told Graham, I would *feel* it if he was, the same way Grey had felt my powers. Wherever he was, whatever he was up to, he was doing it from the shadows. That was his MO.

My phone buzzed, rumbling across the table and startling me.

"Mac? Did I wake you?" Deputy Wallace's normally bombastic voice was subdued. She sounded as exhausted as I felt.

"Hey, Cynthia. No, I've been up for a while." It wasn't a lie. Two days was arguably "a while."

"Do you have some time today to help me sort through my grandmother's things?"

Her request had come sooner than I expected. Packing and organizing the contents of Elizabeth's shop sounded like it would take way more energy than I currently had available, but I struggled to come up with a valid reason to bail on a promise.

We made plans to meet at The Enclave in an hour, which

would theoretically give me time to breakfast and shower. After another high-powered dose of sugar and caffeine, I thought I would be strong enough to handle the task ahead. But when Wallace let me into the day spa's waiting room, the sorrow weighing down her features immediately spread to my own.

My heart ached as I stared around at the empty chairs. Standing here in a place that was heavy with every smell I associated with Elizabeth—frankincense, lavender, lemon—made her death feel more real than even her funeral had. This room should have buzzed with her energy. Instead, it just felt… lifeless.

"Thanks again for helping me with this. I brought some packing supplies." Wallace pointed to a stack of flattened cardboard boxes on the counter.

"No problem," I assured her. "We'll sort through it all together."

She pressed her lips into a thin, joyless smile. "Grandma's will said to sell as much as we can, so I guess just try to box similar things up together. I'll take everything to my house and deal with it when I get back."

"Back? From where?"

"We're going to go spread—" Her voice cracked. She cleared her throat and started over more quietly. "We're going to spread her ashes into the ocean. My whole family."

"That sounds really nice. When are you leaving?"

"Tomorrow."

"Well…" I gazed around the room and tried to nudge my worn-out brain into waking up a little more. "Let's get started."

For the next several hours, we moved from room to room, categorizing and boxing up everything in the spa. Elizabeth had managed to organize a lot of things into a relatively small space, and her personality shone through in unexpected places. The drawers beneath the counter in the waiting room were mostly filled with business supplies like envelopes and blank appointment reminder cards, but there were also a few pieces of jewelry made from black tourmaline and a dozen tiny bottles filled with her own personal blend of essential oils.

I tucked the oils into a tote bag for Wallace to take on her family's trip. I didn't know how many people were going, but I felt sure Elizabeth would want her descendants to use the oil and think of her. As an afterthought, I grabbed a sticky note off the countertop and scrawled a quick message for her family: *Elizabeth was a healing presence in the world. She will never be forgotten.*

Together, we pulled the posters of lotus plants off the walls and rolled up the rug on the floor. We packed away towels from the massage room, cat treats and dog bones from the furrapy room, and cleaning supplies from the bathroom.

"There's no bedroom," I realized. "I thought she lived up here."

"No, her house is down at the edge of town. The forest grows right up to her property line, and wild animals are always coming into the backyard. She says—" Wallace had to pause and clear her throat again. "She always said she had the best neighbors because they either had four legs or feathers."

That made more sense to me. When I heard how Elizabeth died and where they found her, I had imagined her walking all the way across town from The Enclave to get to the woods. But if she only had to go out her own back door…

"Hey, this is going to sound like a really weird question, but did your grandma have a wooden jewelry box?"

Wallace thought for a moment. "Yeah, she did."

My pulse quickened. "What did it look like? Small and square?"

"No, it's pretty big. Like the size of a phone book. It has a little heart cut into the top." A wistful smile settled onto her lips. "I remember looking at her jewelry through the heart-shaped glass. My grandpa gave her a new wedding ring every ten years, so she had a little collection of diamonds to mark how many happy decades they had before he died."

"Oh. And that was the only one?"

"Yeah." Wallace narrowed her eyes. "Why?"

"It's just a feeling I have. I can't shake it."

"About her jewelry?"

"No, not that." I hesitated, not sure how much I should tell her. But even in grief, Wallace's large eyes held the same inquisitiveness they always did. I could tell I had piqued her curiosity, and if anyone would believe my wild theory, it was her.

"What is it?" she pressed, voice rising.

"Remember last month, how that little box got stolen out of Graham's garage? I think I know who did it. There's a psychic named Anson Monroe who used to mentor my mother, way back when I was a kid." I took a deep breath. Wallace had been open to all things paranormal in the past, but what I was about to tell her pushed the boundaries, even in Donn's Hill. "He can astral project. I would be somewhere, and then I would see him. And he talked to me."

She looked confused. "Some guy who used to know your mom?"

"He pretended to be a ghost named Horace haunting the Oracle Inn last month. He told me he could help me clear my name when Raziel was murdered, but only if I went out past Moyard and got him this little wooden jewelry box from the woods. I went out there, and it called to me."

It felt so good to be telling her everything. Graham knew it, but he was like me: powerless to do anything about it. Deputy Wallace could do something. She could help.

The words tumbled out too quickly. My drained mind couldn't keep up, and it kept skipping forward just to give my mouth something to say. "Then the box got stolen, and that van Graham and I found? The one that caught fire? It had New Mexico plates. And that was too weird. I mean, *I'm* from New Mexico. So we took a chance. We had to go. And the girl, the one who was in our yurt before us, she died. Of exposure, just like my mom. And she had a box. A wooden one, just like Horace made me get." I sucked in air. "And that box called to me too. Just like the first one. *He's* doing it. Horace. Luring people—women, I guess?— outside with the box. And then he kills them. He did it to my mom and Camila and then Elizabeth."

When I spoke her grandmother's name, Wallace's eyes flashed. Her jaw clenched, and her voice hardened. "You think this Anson Monroe guy murdered my grandma?"

I panted slightly as I nodded. Recapping the bizarre events of the past week had sapped the few drops of energy I had left, and I desperately wanted to sit down. There weren't any chairs in the little hallway between the treatment rooms, so I crumpled down the wall until my legs rested on the floor. My stomach growled noisily, and I tried to remember the last time I ate a real meal.

Wallace towered over me, hands on her hips. "And if I'm following you correctly, this guy also killed your mom?"

I nodded again. How long would it take me to get home? I couldn't wait to be in bed.

She made a strange sound, like she was trying to get something gross out of her throat. "Unbelievable."

"What?" I squinted up at her. "It all happened."

"Not your story. *You.*" Her eyes burned with anger. "How dare you pull my grandma into your twisted, egocentric delusions? My grandma is dead, Mac. She's gone. She died alone in the woods. Nobody was with her. None of us got to say goodbye. Isn't that horrible enough without pretending she was murdered?"

My head spun. I couldn't understand why she was so upset. "Cynthia, I don't know what I said, but—"

"Save it. Just… save it, okay?" She rested a hand on her forehead like she was taking her own temperature. Tears glistened on her cheeks. "And just go. I don't need your help anymore. Leave me alone."

I staggered to my feet and reached a hand toward her.

She slapped it away and turned her back on me. "Go. Now."

There seemed little point in arguing. Head pounding, belly empty, and desperate for sleep, I stumbled out of the spa and down the stairs in search of rest.

CHAPTER TWENTY-ONE

My fatigue was so complete that I had no memory of getting back to my apartment. As I lay in bed, every muscle in my body ached. My mind begged for sleep. But just like every night since Elizabeth's memorial service, fear kept me awake. Sleep tugged at me the way those jewelry boxes had, pulling me toward it, enticing me along. But the more tired I grew, the more apprehensive I became. I couldn't let myself drift off into unconsciousness. Every time I felt myself nearing the edge of that cliff, I pulled back.

Just dive off, a voice inside me urged. *Come on in. The water's fine.*

I jerked myself into full wakefulness for a few seconds, determined not to lose myself in the great, ghostly river Grey had described. But within moments, my exhaustion coaxed me toward sleep again, only for my fear to yank me back.

Rinse and repeat.

Eventually, though, it wasn't my choice anymore. I had been awake for days, far longer than anyone should be. My fatigue was too strong. My anxiety lost the battle, and my eyes closed.

When they opened, I was standing in the backyard of Primrose House, facing the large window overlooking the lawn. I could see myself in the glass, wearing the same clothes I had worn to help Wallace. Well, almost the same. My purple zippered hoodie was now a dark charcoal, and my blue jeans were a pale nickel. Like the last time I slept, the world around me was a study in gray scale, and no sound reached my ears when I clapped my hands in front of my face.

A deep crease formed between my reflection's eyebrows. The silence and the lack of color were exhausting, and it wasn't fair. Even in my dreams, I felt tired. Why couldn't I dream about taking a nap in a hammock or curling up with a good book on a warm window seat?

I tried to imagine myself somewhere else. Anywhere else. I would take my old recurring nightmare about falling down the stairs over this. But no matter how many times I closed my eyes and pictured myself on a white sand beach, I opened them to my monochrome reflection in the kitchen window glass.

What if the ghost at the Ace of Cups wasn't just an imprint, a movie playing over and over? What if his spirit was trapped in a loop, and every time he closed his eyes, his mind put him back in the same spot? If I died here, would the same thing happen to me? Would my mind just get stuck on repeat?

Someone tapped me on the shoulder, and I turned to find Camila Aster looming over me again. I hadn't seen her in the reflection. I wondered if she could see herself, but like last time, there was no way to ask.

Her brows scrunched together as she glared at me.

"I'm not exactly overjoyed to see you either," I said silently.

She mouthed something back. Like before, I couldn't make it out. She lifted and dropped her shoulders in an exaggerated sigh, making her feelings crystal clear.

In college, I had a roommate who claimed all dreams were just the result of our brains trying to process and catalogue everything we'd seen that day. Sometimes, things we hadn't consciously noticed, but which our eyes had seen, would pop up. If we saw that same thing later—like, say, a billboard for a new company—it would feel like déjà vu.

If any of that was true, I couldn't figure out why I kept dreaming about this woman I had never met. As I stared at her, puzzling over it, the memory of my conversation with Grey came back to me.

Visitations are very common, she had said. *Most people dismiss them as just dreams.*

"Holy crap," I said. "This isn't a dream."

Camila's eyes widened. I felt mine growing larger too.

I hadn't just said it.

I had *heard* it.

"This isn't a dream," I said again, louder. "This is a visitation."

She shook her head and tried to say something. I still couldn't hear her. Frustration clouded her face again. I shuffled my feet along the grass and couldn't hear the crinkling of the leaves either. But I could hear myself. That alone made me feel a little less like I was about to lose my mind.

"Why are you here?" I asked.

As before, I couldn't follow what she was trying to tell me. Her lips moved, but it was pointless. I stared at her glumly. Talking to her was as worthless as sending texts to Kit's phone in France.

"I wish I could hear you," I said. "I'm guessing you don't have anybody to complain to about your day, right?"

Her short curls bobbed as she silently chuckled. Then her face lit up. She held up her bony hands, palms toward me and long fingers spread wide. She looked at her hands, then back at me, and gave me an encouraging smile.

"Uh…" I squinted, trying to figure out what she was trying to tell me. "Ten?"

She punched the air and nodded enthusiastically. Then she closed her hands into fists and flashed her ten fingers at me twice.

"Twenty?" I guessed.

I thought she might collapse on the ground with relief. The frustration on her face had vanished, replaced by the tight eyes and pursed lips of determination. Holding my gaze, she slowly raised her arms into an exaggerated shrug.

"What?"

She shook her head.

"Um… How?" I guessed. "I don't know? I don't care? Confused?"

I rattled off possibilities in rapid fire, but each one was met with another negative. I was already starting to feel discouraged, but Camila kept a smile on her face as she urged me to keep going. I had always hated games like these, but with a partner like Camila cheering me on, maybe it wouldn't have been so annoying to play party games like charades and twenty questions—

"Questions!" I shouted. "Twenty questions!"

She winced at my volume but clapped soundlessly.

I understood her meaning at once. I couldn't hear her speak or read her lips, but that didn't mean we couldn't communicate. I just had to ask the kinds of questions she could answer in a way I could more easily understand, like a nod or a headshake.

"Okay," I said. "Let's start over. Do you know where we are?"

She answered with a half frown and a half shrug. She pointed at me and then the house before tilting her head to lay it on a pillow made from her hands.

"Yeah, this is my house. And we're a long way from New Mexico." I wanted to ask why she had followed me here but had to rephrase it. "Did you come here on purpose?"

She shook her head firmly. Definitely not.

My stomach sank. I had a feeling that, as per usual, I had accidentally brought a spirit home with me. As a professional ghost hunter, I really had to get better about not letting my work follow me home.

"Did I bring you here?"

She nodded.

"With the box?" I guessed.

She nodded again. Her nostrils flared, and anger sparked in her eyes.

I drew back. "Are you mad at me?"

She shook her head and heaved another silent sigh. Whatever she was upset about, it would take more than a yes or no to tell me.

"Is the box yours?" I needed to know where she had gotten it, but one step at a time.

She crossed her arms into an *X* in front of her face, then drew them downward quickly as she shook her head. It was the most emphatic no yet.

I frowned. "Did you find it?"

After nodding, she shivered and rubbed her arms.

"Are you cold?"

She shook her head and pointed over her shoulder with her thumb.

"Oh, you *were* cold."

Camila took a few steps toward the house, then pantomimed seeing something on the ground and reaching to pick it up. She sank to her knees, curled up on her side, and froze there.

The pieces clicked into place in my mind. It was exactly as I had imagined. "The box called to you. You went out into the cold to find it. And…"

I didn't finish the sentence. It felt too strange to tell someone she had died. Besides, unlike the ghost at the Ace of Cups, I was certain Camila knew exactly what her situation was.

I was right. She nodded sadly.

"Did you see anybody that night?"

She shook her head.

"Nobody at all?" I pressed. "A man with an old-fashioned brimmed hat and glowing red eyes?"

Her face scrunched up as she thought. After a few seconds, she shook her head again.

"What about before that? Did you see any strange men around? Older men?"

She gave that plenty of thought as well but ultimately signaled that she hadn't.

Despite the heavy subject matter, our strange little game of charades was weirdly fun. I felt myself warming up to the challenge of conversing this way. Wanting to keep the game going as long as I could, I asked something lighter.

"You're from Georgia, right?" I didn't mention where I had read that particular piece of information.

Even in the muted colors of a grayscale world, her face lit up when I mentioned her home state. She nodded.

"I've never been there. What's it like?"

She didn't balk at the open-ended question. She rubbed her hands together and took a moment to strategize. Then, like a swooning damsel, she laid one wrist against her forehead and fanned herself with her other hand.

"Hot?"

She nodded and held up a finger. With a huge smile, she rubbed her stomach and pretended to swallow something.

I grinned back. "But the food is great. That's enough to get me to go anywhere."

Despite not being able to hear it, her laughter was contagious. As we stood on the back lawn giggling together, Striker stepped daintily out the cat flap in the kitchen door and sauntered over to us on silent paws. Like the last time Camila visited me, the brown and cream in Striker's fur had been muted into swirling gray tones. I reached down to scratch her between the ears, and she plopped down on my bare feet. Her silky fur dusted the tops of my toes, but I realized I could feel neither the warmth from her body or the cold from the grass. I could only sense the rumble of her purr.

Dream visitations had their benefits, I supposed. If Kit and I were standing outside in the middle of the night, I would have had to cut our conversation short ages ago to go inside and get a coat and some slippers. Or, more likely, we would both go into the kitchen to chat over steaming cups of hot chocolate and whatever baked goods our housemates had left lying around.

"Do you want to come inside?" I offered. "I know you don't actually need food anymore in the real world, but this is mostly in my head, right? If I can dream it, you can eat it?"

I expected her to laugh, but her brows drew together, and she pursed her lips. Her sudden unhappiness startled me.

"Sorry. That was probably really rude, huh? I didn't mean to remind you—"

Camila cut me off with a wave of her hands. She pointed at my head and gestured at the yard. Her eyes flashed. Whatever she was trying to tell me, it was important.

"Um... You don't want to be in the yard anymore? We can go somewhere else."

She lifted her eyes to the sky and mouthed something.

"Hey, we were getting pretty good at this," I reminded her. "Don't give up now. Let me try again. I can get it."

The irritation on her face was plain, and I suddenly felt like I was missing something very obvious. I dipped my chin and focused on her face, determined to figure out what she was intent on telling me.

As she had done earlier, she made a pillow out of her hands and rested her head on them with eyes closed.

"Sleeping."

She straightened up and clapped her hands. Then she made another X with her arms and pulled it apart. A definitive no.

"Not sleeping? Wait… I'm not sleeping?"

She pursed her lips and shook her head, looking strangely apologetic. My stomach dropped. If this wasn't a dream visitation, I could only think of two possibilities. One: I had died in my sleep, and Camila, for some reason, was here to help me cross over. But this was the second time I had seen her, and death was kind of a one-time deal. That only left scenario number two.

"This is real?"

As Camila nodded, her eyes lightened from a dark gray to a nutty brown. Her skin warmed, and all around her, color flooded back into the world. Primrose House was once again a sunny yellow, and the leaves on the ground took on their familiar fall shades. It was like the entire world was shouting at me, "Yes, dummy, this is real!"

Joy soared through me at the sight of all that color. I turned slowly where I stood, drinking in the intense rainbow around me. It was like standing in a piece of art, and the subtle variations in everything from the blades of grass to the tiny pebbles in the concrete made me want to take up painting.

Then I saw myself in the kitchen window. All of my color had come back too. My brown hair, my pink lips, and the purple in my sweatshirt.

But there was one color that didn't look right.

Instead of their usual blue, my eyes glowed crimson.

The shock sent me soaring back into wakefulness. Afternoon sunlight flooded my apartment. A shrill beeping pierced the air. Graham was leaning over me and shouting my name, shaking my shoulder with one hand and clutching Striker with the other.

"What is it?" I mumbled blearily. "What's that sound?"

"Fire!" He pulled me out of bed and handed me a pair of shoes. "Go!"

CHAPTER TWENTY-TWO

The acrid stench of smoke stung my nose as soon as I stepped out of my apartment. I raced down the stairs as fast as I dared, while Sister Mary Bernadette's voice screamed in my memory of elementary school fire drills. *No running! Get low! Find the closest exit!*

It took far too long to reach the ground floor, and all the way down the stairs, my eyes were locked on the black smoke curling around the arched doorway leading into the kitchen. By the time my feet hit the foyer, I was in a full panic. A single thought—escape—propelled me forward, and I made straight for the front door. Striker shot past me, and I glanced toward Graham, grateful beyond words that he had made sure to grab her.

But Graham wasn't next to me. He wasn't following me through the front door. As I watched, he ducked into the kitchen.

He had gone straight into the source of the smoke.

"Graham!" I shouted.

I hovered on the porch, unsure whether to continue fleeing onto the lawn or go after him. The shrill beeping of the fire alarm felt like the ticking of a clock that was counting down to disaster.

Counting down to his death.

Just as I was about to throw myself back into the house, he ducked his head through the kitchen doorway.

"It's okay!" he called. "Come give me a hand."

In the kitchen, a cookie sheet sat at an angle in the sink. The faucet was on full blast, and two charred black triangles hissed against the cold water.

Graham climbed on top of the table. "Spot me for a second, okay?"

He stretched to his full height and managed to press the fire alarm's reset button. With the beeping silenced and the smoke being pulled out of the house through the open doors, the fog began to clear from my brain as well. I guarded him with my hands as he climbed down from the table, as if I could catch him if he fell.

He took off his glasses and wiped the sweat from his face with his sweater sleeve. "I won't pretend that didn't scare the crap out of me. Are you okay?"

"Yeah. Shaken, but fine." I went to the sink and prodded the triangles. "Ew, this poor pizza."

"Did you forget to set a timer?"

I raised an eyebrow at him. "Me? I thought it was you."

"I could have sworn I heard you down here banging pans around an hour ago. I've been cleaning my apartment—I haven't been cooking."

"Then it must have been somebody else."

"Nobody else is home." Concern clouded his features, and he reached out a hand to feel my forehead. "Are you feeling okay?"

I sank down into a kitchen chair and cradled my head in my hands. Had I come home, put pizza in the oven, and then gone upstairs to climb into bed? I couldn't remember. I just remembered finally falling asleep, and—

The memory of the red eyes in my reflection sent me bolting

back upright. Slowly, I turned to Graham, but the words caught and croaked in my throat.

"What?" he asked. "Are you going to throw up?"

Before I could answer, he slid the kitchen garbage in front of my feet. The stench of a rotting banana peel wafted up my nostrils, and I shoved the can away.

"No, I'm fine. Just listen. I think…" I paused. "I think I just astral projected."

I walked him through my encounter with Camila Aster— which I now refused to think of as a dream—in as much detail as I could remember. When I told him about my eyes glowing red, he frowned.

"Couldn't it have just been a dream?" he asked. "You've been having nightmares about Horace all month."

"This was different. It didn't feel like a dream. Or look like one. Or even sound like one. It didn't exactly feel real either, but…" I trailed off, unable to organize my thoughts about the experience I had just had while asleep.

I wished it had lasted longer.

I wanted it to happen again.

"Mac." Graham's voice was gentle. "Your mom chased astral projection for years. You don't even know if she ever accomplished it. How likely is it that you would do it without even trying?"

For some reason, his words stung. I wanted to slap them out of the air. Sure, on the surface, they made sense. But my gut rejected them. I knew what I had experienced. Nobody I knew *tried* to be psychic. They just were. And in my case, I suddenly lost the gift, only to discover it all over again. I hadn't done any of it on purpose.

Logic didn't apply to the spiritual realm.

Graham was still trying to talk me down. "How long has it

been since you got a good night's rest? You barely slept in New Mexico, and you've looked exhausted since we got back."

"I know." I fell silent for a moment and considered his argument. It had been over a week since I'd gotten my preferred nine hours of uninterrupted hibernation. But sleep-deprived or not, I *knew* I had astral projected. I felt it in my gut. I just had to do it again, while fully rested this time, and then he would believe me. "It's weird, but something changed during that nap. I feel like I can sleep again. I'm excited to."

A car door slammed out back. A minute later, Reggie stepped into the kitchen, holding a bag from the deli in his hands. "What stinks?"

"Pizza," I said, pointing to the charred pan in the sink. "Want some?"

He scrunched up his face. "No, thank you."

"How's the writing going?"

"Fine." Reggie moved for the foyer, then paused. After a moment, he turned and looked at me with a curious expression. "Your name is Mac, right?"

I laughed. Of course he wasn't sure who I was. To him, I was just the idiot on the third floor, the dunce who couldn't take a hint and kept asking him about his books.

He didn't seem fazed by my laughter. He simply looked at me expectantly.

"Yes," I finally answered. "Mackenzie Clair."

"Oh, good. I'd like you to sit down with me sometime and tell me about the Franklin cabin."

My eyes popped. "What?"

"Not today, of course." He hefted the deli bag. "I've got to finish my lunch and get back to work. But sometime soon."

Without waiting for a reply, Reggie nodded to Graham and hustled into the foyer.

As I stared after him, my shock and irritation grew into suspicion. What did he want to know about the Franklin cabin? And why did he want to know it? That place was deeply, inextricably intertwined with Horace in my mind. He had first appeared to me in the Franklin cabin, and the van with New Mexico plates had been hauling furniture and wood paneling stripped from the cabin when it crashed.

"How does he know about that?" I asked aloud.

Graham shrugged. "Everybody knows about it. Your investigations there are famous, especially around here."

I didn't buy it. With my eyes locked on the doorway through which Reggie had just passed, the wheels in my mind turned. If Anson Monroe killed Elizabeth—which I believed was true, despite Wallace's skepticism—then at some point, he left New Mexico and came to Donn's Hill. When did he get here?

Could he have come to town with a moving truck the very same day Graham and I left?

"All right, Detective Mac," Graham said. "I know what you're thinking."

"What?"

"You had this same look on your face yesterday when Lucy brought up Seattle. I saw your eyes snap right to Fred. You thought he was Horace." He tilted his head. "Or do you still think so?"

"I did for a second, but I've never gotten anything but good vibes from Fred. Reggie, on the other hand…" I ground my teeth together. "Not so much."

"But we know Horace is Anson Monroe, and we know Anson Monroe was already old when your mom died. Right?"

"Right."

"Reggie's only in his fifties. He would have been my age back then."

"Do you have any idea how ancient we probably look to eight-year-olds? We could go down to the school and take a survey, and I guarantee at least half of them would say I'm old enough to be a grandma. It could still be him."

"Mac," Graham said gently. "I did a background check on Reggie when he applied for the lease. He's never lived in New Mexico or Washington. He's from New Jersey."

"Since when did you start doing background checks on people? Did you do one on me?"

"No, but when you signed your lease, the love of my life wasn't living upstairs yet." He smiled. "Do you think I'd let just anybody move in here now?"

My cheeks warmed. I stared at him. The L word was nothing new between us; we said "I love you" to each other all the time. But *love of my life*....

I shook my head, refusing to be distracted from my point by his romantic language. "I could still be right. Horace could be way younger than we think he is. And what, he's capable of astral projecting but not faking an identity that can pass a background check?"

He sighed and walked over to me to rest his hands on my shoulders. "Okay, I'm not trying to treat you like a toddler here, I promise. But you are tired with a capital *T*. You need a meal and a nap."

"What?" I raised an eyebrow at him. "No juice box?"

* * *

AFTER A SANDWICH that didn't require the oven to prepare, I headed upstairs to try to get a little more sleep. With luck, I would do more than rest. I couldn't wait to astral project again and continue my charade-like conversation with Camila.

But halfway up Primrose House's grand staircase, I paused. I stood on the second-floor landing, listening to the clatter and pings of Reggie's typewriter from his apartment, and stared up at my door on the floor above.

After having to run down so many stairs while the fire alarm screeched at us, my apartment suddenly felt needlessly, dangerously far away from the front door. What if the fire had spread through the kitchen before the alarm went off? What if Graham hadn't been home to wake me? The knowledge that I might not have made it out alive sent a shiver down my spine, and I turned on my heel and went through Graham's door instead. Sleeping had been hard enough lately without having to worry about getting trapped up on the third floor.

I woke ten hours later, well-rested but frustrated. My dreams had been nonsensical and pedestrian and mostly centered around food. The next night was the same, and the night after that. I felt my physical energy returning, and my head cleared enough for me to realize exactly how insensitive it had been for me to tell Deputy Wallace my theory about her grandmother's death. But each night I spent in Graham's apartment was one without any supernatural occurrences at all.

It wasn't something I expected to miss, but I ached for it.

Was I losing my psychic abilities all together? Had I somehow burned through a lifetime's supply of seeing the dead, all for two trips into the astral plane? No, I decided. That couldn't be it. Horace had appeared to me multiple times, for long visits. So unless he had some kind of spiritual generator recharging his psychic batteries, it had to be something else.

Three days after the fire, I decided I needed to recreate similar circumstances to the last time I had seen Camila, starting with my sleep locale. But key to astral projecting would be feeling safe enough to sleep at all, so I requested a few changes to my apartment. That same afternoon, Graham installed a retractable steel ladder, which could be tossed out my turret window in an emergency, and replaced the fire extinguisher in my kitchenette.

"What do you think?" he asked.

I inspected the recharge date on the extinguisher and nodded. "Thank you. I know it's silly, but—"

"It's not silly," he said firmly. "The apartments up here always should have had escape ladders. I feel awful thinking about what could have happened if that fire spread."

"Do you need help switching out any other extinguishers or anything?" I asked, feeling bad for forcing him to drive to the home improvement store in Moyard.

"That'd be great, thanks."

As we headed for the second floor, the front door slammed.

"Hello?" a familiar voice called.

My pulse quickened, and I raced down the stairs until I could see who waited in the foyer. Her green hair came into view first, followed by a pair of shining brown eyes.

"Kit!" I shouted, bounding the rest of the way down for a hug.

She dropped a heavy suitcase onto the floor and held out her arms. "Honey, I'm home!"

CHAPTER TWENTY-THREE

"I can't believe I have to stay at the Oracle Inn," Kit grumbled.

I hid my smile behind my beer glass. "Well, you did move out. What was Graham supposed to do? Keep the apartment open forever?"

"Yeah, basically."

The two of us sat at my favorite table in the Ace of Cups, a little curved booth in the corner where the ceiling was at its lowest. I was working my way through every appetizer on the menu while Kit sullenly poked a serving of shepherd's pie with her fork.

"You could stay at your dad's," I suggested.

She cringed. "Are you kidding? With Penelope there all the freaking time? Gross."

"What are you doing here anyway? I thought you were in France."

"We finished that shoot, and now we're on a little production break." Her lower lip plumped into an exaggerated pout. "What? Is it a crime to come home when I can?"

"Honestly, I'm shocked you came back at all." I swallowed a

fried pickle slice. "I figured once you got to Paris, you would never leave."

She cracked a smile for the first time since Graham had broken the news that Primrose House didn't have any vacancies. "It was pretty awesome. I thought it would be way crowded, but I guess not many tourists pick November for their big vacation. Our showrunner, Angel, has been there a lot and knows all the best restaurants. This one place had a pizza called fruit d'mer with the craziest kinds of seafood on it. We went back there three times —I wish you could have tasted it."

"Gross, no way. Even my gluttony has its limits."

"No, it was great. And the pastries, Mac." She rolled her eyes up to the sky and let her mouth hang open. "They're unbelievable."

"I bet," I said, not quite able to keep the envy out of my voice.

Kit's eyes softened. "I wish you had been there. We need to plan a trip together or something. It's weird not seeing you every day."

"Same." Feeling mist at the corners of my eyes, I cleared my throat and steered us into less emotional territory. "So what were you filming there anyway?"

She looked around and lowered her voice. "I'm technically not allowed to talk about it until it airs, so keep your trap shut about it, okay?"

"Deal," I whispered back.

"Okay. You know how Amari's whole vision is to carry on Raziel's work and expose frauds in the paranormal community?"

"Yeah."

Amari's old boss had made it his life's work to out fake psychics. He was especially incensed when charlatans, as he preferred to call them, tried to make money off people's grief. It was a noble mission, but his cocky attitude didn't make him many friends, and his life was cut short when one of the phony fortune-tellers he threatened to unmask killed him.

"Well, down by the Saint-Ouen Cemetery, there are these antique markets," Kit said. "Mostly they're outside, even in the winter when it's snowing. But if you know the right people, you can get into these special backroom bazaars. They don't sell the kind of stuff tourists want to haggle over."

I leaned forward, drawn in by the picture she was painting. Like her father, Kit had a knack for telling a good story. "What do they have?"

"Amari's contact claimed the black market was selling body parts." She took in my facial expression and quickly clarified. "Not, like, entire arms or anything. More like jars of powder that are supposed to be dried organs. Fingernails. Uh..." Her face flushed. "Various liquids."

"Gross. That can't be legal."

"Nope. Not even a little bit. And to get in there—it's like something out of the movies. Back doors, secret passwords, huge beefy dudes guarding every entrance."

My mouth fell open. "You didn't go in there, did you?"

"Man, I wish! There's no way our crew could get inside with our cameras and everything. Amari had to go in alone. Check it out." She pulled out her phone and showed me a photo of Amari wearing a pair of thick, black-framed spectacles that could have come out of Graham's wardrobe. Kit pointed to the edge of the glasses, where the frame met the hinge. "The camera's right there. I couldn't even see it when she was standing right in front of me."

"Seriously? They have that James Bond stuff in real life?" I suddenly pictured everyone on the *Soul Searchers* crew wearing identical pairs of spy glasses. It would be weird to see Yuri in anything other than his classic double-bridged wire frames, but it would quadruple the video we could capture during investigations.

The real question was: did they make something similar for cats?

Kit was nodding. "They're not even that expensive."

"How did the footage turn out?"

"Surprisingly good. Amari went in there alone, and it was like a total sting. She speaks French really well, and she got all these vendors to tell her about the illegal stuff they were selling—or pretending to sell. I'm still not sure if any of it was real. Meanwhile, I was sitting in a Mercedes delivery van with the rest of the crew and our interpreter. I felt like I was in the CIA or something."

"That sounds incredible." I blinked a few times, genuinely concerned that the whites of my eyes might be turning green.

No wonder Kit left. We couldn't compete with adventures like this.

"What are you guys filming next?" I asked, dreading the answer.

"Dunno. Amari's putting together the schedule. I know we're going to try to pack a couple things between the holidays, but that's it."

"Oh, I assumed you were doing the scheduling."

"What, you think I'd get lured away from the best show in the world just to do the same job I did before? No way. I'm first A.D."

"Oooh, fancy." I popped a french fry into my mouth. "What's that?"

"Assistant director. Imagine my dad is the director, and your job was to handle all the logistics of the shoot and communicate what he needs to the rest of the crew."

I frowned. "That's exactly how things work right now."

She rolled her eyes. "No, like… combine what you do plus everything Dad does except for the actual directing."

I still didn't get it, but I pasted on a grin and patted her hand. "And I bet you're the best first A.D. ever."

"Thanks." She jangled the ice cubes in her now-empty tumbler. "I'd give a toast to myself if I could get a refill around here. Where'd our waitress go?"

I raised a hand toward the bar, where a tall guy with sandy brown hair was minding the taps. He returned my wave and, a few minutes later, delivered another martini on the rocks to our table. It was only then that I paid attention to the details of his face.

"Noah?" I asked. "You work here now?"

The new *Soul Searchers* cameraman gave a slight bow. "We can't all be psychic, but at least some of us can pretend to be psychic bartenders. Besides, I heard moonlighting was the Donn's Hill standard."

Kit raised her glass to him. "Whatever your other job is, you make a mean martini. Nice work."

"Noah is the new Mark," I told her. "He just moved here from LA."

Her smile faded. "Oh. Well… welcome to Donn's Hill. How do you like it so far?"

"It's good. People tip better here than I expected, so I can't complain. Well, except for one thing. Everyone's obsessed with the idea of this ghost upstairs." He leaned onto the edge of the table and lowered his voice conspiratorially. "Okay, you con artist, spill. How'd you do that the other night? Was there a little motor on the door or something?"

Kit frowned. "What the hell are you talking about?"

"Miss Mackenzie here saw a ghost, but all the camera picked up was a door opening and closing on its own. Alexi was all excited about advertising the haunted apartment, but all the spooky stuff stopped right after we cleaned up our gear. What a coincidence, right?" He winked at me, then glanced toward the door and took a step back from our table. "Whoops, speak of the devil. Boss is back. Better get to work. Whistle if you need anything."

Kit's eye daggers followed him across the room as he returned to his post behind the bar. I stared after him as well. I had been sure he believed us after the investigation, but now he was back to calling me a fake.

"Has your dad ever had to fire anyone before?" I asked.

Before Kit could answer, the Ace of Cup's owner slid into the booth across from me and punched Kit's shoulder.

"I was hoping that green hair belonged to you," Alexi said. "What are you doing back in town?"

Kit shrugged. "Just a quick visit while I had the chance."

"Oh, bummer." Alexi leaned forward and stole a fry off my plate. "I was hoping the good California weather chased you back here to stay."

"Pfft." Kit swatted the air in front of her face. "Fat chance. Besides, where's anybody supposed to get a decent drink in this town?"

"You'd better be kidding." Alexi eyed her newest bartender. "I took a gamble on that guy."

"I kid, I kid," Kit said. "He's fine. Great drink, great service."

Relief washed across Alexi's features, and she sank back against the suede seat. "Phew. You had me worried there. I mean, what's the point of having a bartender who looks like Cary Elwes if he can't even pour a good drink?"

"Who?" I asked.

"Noah."

"No, I mean who does he look like?"

"You know, the actor." Alexi waited for me to catch on. When I stared blankly at her, she said, "Cary Elwes? *The Princess Bride*?"

"Oh, that guy." I squinted at Noah. From the right angle, his face did sort of look like Westley from the movie, minus the mustache and at least ten years older. "Thanks for saying that. I couldn't figure out why he looked so familiar. It was really bugging me."

"He's been killing with the ladies in the brunch crowd. It's a sad truth that cute bartenders get more tips, but"—Alexi tossed her curls and mimed checking her nails—"I'm not complaining. Speaking of which, I better get back to work."

"Hey, is it true there hasn't been any more paranormal activity upstairs?" I asked. "Noah said something about the occurrences stopping."

"That bum." Her eyes narrowed. "He wasn't supposed to say anything. Yuri and I decided not to tell you, so when you came back to investigate, it would be a little more…"

"*Cinéma vérité*?" Kit supplied.

"Sure," Alexi said. "I was going to say 'in line with the first time you were here,' but whatever floats your boat, *madame*."

I frowned. The way Yuri had explained the residual haunting, it didn't seem like the kind of thing that would just up and resolve itself. I had expected to have to do a cleansing or something if and when Alexi decided she didn't want a ghost for a tenant anymore.

"Would you mind if we went up there and checked it out?"

"Sure. The door's unlocked. Have at it." She stood and pointed a finger at Kit. "But don't even think about sneaking out of town the way you snuck in. I better see you before you head back."

Kit grumbled something unintelligible into her glass before drinking deeply. We stopped at the bar for refills, then headed up to the apartments on the second floor. Kit followed after me in moody silence, saying nothing as I filled her in on the *Soul Searchers* shoot and the ghostly miner who seemed to be stuck in time.

At last, as we settled cross-legged onto the floor to wait for the miner to make his nightly rounds, I couldn't take her silence any longer and demanded, "Okay, what's going on? What are you so salty about?"

"Nothing." She pursed her lips and looked away.

"Is everything okay with Amari?"

A smile flitted across Kit's lips at the mention of her girlfriend, and she relaxed. "Yeah, everything's good."

"You haven't taped a line down your half of the apartment yet?"

I was only half kidding. Kit was one of the most generous people I knew, always giving freely of her time and her talents to anyone who needed help. But she was also strangely stingy when it came to things like specialty coffee creamer or her favorite cookies, marking her food at Primrose House with a thick black permanent marker. She was also fiercely protective of her personal space, preferring to hang out in the common areas of Primrose House or at my place so she didn't have to play hostess. I had a hard time imagining her sharing a home with someone.

"I thought it would be weird, living with someone else. Especially since we work together too. You would think we'd get sick of each other, but it just feels right." Her eyes gleamed mischievously. "What about you and Graham, huh? When are you two finally going to bite the bullet and move in together?"

"Give it a rest. You just want a room to open up so you can crash there whenever the mood strikes you."

"It would be a pretty sweet fringe benefit," she admitted. "Well, if you two aren't shacking up yet, what's going on? Anything new besides, you know, how freaking fast you and Dad replaced me?"

I flicked the side of the glass sitting beside her foot. "Um, are you that drunk already? You quit, remember?"

"Whatever." She leaned back against the cabinets and folded her arms across her chest. "I don't want to talk shop anyway."

I hadn't wanted to dive into what was going on in my life until I got to the bottom of what was going on with hers. Randomly showing up back here with a surly attitude didn't feel like normal Kit behavior, but clearly, she wasn't ready to open up yet. So, eager to finally tell someone who would believe me, I leaned forward and dropped my bombshell.

"I astral projected the other night."

As quickly as I could, I described my experience. I expected Kit's jaw to drop or for her to leap up excitedly and announce she was coming back to work with the *Soul Searchers* so she could be part of filming the research into this groundbreaking discovery. But she just narrowed her eyes and smiled indulgently.

"That's... not possible."

"What?" My shoulders sagged. "Of course it is. Horace did it multiple times."

"Yeah, but he's on his own level," she argued. "Amari's been trying to find anybody who can prove they can really astral project, and nobody's willing to do it on camera. A lot of people claim they could if they wanted, but you know what that means."

"I'm not making this up. I *did* it, Kit."

She pinched her mouth with one hand. "Sorry. I didn't mean it like that. I'm just saying—maybe you think you did it, but it was just a dream. You have crazier, more vivid dreams than anybody I've ever met."

I felt the irritation settling onto my face and dragging my features toward the ground. As surprised as I had been by Graham's skepticism, hers was even more unexpected. She traded her life in Donn's Hill to go chasing the paranormal all over the globe, but she couldn't believe I was capable of doing something extraordinary?

Kit stuck out one leg and nudged my knee with the toe of her Vans. I shifted my weight onto my other hip, moving myself out of her reach, and turned my face to the side.

"Look, I'm sorry," she said. "This new show… we sort of take Dad's 'supernatural second' method to the max. It's more like 'supernatural never.'"

I said nothing.

"I believe you." She kicked my knee lightly, and I grudgingly looked at her face. Her brown eyes were round and sincere. "I do."

"Promise?"

She grinned. "Do me a favor. Pull a Horace. Show up in my hotel room with creepy red eyes and prove it to me. It'll be worth having to pay Penelope for new bedsheets."

The tension between us broke, and we got down to the business of making up for lost time. As we waited for the apartment door to be opened by a ghostly hand, she caught me up on life in LA, and I told her everything that had happened to me in New Mexico.

"You seriously brought another one of those jewelry boxes home?" The expression on her face was part shock, part morbid interest. "After what happened last time?"

"This one feels different," I protested. "I didn't pass out when I picked it up, and I haven't been getting those weird headaches. And you should see the way Striker acts around it. She's not afraid of it at all."

"That's so weird." Kit chewed one black-painted thumbnail. "Or maybe not. I mean, Amari is dead certain the other box held some kind of angry spirit. Striker probably felt that."

It made sense to me. Of course Striker would be more friendly to a box haunted by someone like Camila.

I glanced at my watch. Kit and I had been at the bar for hours, and it was now long past the time the miner's ghost should have come to his room, stepped out, and returned. But the door hadn't opened since we'd come in here.

"Hey, will you humor me for a minute?" I asked. "Can we do a quick little séance?"

"As if I would say no." Kit scooted forward until her knees touched mine.

We grasped hands, and I followed my normal breathing ritual until I was in a relaxed, receptive state. It wasn't hard to get there; the weeks apart from Kit had left a mark, and hearing her laugh and trading jokes with her was like a healing salve that soothed my soul. I found it easier than usual to calm my mind and reach out with my other senses.

Still... I felt nothing.

We sat in silence for over half an hour as I pushed my psychic energy as far as it could go, grasping in the darkness for any trace of the young miner who haunted this place. I pictured him in my mind as I'd seen him before: gaunt, sluggish, sick.

Nothing.

"Damn it," I muttered.

Kit's eyes fluttered open. "No dice, huh?"

"Nope." Disgusted, I heaved myself off the floor and kicked the edge of the cupboard. I felt like all the energy I had summoned within myself to try to make contact with the spirit was now trapped inside me like an overinflated balloon, and I prowled back and forth across the room in a vain effort to work it off. "This is ridiculous. We were here, and there was a ghost. Now I'm back, and there's nothing. How is that even possible?"

Kit got to her feet more slowly than I had. A troubled look grew on her face, and she cradled her chin in one hand. "That is pretty weird. And this isn't even the first time this has happened, right?"

I stopped pacing. "What do you mean?"

"This is just like the Franklin cabin. One day it's haunted by a violent poltergeist, and the next..." She snapped her fingers. "*Poof.* He's gone."

My eyes went wide. She was right. This was exactly like what had happened back then. Sometime between our investigation and tonight, someone had come along and banished the spirit.

No. Not someone.

Horace.

CHAPTER TWENTY-FOUR

After dropping Kit off at the Oracle Inn, I raced home to Primrose House. I was desperate to be asleep in my own bed, where I had the best chance of astral projecting. As amazing as it had been to spend the evening in Kit's company, I couldn't wait to see Camila.

I needed to be sure she hadn't disappeared too.

To my relief, she was already waiting for me in the backyard when I finally fell asleep. The world was gray scale again, but with a thought, I forced the color to come flooding back into my surroundings.

"You're here," I breathed.

Camila raised an eyebrow. I could practically hear her thoughts: *Where else would I be?*

"Don't worry about it. It's a long story anyway. I'm just glad to see you."

She grinned and held up her hand for a high five. As before, our hands didn't make a sound when they slapped together, but her palm was surprisingly solid when I touched it.

"Oh," I said. "I'm not in my body, right? Of course we can touch. I'm basically just like you."

She rolled her eyes and gave a chuckle I couldn't hear, as though I'd said something ridiculous. Then, eyes locked on mine, she slowly became more transparent. Graham's garage became visible through her body.

A moment later, she was gone.

"Holy crap," I said, hoping she could still hear me. "Did you just disappear on purpose?"

I blinked, and she appeared in front of me again, just an inch from my face. I shrieked and leapt backward. Camila doubled over in silent laughter, her shoulders shaking with mirth.

"Very funny," I said dryly.

If Kit scared me like that, it would have kicked off a prank war that lasted for days. But Camila had the unfair advantage of being a ghost. Scaring her felt impossible.

Unless...

"How did you do that?" I asked. "Did you just think it, and it happened?"

She shrugged and nodded.

If she could do it, I felt sure I could too. After all, we had just proven that our bodies, if you could call them that in the astral realm, were the same.

I stared at her as I tried to focus on disappearing from view. I imagined fading away into the surrounding scenery like a wraith, leaving behind no trace of myself. I felt my features scrunching together as I poured all my effort into doing what Camila had done, and I was sure the stress vein I inherited from my mother was popping out of my forehead.

As Camila watched me, her expression slowly turned from mild amusement to genuine surprise. Her eyes bugged out, seeming to lose track of me in the darkness.

"Mac?" she mouthed.

"Did it work?" I asked. "Can you still hear me?"

She didn't respond. My chest swelled. Kit might have just

spent the week doing paranormal espionage in Paris, but she couldn't do *this*.

I looked down at my hands to see if I could still see myself. I didn't notice any difference; my arms were pale but solid as ever.

It was payback time.

When I looked at Camila to plot my approach, she was staring straight at me. An enormous grin stretched across her face, and when I locked eyes with her, she dissolved back into silent laughter.

I hadn't disappeared at all.

"Oh, that's low," I said as my shoulders deflated. "Was that part of your plan all along?"

She was too busy cracking herself up to answer. I fought the smile trying to creep onto my face, determined that when she finally managed to collect herself, she would see how unfunny I found her little trick.

I lost. It was impossible to stay angry in the face of this much joy. I wondered when she had cooked up this scheme and how long she had been waiting to try it out on me. I got the feeling she didn't get to socialize much in the afterlife. Donn's Hill might have been the most haunted town in America, but Primrose House didn't exactly have a history of paranormal activity. The only exceptions I knew of were Camila herself and a ghost named Tom Bishop—but he had been haunting me, not the house.

Tom had hung around until his killer was brought to justice. I wondered what unfinished business was tethering Camila to this world.

When she eventually calmed down, I asked, "Hey, when you, um... Well, after that night in the desert, did you stay here on purpose?"

Her eyes narrowed, and she frowned.

"What I mean is: why haven't you moved on?" When she didn't answer, I said, "Oh, right. *Can* you move on?"

She shook her head, then wrapped the fingers of her left hand around her right wrist. She pulled away from me, but her wrist stayed in the same place.

"You're stuck."

Another nod.

"Can you leave the yard? You can go in the house, right?"

She pointed to the house and nodded, then pointed to the street and shrugged.

"Let's test it out," I suggested.

With Camila following me, I marched out toward the edge of the property line. I couldn't wait to get to the inn so I could fulfill my promise to Kit and prove I was capable of doing this. But the closer I got to the road, the slower my legs moved. It felt like trying to walk through waist-deep mud. I pushed myself forward, but something tugged at the back of my belly button. There was too much resistance around me. Straining against it was physically painful, like there was a hook inside me holding me back.

I couldn't get to the street.

"Is that what happens when you try to get out there?"

Camila tried to get past me, and it was strange to see the limitation kick in from the outside. She, too, struggled against an invisible barrier, and if her hair had been blowing behind her, I would have thought she was fighting against a strong wind. After a few seconds of walking slowly in place, she turned toward me and heaved one of her silent, exaggerated sighs.

Experimentally, I probed the boundaries of the yard. I could walk out into the street in front of the house but couldn't get all the way to the sidewalk beyond. At the sides of the yard, I could get farther to the east than to the west before the invisible tether in my stomach pulled me back. I stood on the front lawn, hands on my hips, and glared at the house.

"It's like there's an anchor in there keeping me down," I complained, rubbing my stomach with one hand.

I wondered if the ache in my belly would still be there when I woke up. When I was in elementary school, the other kids used to say that if you died in a dream, you would never wake up again, which was a delightful thought to have pop into your head as a six-year-old at bedtime. But I wondered now if there was any truth to it. If something happened to me on the astral plane, would it affect my body in the real world?

My body.

That was it. The thing anchoring me to Primrose House—the thing trapping me in the yard—was my body. That blogger was right; astral projection required a separation between the spiritual self and the physical form.

I wouldn't be able to leave the yard until I broke free of that restriction.

But when I pulled away from that anchor, it hurt. Grey's words flashed through my mind as the pain flashed through my belly. *If you dive too deeply, you can get swept away.*

Her warning conjured an image in my mind of my spirit disconnecting so completely from my body that I could never climb back into it again. I imagined going upstairs and seeing myself lying motionless in bed, just waiting for Graham to come find me.

Would losing me destroy him as completely as losing him would do to me?

I couldn't risk it. I shrank back from the edge of the yard and retreated to the porch below my apartment. Camila perched on the railing. Her dark eyes overflowed with sadness as she watched me.

"What can I do?" I asked her.

She shrugged. I got the feeling she was even more confused than I was. And I didn't blame her for looking more depressed than a cat who hadn't been fed in four hours. She was as trapped here as I was.

"I'll figure it out," I promised Camila. "There's a way around this. There has to be."

She nodded but looked unconvinced. As she faded into the night sky behind her, I forced myself to wake up.

Morning light shone through my turret's windows. Striker purred throatily above my head. But the cheer around me couldn't penetrate the clouds hanging over my mind. Once again, I was sure I had astral projected. But I didn't have any way to prove it, and neither of the two people closest to me believed I was doing anything more than dreaming. On top of that, nobody else seemed to think there was anything suspicious about Elizabeth's death.

The only person I could talk to about any of it was a dead woman who couldn't talk back.

I groaned and rolled over. What was the point of getting out of bed?

Striker stretched and hopped down to go investigate her food bowl. I watched her glumly, envious of the simple life of a cat, especially a cat with a good home. When she was hungry, there was food waiting for her. When she was bored, there were dozens of toys and a willing human to entertain her. There wasn't anything to be sad or stressed about.

And then there was my life. Sure, in the grand scheme of things, I was incredibly blessed. I had a roof over my head, the perfect job, and my health. I had the love of an amazing, kind, creative man, and I had the world's best cat.

All the same, something was missing.

I didn't believe in curses, but I was starting to feel like I must have gotten on somebody powerful's bad side. Every time I found someone to confide in, someone who actually understood what it was like to walk a tightrope between living in the normal world and dealing with the supernatural, life took them away from me. If they weren't dead, they were in prison.

I wished I had gotten Grey's phone number. I wasn't even

sure Grey was her real name. She had seemed so nervous about being in Donn's Hill, so anxious to get out of town. If she had wanted me to be able to find her, she would have made it easy.

That was part of the problem. Like Amari had once said, most genuine psychics didn't exactly put up billboards. As far as I knew, there wasn't some kind of online support group I could rely on. How was I supposed to find someone to talk to about all this?

"Damn it, Gabrielle," I told the ceiling. "I wish you were here."

I sat up. Gabrielle couldn't come to me; the best she could do was call. And the prison wouldn't let me call her when I needed to talk, but they *would* let me visit.

I didn't need a crystal ball to see another road trip in my future.

CHAPTER TWENTY-FIVE

As much as I wanted to jump into Baxter and go see Gabrielle the instant I got out of bed, the trip would have to wait until the next day. Fridays were Yuri's half day at Donn's Hill High School, and he liked to schedule short shoots for his afternoons off. I wouldn't have time to make it back before I was due at The Enclave, so I spent the morning catching up on housework and reading the visitation guidelines for the prison that had been Gabrielle's home for the last six months.

When it was time for me to head to work, Graham tagged along with me. He had joined us to film an episode before—one that required a total of nine participants for a séance. We weren't doing anything so exciting today. I was still waiting for responses back from the feelers I had put out to the owners of a few reportedly haunted places, and until I was able to populate our production calendar with more interesting investigations, we were stuck continuing our assignment from Penelope: shooting more promotional featurettes about local psychics.

Stephen Hastain opened his door with a nervous wave. "Hi, guys. Eh... make yourselves at home, I suppose. I'm at your disposal."

Graham clapped him on the back. "Don't tell me you're afraid of being on TV."

"I'm not." Stephen's hands shook as he gestured for us to walk ahead of him into his reading room. "Just feeling a tad off today, that's all."

I had been in his shop before but never for a reading. The one and only time he had cast his runes for me, we sat in his kitchen upstairs. That day, he predicted I would soon take a journey, and a month later, we traveled to New Mexico. He had also told me an unseen force was pulling strings and manipulating events in my life. That reading had solidified my belief that Stephen was the real deal, and I was glad he had been included on the list of psychics to film. If he'd been overlooked, I would have lobbied to get him on there.

Today, I surveyed the decor through the eyes of a television producer. Or at least, the way I thought a producer might look at things. The walls had been painted a very pale shade of yellow and hung with large tapestries. Each of the wall hangings displayed various runic alphabets on rich backgrounds of maroon, forest green, ocean blue, and black. Stephen had taken a minimalist approach to furnishing the space, leaving most of the floor open apart from a round wooden table and a hodgepodge selection of mismatched dining chairs. In the center of the table, eight small velvet bags waited atop a black and silver cloth.

I slung my bag over the back of one of the chairs and took a seat. "Where's Fang? I figured he'd beat me to work since he lives here and all."

"Oh, Fang moved out." Stephen rubbed the back of his neck and checked out the front window. "He's living in that new apartment complex over by the gas station."

"Really? I figured those would be pretty expensive."

"They are. He's subletting a room." The rune caster shuddered. "Ugh, roommates are the worst. Why'd'ya think I live in that kip upstairs? The rent everywhere else in this town is outrageous."

"Well, not our house." Graham grinned. "But only because I like renting to weirdos with no money."

"Hey." I lifted a hand to swat his arm, then relented. "Never mind. I'm both of those things."

"And you're my favorite tenant," he said with a wink.

"Well, if I'd met you before I signed the lease on this place, I could have been one of those weirdos." Stephen smiled weakly. "Just goes to show, the runes don't always lead you right."

As we bantered, the tension in his face eased somewhat, but his eyes kept darting to the little sacks in the middle of the table. Each of the eight was tied with a different colored string corresponding to the runes it contained. I wondered which set he would be using for the demonstration today.

Yuri arrived promptly on time with our new production assistant and a cart full of gear in tow. Fang immediately got down on his hands and knees to check beneath the table.

"Where's Striker?" he asked.

"Her particular set of skills isn't required for a shoot like this," I said.

"Oh." Fang stood, disappointment all over his face. "I saw her in Elizabeth's episode, so I thought she'd be here. I wanted to show her something."

A warm feeling spread through my chest at the memory of that day. "That's because Elizabeth said, and I quote: 'Only way I'm doin' this stupid thing is if the little puff sits in my lap.'"

"I'd say the same if I wasn't so allergic to cats," Stephen said. "It's bad enough Mac always shows up with a sweater made out of fur."

"If you're so allergic, how come every time you visit Graham's studio you feed her half a bag of treats?" I teased.

He looked stunned. "You mean we don't have to give the little queen everything she wants? I honestly didn't know I had a choice."

"What did you want to show Striker?" I asked Fang.

The young production assistant bounded across the room and dug his cell phone out of his pocket. He held it up in front of me, displaying a photo of a thin black cat with startlingly large green eyes. The cat's ears were both notched and scarred in several places, and his long fur was dirty and matted.

"This is Shadow. He's a lot friendlier than he looks," Fang said happily.

"Congratulations! You're now the proud property of a cat." I tested out a few ways to tactfully ask why Shadow looked so unhealthy, finally settling on, "Did you get him from the animal shelter?"

"No, he just sort of showed up the day I moved into my new place. He's a real loudmouth—he sat outside my bedroom window and shouted at me until I opened it and let him in." Fang smiled down at the photo with paternal pride. "He comes in whenever he wants now, and he eats the food I leave on the floor. He won't let me pick him up yet, though. Do you think he ever will?"

"Maybe. Striker is my first and only cat, so I'm not really an expert. I hope he does."

"Me too. I'm going home to visit my parents next week, but when I get back, I want to take him to the vet and make sure he's healthy."

My heart swelled. I wanted to hug this kid. He had gone from fleecing tourists to literally opening his home to an animal in need.

His eyes darted to the door, and he lowered his voice. "Don't say anything, okay? I'm not supposed to have pets."

I mimed zipping my lips. "Your secret's safe with me."

"Mac?" Yuri called. "Would you help bring in the rest of the gear? I want to show Fang how to rig up the lighting."

"Sure thing." I gave in to my earlier urge and gave Fang a quick sideways hug. "Give that to Shadow for me, when you can."

The men started setting up the lights, and I pulled the empty cart back out to the street. There, parked against the curb, was something I had never expected to get to see again: a black cargo van with a smashed-in front fender and Kit behind the wheel.

I opened the passenger door and climbed inside. "You got it running again!"

The *Soul Searchers* van had taken a lot of damage when it crashed into a tree the month before. Kit had been driving, and the official accident record stated that she lost control of the vehicle. But I maintained that something else had taken over, yanking us toward it when it sensed we were near.

"I can't take any credit. Dad loaned it to the auto shop class at the high school, and they did all the repairs." She ran her hands down the sides of the steering wheel. "Man, I missed driving this thing. I wish I could've taken it to LA with me."

"But then what would your limo do all day?" I joked.

Her only answer was an epic eye roll.

I nudged her knee with my foot. "So are you helping with the shoot or just chauffeuring the crew?"

"Is there even room for me anymore?"

"Of course, doofus. You can help me carry this stuff in, for one."

Together, we loaded the remaining equipment cases onto Fang's handcart. Kit steered it up the path to Stephen's shop, grunting a grudging approval at the easy way the little four-wheeled contraption handled.

We set up to shoot in a three-camera interview style just like the one we had used with Alexi at the Ace of Cups. Fang was a fast learner, and he quickly had Stephen mic'd and ready to go. Kit pitched in, mounting cameras and positioning lights, but her efforts didn't last long.

When Noah arrived with an apology for letting his bartending shift run long, he moved through the room, changing Kit's camera settings and rearranging the tripods.

"Sorry," he said, ducking his head. "I'm just used to things being a certain way. I'm sure you're the same way on your shoots."

"No problem." Kit pulled her lips into a thin smile that disappeared the second she turned her back on him. She stalked past me toward the back corner, and I recognized a muttered Russian obscenity as she passed.

Before long, we were filming what felt like a fairly casual conversation between Yuri and Stephen, who sat on opposite sides of the large round table. The rest of us sat around the room, spectators and, in Graham's case, silent cheering section for his surprisingly camera-shy friend. But the longer the two men talked, the more comfortable Stephen became, and soon he was relating his rune-casting history with a genuine smile.

That is, until Yuri asked if he would mind doing a reading for the camera. At that, Stephen's face paled.

"Eh, sure." He reached a shaking hand across the table toward the sacks of runes, then stopped himself. "Whoops. Why don't you go ahead and pick a bag? Any of them that calls to you."

If Yuri noticed Stephen's sudden nervousness, he didn't acknowledge it. He smiled warmly and leaned forward to pluck out the bag tied with a thin piece of red string.

"Elder Futhark," Stephen murmured. "Good choice. Any questions you want answered? Anything on your mind, maybe?"

Yuri cupped his chin in his hand. "Nothing in particular. Could you look ahead? Tell me what the future might hold?"

With zero pomp or pageantry, Stephen tossed the bag of runes onto the table. Three small wooden rectangles shot out and flew in every direction. The first skidded to a gentle stop in front of Yuri. The second skittered off the edge of the table and landed a few inches away from my shoe; the symbol resembled a backward *Z*. The third bounced off a nick in the table's battered surface and reversed course, coming to a halt beside Stephen's hand.

Yuri bent over his rune and adjusted his glasses. "Interesting. It looks like a capital *F* with the horizontal prongs pointing downward. What does it mean?"

Stephen didn't answer. He stared down at the rune beside him. His clammy palms left his curly hair damp and stringy when he pushed his clawed hands backward through his scalp, and a few beads of sweat broke out along his forehead.

Graham moved across the room, heedless of the cameras. "Stephen, are you okay?"

"No." Stephen's voice was dry and raspy.

I hopped out of my seat and grabbed a glass of water. Stephen accepted it gratefully but had to use both hands to bring it to his lips. As he drank, I examined the rune in front of him.

It was composed of one long vertical line with two shorter lines that jutted off to the right at opposing angles. The smaller lines formed a triangle about half as tall as the primary line and were perfectly centered on it, like a sideways drawing of a witch's hat.

I had seen this one before, several times.

It had been burned inside Camila's jewelry box and painted on Horace's ceiling.

This was the third rune of the word Stephen had identified as a spiritual invitation. But for whatever reason, this single symbol seemed to have knocked the air out of him even more than seeing the full word had done to me in New Mexico.

"What is it?" I asked.

"*Thurisaz*," he whispered. "Always, always *thurisaz*."

His voice quavered, as though he was about to start crying. I shot a worried look in Yuri's direction.

"Noah, let's cut the cameras," Yuri said quietly.

"I'm sorry." Stephen stood and gripped the back of his chair for support. "I think I need to go lie down."

"We'll take you upstairs." Graham took hold of Stephen's arm and nodded me for to take the rune caster's other side.

Together, we supported Stephen up the narrow staircase to his apartment. I expected him to feel better once we were away from the cameras, but his whole body shook as he lowered himself onto the sofa in his living room. With a deep, guttural sigh, he cradled his head in his hands.

"You don't look so good," Graham told him, worry etched across his narrow face. "Maybe we should take you to the hospital."

"I'll be fine. It's not my body." Stephen lifted his head and locked eyes with me. "Mac knows what I mean."

"I do?" I stared at him, puzzled. It took me several moments to realize what he was talking about. "Oh. You're out of bent spoons."

Disappointingly, neither of them laughed. They just watched me, saying nothing.

"You know," I said. "Spoon theory?"

Graham shook his head. "I don't get it. Is this some sort of coffee analogy? Because I can go grab a to-go mug from the Ace of Cups if that's what you think Stephen needs."

"No, it's a chronic illness thing. My dad started talking about it after he developed his heart condition. A spoon is like… a unit of energy. Dad said his younger self was spoiled with unlimited spoons. He could spend weeks in the hot desert on a dig, stay up all night with the other grad students, and hit the ground running the next day. But when he got older and his condition got worse, he started every day with fewer spoons. He had to be smart about how he spent them—less time in the field, more time in the classroom." I shrugged. "Stephen looks as wrecked as my dad did when he overspent his spoons."

Stephen chuckled weakly. "And my spoons are bent because you think I'm psychic. Cute."

I frowned down at him and crossed my arms. "Well, isn't that what you meant? You burned through all your psychic energy, and now you're beat, right?"

"I keep telling you. I don't have that kind of gift. The power doesn't come from inside me—it comes from the runes. I just read them." He collapsed back against the cushions and flung an arm over his eyes. "But can't a road feel tired when too many feet have trod upon it?"

I perched on the arm of his couch and considered his words. He always said anyone could read runes or cards or palms, as long as they were open enough to what the instruments were telling them. But as far as I was concerned, there was no difference between what he did and what I did. Not really. For whatever reason, by accident or by design, I was able to be more open to what the spirits around us were trying to say.

Now seemed like the wrong moment to try to argue the point, however.

"Have you been doing a ton of readings lately?" Graham asked.

Stephen dropped his arm from his face. "No more than usual. Business has been good, but last night wasn't anything special. It wasn't until this morning that..." He trailed off, face draining once more.

I touched his shoulder. "It's okay. Tell us about it."

"I read my own runes every morning when I wake up. Just to check in with myself, prepare for the day ahead. But today..." He shuddered. "Today, I read them four times. No matter which set I used, it gave me the same message. *Thurisaz.* The blackthorn. Even my curio set kept spitting out that damn seashell."

"What does it mean?"

His brown eyes filled with fear. "Something bad is coming. And I don't mean a poor harvest or a bad investment. The runes don't hammer you over the head about something unless it's really, really important. This… If this were a sound, it'd be a death knell."

I swallowed. "It could be a coincidence."

But I didn't really believe that. And from the way his hands trembled, it was clear Stephen didn't believe it either.

"I'll be all right," he said, stretching out on the couch and pulling a blanket over himself. "I just need a good nap."

Graham and I headed back downstairs, where the *Soul Searchers* crew was loading out our gear. Kit didn't bother trying to help; she marched out to the van with nothing but her keys in her hand and waited, engine idling, for the rest of us to bring out the equipment cases.

"Should we try again another day?" I asked Yuri as he closed the cargo door.

He dusted his hands off on his thick wool coat. "I don't know. We might be able to use what we have and splice in some stock footage of rune casting. I can check with the editing team and let you know. Will Stephen be okay?"

I glanced back up the walkway to his salmon-pink building. "With a few days off, I think so."

"He scared me in there. He looked the way you did at Cambion's Camp last month, just before you fainted."

That wasn't a memory I particularly loved looking back on. I had felt completely drained after that. More evidence, I decided, that Stephen was psychic. When he felt better, I'd tell him so.

"Any word on other bookings?" Yuri asked.

"Still waiting to hear back. Is it usually this slow?"

"It can be. Keep looking. Cast the widest net you can. Let me know if you need help."

He climbed into the van, and he and Kit pulled away. Fang and Noah trudged away up the footpath toward the Ace of Cups. I thought about joining them for a drink, but instead I headed back to Stephen's shop.

Graham was in the bathroom, rinsing out the water pitcher and glasses. Someone—probably him, as it was the considerate thing to do—had already cleaned up the runes, including the one that had landed on the floor by my foot. I leaned over the table, grabbed the red-stringed bag, and dumped it out.

I smiled smugly down at the messy pile of runes. If Stephen was right and just anyone could get the same message out of them, I would have expected *thurisaz* to be resting right on top, but I had to dig to find it. I filed that away in the "can't wait to say I told you so" drawer and sifted through the pile for the other two runes he had drawn during our reading.

It didn't take long to find the one Yuri had described, but once I saw it for myself, I nearly dropped it out of reflex. The strangely tilted capital *F* was the second symbol in Horace's sequence. I stuffed it back into the pile, not wanting to see it anywhere near *thurisaz*. I plucked out the backward *Z* that had flown my way in the reading and turned to the cream-on-crimson tapestry that displayed the Elder Futhark alphabet.

"'*Thurisaz*,'" I murmured when I found Stephen's rune, reading the cramped text aloud. "'The thorn. A warning or a temptation. Tread with care.'"

Yuri's rune was similarly ominous. *Ansuz: watch for the signs around you. Ignoring an unpleasant message will only make things worse.*

I gulped as I searched for mine. After those last two, I wasn't sure I even wanted to see what it meant. Given the way my life had been going lately, it couldn't be good. But as the *ansuz* rune warned, it was better to know.

The backward *Z* was called *eihwaz*. According to the tapestry, it meant: *Change. Transformation. Embracing these will give you the power to deflect unexpected attacks.*

An incredulous laugh burst out of my mouth.

What had I been doing this entire year if not changing? The things I had experienced—all the loss, all the heartbreak—had shattered me. I'd done my best to put myself back together, but I knew not all the pieces were exactly where they had started. My old self wouldn't even recognize the new me.

I had evolved. But right now, I felt more vulnerable than I had in my entire life.

"Everything okay?" Graham asked from the doorway.

"Fine." I shoved all the runes, including *eihwaz*, back into their bag. "Stephen was off today, I think. That reading didn't make any sense."

I should have had more faith in him. Stephen's readings were always dead-on.

CHAPTER TWENTY-SIX

Compared to the trek to New Mexico, the three hours to get to the Cronus County Women's Correctional Center the next morning was a breeze. Guilt weighed on me as I pulled off the freeway; this was something I could have easily done months ago. But like facing the reality of Elizabeth's death, I hadn't been in a hurry to confront Gabrielle's true circumstances.

I parked in front of a wide brick building that could have been a nursing home if it weren't for the tall security fences that ran along the edge of the parking lot. Inmates dressed in orange pants and heavy brown jackets milled around a large shadeless field on the other side of the barrier. Beyond them, the building bent in an *L* and stretched on for quite a ways. Whether it was the guard towers, the razor wire, or just the general aura of the place, an uncomfortable tension squeezed my chest.

The check-in procedure did nothing to calm my nerves. The visitor's form they asked me to fill out reminded me of the patient history forms at hospitals, which I mentally bumped out of the number-one spot on "Mac's Least Favorite Places to Visit" list in favor of this experience. After a metal detector and a full-body pat down, I stashed my phone and purse in a small locker and sat down at my designated table to wait for Gabrielle.

The last time I'd seen her, straight black hair had fallen to her waist, and only a few sprinkles of white had hinted at her age. She'd preferred simple floor-length dresses, as long as they had pockets, and always struck me as someone who had somehow slipped through a portal from a world with a lot more magic and mystery than our own.

The woman who approached the table now had ultrashort gray hair with barely any black left at all. She wore bright orange scrubs, plain black shoes, and no jewelry. Only one thing about her was the same: piercing green eyes that lit up when they met mine.

"They told me you were here, but I didn't believe them," she murmured in her softly accented, melodic voice. "I thought there had been a mistake."

I stood up on shaking legs. "Are we allowed to hug?"

"If you like," she said.

After a moment's hesitation, I stepped forward and pulled her into a quick embrace. Out of instinct, I inhaled, expecting to detect the lingering scent of nag champa. Her skin smelled clean, like Ivory soap, but nothing like her shop.

Nothing like the old Gabrielle.

We broke apart and mirrored each other's movements as we took our seats on opposite sides of the rectangular steel table.

"Your hair," I said. "It's so short."

She ran a hand over her nearly shaved head. "My ends kept splitting, and it was impossible to manage. It's easier this way."

"It looks good on you."

"Thank you. You're looking well. So much like your mother, as always." Gabrielle stared at me, eyes wide with wonder. "How are you?"

Inexplicably, the question triggered a rush of emotion. I

opened my mouth to answer but had to quickly close it again as my eyes filled with tears.

She stayed silent as I cried myself out. It took a few minutes, and when I finally raised my head to look at her, she was sitting calmly with her hands folded on the table in front of her. Her eyes glistened, but I was the only one who actually needed to wipe any tears away.

"I'm sorry," I said at last. "I don't know what that was."

"Don't worry about it. I hear it happens all the time."

I glanced around at the other tables, but nobody else was crying. Maybe they were here often enough to get used to it.

"Do your other visitors bawl like babies when they walk in the door?"

"I haven't had any," she said matter-of-factly.

"Oh." The guilt I'd felt on the drive up here roared back to life. "I didn't know."

She shrugged. "My attorney is here regularly, which is more than some can say."

"How's that going?"

"We have reached an agreement. I will plead guilty to two counts of involuntary manslaughter, in addition to conspiracy to commit a felony."

"So there won't be a trial after all?"

"No."

Relief flooded through me. Deputy Wallace had predicted this outcome, but I'd still envisioned Gabrielle's fate being decided by a jury. I had been terrified by the prospect of having to testify against her. Not only had I found the bodies of both her accidental victims, but I had been the one to stumble onto the stash of secret audio recordings that incriminated her in a multistate burglary scheme. I'd given the details of those discoveries to the authorities multiple times but never from a witness stand.

And never in front of my mother's oldest friend herself.

"Have they already sentenced you?" I asked.

"We have agreed to five years in prison, with the possibility of parole after three."

"Wow." My mind raced. "So you could be back home in just a few years? What will you do? Donn's Hill is changing a lot, but I can help you look for a place to reopen the store—"

She held up a hand to cut me off. Her eyes were cast downward onto the scratched-up table. "Mackenzie, I can't return to Donn's Hill when I'm released."

"What? Why not?"

"Can you really not understand why?" Her voice broke, and her shoulders shook gently. "How can I rejoin that community after all the damage I have done? Penelope has been more generous to me than I deserve. Would I repay her kindness by forcing her to see my face on a daily basis? No. I love Donn's Hill, but part of my penance must be that I can never go back."

I could hardly speak around the lump in my throat, but I managed to choke out, "Where will you go?"

"I don't know. I have a long time to decide. By then, it might be time to go home, back to Spain. Who knows?"

Tears spilled down my cheeks once more. I felt so naive. Of course she wouldn't come back. What was she supposed to do, buy the Oracle Inn back from Penelope so she could turn it into a bookstore and séance room again? And five years was a long time. Even more could change between now and when she got out of prison.

Time didn't stop just because she was gone.

"I'm so sorry," I said.

I didn't specify what I was apologizing for. Not helping cover up for her crimes? Maybe a little bit. But mostly I was sorry I hadn't moved to Donn's Hill sooner, that my mother hadn't lived long enough to help Gabrielle when she needed it, and that there was absolutely nothing I could do to turn back the clock and change any of this.

She smiled and squeezed my hand. "You have nothing to be sorry for. And I'm so happy you're here. Please tell me everything that's going on in your life. How is Striker?"

"Spoiled rotten, especially since we got back from New Mexico. Graham feels guilty for taking her on such a long car ride, so he's been giving her even more treats than usual."

"I wish they would allow animal visitors," she said wistfully. "I would love to see her sweet face."

I reached into my pocket for my phone before remembering it was locked up outside the visiting room. "I'll mail you some photos," I promised.

"I would like that. And how was the trip? Did you get to show Graham where you grew up?"

"I did. In some ways, it was really nice. But it was also…" I sighed, unable to find a word to describe all the ways things had gone off the rails.

"I imagine it was difficult to relive those memories."

"No, that's not it. Things just felt… *wrong* there. Last month, I saw signs in everything, and all of them pointed me back home. I convinced myself that going to New Mexico would let me find the answers to all my questions. I thought I could figure out who Horace really is and get strong enough to beat him at his own game. And now I know who he is, but I'm no closer to actually finding him. And—"

"Wait." Gabrielle held up her hands to stop me from speaking. "You know who he is? This psychic who pretended he died in my attic?"

I nodded. "His real name is Anson Monroe."

"Anson Monroe? Not that old Seattle mystic."

"You knew him? My mom was working with him to find a way to walk the astral plane."

"Yes, she told me all about it. He had several students but wasn't able to help any of them cross over. She was bitterly disappointed. Apparently, he never managed to do it himself but thought a younger person could be more successful."

"Well, did you know he moved to New Mexico after that?" A hard lump formed in my throat, and I had to work to push the next words around it. "Or that he killed her?"

Gabrielle looked as stunned as if I had just slapped her across the face. "What? How?"

"The same way he killed Elizabeth Monk and an astronomer named Camila Aster: by luring her out into the cold and leaving her there to die."

She stared at me for several silent seconds before slowly shaking her head. "I don't believe it. Upset as your mother was that she couldn't reach the astral plane, she spoke glowingly of Anson. He was like a father to her. What you're describing—multiple murders—that's a serial killer. I don't think Anson would be capable of something like that."

"But you never even met him," I argued.

"True." A troubled look crossed her face. "And I suppose we don't even know what we're capable of doing until the moment arrives."

I said nothing. We had strayed dangerously close to a truth that I had to carefully avoid acknowledging whenever I thought of or talked to Gabrielle: technically, she was a killer. We sat in an uncomfortable silence for a few minutes before she found another subject.

"Have you seen him again?" she asked. "Anson or Horace or whoever he is?"

"No." I touched my necklace. "Either because he can't get through my protections or because he hasn't been trying. He's powerful. I didn't really appreciate how powerful until I started astral projecting. He can travel through the astral plane so easily, but I can't even leave my own…" I trailed off, alarmed by the sudden look of horror on Gabrielle's face. "What?"

"Don't 'what' me." She glanced from side to side and lowered her voice to a near whisper. "How did you do it? For God's sake, tell me you're not using those flying ointments. They're poison, Mackenzie."

"I haven't— Wait. You believe me? That I've done it?"

"If you say you have." She frowned. "Have you?"

After having to explain my experiences and defend my instincts to everyone else, it was so refreshing to be taken at my word that I nearly burst into tears again.

"I did," I whispered, voice cracking. I cleared my throat and told her about my midnight walks with Camila, walks that couldn't extend much past the Primrose House property line. "It's exhilarating. I would do it every night if I could just figure out how. But I feel like I should be able to go farther. Horace did. I mean, I don't know where he was when he was visiting me last month, but I assume he was in New Mexico, and—"

Gabrielle clucked her tongue. "Assumptions can be dangerous under the best of circumstances. In the psychic realm, you can't afford to guess. How far would you say you're able to travel?"

"I don't know." I pictured the three stories of Primrose House and estimated the size of the yard. "A hundred feet?"

"How do you know Horace wasn't that close each time he astral projected to you?"

I stared at her. I'd assumed Horace had arrived in Donn's Hill just before he killed Elizabeth. Was it possible he'd been nearby this whole time? Had he been lurking somewhere in town, waiting for me to leave so he could target Elizabeth while I was gone?

No. That couldn't be right. I would have felt him. I would have sensed—

My blood went cold.

Horace's location hadn't been the only thing I'd made an assumption about. Since Elizabeth's funeral, I had been sure I could feel another psychic's energy. I was positive I could sense someone the way Grey sensed me. My evidence was the way I felt around Stephen: he had so much verve, he was practically magnetic. Whatever his mood, it was contagious. It spread through the air to everyone around him.

But what if that was just charisma? After all, I felt the same way around Kit. When she was laughing, I was laughing.

And here I sat, mere feet from the most powerful medium I had ever known, and I felt... nothing. No waves of psychic energy rolled off Gabrielle. The truth slammed into me with so much force that all the air left my lungs in a single rush, and I had to gasp in a replacement breath.

Horace could be in this room with me right now, and I would never know it.

"Are you all right?" The divot between Gabrielle's eyebrows deepened. "You look pale."

"I'm fine. I just need to think."

My mind raced. Horace had appeared to me three times. Once at the Franklin cabin beside Lake Anam, once in the attic suite at the Oracle Inn, and once in Elizabeth Monk's day spa. He could have been anywhere in The Enclave and reached Elizabeth's shop, and there were plenty of places to hide in and around the inn. But could he have gotten anywhere near the cabin without us knowing?

It was too unlikely. Maybe he hadn't been all the way in New Mexico, but he hadn't been in the same building.

"Okay. Maybe he was closer than I thought. And maybe—" My fingernails scratched the metal tabletop as my hands curled into fists. Anyone I had mentally cleared of being Anson Monroe based on not getting a feeling from them could still secretly be the old psychic. But Gabrielle couldn't help me with that. There was only one thing she might be able to do for me. "Maybe I don't know what name he's wearing around Donn's Hill, if he's even still there. But there's got to be a way to go farther in the astral plane, right? That much I know for sure."

She exhaled loudly through her nose. "Well, there's a reason the lore around flying potions exists. Conventional wisdom, such as it is, says that the living body is like the anchor on a ship at port. It keeps the tide from carrying everything away. You're strong enough to have an anchor chain of one hundred feet. Anson—if he truly is Horace—must be nearing a hundred by now. If he's been studying the craft since he was your age, he's had decades to forge a chain. His would be far, far longer than yours."

"There's got to be a shortcut, though, right? Some way I can catch up?"

"I don't know. None of us, no matter how strong our gifts, can know everything. But I do know this. Everything has a price, and everyone must pay it. I bought my power—my strength—through a lifetime of practice. Time is the most valuable currency, even more than natural talent." Her eyes darkened. "If you want to find a shorter path, I fear the price would be very, very high. And I don't think you would be willing to pay it."

A buzzer sounded, jolting me half out of my seat.

"Time's up," one of the guards called.

Gabrielle stood. "Thank you so much for coming. It means the world to me."

"I'm really glad we could talk. Can I come visit again?"

"I hope you will."

We kept our goodbye short; the looming presence of the prison guards made loitering feel like a terrible idea. I watched her walk away from the table with more spring in her step than when she arrived, and I resolved to visit her at least once a month, if not more often.

When I collected my things from the visitor lockers, a voice mail message from Deputy Wallace waited on my phone. I tapped the button to play it with some trepidation. For all I knew, she was calling to give me a well-deserved lecture about how insensitive I had been the day we cleaned out Elizabeth's shop.

Her message was short. "Will you be home later? I have something for you."

My mind ran through a few possibilities. What did she have? Something of Elizabeth's? Something from the coast where they had spread her ashes? None of those things sounded like something you would give a friend unless you were willing to forgive their jackassery, which gave me the courage to call Wallace before pulling out of the parking lot.

"Hey, I got your message," I said when she answered. "I won't be home for a few hours. Are you working today? I can come down to the station."

"No, I'm off. I'll just meet you at your house."

Excited as I was to see her again, any curiosity about what she was planning to bring me was quickly swept away by the things Gabrielle and I had talked about. As I drove, I tapped a thumb impatiently against the steering wheel. I wanted to be home, sitting with a notepad on my turret window seat. I desperately needed to be able to draw a big fat vertical line down the middle of a sheet of paper and organize my thoughts into what I knew for sure versus what I could only assume to be true.

Gabrielle was right. It wasn't safe to operate on assumptions. But until I could be home with a pencil in hand, I would have to do my best with my easily distracted brain. I thought about what I knew as I headed back to Donn's Hill.

First, I had Horace's real name: Anson Monroe. I didn't know how far he could travel or how he managed to erase sixty years from his face in the astral plane, but if I had more time to practice, I was sure I would be able to do both things too.

I was also certain Horace was behind the jewelry box Camila found in the desert. There was absolutely no way a box could look identical to the one Horace had sent me to find *and* have runes matching the ones on his ceiling. That was an assumption I was willing to make.

Thanks to Stephen, I also knew what those runes meant. *Invitation.* I felt—but wasn't sure—that Horace had done something on a level I hadn't even known was possible to make those runes attract his victims. Whether it was luring Camila out of a yurt, drawing Elizabeth into the woods, or getting my mother to stop her car on the side of a desert highway, he had figured out a way to work some kind of twisted magic in the waking world.

Six months before, I would have called it impossible. Magic was for storybooks. Even Gabrielle said witches were just misunderstood psychics. But everything we did—speaking to the dead, divining the future, walking through dreams—would all be dismissed as pure nonsense by the Mackenzie Clair who had lived in Salt Lake City.

Yet here I was.

Deputy Wallace's black SUV sat in front of Primrose House when I got home. I parked Graham's Geo and walked around to meet her on the wide covered porch by the front door. I still wasn't used to seeing her out of uniform. Her Levi's, cowboy boots, and Carhartt jacket made her look more like a rancher than a law-woman, and for the first time since I had met her, her black hair fell down her back in loose waves.

I rubbed my arms, which were warm enough in my sweater and light jacket for a brief visit outside but not much else. "Want to come inside for some coffee?"

"No, this won't take long." Wallace leaned back against the porch railing and studied me. Her dark eyes were intent, as though she was trying to see past the concerned expression on my face to something deeper inside me.

"Listen," I said, needing to get my apology out before she found or didn't find whatever she was looking for. "I am so, so sorry for everything I said. That wasn't the time or the place for it. I should have just been there for you and helped you remember your incredible grandmother for the way she lived."

Wallace pursed her lips and nodded slowly. "Yeah. You should have. But I appreciate what you did, sending the oils with your note."

"No problem," I murmured.

We stood in silence. The wind picked up, and a few stubborn leaves drifted downward from the tree beside my turret. I thought about inviting her inside again but decided against it.

"How was the trip?" I asked.

"Hard." She gazed out at the street. "Not my favorite family vacation. But it gave me a lot of time to think, especially about our last conversation."

My stomach twisted itself into a pretzel as I waited for her to continue.

She kept her eyes trained on the falling leaves as she spoke. "You're like a dog with a bone, Mac. When you've got some wild idea in your head, you can't let it go. And most the time, I don't think that's a bad thing. But this obsession you have with Horace isn't healthy." When she turned back to me, her dark eyes had hardened. "He didn't kill my grandma. What happened to her... It was horrible. And for the rest of my life, I'll ask myself what I could have done to prevent it. But you know what'll help? Not thinking about you running around, fixated on some guy who may or may not even exist and thinking he murdered her."

I stared at her, stunned. It sounded like she didn't think Horace was real at all. Did she think I imagined him? Did she think I was delusional?

"So I'm here to help you shake off this obsession." She

reached into her breast pocket, pulled out a folded sheet of white paper, and dropped it into my hand.

I opened it gingerly, half expecting it to be a referral to a mental health specialist. Instead, I found a government form. The lines were grainy, probably from being photocopied one too many times. At the top, capital letters spelled:

CERTIFICATE OF DEATH
STATE OF NEW MEXICO

A few rows down, in the box titled Name of Deceased, was the name that had been dominating my mind since I found his letter to my mother.

MONROE, ANSON

"He's dead?" I whispered. My hand crept up to the necklace around my neck. If he was dead, I didn't need to wear this anymore. I didn't need to be afraid.

Then I saw the date of death.

It was a year and a half after my mother's.

My head snapped up. I narrowed my eyes at Wallace. "Where did you find this? It can't be right."

"I had my partner track it down for me while I was gone. He got it straight from the New Mexico Department of Health. It's real, Mac. Anson Monroe has been dead for almost twenty years."

CHAPTER TWENTY-SEVEN

I clutched Anson Monroe's death certificate in my hands, staring down at the date he died until the frigid autumn air made the joints in my fingers ache. Wallace had long since left, having done what she came here to do. It was clear from the pitying look on her face that she expected this news to force some kind of reckoning within me and make me decide Horace was just a figment of my imagination.

As I trudged up the stairs to my apartment, I checked my memories. Wallace couldn't be right. Horace was very, very real.

True, only one other person said she could see him, and she had been lying. But that didn't mean *I* hadn't actually seen him. And just because nobody else had been with me any of the other times he appeared—

I drew to a halt on the second-floor landing.

She hadn't been in the room while Horace was there, but Elizabeth walked in right after he vanished from her massage room the month before. And she had been able to smell something. She hadn't known what it was, but she hadn't liked it.

That wasn't in my imagination. The memory of Elizabeth

covering her nose at the strange, bitter scent Horace left behind was all the proof I needed.

He was real.

He wasn't Anson Monroe, but he was real.

And Graham had been with me in that basement. He had photos of the strange mix of runes and symbols Horace left behind. So *that* was real.

I sprinted the rest of the way up the stairs and dug out the box of letters from Darlene's house. There, on top of neatly bundled stacks of correspondence, was a slip of paper with an address on it. Graham and I had both assumed the address belonged to Anson Monroe, but if he had been dead for two decades, the house belonged to someone else.

Whoever owned it had to be Horace.

I lifted out the piece of stationery and took a photo of it, then sent the picture to Wallace.

Thanks for looking into Anson for me. It really means a lot, I typed. *I hate to ask, but I need one more favor to put my mind at ease about all this. Are you able to find out who this property in New Mexico belongs to?*

After hitting send, I sat on the floor with my back against my bed frame, clutching my phone in my hands and staring at the screen until my eyes burned.

After what seemed like an eternity, Wallace replied, *I'll try.*

As I moved to put the address back in the box, the matching handwriting on the top letter caught my eye. I pulled out Anson's note to my mother and reread the brief message.

I'd like to pick up our work where we left off—I think we can crack it. You always were my most promising student.

Anson's death certificate had been issued in New Mexico, so he must have followed through on his plans to move there. That would explain why he was able to attend my mother's funeral as well. What were the odds he moved that far without starting to work with my mom on astral projection again?

It didn't seem likely. They had to be working together. And if they were, he could have had something to do with her death.

No, that didn't feel right. I knew I was making another assumption, but I preferred to call it following my gut. The circumstances around my mother's death were too eerily similar to Camila and Elizabeth to not be connected. Horace was the link.

You always were my most promising student.

The letter dropped out of my hands and onto the floor.

My mother wasn't Anson Monroe's only student.

Who else had been learning from him in Seattle and New Mexico? Who else had been trying to unravel the mysteries of astral projection?

Did that person manage to cross over before or after they started calling themselves "Horus"?

Before or after they killed my mother?

The letter tore along the decades-old fold lines as I gripped it. All I had were questions. Every answer took me five steps in the wrong direction.

Horace could be anyone.

He could be anywhere.

The only way to reach him was the way he had reached me: through the astral plane. But even after talking to Gabrielle, I was no closer to figuring out how to get to him in either world.

My phone pinged. Another message from Wallace waited on the screen: *NM property tax office is closed. I'll call again on Monday.*

Monday. Two full days away. And even if she was able to get me a name, what then? Back to looking through phone books and combing through social media, hoping they used their real name on their profile and a Horus beak as their picture or something?

Wallace was right. I was a dog with a bone, and there was no way I could sit on my hands for two days just waiting to find myself at another dead end. No. I might not be able to go to Horace, but that didn't mean I couldn't bring him to me.

Horace wasn't the only psychic who knew how to set a trap.

Two could play at that game.

CHAPTER TWENTY-EIGHT

"Um…" Graham frowned down into the mug I had just handed him. "I appreciate the gesture, but I really shouldn't be drinking coffee this late. Want some Sleepytime tea instead?"

I positioned a hard metal folding chair next to my bed. The sky outside my turret window was dark, and the rest of Primrose House was asleep, but I was keyed up with an electric, nervous energy. Striker stood on my pillow, yellow eyes alert and excited. I felt certain she could sense what I was up to, and I got the feeling she approved.

I flicked the side of Graham's mug. "Drink it. I already had three mugs of Sleepytime, but I need you to stay awake for a while."

"Why?"

"I just need you to watch over me while I'm sleeping." I lifted my hands to my necklace, intending to pull it off over my head.

Graham's hand shot out, pinning the black tourmaline to my chest. "Whoa, what? Why are you taking that off? I thought it was the only thing keeping Horace from just popping in here and harassing you."

"It is. And that's exactly what I want him to do."

"*What*?"

Irritation crept up my back. I didn't have time to explain every single detail of my plan. Now that I knew how to finally get to the bottom of Horace's real identity, I just wanted to get it over with.

Plus… I couldn't wait to get back into the astral plane. I needed to be there in that strangely silent world, working to make myself stronger. Every second I spent on the astral plane was currency, and just like Gabrielle had told me, I needed to pay the price for more power. I finally understood why people put in the time to master a musical instrument or why Graham dedicated so much of himself to his art.

Being a psychic was my calling. Walking the astral plane was my purpose. Once I embraced that truth, I knew it was the only way I could unmask Horace once and for all.

Graham, however, still hadn't even accepted what I could do. That was the first thing I needed to fix if I was going to pull this off.

"Look," I told him. "One of two things is happening. Either I'm just having super vivid dreams about a dead woman I've never even met, which I will admit is entirely possible. Or—and I really, really need you to get on board with this—I'm astral projecting in my sleep."

He opened his mouth to say something, then apparently thought better of it. I waited until his lips closed again to continue.

"If I'm wrong," I went on, "Horace won't be able to do anything to me. He'll just show up, and I'll be sleeping, and you won't even know he's here. The worst he can do is give me screwy nightmares, which I'm pretty sure he was doing to me last month anyway."

"And if you're right?" Graham asked softly. "Can he hurt you then?"

I paused. I had been avoiding asking myself that same question because I couldn't answer it. Camila had been able to touch me, but the "me" that existed in the astral plane didn't have a physical form to harm.

"I don't think so." I bit my lip. "At least, I hope he can't."

"That's not good enough. If you don't know for sure, then it's not safe."

"I don't know *anything* for sure. And I'm sick of it!" My voice rose to a shout. I took a breath and made the effort to lower it again, then retrieved the death certificate Deputy Wallace had given me from my counter. "Anson Monroe is dead. He was my one lead to Horace in the real world. I'm out of options, Graham. Either I get some answers straight from the bird's beak, or I don't get them at all."

His jaw clenched and unclenched over and over as he stared down at Anson Monroe's name. When he eventually met my eyes, a deep crease of worry had formed between his heavy brows. "Does it have to be here? Let's go to Moyard, rent a hotel room. Whatever we have to do to keep him out of our home."

I shook my head. "I don't know why, but I can only astral project from my own bed. And it's not like our house is some super-secret location he doesn't know about. Somebody had to put the first jewelry box back in our house, and I'm betting it was the same guys who stole it out of the garage after that. You don't think they gave him our address or got it from him?"

He said nothing, but I could see the wheels turning behind his glasses. Another rebuttal was inbound.

"I can't stay awake forever," I pointed out. "Either this happens now—on purpose and with you watching over me—or it happens next time I fall asleep."

It was a low tactic, essentially using the same argument I had used against him outside Horace's house. But it had worked then, and it wasn't any less true now.

"Fine." He marched over to my kitchenette, filled a large tumbler with water, and plunked down into the folding chair beside my bed. "But if you so much as snore funny, I'm dumping this on your face to wake you up."

I grimaced and took off my necklace. "Deal."

IF YOU NEED proof the universe has an ironic sense of humor, just try super hard to fall asleep sometime. Really work at it, especially with two weeks' worth of fear and anxiety pumping through your veins. I lay in bed for a good hour, squeezing my eyes shut and telling myself to disconnect from my body. I imagined opening my eyes in the yard like always, except this time I wouldn't even wait for Camila. I was going to run straight back into the house, up the stairs, and here to my apartment so I could be close to Graham. That way, if anything happened, he would know.

I hoped.

For a moment, I thought I felt the familiar pull of sleep, but it was no good. My eyes popped open, and I glared at the sloped ceiling. Beside me, Graham hunched in the folding chair and chewed his thumbnail as he watched me.

"It didn't work," I said. "I'm too excited. I think I need more tea or something."

He didn't respond.

"Hey." I sat up and frowned at him. "Are you okay?"

He still didn't say anything, and his eyes didn't follow me as I rose. They stayed fixed on my pillow.

I looked back, following his eye line, and saw myself asleep in bed. There was something wrong about it, something off-putting. It took me a moment to realize I had never been this close to my own face unless it was reversed by a mirror.

But this wasn't a reflection. I was sitting on top of my own body.

I was astral projecting again.

Well, either that or I was dreaming about astral projecting and sitting on top of myself. But this didn't feel any more like a dream than the last two times had. The world around me was crystal clear, in vivid but real colors, and silent except for the sound of my own voice.

I climbed out of bed and looked back at my body. My eyebrows were drawn together, and my mouth hung slightly open. It wasn't a very flattering expression. Did I always look this concerned and stressed out when I was snoozing away? No wonder I slept like crap most of the time.

Striker curled around the crown of my head, her furry belly perfectly positioned to soak up all the heat escaping out of my body's chimney. But she wasn't sleeping. Her yellow eyes were bright, alert, and focused on my astral form.

"Hey, buzzy bee," I whispered. "Can you hear me?"

She lifted her chin, and though I couldn't hear it, I was certain she had just trilled in response to my question.

Graham glanced at her, then cast his eyes in my direction. He shivered and said something to her that I couldn't hear, but if I had to guess, he was probably asking what she was looking at.

I stared at her. She was clearly still in the waking world; Graham could see and hear her. But she could see and hear me too. Was she astral projecting? How could she do that and still be awake?

Or—and the thought sent a strange chill down my spine—did cats constantly exist in both places? Could they see both the living world and the astral plane in tandem?

Was that what *I* was really doing when I saw a ghost?

Something grazed the side of my arm. I jumped and spun

around, but it was only Camila. She winced apologetically and mouthed, "Sorry."

"It's okay," I told her.

She looked excited to see me again. Her brown eyes glittered like Striker's, and she smiled happily around my apartment. I wondered if this was the first time she had ever been up here. On past nights, I always saw her in the backyard. I wanted to ask her, but there wasn't any time to play our usual pantomime game.

"Hey," I said. "Remember that man I was asking you about? The one with the hat and the red eyes?"

She nodded.

"I'm going to try to get him to come here." I pursed my lips. "I don't think you should be around for his visit. He's dangerous."

Her eyes narrowed, and she considered me for a few moments. Then she planted her feet, crossed her arms, and cocked her head to one side. I was getting pretty good at reading ghostly body language, and her message was clear.

Bring it on.

I shook my head. "I'm not kidding. He's the most powerful psychic I've ever heard of. He can do some impossible things in the waking world, the kind of stuff you can do in here. I have to assume he's capable of even more than that on this plane. Plus, he left that box for you to find. He could be after you. If he gets here and figures out I have it…"

The look on her face made me falter, and I trailed off. Her eyes were growing narrower and narrower, and I realized every word out of my mouth was just making her more determined to stay. She walked toward me, then made a gun out of her fingers and struck a pose like one of Charlie's Angels.

I couldn't help but crack a smile. I glanced at Graham, who was still staring at my sleeping body. He clearly couldn't see my astral form. It might be nice to have someone around who could —besides Striker anyway.

"Okay, fine," I said. "But you have to hide. Do your disappearing act, okay?"

She gave me a double thumbs-up, then walked over to my kitchen cupboards, placed her hands on one of the doors, and slowly faded out of sight.

"Great," I muttered. "There's a ghost in my cabinet. Definitely not going to be thinking about that every time I need to grab a plate for the rest of my life."

With Camila safely secreted away, I prepared myself to do something I never imagined trying to do on purpose. Striker hopped off my pillow and scampered to my side, winding between my legs. Her presence bolstered my confidence. With her and Camila on my side, it would be three against one when Horace got here. I liked our odds.

I took a deep breath, centering myself the same way I would if I were back in the waking world and about to call to a spirit during a séance. Then, raising my voice as loud as I could manage, I shouted, "Horace!"

I pushed his name outward with all of my strength, forcing it through the walls of Primrose House and far beyond the boundaries that limited my travel in the astral plane. Wherever he was, whoever he was, I needed him to hear me.

"Horace!" I shouted again.

For a few moments, nothing happened.

Then Striker growled. She stood between my feet, fur standing on end as she huffed at something directly behind me.

"Mackenzie," someone purred in my ear. "I've been looking for you everywhere."

Bile rose in my throat at the sound of his voice. It took real effort to force my feet to move, and neither my neck nor my torso agreed to cooperate with my need to look behind myself. Inch by inch, I swiveled on my tiptoes and turned around.

His face was inches from mine. He stood as close to me as

Camila had been when she startled me a few nights before. But the fear I felt now wasn't the heart-stopping jolt of a jump scare. This was deeper, like the dread that immobilizes a pedestrian when they see a truck bearing down on them too quickly to stop.

Horace terrified me to my core.

I had never been so close to him before. Even when he appeared beneath my massage table, a few feet had separated us. I had no choice but to look at his face; it took up my entire field of vision. But despite the lack of distance between us, it was still difficult to make out the details of his features. They were fuzzy. Blurred. Whether it was the way his eyes burned like a pair of brake lights in the darkness or the shadow his flat-topped, brimmed hat cast over his features, I felt like I was only able to discern the parts of him that he was willing to let me see.

What did he really look like? How much of this was him? Was he asleep somewhere in a Zorro costume, or did the cape and the hat just pop into existence whenever he wanted them to?

The crimson glare in his eyes faded, and his face registered genuine surprise. "Look at you, red eyes all aglow. I knew you were powerful, but you seemed so raw the last time we met. So"—he licked his lips—"untamed."

As he spoke, the air around me thickened. It pressed in against me like humidity on a hot day. My arms grew heavy, and even holding my head up became more difficult.

Silently, I swore. I had suspected he would be even more powerful in here, but it would have been nice to be wrong. I was, however, a little relieved I could hear him speak. I'd played enough of Horace's games; we didn't need to add charades to our repertoire.

"I never thought you would find your astral form so quickly," he said. "How did you do it?"

Good question, I thought, happy not to have the answer. The spiritual energy rolling off him was strong enough that I worried I would blurt out anything he wanted me to tell him. Not knowing how I'd reached this point made it easier to play it coy.

"You have your secrets," I said. "I have mine."

"So I see. Well, the jig is up, I suppose. There's no more point pretending to be a ghost."

"No," I agreed. "So why don't you take off that costume?"

He chuckled, and his cape blinked out of existence. He ran his fingertip along the brim of his hat. "You'll forgive me for keeping this. I'm rather fond of it."

I tried and failed to keep the awe off my face. He really could change his appearance in here. He could literally be anyone, look like anything. Meanwhile, I stood in the same charcoal jeans and Pink Floyd T-shirt I had been wearing when I visited Gabrielle at the prison that morning.

Would I ever get to his level?

"Thank you for inviting me into your lovely home." His lips twisted into a judgmental sneer as he gazed around my apartment. When his red eyes landed on Graham, they lit up with interest. "And who is this, watching over your sleeping body so sweetly?"

Graham's name nearly flew out of my mouth. I swallowed it back just before it left my lips. The air grew heavier by the moment, and I was already starting to feel exhausted. This conversation was burning through my energy way faster than my chats with Camila did, and I had a sneaking suspicion he was doing that on purpose. Would I run out of spiritual stamina at some point? What would happen then? Would I wake up?

Would I die?

I'd rather not find out. But there were several things—one in particular—I did need to know. I had to figure out as much as I could about his real identity as fast as possible.

"How old are you?" I asked. "You're clearly way better than me at this. How many years did it take you to get so strong?"

"Ah, I see." He strode across the room and leaned against the wall beside my bathroom door. His pose was casual, with one bent leg propping him up against the plaster. "You want a teacher."

"I just want to know how you travel so far." I decided it might be worth showing one of the proverbial cards in my hand, just to get him to show me a little more of his. "Is it the runes? *Lathu*?"

That earned me a raised eyebrow. "How do you know about that?"

"I know things," I hedged.

He considered me for a moment before a strange smile spread over his face. He shook his head ruefully. "You kept the box, didn't you?"

My heart leapt into my throat, and my poker face slipped. How did he already know about Camila?

"I should have known," he said. "That's where you're getting the energy to walk the astral plane. I thought it burned up with Cyrus and Shawn."

Cyrus and Shawn?

The guys in the van, I realized.

I had been right; they were working for him. And he wasn't talking about the box I'd found in New Mexico. He meant the jewelry box he left for me to find in the woods the month before. His original assumption had been right—that box did go up in flames—and I could only hope the sudden stunned expression on my face read as surprise that he had guessed my big secret rather than fear that he might discover Camila.

"Did you keep the rest of it too? Is the Franklin boy here somewhere?" He closed his eyes and seemed to be concentrating on something. When he opened them again, he pushed out his lower lip and nodded approvingly. "I'll admit, Mackenzie. You impress me. First, you find a way to disappear from my sight completely, and now you've managed to hide one of my own vessels from me. But it doesn't matter—I'll find it soon enough."

My mind raced. I couldn't follow everything he was saying, but I knew I needed him to keep talking. I latched on to the one piece of information that made sense to me. "So your goons are who banished Richard Franklin from his cabin for me, huh? I should have thanked them when I had the chance."

Horace scoffed. "They only used the tools I provided them. Not anyone can do what I do. A child couldn't draw my runes with a stick in the mud and expect anything to happen. The symbols themselves are meaningless in the wrong hands. It takes power to create power. My runes—my magic—they work because I will them to."

"But you said I'm powerful," I pressed. "Tell me who you really are. We could meet up in the waking world. You show me how to get stronger, and then we can do like you said. Use my power to make more power."

"Oh, that's exactly what I'm going to do." He pushed himself off the wall and started walking toward me.

"So you'll teach me?"

"What would be the point?" He tilted his head, his lips curled into a sinister smile. "You can only fatten a calf so much before it's fit for slaughter."

My spine stiffened. "So that's your plan? Kill me, the way you killed my mother?" I took another gamble. "The way you killed Anson Monroe?"

He drew to an abrupt halt halfway across the room. His eyes narrowed into thin slits. For a moment, I wondered if he was about to ask me how I knew that name.

Then I was on the floor.

Horace straddled me, the weight of his body pinning me to the braided rug. I hadn't even seen him move, but he had closed the distance between us in the blink of an eye and wrapped his hands around my throat.

I gasped for air. I felt my eyes bulge as panic built up inside me.

"We don't need to breathe, not when we're like this," he hissed into my ear. "But you have to be more careful, Mackenzie. What happens on the astral plane is mirrored in the waking world."

I couldn't move my head, but I could see the bed out of the corner of my eye. Graham stood over my body, holding me in a half-sitting position and shaking me from side to side. The empty water glass rolled silently across the floor toward me.

"Isn't that sweet? I wish you could hear him desperately screaming your name. He's trying so hard, but nothing out there can wake you while you're in here." Horace leaned back from me, and the pressure against my windpipe increased. "He'll be so heartbroken when you die."

I felt myself choking. A strange feeling grew behind my belly button. It was the same sensation I'd noticed when I was trying to leave Primrose House the other night with Camila.

It was the feeling of pulling too far from my body.

As though someone was slowly turning up the volume on a car radio, sound flooded my ears. I could hear everything around me, from the glass rolling along the floor to Graham's panicked shouts.

"Mac! Mac!" he bellowed. "Wake up!"

This is it, I thought. *I hope my parents are waiting for me.*

My eyes slipped closed.

The ambient noise faded away.

The pull from my body weakened.

Then Striker screamed.

Her wild howls sounded like five cats at once. My eyes flew open just as she leapt into view, claws out and tail thrashing. She headed straight for Horace's face, but he slapped her away with one hand as easily as swatting a fly. Her snarls abruptly cut off, but I didn't have the energy to move my head to see where she went.

"I don't have a box handy," Horace said as his second hand rejoined the first at my throat. "But your spirit will stick around here for a few hours at least. There will be plenty of time for me to collect you and the others—"

His words were abruptly cut off as something slammed into him from the kitchen. Horace went flying, straight toward my wardrobe, and passed through it to the hallway outside my apartment.

Camila's face appeared above mine. She looked back at Graham, who was still shaking my unconscious form on the bed. She grabbed my face in both hands, brought her lips so close to my ear that they brushed my skin, sucked in air, and screamed, "Wake up!"

Her voice knocked me out of the astral plane. I sat up, gasping and clutching my neck.

"Mac!" Graham gathered me to him. Then he pushed me away and searched my eyes. Tears poured down his face, and his hands trembled as they gripped my shoulders. "God, I thought I lost you."

"Brrrlllll," Striker trilled from my pillow. She stood and stretched—first her front legs, then her back ones—and twisted her head to lick the back of one of her shoulder blades. When she was finished, she glared at the wardrobe, yellow eyes filled with indignation.

"My necklace," I croaked. For all I knew, Horace was still just on the other side of my apartment wall. I needed to protect myself from him before he came back.

"Here." Graham slipped the cord over my head.

The familiar weight of the black tourmaline against my chest comforted me, but it did nothing to soothe the burning in my throat or the bruises on my ego. Every muscle in my body shivered at how close I had just come to death. I had nearly lost everything… and for what?

I was no closer to learning Horace's real name, and now he knew I could astral project. I had thrown away my one advantage —the element of surprise—for nothing.

No. Not nothing. In the end, he had let a few things slip. And those details were the guide I needed, the picture on the front of the puzzle box.

Now I knew how the pieces were supposed to fit together.

Graham's fingers grazed the sides of my neck as he inspected me. "Your skin's all red. What the hell just happened?"

"Horace tried to kill me." My voice was raw and husky, like I had been screaming along with the lyrics at the world's longest concert. I pulled my knees up to my chest and hugged them to my body. "And he's going to try again."

CHAPTER TWENTY-NINE

I turned Camila's jewelry box over in my hands. I had started thinking of it as hers because I found it in her luggage, but now I knew it belonged to her in a way no piece of property had ever belonged to me. The way Horace talked about coming back for "the others" made me sure of it.

Graham nodded down at the box. "So she's in there right now? Like a genie in a bottle?"

We sat together on the floral couch in his apartment. As soon as I had felt strong enough to walk, I insisted we go somewhere—anywhere—other than the place Horace tried to kill me. Striker assumed her favorite position on my lap, and her claws pierced the skin on my belly again and again as she kneaded me. It was her ritual whenever I was sick or upset, and I never had to heart to tell her to stop.

"I don't think she's trapped *in* it," I said. "I think it's more like how, when I'm astral projecting, my body is my anchor. Somehow, Horace anchored Camila's spirit to this box after it detached from her living body."

He stared at me. "He can do that? How?"

"I think it has something to do with the invitation rune. They must do more than just lure his victims to the box."

"So it's a mousetrap," he said softly. "Only it's both the cheese and the bar that snaps the poor thing's neck."

I shuddered. His analogy was uncomfortably accurate.

"I'm sorry I didn't believe you," he said. "It's not that I don't think you're capable of doing whatever you set your mind to. I just think… Well, I think I didn't want it to be true. It's pretty terrifying to know that when you go to sleep, your spirit is getting up out of your body and running around with ghosts."

That made me laugh. "Sure, when you describe it like that. But it doesn't feel scary when it's happening. I mean, it hasn't before tonight. Mostly, it's just been exciting. Exhilarating. Like being on a roller coaster."

He flashed his dimples. "Just don't turn into some kind of paranormal adrenaline junkie, okay? I like it best when you're in the living world, with me."

Striker hopped off my lap and used her claws to pull herself up to the back of the couch, where she curled into a ball and flopped one paw over her eyes to block out the light from the reading lamp.

"She looks exhausted," Graham said.

I gently pulled one of her ears. "She came to my rescue again, just like the very first night I lived here. She's incredible."

"She's fierce, that's for sure." He ran a hand down her silky back, then frowned. "She was so agitated around that first box, but she doesn't mind this one at all. It must feel different to her."

Kit had theorized the same thing, that Striker could tell Camila's jewelry box was associated with a kinder spirit. But Graham's words resonated differently with me in light of my conversation with Horace.

It must feel different to her.

You've managed to hide one of my own vessels from me.

The box didn't just feel different to Striker. It had felt different to Horace too. He hadn't been able to sense it in my apartment. Why? What was different about this box, other than the spirit anchored to it?

The answer took me longer than it should have to puzzle out, especially given that it was one of the first things I had noticed about this box back when I found it.

"Remember how the box we found at Cambion's Camp had the Seal of Solomon carved into the bottom?"

Graham was more familiar with the symbol than I was, having been commissioned to add the two interlocking triangles that comprised the six-pointed star to a number of different sculptures over the years. He'd also been with me when Kit's girlfriend, Amari, explained the legend behind the symbol, that it was used to trap demons in the ancient world.

He seemed to understand where I was going with my question and reached over to pluck the box from my hands, then flipped it over to check the bottom. "This one doesn't have it."

"Yeah. So what if that was more than just the name of the symbol? What if it was an actual, literal seal?"

Graham frowned and gave the box back to me. "That's a depressing thought. But I don't get why it's not on this one. He had to kill her to trap her, right? Why go to all the trouble of murdering somebody and then just leave the box lying around in the desert for anyone to find?"

"I don't know. Maybe he didn't have the chance to collect her." I thought back to our conversation with Fred Hawkes about how his wife had found Camila just hours after she died. Had Horace been counting on a larger window to collect his prize?

Then I remembered something else Fred had told us that day about their competitor, Arcane Oasis. The motel had been forced to close after people kept disappearing. How many of those tourists had been drawn into the wilderness by a *lathu* rune in a jewelry box? It must have been a fertile hunting ground.

Or maybe Horace wasn't a hunter. Maybe he was a trapper, and the boxes were carefully placed near his victims, easy to collect at his leisure.

That felt the most true, especially given that he hadn't originally come to Donn's Hill himself. He sent his errand boys to collect everything from the Franklin cabin, and they'd been the ones to move the original jewelry box around like a token in a board game. He had confirmed it himself: they were bringing "his" spirits back to him.

The box from Cambion's Camp must have come from his house in New Mexico. That was where he marked them. He had emptied the house of every stick of furniture, except what remained in the basement. He didn't need the two extra beds and the two dressers anymore, not when Cyrus and Shawn were never coming back to use them.

I shivered. Had they worked for him by choice? Lived in his basement of their own free will? Or had he kept them trapped somehow, kenneled like a pair of hunting dogs when they weren't out retrieving his prey?

And why had he been willing to let his lackeys bring one of his trapped spirits to Donn's Hill? Why was he toying with me? What made me different than his other victims?

Why was he killing at all?

I sighed. "Gabrielle tried to warn me about the danger of making assumptions, and I just keep making them anyway. I need to confirm some things or I'll never figure this out."

Graham's face paled. "Not by summoning Horace again."

"No, nothing like that. I need to talk to Camila."

There was no more time for games like twenty questions. I needed to be able to communicate with her as clearly as possible.

I needed to be able to channel her the way Gabrielle channeled spirits at her séances.

But I couldn't.

I gripped the box in my hands, nearly scratching off some of the varnish with my nails as my fingers curled into frustrated claws. I hadn't been able to channel the ghost of the miner at the Ace of Cups, and he had been sitting right in front of me. I wouldn't be able to channel Camila now.

There wasn't any point in even trying.

"Who should we call?" Graham asked.

"Call? For what?"

"For the séance." He pulled his phone out of his pocket. "Do you want nine again, like at the cabin?"

I stared at him. He seemed to have followed my train of thought halfway to the obvious conclusion, but he must have gotten off at a station that still had some optimism left.

When I didn't answer, he frowned. "You need to be able to ask her questions, right? And you haven't been able to hear her on the astral plane, so a séance would be the next best thing... right?"

"It won't work." I glared down at my socks, disgusted by my lack of power. "It never works."

"You're not even going to try?"

"I will. Tomorrow or the next day, I'll astral project again and try to talk to her there."

"You're going back again?" His eyes went wide behind his glasses. "Mac, Horace knows you can do that now. What if he's just waiting for you in there?"

I touched my necklace. "This will protect me."

"How do you know that? You took it off while you were awake, and you put it back on while you were awake. We don't know that it's not just luck that kept him from wandering over to the house while you were astral projecting before, but if he's half as smart as I think he is, he'll be projecting into your apartment every single night, just waiting for you to fall asleep."

The thought sent a shiver down my spine, and my shoulders trembled. Graham was right. It wasn't safe for me to visit Camila anymore, not until I figured out who Horace really was and how I could protect myself from him.

If I wanted to talk to her, I had to do it the old-fashioned way. Gabrielle's way.

"Okay." I slid off the couch and onto the rug, then set Camila's jewelry box in front of me. "But don't call anybody else. This will just be you, me, and Striker. I don't need a huge audience when I fail again."

Graham joined me on the floor and took my hands into his. Striker hopped down off the couch a second later, climbing into my lap and settling into a compact loaf with her paws tucked beneath her chest. They were ready—more ready than I was.

With a deep sigh, I closed my eyes and began to center myself with Elizabeth's measured breathing exercises. I didn't expect anything to happen, but I figured I might as well go through the motions. After all, this was practice. This was putting in the time.

Maybe if I do this for twenty years, I'll finally channel a dead bird or something, I thought bitterly.

A few minutes into calling out half-heartedly with my psychic senses, I already wanted to throw in the towel. I could sit here and burn through all the bent spoons in the world, but it wouldn't make a difference. Camila wouldn't show.

Just as I was on the verge of letting go of Graham's hands, Striker began to purr.

My eyes flew open.

Graham's living room didn't look right. The high-ceilinged room was still cluttered with cast-off furniture that didn't match his personal style, and every surface was covered in unsold vases and statues. But everything outside of our tiny circle was muted by a thin layer of gray mist, like a photograph covered by a sheet of vellum.

The veil, I realized.

An icy bolt of shock shot through my body. I had always thought of the veil as a metaphor, something a psychic could pierce through to the other side and sense the unseen. But as Camila appeared behind Graham and stepped through the mist to stand behind him, I was forced to acknowledge that—as I had been on so many things—I was wrong.

My ghostly friend's thin face was filled with worry. Her eyes glistened with tears as she looked me up and down like she was inspecting me for damage, and her arms were wrapped around her torso in a tight self-hug.

Still stunned to see her standing there at all, it took me a few seconds to get my mouth to move.

"Are you okay?" I finally asked.

She nodded and gestured at me with an impatient hand.

"I'm fine," I said. "Thanks for saving me back there."

Graham twisted, looking behind and above himself. "I can't see her," he complained.

"That's okay. If this works, you'll be able to hear her."

Camila tilted her head and raised one eyebrow.

"Bear with me here," I told her. "I've never done this before, and I'm pretty sure you haven't either. But I've seen it, and I know it's possible. Now that you're here on this side of the veil, I think you can…"

I hesitated, not quite sure how to describe it. At my very first séance, I had witnessed Gabrielle speak for a spirit. The ghost had sat inches from her face, eyes locked on hers. When she spoke, her voice took on a strangely doubled quality, like a musical instrument with two reeds. If I listened closely, I had been able to hear the dead man's voice behind her own.

"You can borrow my voice," I finished.

Camila still looked confused. My shoulders sank a few inches. I hadn't expected to get this far, and now that we were here, neither of us had any clue what to do next. Some psychic I was.

"I, uh…" I cleared my throat and raised my voice. "Camila Aster, if you can, I invite you to speak through me."

That did it.

With no warning, Camila flew forward. Instinctively, I recoiled. She was moving too quickly; she wouldn't be able to stop before she slammed into me.

And she didn't.

She collided with me.

Then, after a pause that lasted less than a breath, she possessed me.

My skin tingled as Camila passed through it, and I felt suddenly cold. My stomach twisted as her energy connected with my gut, and my lungs compressed. There wasn't enough room inside them for her *and* for air. I gasped, scratching at my throat, and my eyes watered.

Graham leapt to his feet. "Mac! Are you okay?"

I shook my head. No, I wasn't okay.

I was drowning.

I was dying.

Then, as suddenly as the pain had begun, it stopped. I could no longer *feel* her spirit inside of me—not the way I had a moment before—but I knew she was there. I sat, stunned into motionlessness for a moment. When I had seen Gabrielle channel a ghost, it didn't seem like he had literally inhabited her body. I didn't know if the difference was because of my lack of experience or what, but if I'd known it would be like this, I wouldn't have signed up for it.

When my body finally let me move again, I straightened my spine and took a long, deep breath, savoring the sweet feeling of oxygen in my lungs.

"Sorry," I heard myself say.

I clapped a hand over my mouth. Graham hovered over me, looking unsure.

"Mac?" he asked.

"Yes," I said at the same time a slightly higher voice said, "No."

He backed away from me, eyes bulging.

"It's okay," I said. My voice sounded strangely flat without Camila's ringing behind it. "I didn't expect it to feel like this, but I'm fine. Camila is here. You can sit back down."

"Brrrllll," Striker agreed, still purring loudly and steadily.

Graham's legs shook as he lowered himself to the ground. "Should I talk to her?" he whispered.

I blinked. I was the one with the questions, but it did feel a little strange to ask them of myself.

"If you want," I said.

"I don't know what to say."

"It's okay." I cleared my throat again. "I'll do it."

It took me a few moments to gather my thoughts. If I let myself worry about what was happening right now, everything scattered. But the reality of it kept barging into my mind, over and over.

Would the Mackenzie Clair who had arrived in Donn's Hill in the back of a pickup truck have believed this if she saw it? Would the woman who had been terrified beyond words by her first encounter with a poltergeist have been capable of doing something like this?

No way.

That Mackenzie was still deep inside me. She still made up the core of my being. But over the last seven months, I had been growing. Without even noticing, I'd been bulking up. And now, suddenly, I had the psychic power to channel a spirit.

The suddenness of it bothered me. I couldn't focus on it,

though. I had no idea how long I could maintain this, and there was just too much I needed to know.

I took another deep breath. "Okay, Camila. Fill me in. What happened to you on your trip to New Mexico?"

The answer came from my own mouth in double timbre. "Thank goodness you can actually hear me! Do you know how hard this would be to act out?"

Even though we were talking in such a weird way, she still managed to make me laugh. Between that and the stunned expression on Graham's face, I struggled to focus on her half of my voice. I closed my eyes, tried to pretend we were just chatting over the phone, and concentrated. I wasn't sure if she always had this much to say or if she was just excited to finally be heard, but her words flowed in a steady rush.

"I was down there to check out the Very Large Array. You know, the one SETI uses? It's been on my bucket list forever—holy crap, I just realized I kicked the bucket while I was checking something off my bucket list. How unfair is that? And I didn't even get to see the VLA, because the first night I was there, I walked out a little ways to do some stargazing, and I got this random urge to walk down by the river even though I'm honestly terrified of drowning. Then, a little before the river's edge, I got another wacky urge that I should start digging, and I listened to it because I was sure—totally, completely positive—the aliens left me a message buried in the ground. When I found the little wooden box, I freaked out. Then I blacked out.

"Next thing I knew, I was standing over myself, looking down at my own body. I was pretty close to my yurt, so I think I must have tried to crawl back or something. Then I felt this weird sensation. You know the way water looks when it drains out of the tub? It was like that, only it was *me*, and I was draining into the little box."

My mouth stopped moving, and I shifted uneasily. The pulling sensation she was describing reminded me a little too much of the way I felt when sleep—or rather, the astral plane—tugged at me in the days after Elizabeth's funeral.

"Are you... okay with all this?" Graham asked. "You sound way more cheerful than I think I'd be about it."

A wave of cold washed over my body. Camila's sorrow over the loss of her own life rushed into me like a crashing wave, and I had to gulp back tears.

"Of course I'm not okay," she said with my voice. "I'm dead. But what can I do about it? Nothing. And don't get me wrong, I was mad at first. Furious, actually. I was stuck at the yurt resort, alone, watching the dude who runs the place pack my stuff wrong, watching him try to find a place to send it back to. I tried to leave him a note to tell him just to burn it all, but I couldn't figure out how to pick up a pen."

"There's no one who would want it?" I asked.

Her answering "nope" was terse and clipped, and I didn't press the subject.

"We'll tell him," Graham promised. "I don't know if he'll believe us, but we'll try."

"Thanks," she said. "Being a ghost isn't all it's cracked up to be. I kind of get why the old lady haunting my laundry room is so pissed all the time, but I'm trying to make the most of it."

I wrenched control of my voice back from her. "Wait, what old lady?"

"Back in Gainesville, every time I went downstairs to do the laundry, I could feel eyes in the back of my head. When I turned around, nobody was there. But then, a few months after I moved in, when I looked over my shoulder, I saw a woman standing there. Just standing. She watched me do my laundry with this mean look on her face, like she hated the way I was measuring the detergent. I asked the other tenants about her, and one of them told me the building is supposed to be haunted by the old lady who originally built the house. I guess she's mad they turned it into apartments or something."

She said it so matter-of-factly, but her words took the mental puzzle I'd been working on and rotated it around. Suddenly, the picture made so much more sense.

Camila was a psychic.

Horace wasn't just sprinkling his jewelry boxes everywhere he could. He was targeting psychics, and he laid his traps where they were most likely to be. That's why so many people disappeared from Arcane Oasis. And once they shut down, he moved on to other out-of-the-way motels that appealed to those adventurous souls with eclectic tastes.

My mind raced, trying to process this new information and snap the pieces together as fast as I could. If he was targeting psychics, Donn's Hill was certainly a fertile hunting ground. Did he know Elizabeth was an Empath? Had he gone after her specifically, or had he cast a wide net and happened to catch her?

Of course he knew she was an Empath, I realized with horror. *You advertised it around the country.*

Our videos. We might as well have sent him an embossed invitation with a list of names and cordially invited him to come pick off every intuitive in town. He must have seen Elizabeth's video and come to add her to his collection. He only knew she existed because of us.

She was dead because of me.

The guilt came swiftly, settling over me like a heavy cloak and tightening around me like a vise. Blackness closed in at the edges of my vision. My fingernails clawed into my knees through my jeans.

Then, just as I thought I was about to faint, a sudden vision flared into my mind. I saw Stephen sitting at his rune-reading table, surrounded by cameras. We had made a featurette of him too.

And it was set to air on Monday.

"I have to tell Yuri," I gasped. "We have to pull Stephen's video."

I was halfway to my feet when Camila yanked me back to the ground with my own muscles.

"Hey, what about me?" her high voice echoed behind my own. "You promised you'd help me break free, remember? I don't want to be stuck here forever."

She was right. I had told her I'd figure out a way to help her move beyond the boundaries of Primrose House.

"Do you even know how to do that?" Graham asked me.

I stared down at her jewelry box for a few seconds, then answered his question in a flat, hollow tone. "I do. I've seen it happen. You were there."

To Camila, I said, "If I'm right, this is a one-way street. Are you sure you're ready to move on?"

The responding laughter was quick and harsh. It wasn't a sound I'd ever heard come out of my mouth before, and from the way Graham cringed away from me, I could tell he wasn't used to it either.

"Okay," I said. "Silly question."

At that moment, my spirit reached its limit. My vision fuzzed, and a wave of nausea rocked me. I reached out a hand and steadied myself by gripping the couch beside me. Bile welled up my throat, and I thought I might be about to throw up.

If I had been in full control of my own body, I would have grabbed the nearest concave-shaped thing to me and bent over it. But my unexpected copilot had other ideas, and she tipped my head backward.

Then, mouth pointed straight up at the ceiling, I *did* throw up. Only it wasn't vomit that rocketed upward; it was Camila's spiritual energy. The gray mist around us lifted, and I collapsed onto my back with a noisy sigh.

Graham peeked out from behind his arms, which he had flung over his head in anticipation of something horrible raining down from above. "Are you okay? Is she gone?"

"I think so." My voice sounded normal to my ears—full and slightly high pitched, not musical but not disagreeable. I laughed at how good it felt to speak as just one person. "Yes. It's just me now."

Striker stood and trotted up my chest to my face. Her little pink tongue darted out once to lick my forehead. Then she walked over to the kitty bowl Graham kept by his kitchenette, nudged it with her nose, and yowled.

I pushed myself back up into a sitting position, arms shaking. "You too, huh? That really took it out of me."

My stomach growled, but I didn't feel right taking care of my own needs until Camila was free.

"Do you have any gasoline?" I asked Graham.

CHAPTER THIRTY

Yuri didn't seem to mind at all that I called him in the middle of the night to demand, citing zero tangible evidence, that he stop ScreamTV from airing Stephen's featurette. He promised to do everything he could as soon as their offices opened.

"You're sure we're not too late?" I asked.

"Positive," he assured me. "I will call you back in the morning and let you know how it goes."

Now, as the first light of day painted the sky a rosy gold, Graham and I stood in the same place I always met Camila in my dreams: halfway down the walk from Primrose House to the garage. Her jewelry box rested on the pavement in a small metal pan and was covered with a thin layer of charcoal lighter fluid. The latter had been Graham's idea; he assured me it would burn just as well as gasoline without taking off anyone's eyebrows.

"Ready?" he asked.

I turned the box of kitchen matches over in my hands a few times. I was sure this would work; just the month before, I had seen what happened when one of Horace's jewelry boxes burned. The spirit inside had been released, and it quickly faded from the living world, passing through the veil to whatever awaited it beyond.

Camila could do that too. All she needed was a little help from me.

But was I ready?

Could I do it?

The other ghosts I'd banished had been strangers to me. I hadn't known them. I hadn't laughed with them. I couldn't call them friends. This was different in every possible way.

Tears stung my eyes as I stared down at the prison containing Camila's spirit. Logically, I knew what I had to do. But my heart ached, raw from a year of loss and pain and far too many goodbyes.

At least in those cases, the final decision had been left up to fate, not to me. Now, as I stood above my friend, the choice was literally in my hands.

What if I kept her here? a tiny voice inside me asked. *Just for a while?*

The thought sickened me, but I found myself considering the idea nonetheless. How terrible of an existence was it, really, being anchored to the astral plane? Was it painful? Could she find enough happiness to make it worthwhile?

Then I saw Horace's face again, the way his lips twisted into a gruesome grin while he curled his hands around my neck. I heard the echo of his voice as he mused about coming back to fetch me into one of his little boxes. I shivered. I wouldn't choose that existence for myself.

Bottom line: Camila wanted to be free. She had made her wishes abundantly clear, and letting her go was the only way I could protect her from being scooped up by Horace and added to his twisted collection. Who knew how many spirits he had managed to trap over the years? A hard lump worked its way up my throat as I counted the few victims I could name. Elizabeth Monk. Anson Monroe.

Evelyn Clair.

If he had succeeded tonight, my name would be on that list. He would have trapped me forever, just like the others, and gotten Camila in the bargain.

Bile flooded my mouth. Before I could change my mind, I struck a match and tossed it onto the jewelry box.

Then another.

And another.

The lighter fluid ignited with a sudden burst of yellow flame. The box charred at the edges, and as it burned, Camila's energy tickled my cheek, like fingertips stroking down my skin. I raised my hand to touch hers but found nothing there.

A sob escaped my throat. Was this it? After everything we had gone through together, she was disappearing, just like that?

The box crackled against the cold as it burned. I took a step forward. It couldn't be too late. I wasn't ready. I needed more time to say goodbye.

Graham touched my arm. I stopped moving. I felt, rather than saw, her spirit rising toward the dawn.

Then I felt nothing.

She was gone.

A sudden sorrow welled up inside of me, and as I stared at the horizon, my breath came in shuddering gasps. I had been wrong before: death wasn't a one-time deal. Not for everyone.

Camila Aster had died once in the New Mexico desert and again in the backyard at Primrose House.

And for that second death, I mourned alone.

CHAPTER THIRTY-ONE

It was with a subdued energy that I made breakfast that morning. Graham offered to cook, but I was convinced having something to do with my hands would help prevent any more tears from falling.

It didn't.

My movements felt pointless as I stirred the vegetable hash. My eyes couldn't focus on what my hands were doing. I couldn't see anything in the real world in front of me. I only saw Camila's spirit rising toward the sky, away from the material plane.

Away from me.

It had been the right decision. I knew that. There was no question. It would have been completely selfish to keep her around—in a partial state of being—just because I enjoyed her company. As her friend, the best thing I could do was make sure she could truly move on to a world without pain.

But that didn't stop my heart from breaking.

I blinked back the tears and wiped my nose with the end of my sleeve. "Stop being ridiculous," I muttered to myself as I spooned the veggies onto a pair of plates. "She was dead before you even met her."

I tried to focus on the one scrap of good news I'd gotten so far that day. Yuri had been able to stop Stephen's featurette from airing by telling the network there was a legal issue with some of the footage, and we needed more time to make sure we weren't violating any trademark laws. Fear of a costly lawsuit helped ensure that Stephen's episode wouldn't be seen by anybody anytime soon. That bought me more time to work on the Horace problem, and tomorrow Deputy Wallace would be able to call someone in New Mexico and find out who owned Horace's house.

Tomorrow, we'd have a real lead.

A gust of wind nearly knocked the plates out of my hands as I carried the food out to Graham's garage. The Pixies were singing about mountains on Mars, but the music was turned down low. Graham stood with his back to his workbench, arms folded and wearing his bad-news face as he talked to a sullen-looking Kit.

"I'm sorry," he said. "Reggie signed a lease on your apartment all the way through the spring."

"What about the butler's pantry?" she asked.

"Some friends of mine are staying there another few days—"

"And then it'll be free?" she interrupted.

He shook his head. "No, once they're gone, I've already got another renter lined up to take the space."

I handed him a plate and offered the second one to Kit. She looked at it, hesitated, then picked up the fork.

"What's going on?" I asked as she ate.

"Kit wants to move back in." Graham looked pained. "There's just no room."

"What?" I stared at her. "You don't want to live in LA anymore?"

"It's not like that," she said around a mouthful of hash. She swallowed and continued. "I was just talking to Amari about our production schedule, and there are big chunks throughout the year where we're not filming. And when we are working, it's not like we commute from home to an office every day. We're on location. The show pays for our hotels and stuff, so I convinced Amari we should just live in Donn's Hill whenever we're not traveling."

The tears I had just worked so hard to contain spilled down my face again. I threw my arms around her. "Seriously? This is the best news ever. I'm so happy."

She pushed me away gently. "Well, it *would* be awesome news—if we had somewhere to stay."

"There are those new apartments by the gas station," Graham suggested.

Kit made a face. "Ew. So some big company can be my landlord? No thanks."

I shrugged. "I heard they're really nice. There's a pool and everything."

"Or…" A sly grin curled at the corners of her mouth. "You two could do what I've been telling you to do all freaking year and just move in together."

It wasn't the first time she had suggested this. Ever since Graham and I started dating, Kit had been teasing me about giving up my turret room and moving into his place. On paper, it made sense; his apartment was much bigger than my little studio, I would save money on rent, and we basically lived together already anyway.

But my apartment was special to me. It was the first place I had ever really, truly lived on my own. I had gone from living with my dad to crowded college dormitories, then to a string of apartments with a terrible boyfriend. In spite of its small size, that third-floor room had given me the space I needed to work through a lifetime of baggage. It was where Striker had made it clear that she was adopting me. I never thought I would leave it.

Until now.

This morning, the thought of sleeping in the room where Horace tried to choke me to death held zero appeal.

As casually as I could manage, I glanced at Graham. We had never seriously talked about consolidating apartments. Going from two separate units in the same building felt like less of a gargantuan relationship change than most couples had to deal with at this stage, but it still felt like something that warranted a serious discussion. I didn't want to pressure him into it if it wasn't something he was ready for.

Graham's entire face was aglow. He looked like someone had just handed him a magic wand that solved every problem in the world, and he couldn't wait to start using it.

"What do you think?" he asked. "There's a lot more room for bookshelves in my living room, or we could turn my spare bedroom—I mean, *our* spare bedroom—into a library or an office."

A heavy weight lifted off my shoulders. I pulled him in for a kiss. "I'll move in today."

"I THOUGHT YOU WERE KIDDING," Kit said as she tossed clothes out of my wardrobe and onto my bed an hour later.

"Well, I'm not. You can move in tonight if you want." I dragged my laundry basket over to the turret so I could empty my bookshelves into it. I had been so excited to fill these when I first got here, and now I couldn't wait to drag all my books down to the second floor. It took all my willpower not to get out my laptop and start shopping for new floor-to-ceiling shelves to put in Graham's spare bedroom.

The act of packing was exhilarating. It gave me a sense of freedom and purpose. And knowing I was only carrying things down one flight of stairs erased any of the typical anxiety that accompanied boxing everything up. Striker also didn't appear to have any qualms about moving; she had immediately curled up in the exact center of Graham's bed as though she knew it belonged to her now.

"I'll sleep here tonight for sure." Kit put her hands on her hips and surveyed the space. "The light in here is great. I'll have to ask Amari to ship out my easel."

"What a wonderfully bohemian life you'll be living," I teased. "Traveling the world and spending your off weeks here in the heartland, painting soup cans."

"Or I could moonlight like most good Donn's Hill residents do."

"Hey, is that a dig? Some of us are pretty satisfied with our one job."

"Some people are happy being bored, I guess," she said with a theatrical sigh. "I don't know how you manage to fill your time on days you're not working with my dad."

"Um…" I gestured at the pile of books around me, some of which had actually made it into the laundry basket without me thumbing through them to find my favorite scenes. "I read. You could try it sometime."

"Why read when I could be doing what I love, with the people I love, no matter where I am?" She raised her eyebrows expectantly, like there was some hidden meaning there I was supposed to understand.

"I don't get it."

"When I'm out there, I'll do *Hidden Truths*. When I'm home, I'll work on *Soul Searchers*. Don't pretend you don't need my help. I know you haven't booked any new investigations since Dad promoted you."

I pursed my lips. Her words, while true, still hit me in a soft spot. For whatever reason, I wasn't getting any responses from my inquiries about filming various places. As much as I hoped it was because everyone was so busy preparing for Thanksgiving that they were ignoring their inboxes, part of me suspected I wasn't very good at communicating why they should let us shoot our show on their property for free.

"Or I could run the cameras," she suggested. "I did it before we hired Mark, and I've only gotten better since."

Dump Noah, the king of skepticism, and hire Kit? Now that was tempting. "Would your dad fire somebody just to get you back, though?"

"That wouldn't be the only reason. Noah's crap. Did you see the settings he's using? It's like he doesn't even know what he's doing. There's only so much you can do in the editing room. Stephen's episode is going to look terrible."

Her arguments brought a smile to my face. The teeny, tiny spiteful spot at the core of my being wanted to rub her face in the fact that she had totally bailed on us not one month before. Her arguments for coming back reeked of desperation, and it wouldn't take much needling to really bother her.

But beneath the hurt of saying goodbye, I understood why she did it. Who could resist working their dream job side by side with their dream partner? And I had missed her enough that there was no way I could suppress my elation that she was coming back, even if it was only part time.

"Count me in," I told her. "But you have to be the one to get your dad on board. Now you grab those hangers, and I'll get these shirts."

Together, we ferried my clothes down the stairs and into Graham's closet. Reggie's typewriter clacked and pinged nonstop as we passed Kit's old apartment.

She grinned at the sound and tipped her head toward the door. "I should hate that dude for swooping in and snatching up my lease, but this way I get the coolest unit in the house, and you and Graham can canoodle together properly."

I lowered my voice to be sure Reggie wouldn't be able to hear me. "You'll hate him anyway, soon enough. Just brace yourself for some insults and talk to him for five minutes."

"That bad, huh?"

"Yup."

She carried another load of my clothes down to Graham's, and I tried to get serious about packing my books. There weren't many, but each one triggered a slew of memories, especially the little stack I had crammed into my small nonfiction section. When Kit came back, she settled onto the floor beside me and started piling classic novels into the hamper as I flipped through a semi-recently acquired textbook.

"Remember this?" I held it up for her approval. "*Haunting Hypothesis: The Application of the Scientific Method to Modern Paranormal Investigative Techniques*."

She chuckled and reached for it. "Oh, yes. Dad made you read this, right?"

"Yeah. I swear, if a poltergeist hadn't shown up that same day, this book would have bored me right out of being a paranormal investigator."

"Do you want to keep it, or should we just chuck it?"

I stared at her. "Did you seriously just suggest throwing a book in the garbage? Heresy."

She held up her hands in defeat, and the outdated text made its way into the hamper. I pulled another one of Yuri's recom-mended books off the shelf. It was one of a few that *Haunting Hypothesis* frightened me away from reading, lest I accidentally bore myself to death, and I had forgotten it existed as soon as I shelved it. According to the inside flap, *Unlocking the Third Eye* covered everything the reader needed to know about psychic powers, abilities which the author claimed to be a "first-person witness" to and "the world's foremost living expert" about.

His name and photograph, printed beneath the book's description, sent me rocketing to my feet.

"What's wrong?" Kit asked, voice sharp with alarm.

I handed her the book and tapped the author's name at the bottom: Reginald Albertson. "This is the guy who's living in your apartment."

Kit followed me as I marched down the stairs to the second floor. The typewriter fell silent when I knocked, and I heard a short, irritated grunt. A moment later, Reggie yanked open his door a few inches, just enough to expose his round, florid face.

"Yes?" he growled.

I held *Unlocking the Third Eye* the way a vampire hunter might wield a large cross. "Did you write this?"

His small eyes widened farther than I thought possible, and his jaw fell slack. He looked from the book to me and back again. The silence verged on uncomfortable when he finally asked, "Did you read it?"

His question brought the awkwardness of the moment into full bloom, and I felt my cheeks redden.

"Well... no," I admitted.

"She forgot she had it," Kit piped in helpfully from behind me.

To my surprise, Reggie chuckled. He pulled the door open and gestured for us to enter. "Come on in. I've got some coffee brewing."

He had taken a much different direction decorating the small apartment than Kit had done before him. Her focal point had been the pair of enormous monitors where she edited *Soul Searchers*. His was a simple white desk, atop which sat his typewriter and several stacks of paper of varying heights. A pair of microfiber love seats faced each other over a marble-topped coffee table by the window, and the other two walls held tall shelves that were packed with books.

I still wasn't completely sure Reggie didn't like to spend his evenings murdering psychics, so I left the door open. Kit flopped onto one of the love seats, and I sat beside her gingerly. Reggie joined us a moment later with a wooden tray holding his French press and three mugs. He was midpour when Striker hopped up onto his desk on quiet paws and began sniffing the sheet of paper in his typewriter with interest.

Reggie's voice was cautious as he greeted her. "Hello, kitty cat."

Striker's ears pointed toward him, and she tilted her head. The sound of her purring filled the room.

I stared at her. Unlike me, who had to leave my body to walk the astral plane, Striker seemed to move through it and the real world simultaneously. She had seen Horace last night. Had she been able to see through his disguise? Would she know if this man standing in front of us was the same person who had backhanded her while trying to kill me?

She would. I knew it. And if he was standing in front of us now, her claws would be paw-deep in his face.

"She wants the paper." I relaxed into the deep couch and propped my head on my fist. "It's this thing she does. She wants you to crumple it into a little ball so she can chase it around."

"Oh." Reggie glanced at the typewriter and winced. "Well, she can't have that one, but I've got a few in my wastebasket."

He retrieved a crumpled ball of paper from the garbage can under his desk and hesitantly threw it out his open apartment door. Striker bolted after it, and I heard her quick feet scampering down the hallway as she knocked the ball around. He sat back down with us and finished pouring the coffee, but his hands shook as he passed the mugs around.

"Are you afraid of cats?" I asked.

"A bit. There's something otherworldly about them. I know

it's not their fault, but I always feel like they're looking through me. Judging me."

"They are," I confirmed. "At least, Striker is. But she seems to like you. She also thinks every apartment in this house belongs to her, so if you leave your door open, you might find her sleeping on your bed."

"It's the best," Kit said. "It's like having a cat, but Mac deals with all the gross stuff like litter boxes and vet visits."

"From what I hear, you're quite capable of dealing with a number of things," he told me. "I'd still love to hear about your experiences with the poltergeist at the Franklin cabin."

I tilted my head. "Okay, but first I need you to explain a few things. Why have you been so rude to me?"

"Rude?" He blinked a few times. "I've been rude?"

"Well... yeah. I mean, you acted like I wouldn't want to read your books, but you write about psychic phenomena, right? And I'm a psychic."

A divot formed between his eyebrows. "Well, I didn't know you were psychic when we met. My books are fairly niche; most people genuinely aren't interested. And now that I know you're a medium—"

"She also astral projects," Kit put in.

"Really?" Reggie leaned forward eagerly. "So which is it? Flying ointments or raw power?"

I frowned. "Well, I didn't use one of those ointments. So... power, I guess?"

He narrowed his eyes. "You're not sure?"

Kit elbowed me. "Everything this one does is unconscious. We took her to the Grimshaw Library earlier this year, and she saw a ghost without even trying."

"Hold on." Reggie retrieved a black Moleskine notebook from one of the shelves. "Do you mind if I take some notes? *Unlocking the Third Eye* was more focused on the showy side of psychic phenomena, the things skeptics might call parlor tricks. The book I'm writing now is specifically about psychic mediums, which is why I decided to move here for a while. I've got a baseline knowledge of astral theory, but I'd love it if you could confirm a few things for me."

Compared to our prior exchanges, Reggie was practically babbling. His face was flushed and excited, and I felt terrible bursting his bubble with the truth.

"You probably know more than I do," I said. "Kit's right. I'm sort of just bumbling through all this psychic stuff."

"Oh." He hesitated, pen in hand. Then he shrugged and scribbled something down. "You still have the practical experience I lack. Would you mind telling me what it was like?"

I wanted to go back in time and shake past Mackenzie for letting her bitterness about Kit's departure so instantly color her perceptions of Reggie. His gruff manner hadn't helped matters, but if I'd been willing to put in the effort, I could have had this conversation with him a week before. It would have been nice to be believed by someone in my own house instead of having to drive all the way to Gabrielle's prison just to have someone take me seriously.

But then, I probably wouldn't have gone to see her, so I couldn't hate on my past self too much.

As Reggie filled his Moleskine with notes, I recounted my four visits to the astral plane so far. Kit pursed her lips, and her hand twitched toward her pocket a few times. I was sure she was dying to get this on tape, but I was glad there were no cameras on me now. This wasn't for show. This was for my sanity.

I went into as much detail as I could remember, and walking through each experience one after another helped me take a step back from them. It was easier to put aside my grief and fear, and I was able to examine my experiences through a more scientific lens.

"There's so much about it all that doesn't make sense," I said. "Like, why was I only able to astral project while I was sleeping in my own bed? And it feels like I have this huge gap in my abilities. One day, I can suddenly astral project. A few days after that, I don't have enough power to channel a spirit who's sitting ten feet away from me. A week later, I can astral project *and* channel a spirit all in the same night. That's weird, right?"

He tapped his pen on the end of his nose. "You mentioned you woke up from your first astral experience holding a wooden box, correct? Had that ever happened before?"

My heart stopped. No, that hadn't happened before. I hadn't had Camila's box with me before. I hadn't had *Camila* with me before.

And every time I'd done something extraordinary since then, she had been nearby.

Weeks before, Yuri had told me the reason people looted places like the Franklin cabin was because they believed they could borrow the spiritual energy of haunted objects to enhance their own powers. Yuri dismissed the theory out of hand, and I had done the same, so the truth behind the sudden increase in my own abilities never even occurred to me.

I had been using Camila's energy to power myself up.

The next epiphany to hit knocked the breath out of my lungs. Camila was gone. I had let her go, and because of that choice, I would never astral project again.

I hated how much that filled me with regret. I felt dirty. Using a spirit like that… it felt evil. But I would still miss it. How messed up was that?

The next few realizations slammed into me in quick succession, and they would have toppled me over if I hadn't already been sitting down. What I'd been doing wasn't unique. Borrowing spiritual energy to astral project?

That was Horace's entire game.

Did the spiritual energy eventually run out? Was that why he needed so many of them? He wasn't content to travel around to places that were already haunted to capture lingering spirits, though clearly, he did that too. He was too efficient for that. Why hunt down ghosts when he could make them?

Horace was powerful. I had known that even when I'd thought he was a ghost. But now I knew his power didn't come from inside him. He stole it, along with his victim's lives.

Most importantly of all: like I had accidentally done with Camila, he needed to keep his spiritual batteries close. Any time he did anything psychically strenuous—like, say, astral projecting —they'd be nearby. The lives he had stolen, the people he had murdered, the souls he kept from moving on to the next life... they were still out there with him.

Somewhere out there was the place Horace laid his head to sleep.

That's where I would find the spirits he trapped.

That's where I would find my mother.

CHAPTER THIRTY-TWO

I knew as I climbed into our bed that night that I wouldn't be able to astral project. There was no point envisioning myself on the back path. Camila wouldn't be waiting for me. So as my exhaustion from the day's events tugged me into the arms of sleep, I leaned into it and prayed for a dreamless night.

My psyche wasn't in the mood to give me what I wanted. I dreamed of Horace, waking several times with sweat drenching my back and my legs tangled in the blankets, clutching my throat and struggling to breathe.

The third time it happened, Graham turned on the light. "It's okay," he soothed as I gulped for air. "There's nobody else here. It's just us."

When I finally calmed down, he moved to switch off the lamp.

"Can you leave it?" I felt like a child asking, but I was sure I wouldn't be able to fall asleep if there wasn't any light to hold back the darkness.

"Of course."

With Striker purring comfortably just above my head, I managed to fall back to sleep again. Whether because of the light or because my brain had gotten bored of torturing me, my dreams turned to the more abstract, disconnected scenarios I was used to. Searching through piles of equipment cases for a nonexistent piece of gear. Running down the hallway of my high school, desperate to get to class on time for an important quiz. Calmly listening to Striker explain that she was planning to marry Fang's cat, Shadow, and that as parents of the bride, we were expected to pay for the ceremony.

Then, abruptly, I found myself in the parking lot of the Yurt in Luck Resort.

Bright sunlight shone down from overhead, and the desert plants in the gardens were alive with vibrant red and yellow flowers that hadn't been there when Graham and I visited. The roar of the river was far louder than it was in real life, and the breeze carried the fresh scent of piñon pine. My surreal surroundings were a relief; this was a dream, not an astral projection, and I knew that when I woke, I would feel rested.

Someone tugged at my hand. My mother stood beside me, not looking at me as she yanked me toward the first yurt on the left side. She wore a cream-colored, flowing dress that fluttered around her knees, and her brown hair fell down her back in loose curls.

"Mom." I tried to pull her toward me, but she resisted. I relaxed my stance and let her tug me to the door of the Shamrock unit, the same yurt where I had found Camila's luggage.

My mother opened the door easily, no kick required. The room looked vacant; the bed was made, the chairs were tucked neatly under the wooden table, and the door to the bathroom was closed. I expected her to lead me to the tub where we would find Camila's suitcase all over again, together, but she stopped and pointed at the painting above the bed.

"What is it?" I examined the field of shamrocks, which were even brighter and greener here than they had been the last time I saw them. They were nice, but nothing about them struck me as particularly noteworthy.

"Find him," she said, not meeting my gaze. She kept her eyes fixed on the painting.

I frowned. For a moment, I thought this might be the kind of visitation Grey had described. I just wanted to sit down at the little table and talk to my mom. It would take hours, but I wanted to catch her up on my life and hear more about what hers had been like before I was born. Grey made it sound like a visitation was a conversation, but this felt nothing like I had imagined. As always, my mother felt distant.

Restrained.

"Can you talk to me?" I asked. "Really talk?"

She finally faced me, and her expression was pained. She looked like she wanted to say something—there was a depth of emotion in her eyes that made me think she wanted to say a lot of things—and she gathered both of my hands into hers, squeezing them tightly.

"There's no time," she whispered. "I can't stay."

I felt the truth in her words. Her form shimmered, and her hands felt less substantial around mine than they had a moment before.

She was fading.

"Tell me," I urged. "Whatever you're here to say, just say it."

"He's in trouble." She let go of my hands and pointed at the painting again. "The Irishman."

"Stephen?" Alarm flooded me, and my heart pounded against my neck.

The bathroom door fell open. Camila's luggage lay open on the floor. Her clothes spilled out of it, and sitting on top of the messy pile of T-shirts and blue jeans was a wooden jewelry box with an open lid. I walked toward it, dread building in my belly, and peeled back the red velvet lining.

Horace's runes were there, burned into the wood and fully intact. The world around me faded away until I stood at the edge of a dark forest, holding the box in my hands. Horace was striding toward me across a recently plowed field, his eyes glowing red and his cape fluttering behind him. His lips peeled back, and sharpened teeth gleamed in the moonlight.

"Go!" my mother's voice whispered in my ear.

The frigid air pierced through my pajamas and numbed my limbs. The box slipped out of my fingers. Horace's eyes locked on mine. I turned to run, but my feet were trapped, tangled in vines that snaked out from between the trees. I fell to the ground and thrashed, trying to break free.

"Help!" I screamed. "Help!"

A bright light blinded me. I squinted against it. Graham's face appeared above mine, and his head blocked the glare from the overhead light behind him. His hands gripped my shoulders, and I became aware that he had been shaking me gently.

"Shh, you're okay." He leaned back and sighed. "Everything's fine."

"No, it isn't." I untangled my legs from the sheets and leapt out of bed. "Get your shoes. We have to go right now."

"Mac, it's okay. You were having a nightmare. It was just a dream."

"No." I pulled a sweatshirt over my head. "We have to go get Stephen."

"What? Why?"

"Because if we don't find him now, he's going to die."

CHAPTER THIRTY-THREE

Baxter's tired engine squealed against the cold as Graham pulled out of the Primrose House parking lot. The faded green glow of the dashboard clock read 5:00 a.m.

I prayed we weren't too late.

Our breath made tiny clouds in front of our faces as we scanned the sidewalks for any sign of Stephen on the way to The Enclave. We were bundled up warmly with coats, hats, gloves, and scarves. In the back seat, we had Graham's quilt and a bottle filled with hot water from the kitchen sink. They were the only things we had time to grab on our way out the door.

"You're sure he's in danger?" Graham asked.

"Positive."

I chewed the skin off my lip and replayed what I had seen in my dream. My mother had been so emphatic that Stephen was in trouble. I hadn't dreamed about her since the last night we spent in New Mexico… the night Elizabeth Monk died. The jewelry box, Horace, the cold.

It all pointed to Stephen dying before sunrise.

I kicked myself for not calling him as soon as I knew Horace was targeting psychics. But I had assumed—falling victim, yet again, to the very thing Gabrielle warned me against—Stephen would be safe so long as the episode didn't air. How else would Horace know to target him? Or had Stephen somehow stumbled into one of Horace's traps by accident?

Either way, I should have told Stephen. Warned him. Insisted he come stay with us at Primrose House for... well, for who knew how long. Whatever it took to keep everyone safe.

Graham brought Baxter to an abrupt halt in front of The Enclave. We hurried up the path toward Stephen's building as fast as we could without slipping on the icy cobblestones. I pictured knocking on the door and being met by a messy-haired Stephen, to whom I'd have to explain why we woke him so horrifically early. He would make coffee, and everything would be all right.

But before we even reached the front steps, that optimistic vision vanished.

Stephen's door hung wide open.

"Stephen!" Graham shouted, bounding onto the stoop and into the building in two steps.

I followed behind as quickly as my shorter legs could manage. We found no sign of a struggle, either upstairs or down, but Stephen's bed was empty. All his lights were off. And most worrying of all, his cell phone, wallet, and car keys had been left on his nightstand.

Graham was on the phone with the sheriff's department before I finished searching all the rooms. "I need to report a missing person." He rattled off Stephen's name and address. After a conversation that at once felt far too brief and way too long, he hung up and told me, "They're sending over a deputy. They want us to wait here."

"Wait here? Are you kidding? We need to go out there and find him. Now."

After everything I'd had to talk Graham into doing over the

last few weeks, I expected some pushback. But he gave a single brisk nod and gestured for me to step outside. "Let's go."

On the porch, the futility of our situation hit me. Stephen had left on foot. We had no idea how long ago that was or how far he'd managed to get. The weather had been too cold for snow for days, and the slick sidewalk held no evidence of even our own footprints from just minutes before.

Even if there had been snow on the ground, I was no tracker. Neither of us had ever been trained to hunt anything down. I walked back to the street, senses on high alert until I reached the curb. There, my vision fuzzed. I stared blankly up and down the road. Which way had he gone? Toward downtown or away? Uphill or down? What if I chose the wrong direction and we just got farther and farther away from him until it was too late?

A panicked sob rose in my chest.

"Okay, Mac." Graham turned me to face him and rested his hands on top of my shoulders. "Where do we go now?"

"I don't know." My eyes filled with tears. "I don't know what to do."

"Think about what brought us here." His voice was impossibly calm. "You saw something, right? You were screaming in your sleep, so I know it was scary, but I need you to remember."

Tears dripped down my cheeks as I nodded. "Okay. Yeah. I—I can do that."

Except what if I couldn't? What if it was already too late? What if, right now, Stephen's lifeless body was frozen on the ground, hunched around one of Horace's boxes?

"Oh, God," I groaned. "This is my fault."

"Focus, Mac. Just breathe. In through your nose, out through your mouth." He modeled the slow breaths and watched me as I followed suit. "Good. Again… One more… Now what did you see?"

I closed my eyes. The images came back to me. "I saw my

mother at Yurt in Luck. She took me to the Shamrock room… She said Stephen was in trouble." The more I spoke, the clearer the memory and my voice became. "Then I saw the jewelry box. When I picked it up, it took me—" My eyes flew open. "The field. Horace left the box at the end of the big field outside town by all the new construction. He put it in the little patch of woods behind the new apartments."

Graham drove faster than I thought Baxter was capable of going and definitely faster than was probably safe on icy roads. We tore down residential streets, past dark buildings and an empty schoolyard. The glow from the porch lights and streetlamps was more subdued than usual, as though the glacial temperatures were holding back the light.

My stomach twisted. Stephen was outside in this weather, walking the breadth of the town. He had to be freezing. How long had he been out here? How much longer could he take?

"You're sure it's the field on this side?" Graham said.

"Positive. I remember the trees. Plus…" I fidgeted in my seat. "I *want* to go there. I feel like I need to be heading this direction."

He peered at me from the corner of his eye. "You can feel the runes?"

When I nodded, he took a sudden turn toward Main Street. My gut wrenched, and I felt like I was on a carnival ride that had turned me upside down.

"We're going the wrong way." I resisted an impulse to grab the steering wheel and yank us back on track. "He's the other direction."

"This will be faster. There's no road between the older neighborhood and the woods on that side. It's all farmland back there. Stephen's on foot, so he can climb the fences. We can't."

Baxter's engine roared as Graham leaned on the gas pedal. Within minutes, we were racing down Main Street toward the roundabout that marked the last block of Donn's Hill's ever-expanding commercial district. There, the Main Street Diner sat kitty-corner from the town's only gas station, and a large apartment complex jutted inward onto what little farmland remained inside city limits.

A half mile before the intersection, Graham made another abrupt turn. Ignoring a sign warning PRIVATE PROPERTY, he took us down a dirt road that ran between a giant parking lot and a field, perpendicular to the tree line. My brain sang with relief; we were now headed back in the direction my instincts had been screaming at me to go.

In the distance, a lanky figure shambled slowly across the field toward the trees. It was impossible to tell from this far away, but it had to be Stephen.

Then I felt something else.

Something familiar.

"Stop the car!" I shouted.

Graham swore and slammed on the brakes. Baxter fishtailed on the unpaved road before skidding to a halt in a cloud of dust.

"What is it?" Graham looked around, eyes wide. "Did we hit something?"

I gripped the dashboard and shook my head. Two urges warred inside me. Something called to me from the edge of the field, and I wanted to run toward it. It would be warm there; I could feel it. Warm and safe and the perfect place to lie down and get a rest from shivering in this cold.

But to my left, something else tugged at me. Something strong.

The feeling was a hundred times more intense than what I had felt at Cambion's Camp the day Horace sent me looking for the first jewelry box. I had felt it more recently than that, though. The tidal wave of nausea that crashed into me was identical to the one that nearly flattened me when we were leaving Donn's Hill for New Mexico.

I threw open the car door and dry-heaved over the road. When nothing came up, I shuddered back against the passenger seat and squinted out Graham's window toward the source of my discomfort.

On the other side of the enormous parking lot, a long row of dark buildings stood between us and the highway. Hundreds of Donn's Hill residents called the apartment complex home. And somewhere in there, I was suddenly sure that there was a spiritual force even stronger than the entity trapped in that first box.

No. What I was sensing was too extreme to be caused by a single spirit. There had to be more over there, maybe dozens. All the people Horace had lured to their deaths—the psychics he had murdered—were clumped together, their voices amplified by their proximity to one another.

And those voices were calling to me.

I stared back and forth between the apartments and the form stumbling across the fields. My mother had shown me where Horace was. His astral form was waiting somewhere near the trap he had laid for Stephen. If I took off my necklace, I was sure I would be able to feel his twisted energy lurking just behind the trees.

My hand darted to my chest and gripped the black tourmaline as Horace's words came back to me. *First, you find a way to disappear from my sight...* When I wore this necklace, it did more than just block out any negative energy. On the astral plane, Horace was nothing *but* negative energy. When he was outside his body, he couldn't sense me at all.

And while his spirit waited for Stephen in the trees, his physical body slept somewhere in that apartment complex.

I unbuckled my seat belt.

Graham grabbed my wrist. "Whoa, what are you doing?"

"I need you to do something for me. Call the sheriff again. Get an ambulance out here and go save Stephen."

"Where will you be?"

"There." I pointed toward the apartments. "Horace's body is over there. I can feel it. But his spirit is watching Stephen. When you get there, don't mention me. Just find the box and destroy the runes like you did in that basement, okay? And once Stephen is safe, come find me."

"No way." A muscle twitched in his face. "You're not going alone."

"We don't have time to argue." I yanked my hand away from him, slung my purse over my chest, and got out of the car. "Horace is like a living ghost. If I don't find out who he is now, we'll never know, and he'll just keep hurting people. And Stephen needs your help. He'll die, Graham. There's no third option."

Before he could say anything else, I slammed the door and bolted through the Geo's headlights toward the parking lot. I was halfway to the buildings before I heard Baxter's engine roar to life and tires crunching over the unpaved road. Graham had listened; Stephen was going to be okay.

He had to be.

I had nowhere near as much confidence about my own future. If the timing wasn't just right, if I couldn't find Horace before he returned to the waking world…

There was no point thinking about it. I had made my choice. Now I just had to find him as quickly as possible. I needed to focus on sensing the spirits calling to me and destroy their prisons.

But as I darted through the parked cars, I couldn't help wishing I had taken an extra second to tell Graham I loved him before slamming that door, just in case.

CHAPTER THIRTY-FOUR

Following the ghostly compass in my brain was a strange sensation. It felt like searching for the source of an elusive scent or trying to find the thing in your house that's making the noise nobody else seems to hear. If I didn't focus on it completely, the feeling faded enough to be overtaken by the urge to find the *lathu* rune that had lured Stephen out into the cold. But when I did concentrate on the spiritual energy calling to me, the overwhelming nausea nearly brought me to my knees.

The closer I got to the source, the more difficult it became to push forward. The tourmaline around my neck did nothing to block any of it out, or if it did, what leaked through pressed against me like a giant pair of hands squeezing my skull.

How could Horace stand to be so close to this much energy? How could he relax enough to fall asleep to astral project? If I blacked out from the pain, would I find myself on the astral plane?

I gritted my teeth and concentrated on putting one foot in front of the other until I bumped up against the sidewalk at the end of the parking lot. It took some effort to lift my shoes the few inches required to go from asphalt to concrete, but I soon found myself in a wide, open-air hallway with a pair of numbered doors on both sides. A metal staircase led to more apartments on the floors above me, but I couldn't imagine climbing it without falling backward and breaking my neck.

It felt safer to start my search at ground level. I squinted at the doors around me, most of which sported Thanksgiving decorations—cornucopia wreaths, hand turkeys, and pilgrim hats. But there was one door that looked like it wasn't yet aware that Halloween was two weeks past. A pair of vampire fangs had been taped to the door, perfectly framing the number three.

The pull was strongest here. I stumbled as I approached the door but caught myself on the rough plaster beside it. The voices calling to me were just feet away, right on the other side of this wall.

"Mrrrrooooowwwwww." A black cat growled at me from the far end of the hallway as I steadied myself. It arched its back, and its green eyes flashed, as though it was trying to warn me away from its territory.

My head throbbed like a bass drum, but through the searing pain, I recognized that cat. Fang had shown me a photo of it. I looked from the cat to the vampire fangs and back again.

Fang. This was Fang's apartment. What the hell was *Fang*, that little fake, doing with this much spiritual energy pouring out of his home?

There was only one way to find out. I had to get through that door.

Shadow hissed at me. Apparently deciding discretion was the better part of valor, he turned tail and darted around the corner. An idea wormed its way past the pulsing in my brain. I forced myself off the wall to follow him, turning the corner just in time to see Shadow leap up through a window on the other side of the apartment building.

Fang had made a makeshift cat door with a piece of cardboard, some duct tape, and a cat-flap insert that looked like it was intended to sit in something much thicker. With no regard for the amount of noise I was making or the way this might look to an outside observer, I yanked the cardboard away from the window. The next step took more energy than I thought I had left in me, but I managed to hoist myself up and through the opening, landing on a metal pet dish that thumped softly against the carpet beneath my feet.

Dimly, at the back of my mind, I registered a change. The *lathu* rune no longer called to me. Graham must have destroyed it, which meant he had either reached Stephen or beaten the rune caster to the box. In either case, I prayed he had gotten there in time.

If Horace was out there, he had just witnessed his plan failing. I was sure he would recognize Graham and realize I was behind this turn of events. Would he stick around in astral form to see how I'd managed to stop him, or would he wake up to run before I got any closer?

I didn't love my odds.

The space the absence of the *lathu* rune left in my mind was quickly filled by the increased pressure from the nearby ghosts. They were here, in this apartment. I leaned into the pain, begging it to guide me to its source. But it was all around me now, pressing against my mind from every direction. Forget wading too deeply in Grey's river of spiritual energy; I was a submarine that had sunk to the very bottom of the ocean, and the hull was caving in.

My legs gave out, and I collapsed onto the snow-white carpet. I forced myself forward on my hands and knees, eventually reaching a closed door. I didn't register any of Fang's furniture as my fingers curled around the knob; he could have hung flashing neon signs all over his bedroom, and I wouldn't have noticed. My vision was limited to the six inches in front of my nose as I crawled out of the room.

Carpet.

Carpet.

My shoulder scraped against something. An open doorway, I decided.

More carpet.

Then—cedar.

The woodsy scent of the red boards invaded my nose and cleared my senses. I blinked the tears out of my eyes and focused on the thing in front of me: a large cedar chest. It was open, and I gripped its lip to pull myself to a sitting position. I inhaled deeply, focusing on the smell. It was masculine, like my father's aftershave. Natural, like a peaceful forest.

The scent cleared my head enough for me to fully process what I was seeing. Strange symbols covered the inside of the chest's lid, painted in a thin reddish-brown color that I hoped had come out of a can. Beneath the rim rested rows upon rows of small square jewelry boxes with hinged lids. Ten across, five down, and who knew how deeply stacked. There had to be hundreds of them.

Hundreds.

Horace had *hundreds* of spirits trapped in here.

This time, my stomach found something to vomit up. Yellow bile erupted out of my mouth and spattered across the boxes.

A secret fantasy, one I had buried as far down in my psyche as I could delve, disappeared in a puff of my breath. After channeling Camila, I was sure I could do the same with my mother. No more half visitations where she couldn't even properly communicate with me. We could have a real conversation—one where I could ask her any question I wanted and she could take her time answering.

But to do that, I would have to find the jewelry box that contained her spirit.

I cringed against the returning pressure and lifted a few at random. Each had a different symbol on the bottom, most of which I didn't recognize—glyphs, runes, single alphabet letters, an abstract sketch of a cat. Was it some kind of system? Could Horace pick up a box with a diamond carved into the bottom and know exactly who it belonged to?

My theory was confirmed when I found a box marked with a pickax. I'd been right; Horace had collected the miner's spirit from the Ace of Cups.

There was no time to crack the rest of his code. The moment of clarity the cedar scent bought me had long since started to fade, and the pain came roaring back into my head like a freight train. I gripped the chest with one hand and reminded myself what I had come here to do. It took every ounce of my focus to dip my other hand into my purse, close my fingers around something small and cold, and haul out Darlene's lighter.

The little green head with its oversize black eyes made me think of Camila and her alien obsession. I had set her free, and I would free the others.

"Sorry, Mom," I whispered.

Blue flame erupted out of the alien's head. I lowered it into the chest, where it licked at the unvarnished edge of the center-most box.

Then the cedar chest's lid slammed shut. Pain shot through me. I yanked my aching limbs to my torso with a yelp, dropping the lighter. It bounced off my knee and landed on the carpet.

"I should have known you'd show up sooner or later," a familiar voice said above me.

I jerked my head up, and my eyes went wide.

Noah leaned over the cedar chest, rage tattooed across his snarling face as he reached for me.

CHAPTER THIRTY-FIVE

When the lid slammed closed, two things happened at once. The fingers on my left hand felt like someone had snapped them in half, and the pressure squeezing my head vanished. Whatever Noah had painted on the inside of the chest's lid must have been containing the energy of the spirits trapped within.

The fog in my brain instantly cleared, and I scrambled backward out of his reach, finding my feet faster than I would have thought possible. I backed across the hall and into Fang's bedroom, never taking my eyes off the suddenly murderous cameraman. He wore a pair of sweatpants and a plain white T-shirt, and though there was no trace of his hat or cloak and his face wasn't the same as it looked on the astral plane, there was one thing about him that was instantly recognizable: the cold, sadistic gleam in his eyes.

I had thought Kit was just trying to make space for herself on the *Soul Searchers* team, but she had been right. Noah didn't know how to work the cameras properly. He didn't really have any experience. That had all been a lie, a way for him to get onto the crew. But why? Just to screw with me?

Or to find other psychics to murder?

There was no point in asking. In my heart, I knew it was probably a little of both.

"Well," I said, "I don't know if I should call you Noah or Horace or whatever your real name is."

Noah flashed a humorless smile as he walked toward me. "It's Noah, but I've always hated that name. His story never made any sense to me. He took all that time to build the boat, herded everything that mattered onto it, and then just… let it go? A smart man would have kept it for himself."

"Horace, then."

He hissed through his teeth. "I can hear that, you know. The way you say it, like you're cramming two foul words together as quickly as you can. It's Horus, Mackenzie. Say it with the respect it deserves."

I backed into a dresser and groped for something—anything—I could use as a weapon. Noah might not be able to travel the length of the room in a single blink outside the astral plane, but he was still considerably stronger and larger than I was. If he leapt at me, I needed to be able to level the playing field.

My hands found nothing.

"Sorry, Horus," I said, careful to enunciate the *u*.

He stopped at the threshold between the hallway and Fang's bedroom and inhaled deeply. "I told Fang not to leave his window open for that worthless cat. I should have checked when he left this morning. But don't you think the winter air is… I don't know… bracing? The cold can be so freeing."

I shuddered. "Does he know what you're doing in here?"

"Lord, no. I don't know if it's his youth or his disposition, but the child is pitifully easy to manipulate." His eyes flicked to the window. He darted across the room toward it, blocking my exit and chasing me up onto Fang's bed. "Now, now. Where do you think we're going? I've got a box ready for you, Mackenzie. It took me a few years, but I figured it out. The stronger the psychic, the longer she lasts. And you're ripe for the plucking."

Frustration welled up inside me. I half crouched on the mattress, unsure where to go from here. Should I go on the offensive? Leap off the bed and attack him? Or focus on getting away?

Noah tilted his head, and for a moment, he looked almost nostalgic. "You look so much like her, you know. I'll admit I had a bit of a schoolboy crush. But she was too old for me. Even Anson said so. But then, what did that old man know? He said my ideas were insane."

"What ideas?" I asked, edging the opposite direction. If I couldn't get out through the window, maybe I could make a break for the front door. I just needed a distraction, something to keep him from chasing after me.

"Oh, you know. A little of this. A little of that. Anson didn't like the idea of mixing rune systems or inventing my own. I told him they were just symbols—it's the *intent* behind them that matters. And when I finally found a way to reach the astral plane, after all the time we spent working together, he told me I should stop." Noah shook his head. "Can you believe that? Stop. Like anyone could just *stop*. Now that you've done it, you understand."

I swallowed. I did understand. Even now, lurking beneath the fear and panic that gripped me in this moment, I wanted to do it again.

"Anson was a purist. And a fool. And now he's in—" Noah pointed toward his room, and his smile vanished. "NO!"

He leapt away from me, diving through the hallway. The light on the walls flickered oddly, and I slid to the side to see what had sent him bolting away from me.

The carpet was on fire. The alien head lighter's defective button had gotten stuck, and it spat blue flame toward the cedar chest. The blaze had spread quickly through the small bedroom and licked at the walls. The cedar chest was already charred. Any second now, the fire would eat through the barrier and start consuming jewelry boxes.

I backed away from it, toward the frigid air that poured in through the open window behind me. Noah was right; at this moment, the cold felt like the most freeing thing in the world. It was about to save my life. But as I threw one leg up onto the windowsill, I glanced back through the open doorway.

Noah stood on the other side of the rising flames with a comforter in his hands. Sweat dripped down his face, and he winced against the heat as he used the blanket to swat at the flames in a desperate attempt to put them out.

It looked like it was working.

If he saved the cedar chest, every spirit inside would stay trapped in its prison. Noah would take them and flee, and even with his real name, I would still be powerless to find him.

I might be free, but my mother never would be.

He lifted the blanket, spreading it between his outstretched arms. As he lunged forward with it to smother the fire eating the cedar chest, I bolted back across the kitchen and into the flames.

I had to stop him.

No matter the cost.

My feet crossed the threshold. An explosion pierced my ears, and a blast of spiritual energy knocked me off my feet. I flew backward into Fang's room, tumbling across the carpet before slamming into the wall beneath the window. The impact knocked my breath out of me, and when I sucked in air, it seared my throat. Black smoke billowed out of the cedar chest. Through the haze, I could just make out Noah's body, crumpled against the far wall in his room.

Someone grabbed me beneath my armpits and hoisted me up and through the window. I fell to the ground and clutched at the frosted grass, gasping in the cold—but clean—air.

"Graham?" I asked, raising my head.

I was sure he must have found me and pulled me to safety, but there was nobody around me. I was alone in the field, apart from the green-eyed black cat, who leapt out the window after me.

A shrill noise split the early morning air, jolting me to my feet. The fire alarm screeched, paused, and screeched again. Windows on every floor of the building lit up, one by one, and panicked voices echoed out of the stairwells.

As I watched Fang's neighbors evacuate, invisible fingers touched my cheek. I felt someone cup my face between their hands, then a gentle pressure at my back as though I had been pulled into a hug.

"Mom?"

The pressure increased. I reached my arms out, wanting to hug her back, but my arms passed through the empty air in front of me to circle around my own torso. I squeezed anyway, hugging myself as tightly as I would have hugged my mother if I had been able to see her.

After a long time, I felt her let me go. She brushed my cheek again, and as her fingers left my face, I sensed her rising upward. Her energy drifted toward the sky like the smoke pouring out of Fang's bedroom window.

Tears ran down my cheeks. I knew, deep in my heart, my mother was moving on to a place where no psychic power could reach her. She had lingered on our plane long enough, far longer than she would have done if she'd had a choice.

That last embrace was the goodbye she hadn't been able to give me before she died.

I sank down to the cold ground and let my grief wash over me. Strangers surrounded me, and one of the evacuees wrapped me in a quilt that smelled like freshly washed laundry. Graham came running across the lawn toward our clump, and the panic in his eyes abated when he found my face in the crowd.

He gathered me to him. "Are you all right? What happened?"

"I'm okay." I searched for the words to explain what I had just experienced but couldn't find them.

"Horace?" he asked.

"It was Noah." Shame and anger filled me, momentarily over-shadowing my sadness. "I was so stupid. I thought I would be able to sense him—feel his energy. But all the time, I've been wearing this to block him out."

I ripped the black tourmaline necklace off and let it fall to the ground. Thin tendrils of negative energy pawed at my psyche, but any dangerous or angry spirits Noah had kept trapped in that cedar chest were rising to the sky, hurried into the next world by the flames that freed them.

Gingerly, I felt for any trace of Noah in the apartment. I found none but couldn't be certain what that meant.

"Do you want to go home?" Graham asked.

"Not yet. I need to see." I opened the blanket, inviting him to join me in its warmth.

He stepped inside and wrapped it back around our shoulders. Together, we watched as the firefighters arrived and put out the flames. And as the sun rose behind the trees, we watched them carry a stretcher out of Fang's apartment.

The corpse was hidden from view by thick black fabric.

As soon as the body bag was out of sight, I shrugged out of the blanket and returned it to the woman who had given it to me, then stooped to pick up my necklace. Because it had come from Elizabeth, I couldn't bear to leave it behind. But it went into my pocket, not around my neck.

Horace was dead. I didn't need it anymore.

CHAPTER THIRTY-SIX

The front door of my shop swung open. A bell tinkled overhead as Graham carried in a large cardboard box and lowered it to the ground with exaggerated relief. He put his hands at the small of his back and pushed. His spine cracked audibly, and he sighed.

"If I had known I would have to schlep shipments all over town for you, I would have begged you to open a pillow store," he teased.

I stood up from my desk, which doubled as the checkout counter, and winced. "Sorry. I'm still not used to using this address."

"What's in the box?"

"New journals. A few people have asked for them."

He plucked one out and inspected it. "Not bad."

Through the window behind him, the usual Sunday brunch crowd trooped up the sunny footpath toward the Ace of Cups. The weather outside was still chilly, but the snow was melting, and springtime was steadily marching across Donn's Hill.

I grabbed my pricing gun. If I was quick enough to inventory the new products, I could have them shelved and out by the time the tourists finished their mimosas.

Business had been brisk in the two weeks since my grand opening. It was a relief, especially after everyone in my life had warned me about the risks of going into retail. But those warnings always came with offers to help, and Penelope had generously shared the keen eye for design that made the Oracle Inn such a smashing success as I planned the renovations on the former tarot-card parlor.

Now, after four months of work, only one piece of the shop was still technically unfinished. Tomorrow, an artist would be coming to put the final touches on the gold-leaf design that covered the front window: a cat wearing a crown of sunlight posed atop a stack of books. The words *Tortoiseshell Books and Gifts* arched above her head. *New - Used - Trades* stretched beneath her.

The bell above the door jingled again.

"Hey, Mac." Stephen Hastain helped himself to a cup of the complimentary coffee. "Got any of those new mysteries in?"

"Yep, I left a few for you in Henry's Room." I jerked my head toward the back of the store, where I had converted the former office space into a comfortable reading room. Shoppers could borrow a lovingly used paperback and settle into one of the overstuffed chairs for as long as they pleased or just put their feet up and enjoy the knickknacks and wall hangings that had decorated my father's office in Colorado.

Graham helped me shelve the new arrivals, and we sat down at my desk to split a slice of cake from the Ace of Cups over tea and coffee. Alexi had started making decaf chai just for me, and the blend she used went criminally well with the cream cheese frosting on her chef's housemade carrot cake.

Striker hopped up onto the desk and sniffed at the plate.

Before I could lift her back down to the floor, her little pink tongue darted out and left a wet splotch on the frosting.

I sighed and scraped off the portion she had tried to mark as her own. Her bright eyes followed it all the way into the garbage.

"Brrrlll," she complained.

"I'm not rewarding your bad behavior with a treat," I told her. "At least, not a treat you can't even digest properly. Go find Fang. He knows where your crunchies are."

The young *Soul Searchers* production assistant had taken to hanging out upstairs in what used to be Elizabeth's day spa. Her former waiting room had been transformed into a large, open classroom where anyone could share their knowledge of herbalism, hedgecraft, or any other esoteric topic. On days with no scheduled classes, Fang liked to use the craft tables to make seasonal wreaths and home decor. His passion for crafting had been born when his apartment burned down and he was forced to remake his possessions on a budget. I felt free use of my space was fair penance for the role I had played in destroying everything he owned.

In the back half of the second floor, I knocked out the walls between the treatment rooms to make a single space large enough to hold a low, round table. Eight cushy floor pillows, low-hanging ceiling drapes, and recessed lighting helped create a comforting ambiance in Evelyn's Room. With months of practice under my belt, I had finally been able to channel a spirit again. That time, without Camila's spirit supercharging my abilities, the ghost had politely hovered in front of me and spoken through me from the outside, rather than taking over my entire body, and the *Soul Searchers* had gotten it all on film. When the Afterlife Festival crowds arrived in a few weeks, I fully expected my shop to be one of their top destinations.

Striker hopped off the desk with a huff. The bell above the

door tinkled again, and Kit nearly tripped over my gluttonous feline as the cat scampered toward the stairs.

"Whoa!" Kit steadied herself on a display of Donn's Hill post-cards. After shaking a fist at Striker, she poured a cup of coffee and hoisted herself up onto one of the low, sturdy bookshelves that housed our nonfiction materials.

"Did you guys make it to the airport on time?" I asked.

Kit nodded. "Yep. Amari said she'll call when she gets to Dallas and again when they get to Rio."

I took a deep breath to soothe the envy that spiked in my chest. This was the fourth time Kit and Amari had gotten to film internationally. As much as I would have loved to join them, I had enough going on here. Plus, when they were both in Donn's Hill, they lent their considerable talents to the *Soul Searchers*. Kit's camerawork got better every week, and Amari seemed to be able to talk anyone into letting us film wherever we wanted.

"It's a long trip," I said. "When are you heading out?"

"I'll go next week, once you and I are done filming at the old mill. Amari has a bunch of stuff to get set up before we can really start shooting."

"Tell Mark to check his email when you see him, okay?" I folded my arms across my chest grumpily. "I've been waiting for a reply for like a week now."

A group of customers came in then, putting an end to our conversation. Kit hopped off the shelves and talked a couple from Moyard into buying a tarot card gift set, and Graham helped me ring up a stack of used books for a local teenager whose horror addiction I was stoking on a weekly basis.

When the shop quieted again, I leaned my head against Graham's shoulder. "Hey, do you still want me to tell you when-ever I feel anything strange? Like, any weird urges?"

"Of course." His face was instantly serious, heavy brows knit together above his glasses. "What does it feel like? Another invitation rune?"

I shook my head. "Not, not like that. It's more of a... craving."

The edge of his tension cracked. "Oh, really? Don't tell me it's pickles and chocolate ice cream again. That combination can't be good for you."

"It's not for me." I rested a hand on top of my growing belly. "She's the one with terrible taste. Do you mind grabbing some for me from the store?"

He leaned over the desk and planted a kiss on my forehead. "Anything for you two."

I watched him saunter out the door, then turned my attention back to the store around me. Even if I was the kind of psychic who could see into the future, I would never have been able to predict that my decision to pull up stakes and move to Donn's Hill would lead me right here, to this precise moment. In just under a year, I had gone from skeptic to psychic to paranormal investigator. I'd graduated from carrying my life in a backpack to owning my own business.

And soon, I would go from losing my parents to becoming one myself.

I wished they could see me now. I wished they could hold my daughter when she arrived and marvel at the traits they passed on to her through me. Would she inherit my father's thick hair and freckles? Would she share his love of books and his passion for unearthing the secrets of the past?

Would she have my mother's blue eyes? And would my gifts —my mother's legacy—pass on to my daughter too?

Would ghostly Travelers sit at her bedside, telling her stories as she slept?

I smiled and leaned my head back against the wall behind my

desk. Frightening though my road had been, I looked forward to her walking it with me.

Thank you for reading *Donn's Legacy*! If you enjoyed the book, I would deeply appreciate a short review wherever you love discovering new books. Reviews are crucial for any author, and even a line or two can help another reader discover this story.

Want to know when the next story is on the way and other big news? Join my email list and get a free ebook!

http://carynlarrinaga.com/free-ebook

Join me on Facebook and Twitter to chat about books, cats, horror, and anything else that strikes your fancy!

https://www.facebook.com/carynwrites
https://twitter.com/carynlarrinaga

ACKNOWLEDGMENTS

Well, it's tradition now that I start by thanking Kelly, AKA the inspiration for everything great about Graham. When I threatened to dissolve into a pool of panic that would require me to start sleeping in a bucket, you propped me up and reminded me that there are a lot of reasons to remain a solid being. There's no way I could have done something as productive as write and publish this book if you weren't pushing me forward. I love you!

Enormous feathery thanks to my incredible friend Menum. You and your five crows helped me get my butt in gear and find some momentum, and you regularly inspire me to share my art (such as it is) with the world.

I started writing these books while I was dealing with the pain of loss, and in the years since I finished *Donn's Hill,* we've lost many family members, including kitties. Thank you, Mom and Dad, for grieving with Kelly and me and for always helping us make the impossible decisions about when it's time to say goodbye.

There's a group of truly talented ladies without whom this book would barely be readable. Thank you Kelley Lynn, Jennie Stevens, and Beverly Bernard for your detailed and thoughtful edits. Thanks also to my eagle-eyed ARC readers who caught a few last-minute errors: Travis Poole and Brandy Rood.

Finally, thank you. Yes, you, the person who stuck with me through three books about Mac and Striker and is now reading these acknowledgments. Writing is my favorite thing to do and creating things comes with its own kind of high, but the thing that makes it even better is knowing that somebody out there will read the story, and my words will become images in their minds that are probably much cooler than what I was picturing when I wrote them. Thank you for reading. I wish I could give you a hug.

ABOUT THE AUTHOR

Caryn Larrinaga is a Basque American mystery, horror, and urban fantasy writer. Her debut novel, *Donn's Hill*, was awarded the League of Utah Writers 2017 Silver Quill in the adult novel category and was a 2017 Dragon Award finalist.

Watching scary movies through split fingers terrified Caryn as a child, and those nightmares inspire her to write now. Her 90-year-old house has a colorful history, and the creaking walls and narrow hallways send her running (never walking) up the stairs. Exploring her fears through writing makes Caryn feel a little less foolish for wanting a buddy to accompany her into the tool shed.

Caryn lives near Salt Lake City, Utah, with her husband and their clowder of cats. Visit www.carynlarrinaga.com for free short fiction and true tales of haunted places.

facebook.com/carynwrites

twitter.com/carynlarrinaga

instagram.com/carynlarrinaga

amazon.com/author/carynlarrinaga

goodreads.com/carynlarrinaga

bookbub.com/authors/caryn-larrinaga

SUPERHERO SYNDROME

Tess McBray was dying. The Solstice Syndrome had no cure, and she resigned herself to an early grave. But just when she gave up on survival, all her symptoms mysteriously disappeared.

All but one symptom, anyway. Something is wrong with Tess's hands. They absorb any material they touch, and her skin turns to wood, or steel, or concrete. It doesn't take this comic-book obsessed 21-year-old long to figure out what's going on: somehow, she's developed super powers. And she's not the only one; across the country, people are coming forward and sharing their gifts with the world. In her own city, where the police are battling a human trafficking operation, a masked vigilante called The Fox is saving lives and stopping criminals.

Tess doesn't know where she fits into this new, super-powered world. But when people around her start disappearing, she can't just sit on the sidelines. Teaming up with The Fox to create the world's first superhero duo might be the only way to rid her city of evil and save the people she loves most.

HIDE AND SEEK

Agatha isn't looking forward to Christmas. While other eight-year-olds are hoping for a pile of presents, she just wants her evil stepsisters to leave her alone. Summer and Rain have a cruel idea of what passes for fun, and it always involves tormenting Agatha.

When the three of them get stuck inside their house on Christmas Eve, the twins force Agatha to play a twisted version of Hide and Seek. But they aren't the only things hiding in the house, and someone is about to get more than they bargained for beneath the tree...

GALTZAGORRIAK AND OTHER CREATURES: STORIES INSPIRED BY BASQUE FOLKLORE

Dive into stories about love, loss, greed, and revenge. Meet creatures like the mischievous *Galtzagorriak*, the deadly *Gaueko*, the beautiful *Lamiak*, the legendary *Erensuge*, and the wicked *Sorginak*.

The captivating tales in *Galtzagorriak and Other Creatures* are accompanied by breathtaking illustrations by artist Carina Barajas, and are sure to delight the whole family. Whether you're already familiar with the Basque Country or this is your first introduction, you don't want to miss this collection.